TANGIER GARDENS

...out of the classroom into real life... via plant portals

by Edward Flaherty
The introductory novel in "The Landscape Architect" series

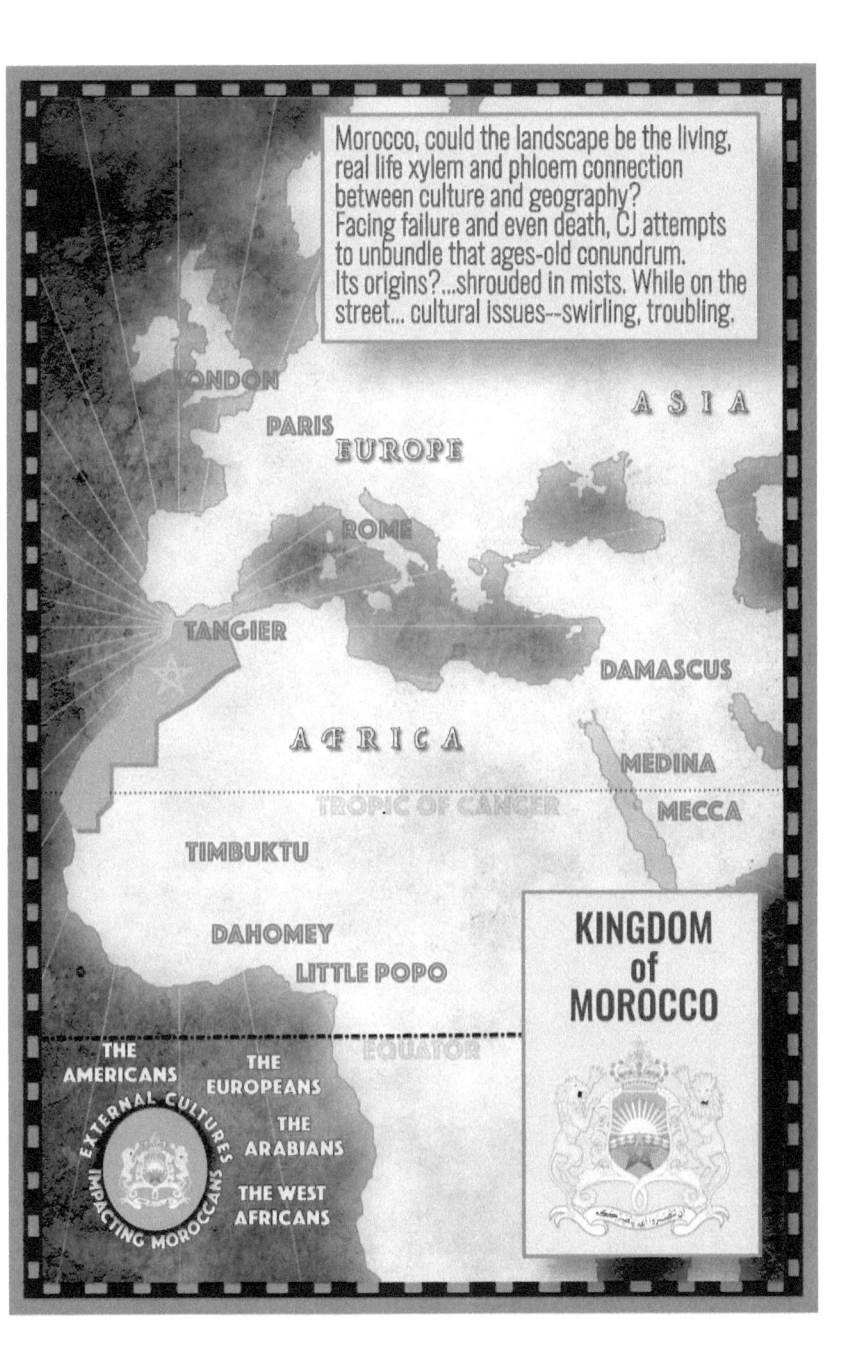

Morocco, could the landscape be the living, real life xylem and phloem connection between culture and geography? Facing failure and even death, CJ attempts to unbundle that ages-old conundrum. Its origins?...shrouded in mists. While on the street... cultural issues--swirling, troubling.

LONDON

ASIA

PARIS

EUROPE

ROME

TANGIER

DAMASCUS

AFRICA

MEDINA

TROPIC OF CANCER

MECCA

TIMBUKTU

DAHOMEY

LITTLE POPO

KINGDOM of MOROCCO

EQUATOR

THE AMERICANS

THE EUROPEANS

THE ARABIANS

THE WEST AFRICANS

EXTERNAL CULTURES IMPACTING MOROCCANS

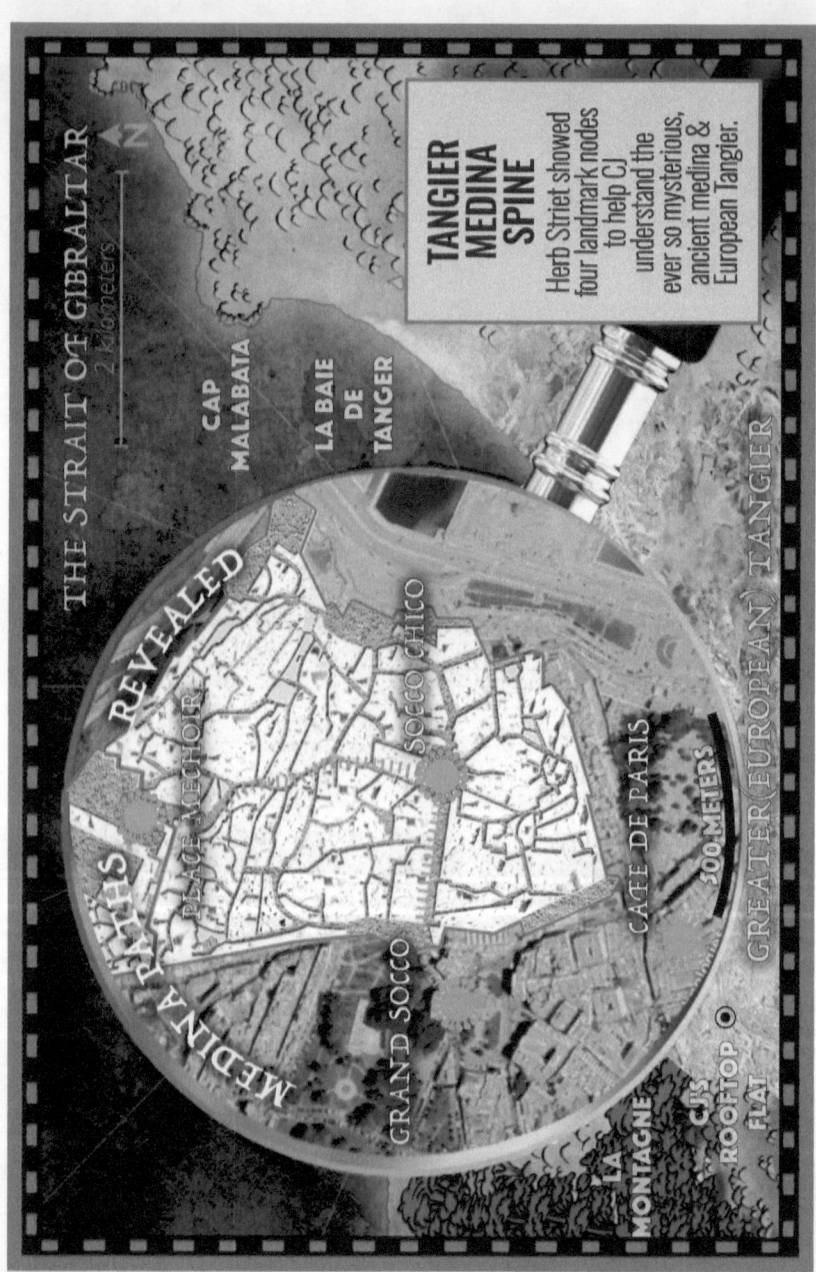

THE STRAIT OF GIBRALTAR

N

2 Kilometers

CAP
MALABATA

LA BAIE
DE
TANGER

REVEALED

MEDINA PATHS

PLACE MECHOUAR

SOCCO CHICO

GRAND SOCCO

CAFÉ DE PARIS

LA
MONTAGNE

ROOFTOP

FLAT

500 METERS

GREATER (EUROPEAN) TANGIER

**TANGIER
MEDINA
SPINE**

Herb Striet showed
four landmark nodes
to help CJ
understand the
ever so mysterious,
ancient medina &
European Tangier.

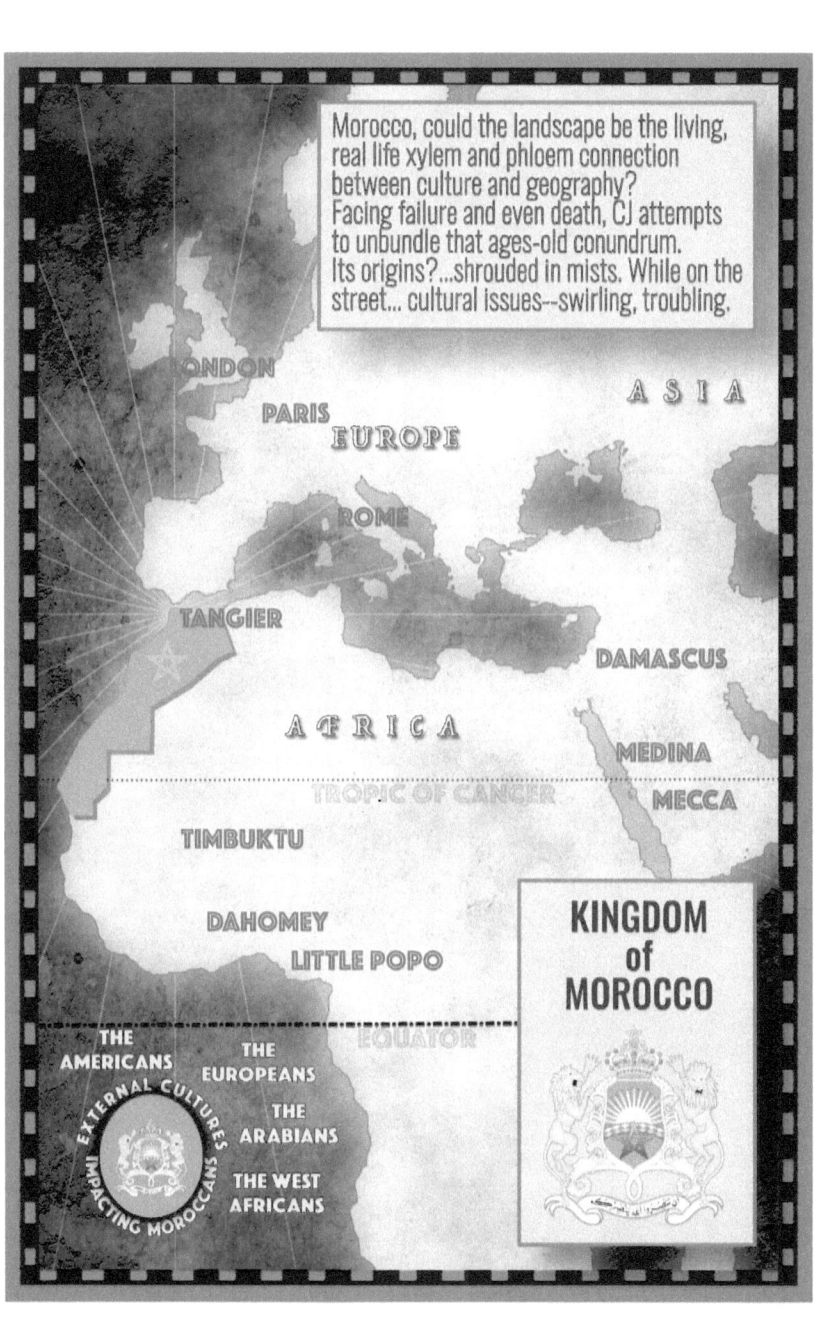

Morocco, could the landscape be the living, real life xylem and phloem connection between culture and geography? Facing failure and even death, CJ attempts to unbundle that ages-old conundrum. Its origins?...shrouded in mists. While on the street... cultural issues--swirling, troubling.

LONDON

ASIA

PARIS

EUROPE

ROME

TANGIER

DAMASCUS

AFRICA

MEDINA

TROPIC OF CANCER

MECCA

TIMBUKTU

DAHOMEY

LITTLE POPO

EQUATOR

KINGDOM
of
MOROCCO

THE AMERICANS

THE EUROPEANS

THE ARABIANS

THE WEST AFRICANS

EXTERNAL CULTURES IMPACTING MOROCCANS

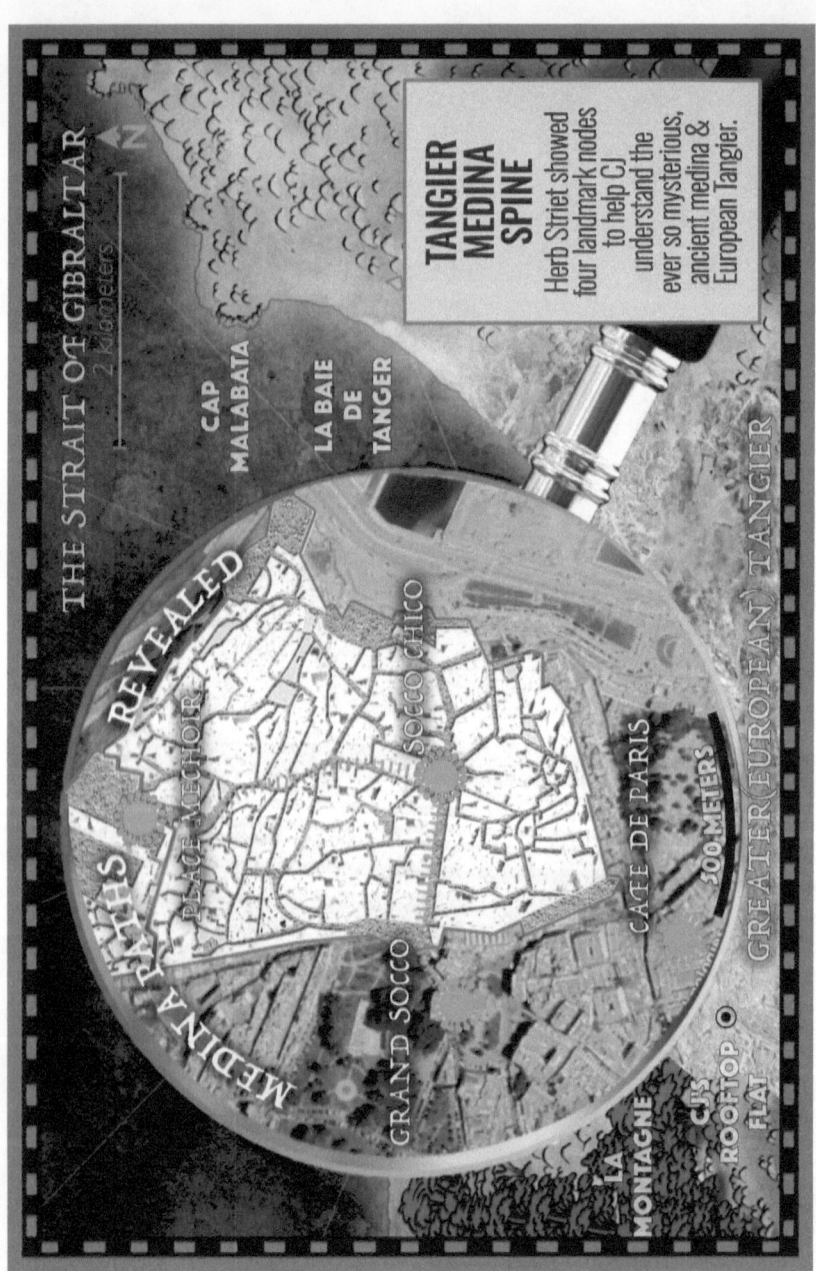

THE STRAIT OF GIBRALTAR

N

2 Kilometers

CAP
MALABATA

LA BAIE
DE
TANGER

REVEALED

MEDINA PATHS

PLACE MELCHIOR

SOCCO CHICO

GRAND SOCCO

CAFÉ DE PARIS

500 METERS

LA
MONTAGNE

CJ'S
ROOFTOP

FLAT

GREATER (EUROPEAN) TANGIER

**TANGIER
MEDINA
SPINE**

Herb Striet showed
four landmark nodes
to help CJ
understand the
ever so mysterious,
ancient medina &
European Tangier.

MEDINA PUBLIC FOUNTAIN

This is what CJ remembered. This is what he based his study on. This is what he was looking for.

VIEW TO THE EAST OVER THE TANGIER MEDINA, LA BAIE DE TANGER, CAP MALABATA, THE STRAIT, SPAIN AND THE ROCK OF GIBRALTAR. CJ COULD SEE IT ALL.

STONESTEVE'S PLACE
next door, no garden

CJ'S ROOFTOP GARDEN SHELTER

Herb Striet, a landscape architect with a green thumb, rented his flat to CJ, if CJ would care for these outdoor plants.

ROOFTOP TERRACE GARDEN

CJ'S RENTED FLAT
bis shelter

4 meters

FRENCH DOORS

WINDOWS

CJ'S WICKER CHAIR

Preface

At the dawn of the 21st century, before the Casablanca 2003 terror attacks and even before the New York September 2001 devastation, Tangier Gardens debuts a series entitled "The Landscape Architect".

In this coming of age adventure novel the American Christopher Janus, a student in his university last year studying landscape architecture, tells us his own story. It is a hard-to-believe story of his term-abroad design study wherein the Moroccan landscape assaults him, forcing him to combat unforeseen challenges to his degree, his professional goals and even his life.

Is the landscape his worst enemy or is he his own worst enemy? Can he design his way out of this conundrum? Could coming of age be more awkward?

Edward Flaherty

Foreword

Dear readers,

For my term-abroad design study, I had to keep a daily diary, submit a weekly SitRep (Situation Report) and make a final presentation.

That was a lot of writing. I got into it. And after all was said and done, after some time had distanced me from the events, I had to look at it again.

Why review it again? Because of the absolute weirdness of it.

While in the process of that review, my search for clarity impelled me to write an autobiographical summary of my six months in Morocco and my "home" in Tangier. I had to make sure I understood just what exactly had happened. Hard to put into words. It began with my naivety and went something like this:

Moroccan dreams... an aphrodisiac of exotic cities, lively marketplaces, spicy aromas...

...enticing...

...beguiling...

...mesmerizing.

But forebodings gathered like storm clouds—thoughts and dreams can be all encompassing. Before I knew it, I had sunk into never neverland—for me it was not JM Barrie. It was Metallica's Sandman. Exit light... Tangier, Morocco, northwest Africa... real life overtook my dreams.

Late night, just off the ferry, hardly put my feet on the ground... when emerging from the dark shadows between faceless port business buildings, surging human swarms "slapped" me around.

Gusty, windswept, drizzly darkness—dim street lights—

strange unknowns.

Dozens of guys surrounded me.

Heads poked into my face, too close.

Shouting, they were, demanding my attention.

I tried to withstand waves of guys crowding in on me.

Good thing I was 6 feet tall. Most of them were noticeably shorter. I looked over the top of them for safety. I only saw hooded people in robes. Hidden faces disappearing in shadowy darkness. Shuffling movements in black and blacker shadows. Nobody paid attention to the harassment maelstrom focussed on me. No relief.

You don't know if you've never been there.

And that was just the beginning.

Follow my path, my dark journey, my search for light,

Christopher Janus

Contents

1-Landscape Architecture   15
2-Strait of Gibraltar   21
3-Meknes—Something Different   39
4-Meknes Deeper   53
5-Speaking the Unspoken   71
6-Rabat   89
7-Tangier   107
8-Tangier Spine   127
9-Kasbah   147
10-Riad Anomalies   163
11-Bookstore Backroom   179
12-Casablanca   193
13-Co-Ca Co-La   213
14-Safely Home   227
15-Hakim ben Wais   245
16-Roller Coaster   253
17-Neil   279
18-Muhendis Abdulwahab   289
19-Zerhoun Sufi   303
20-Making It Work   321
21-Dragon's Blood   333
22-Hibiscus House   347
23-Portals   367
24-The Oval Garden   385
25-Stomata   405
26-Connectors   427
27-Production   451

28-Ohrwurm   477
29-Dreamland   495
30-Iftar   505
31-Home Sweet Home   525
32-Curious Tales   531

"Chocolate and gardens, both have mystical qualities."

1-Landscape Architecture

Getting Started

In the beginning, I learned about suffering when I was young.
   We all do.
Lying.
Cheating.
Hurting.
We have no choice.
Not fun.
Suffering.
All of us.
Anytime, anywhere.
And as I grew I learned...
To ease that suffering.
First there were tales and legends.
Then magic.
Then religions.
Suffering continued.
That is history.
Then I became a landscape architect.
But in northwest Africa, I suffered like never before.
This new suffering?
I couldn't put words to it.
It was... one step beyond.
I'd always enjoyed my views of different cultures, from 30,000 feet. But this time, I felt trapped. Something forced its way in. I didn't like it. It wasn't right.

It?

What was it?

***

Landscape and Gardens

Unimaginable suffering. Not just any unimaginable suffering, but unimaginable suffering from the landscape. That couldn't be... could it? The landscape had always been my muse, my refreshment.

Throughout history, haven't we been searching for freedom from the lie, the cheat, the hurt, the suffering? Long ago, well before the scientific world of ethnobotany, somebody, searching for that cure, may have unfortunately thrown the baby out with the alchemical bathwater. Suffering is still there.

But we have gardens.

Gardens.

Gardens? Everyone likes gardens.

How and why? We may never agree.

But the refuge found in gardens?

Unmistakeable!

Some of us, fully absorbed in garden-world labors of love, spend our entire days nurturing plants—our commitment measured by aches, pains and the amount of earth on our hands by day's end. Others, while engaging in conversations with friends, colleagues, lovers, enjoy simply passing through a quiet garden surrounded by the soothing magic of fragrant flowers. These passers-through might see or smell the garden at most with only two senses. Whereas those who spend day after day nurturing the garden, remarkably experience it through not only their five senses, but also their emotions, dreams... and "beyond".

"Beyond"?

I learned about "beyond" in my Tangier gardens.

My name is Christopher Janus; everybody calls me CJ. Majoring in Landscape Architecture at a Midwest American university, I was in Morocco for a term-abroad design study.

My path to Tangier and its mysterious Hibiscus House was circuitous, awkward. My explorations into those Mediterranean gardens were wrapped in a daily life not only unexpected but threatening.

Something in the northwest Africa landscape overtook me. Suffering arrived.

2-Strait of Gibraltar

Storm on the Strait

Sitting on the dock of the bay in Algeciras, I saw the imposing Rock of Gibraltar. Don Rafael, a Spanish Landscape History Professor, who had been my guide in the Alhambra, told me that, a thousand years ago, the first time the Muslims came to confront the Christians in Europe, they were led by a General Tarek. He named that rock *Jbel Tarek*, Tarek's Mountain. The name, though Westernized over time, still stands. I recalled that same huge Gibraltar outcrop was part of the Greeks' original Pillars of Hercules. This region's cultural roots? Diverse and deep.

I reached into the deepest corner of my food sack and found three lonely chocolate-covered M&M peanuts, my last bites of American culture. Relishing those last peanuts and chocolate, I looked across the strait to Ceuta, a port on the near horizon.

Ceuta was a Spanish outpost on the North Africa coast. Rising above it, the adjacent mountain was the other half of the Pillars of Hercules. In a daze, I stared. Didn't look like the Rock of Gibraltar. It was all... foreign. Shaking myself out of the daze, I inspected the narrow ten-mile-wide strait.

I saw choppy, unsettled waters and felt fast-flowing airs. Together, they gave the Strait of Gibraltar an identity more dynamic than the two-dimensional, flat, narrow body of water shown on every map of this region. I sensed the agitated strait as an impact-absorbing buffer between two incredibly large continents and their complex cultures.

I saw something else in the geography. Not so easily definable... maybe it was just a feeling. This side of the strait, the Rock of Gibraltar was clear, upright, strong. The other side of the strait, the top of that second Pillar of Hercules, was hazy, unclear. The topography had an historical clarity; but spontaneously, I attributed feelings to it. I double-checked myself. How did those feelings arise?

My girlfriend back home, Sachy, used to talk to me about auras visible around people, auras of three character types—goodness, passion and ignorance. But a landscape aura, a geographic aura, a continental aura? Before that day, I'd never even thought about it. I could have sworn I felt some kind of dark and cloudy aura hovering over that North Africa mountain.

I stared at Africa, the continent, looming before me in real time. No worries, right?

Humans had been in North Africa a long time. Eastern Mediterranean Phoenicians two thousand years ago. Middle Eastern and African Muslims one thousand years ago. My thoughts were already adrift in strange cultures. For the first time, I sensed why the university had wanted a team on these foreign projects.

On these term abroad design studies, the university had concluded a team of individuals was necessary to support each other when confusing, cross-cultural tsunamis threatened to turn daily life upside down. I had my own support and reached into my key pocket, fingering the silver Hand of Fatima key ring my mom had given me for good luck. Time to go.

At the Port Passenger Terminal, going through passport formalities, I finally pushed on. In a blustery light drizzle, I boarded the late afternoon ferry, a 4hr trip to Tangier Ville. Crossing the strait, I watched the weather go downhill. By now my mind was swirling with the forebodings. They came as mysteries, unknowns and uncertainties.

What awaited me in Tangier?

For all my time in Morocco with my mom twenty years ago, I'd never been to Tangier. My thoughts continued swirling. Was the deteriorating weather an omen? Naw, couldn't be; Tangier, on the Med, had to be a good thing.

The ferry was crowded with tourists, people with heads full

of fanciful exotic Moroccan marketing images. But in these rapidly deteriorating stormy seas, I could see in their faces they were doing battle with stomach-churning uncertainties. I was part of the crowd. It was either the storm, my own naive ignorance or my irrational forebodings that made me one of them.

The darkening sky, visible only during frequent lightning flashes, was turbulent with racing clouds, rumbling and cracking thunder. Everything felt low, dark and thick. The sun had long since disappeared. Night had come early. Wind whipped up the storm, the slashing rain, the wild waves. Boat rocking. All of us, captive indoors. No escape.

So many people sick from the rough seas. My immediate world had become a harsh rocking blur of personal unknowns and other people blowing lunch. Could not escape the vomit or its stench. It manifested on me most strangely in an odd combination of stomach nausea and spine tingles.

The weather was too rough to go outside. Tried to make an adjustment. I moved near to a locked sliding door that still had salt air blowing through a gap next to the wall. The blowing salt air saved my nostrils from the stench of vomit.

***

Why and How

To isolate from the chaos, I braced myself against the rocking ship movements by leaning against the nearby wall, turning my back to the other passengers. Trying to ignore the sickness around me, I needed another world. So, I pulled out my design study topic statement and forced myself to focus on the details as they had been approved by Neil, my university academic advisor.

Design Study Topic Statement:

The original work, nearly twenty years ago, by a landscape architecture student team term abroad design study in Morocco, graphically documented traditional public water fountains as colorful, intricately designed, highly crafted, local landmarks that functioned as magnets of social activity--places where medina people gathered to collect water for their daily household activities.

Influenced by their efforts, I propose the following: This design study will examine the regional sociological roots behind the physical placement, ornamentation and use of traditional functional water fountains in the Moroccan medina urban public realm, with a view toward deriving a metric of understanding for their physical and cultural components.

Project Location:

Meknes and Tangier, Morocco

The scholarly basis for the design study is identified in the two references following.

1. *The Hidden Dimension* by Edward T. Hall (1966)--Hall, an anthropologist, examined the temporal and spatial dimensions of personal space used by humans in public and in private.

2. *The Social Life of Small Urban Spaces* by William H. Whyte (1980)--Whyte, a sociologist, and highly influential in architecture and planning, wrote this as an acute observer of human urban behavior. He analyzed what works and what doesn't work in small, open, urban spaces.

Project Deliverables:

1. Keep a Project Diary, comprising daily entries of design study activities, as appropriate to site conditions (10% of grade evaluation).

2. Prepare, beginning the first week of August with arrival in-country, a weekly Situation Report (SitRep) email to be sent to the faculty advisor each and every Friday following through to the submittal of the Term Abroad Design Study Final Report (10% of final grade evaluation).

3. Deliver an archivable hard copy and digital Term Abroad Design Study Final Report for placement in the departmental library (60% of final grade evaluation for content, 15% for hard copy).

4. Make a public presentation of the Term Abroad Design Study (5% of final grade evaluation).

Professional Landscape Architect In-Country Advisor/Facilitator
Mr. Herb Striet, PLA (Professional Landscape Architect), ASLA (American Society of Landscape Architects member)

But, under my circumstances on the ferry, I couldn't focus on those academic details. Rather, I recalled about how I had come to this "rock and roll" ferry across the Strait of Gibraltar.

It did the trick—at least my thoughts escaped to another world.

The university department required this self-defined term abroad design study in order to graduate with an undergrad degree in Landscape Architecture. And my path to graduation was the essential first step to my ultimate goal: to professionally practice Landscape Architecture.

My interest in landscape architecture was broad. The profession examined both natural and social sciences as they intertwined in public places. That was clear. Nothing ambiguous there.

I loved landscape architecture work—making gardens and landscapes for people to enjoy. I was eager and motivated to finish this course.

This was my last class after six long years of full-time undergrad studies. The last four years of design studios had been particularly grueling. Traditionally, for each hour of lecture, minimum eight to ten hours of design studio time were required. A typical class had up to five lecture hours per week.

The studio involved gathering massive amounts of natural and social data, assessing those data to develop solutions to the lecture problem—then preparing the graphic exhibits in order to publicly present the solution. Additionally, we were transitioning from hand graphics to computer graphics. Learning the computer interface and achieving high graphic design standards required lots of extra time.

I was nearly burnt out by those intense design studios. Yeah, I was beat, needed a break. So I was eager and motivated to finish this course. Everything had been moving well in my direction.

I was happy with my plans, my design study topic statement and going to Morocco. I was okay with that general idea. So where was the problem?

I had imagined my term abroad design study to be like a six-month vacation on the Med beaches; but... uncertainties, forebodings... omens had begun ominously swirling.

What were these swirling uncertainties that were obsessing me? I had chastised myself for even thinking about "forebodings", about "omens"; but too much negativity had been accumulating— Lazló's description of Morocco's awkward lingering in the 19th century, darkness over African mountains, storm on the strait, people getting sick—seeds of uncertainty had been sown.

Something was bound to go wrong. But I was in the game, and on my way to Africa, Morocco.

I was serious. But, hey, the design topic statement was academic-speak providing viable gravitas and yeah I'd follow the rules. But for me, after six years of full-time university, I was looking for relaxation and sun on Med sand beaches, exotic Moroccan markets and maybe... on the side I'd learn something about the landscape. I was cool with that but...

Hey, it worked. In my mind, I just removed myself from the sickening ferry experience.

By the time we approached the port on the Bay of Tangier the storm had relented, but the sea had not yet calmed. The vomiting continued. The ferry staff could not keep up. We finally docked in the heavily overcast, thick cloud cover and pitch black, dark wetness of the protected Tangier Ville. I cleared passport control without problem. Stamped in 24 June 2000, with a special six-month student visa.

Herb Striet, my in-country Morocco design study advisor, from Meknes, had written me to walk directly to the train station from the ferry because they were close. And if I had to spend a night, stay at the Almohades Hotel because it, too, was close. That seemed simple enough.

Until I left the fenced and barb-wired, official port customs and passport control. What was about to hit me, when I stepped outside of the safety of the government's secure zone...

My footing was a bit unsteady. My "sea" legs were still rubbery even though I was walking on dry land. Then I saw, under a street light, posted at the Tangier Port gate, two military guards with machine guns. What? Why? Could that have been normal? Not cute—just weird.

But, as I passed the street light, within ten meters of the guards, from the shadows, the answers became clear when a surging swarm of truth inundated me. Not the comfort I had expected; I had arrived in Tangier, only to be smashed by a cross-cultural tsunami.

***

Tangier Streets

If you haven't been there...

My land-legs were just returning when...
I was surrounded by guys...
Too many calling, "friend"? What?
Always shouting...
Was I under stress?
Definitely!
These words have described not nearly half of that noisy swarm.

Internally, I was unable to detach or analyze.
What to do?
I tried to pull back; but it was like swatting yellow-jackets. The fury intensified.

Many looked like youth everywhere in Europe. But unlike Europe... they all approached me to talk. Their voices all loud—spoken quickly without hesitation or manners. They were all speaking over each other, and all aggressive.

I heard good English...
Broken street English...
Mixes of four, five and six languages...

I paused to figure out what was going on, to try to be understanding of this strange behavior that suddenly had focused on me. No sooner did I pause than guys started aggressively tugging my arms to get my attention. Then I felt a hand on my bottom—only Sachy does that. I pushed away all the grabbing and touching hands and moved on... but they all returned as quickly as pesky flies. Not like this when I was in Morocco twenty years ago with my mom.

How could I know that any of these strangers was trying to help? I tried to talk with one.

He said, "I know Tangier. What you want? Hotels? *Keef?* Girls? Restaurant?"

That was enough for me. Each choice was like a "pick a door" game show. A stranger named the door and I had to gamble that behind the door would be found the same as he said. I felt a storm of potential danger. No games for me. I was already sick from the ferry trip. These guys made it worse. The unknowns were too much. And it was all in a darker reality.

Up ahead, I could see the train station close by; but on the way more shouting and pushing. I'd had my fill.

I looked off to the side wondering if all of Tangier was like my introduction. In the shadowy distance, I could make out only a steep hillside of crenelated walls and Moorish arch gateways—brightly welcoming? No way! Poorly lighted and darkly nightmarish.

The city and its public streets... the darkest. With every step, I continued to brush off guys trying to help me. I needed to get the train to Meknes.

All this happened non-stop as I walked the five minutes to the nearby train station. Too late. Train station dark and empty. No train until tomorrow morning. Bummer. Still at least fifteen guys rumbling about me outside the train station trying to "help" me.

"Hotel?"

"Guide?"

"Medina?"

"Kasbah?"

"Socco?"

"Hasheesh?"

Hardly could understand what most of them were saying...

Harsh sounds... arguing over each other... probably about what or who was going to have the right to redistribute my meagre wealth. Maybe my backpack acted like a flashing neon advertisement—money here!

Saw a big hotel sign about 150 meters ahead along the coast. Almohades Hotel, the one that Herb Striet had recommended. Guys followed me all the way, unrelenting...

"Hotel?"

"Cheap hotel?"

"Restaurant?"

"Good Moroccan food?"

Some were so persistent...

Too close for comfort...

Hands all over me...

Trying to be my friends!?

"You like hash..."

"You like *keef*..."

"You like girl..."

"You like boy..."

"Come with me, my friend..."

Were these really my friends? Said no thank you again and again but nobody stopped talking. I never thought that the urban landscape could be so off-putting—downright threatening—like gusts in a hurricane—they just kept coming. One after another after another—worse, they overlapped.

"Hotel half price..."

"Best price..."

"Clean..."

"Close..."

"Come, my friend..."

"Good Moroccan hotel..."

Too much. Couldn't think. Too many strangers too close. Felt like I was living a bad dream. Guys trailed me right up to the hotel front door. The Doorman shooed them away. Relieved to get inside the Almohades Hotel. Fortunately, they had a room.

***

The Almohades

I needed space to myself.

I needed time to reflect.

I was sensually and emotionally overcome. There had been no attractive urban markets, no spicy aromas, just intense people crowding in and demanding my attention. I had just been overwhelmed by a strange street culture. I had to describe it as the worst kind of exotic urban landscape. Who were these people? The welcome wagon?

My head spun as I recalled the details. I had asked them politely not to grab at me but they just kept trying to push and pull me into a good deal. A good deal?! These guys were all strangers. If there were 150 tourists on the ferry, there must have been 300 guys—guys, no girls—milling about, waiting at the port to "help" us. Everyone was touching me. No one backed off. As I spoke politely to one, five others rudely interrupted me. Each shouting over the other. No one showed basic concern for my personal space. Very uncomfortable.

I had been taught at school to respect other people's culture. I had assumed other people were taught the same. Somewhere along the line I grew up thinking that everyone, no matter what culture, country or religion, followed the simple golden rule: do unto others as you would have them do unto you. That hadn't happened on my first night arrival in Tangier.

At the hotel front desk, I asked the night manager about the "pestering" I had just felt on the street. As if it was no big deal, he told me it was normal. Normal, I thought?! I asked about the train station and if it would be more peaceful in the morning. He told me it would be peaceful tomorrow. He added, if I was hungry, the hotel had an open restaurant, and if I wanted entertainment, there was a club in the back.

I thanked him and went upstairs to my room. The Almohades Hotel was on the west end of a coastal boulevard overlooking the port and beach on the Bay of Tangier. My room, on the third floor, had that view from its small balcony.

After checking out that view, I examined the room. The room was empty except for a single bed, a single wardrobe and a single towel in my bathroom. No furniture on the room balcony, nothing in the room minibar. Austere to extreme. Will somebody get me a cheeseburger!!

I was hungry, so, after I cleaned up with a much needed shower and shave, I went to the hotel restaurant for a cheeseburger and Coke. No cheeseburgers, but they did have hamburgers and Cokes. Hamburger and Coke were not part of Budgett Meakin's 19th century in the book Lazló gave me in Algeciras. Meakin did, however, describe a 19th century hectic and intense street scene like I had just gone through.

The food actually calmed me, until they gave me the bill. $25 for a hamburger, Coke and fries. That, indeed, was 20th Century plus.

Went back up to my room. The spartan room gave me no distraction. I needed that. Right, I tried to convince myself that I was there to do my design study, not to make a sociological interpretation of street culture behaviors to foreign tourists. I tried to settle.

I would have liked to get in touch with Herb Striet, my in-country advisor, to talk through what had just happened to me at the Tangier Ville port. But Herb Striet was an old-school kind of guy. His only contact detail was a post office box in Meknes. He didn't have a phone, landline or mobile. He didn't have a computer. I could call him a Class A Luddite.

He, no doubt, had his reasons; but that didn't make any difference. He wasn't around the first I needed him. So, I just had to work through it myself. The hotel night manager said everything at the train station should go smoothly. Okay, his statement was encouraging. And I had a full stomach, a quiet room—settling began.

I had a folder with all of Herb Striet's letters. I dug out my last letter from Herb Striet. In it he told me that there were two trains per day from Tangier to Meknes, normally in the morning but sometimes later. A five-hour ride, no changes.

I was still bummed. I had all but forgotten my hopes for the glorious Mediterranean Sea coast and Club Med suntans. Or had I? Nah, I was making a mistake to draw that conclusion so soon. I tried to put it aside. I had to buck up and do my study. In one of his earliest letters, he wrote:

Tangier is filled with scum, human scum. Always been that way. Pirates are pirates. They are only romantic in books.

Tangier got a good turn when it became an independent International Zone in the early 1900s. But its big boost really came in World War II and following through the 1950s.

During those years, every Mo who had one dirham of smarts came to Tangier to take money from the tourists, the crazy infidels. The infidels arrive by the boatload every day and are so stupid they want to give their money away. No matter how much the infidels pretend to whine and protest, in the end the money changes hands and the Mo is victorious. That's the public realm of Tangier.

I remembered that was a shocker. I took that letter to my mom and asked why I didn't have any memories of stuff like that from our visit to Morocco 20 years ago. She said a couple things.

She said first of all that she thought Moroccans showed her respect because she was a mother with her young child, me. I was seven at the time. She also told me that we came and went to Morocco through Ceuta and Tetouan, never visiting Tangier. Also, she thought Mr. Striet sounded like a crusty, cynical old man.

So who was Herb Striet? That's a long story and, in a way, it contradicts my mom's opinion.

A year ago, when I researched the earlier students' term

abroad design study, I found the contact details of Herb Striet, the American landscape architect who had been their Moroccan in-country facilitator. The contact details were scant—a ten-year-old address for a post office box in Meknes.

On a chance, I sent him a postcard. On a chance, I got an answer back. Kismet. Letters ensued. Thus Herb Striet became my real-time connection to Morocco. My contemporary American connection to regional North African culture.

Herb Striet had lived in Morocco for a long time. In his letters to me he wrote that young, American, university-age students had been going to Morocco for decades. They had always fallen into two categories: drug-taking do-gooders; and Peace Corps for social change do-gooders. I read that and thought, not me. Do-gooding did not even enter my mind. I had a goal to become a professional landscape architect.

Be that what it may. Now I was in Tangier. Now I had been initiated to Tangier street culture, the Tangier urban landscape. And now I was exhausted.

Needed rest. Collapsed on the bed. Wondered if Meknes would be like tonight in Tangier. Had I just been welcomed to the real world of Morocco? 19th Century or 20th Century?

Before I knew it, I was asleep. Slept well, except for the flickering dreams... where hooded shadows emerged from the dark clammy rain... where strangers pretending to be my friends hassled me non-stop.

3-Meknes—Something Different

La Gare et al.

Finally, I slept deeply. But after those threatening dreams, upon wakening, I felt disoriented.

I sat up in my bed. I was somewhere in between awake and asleep. The memories of last night's street scene were filling me with a nauseating internal discomfort. I could only just sit there. Strange. I tried to think. I tried to analyze my way out of it. I needed to understand a reality that made sense.

I reviewed my last 18 hours. I had taken the ferry from Spain the day before and I was in Morocco, right? I asked myself, dream, or no dream? I was indeed in the Almohades Hotel in Tangier, Morocco. That was real. But the cloudy disorientation of my sensibilities was still weirdly hovering about me. Nevertheless, I had to start my day.

I washed, brushed my teeth and got dressed. Stepping out on my balcony, in the bright daylight and light drizzle, I could see more details of the waterfront. The coastal boulevard followed the edge of the curving, sandy-shored bay, the Bay of Tangier, and stretched much longer than I had imagined.

Looking out at the bay, I could see to my right, at the east end of the curve, far beyond the city edge, a treeless maquis-covered hill so typical of the Mediterranean landscape. I inhaled the humid misty air and yes it had that maquis blend of brooms, myrtles, fennel, rue, rock roses—what was it? Sweet, tangy, bitter, medicinal—whatever—the essence of health—I needed that.

For a moment, I forgot about the noxious street scene of the night before. Taking advantage of lungfuls of the Med's herbal fragrance, I put on my landscape architecture hat and began a visual assessment of the urban edge along the Bay of Tangier. That was my work. I was comfortable with that. And finally the sour memories of last night dissolved.

On the landward side of the coastal boulevard, non-stop along its full length, I saw hotels upon hotels. They all had views that took advantage of the beach, the coast of Spain and the Strait of Gibraltar. In the middle of the boulevard there was, as far as I could see, a continuous strip of landscaped islands, prominent because of their stately double row of tall date palms—beautiful to see and enticing for taking a walk.

To my left was the train station, in municipal Art Deco style. It had a tall, nicely proportioned, rectangular central hall, with numerous full height vertical windows maybe three stories high. The exterior was rather plain, whitewashed, smooth concrete except for a textured, continuous, high relief, decorative band above the windows. That band was nicely done—an enlarged Art Deco derivative from interlaced geometric bands like I had seen at the Alhambra.

The train tracks ran east out of the train station between the street and the beach, past my hotel and continuing to my right. On the beach side of the tracks was a broad pedestrian-only promenade with alternate rows of date palms and shade trees—very urbane and European in feeling. On the beach side of the promenade, the sand began. Hey, I thought, maybe I would get my Med suntan.

I was feeling better until I saw a horticultural activity I had never before seen. I saw a construction crew planting a new row of date palms. Never seen anything like it. The 6-8 meter long date palms were stacked like telephone poles on a flat-bed truck. All of them were bare root and surprisingly without rootballs. They looked exactly like telephone poles. And they had no crowns—no feathery frond crowns. All the fronds had been pruned off except the newest, youngest, smallest two or three. Ugly they looked.

I planted a lot of date palms in SoCal when I worked there two summers earlier. We never planted them bare rooted, never without rootball. We never brought to a project date palms looking like slender, naked telephone poles.

My guess was it would be two, maybe three years before these date palm crowns looked healthy—with well established majestic date palm frond canopies. Maybe there was local horticultural validity; but I guessed local nurseries never grew date palms to be transplanted for immediate canopy effect.

Then I noticed people. I saw individuals and families walking. At 8AM, the promenade and boulevard were busy with those pedestrians—on their way to where? Work? The Port? The train station?

The station had only two platforms. At this early hour, from the outside, it looked a quiet train station with only one train. On the boulevard below me, I heard no human cacophonies like last night. I could hear only cars and delivery trucks. Not bad, quiet, as last night's desk clerk had told me it would be, so I packed up my backpack and checked out of the hotel.

But as soon as I stepped outside, the bad dream returned. Real life became as if I was the piece of fresh meat that beckoned hungry flies. Bang, they were all around. Again too many guys, too close, repetitiously demanding my attention.

Never before had I felt the distasteful stirring that was welling up inside me. The night before I had tolerance at first; but that gradually dwindled. This day was different. No tolerance, no patience—only a growing disgust at the constant uninvited "helper" invasion of my space, my person. These guys on the street were just as aggressive as they had been the night before. They were determined to "help" me. Help me? I needed help but that was only because of them.

I felt a displacement occurring. It was like an internal slow motion earthquake. It was a drowsy dizziness as guys buzzed all around me. Disgust was metastasising slowly into, I had no other words for it, a gnawing madness. I didn't understand it. What kind of urban landscape feature?

I came to describe it as a cross-cultural dissonance. All my facilities were numbed. Nothing worked. But I had a study to do. I barged through their non-stop pushing and hawking toward the train station.

I entered the station after passing by... what?!... another

armed military policeman. My "helpers" did not enter, clearly put off by the no-nonsense, glaring machine gun man.

Once inside—believe it or not—I saw, by a factor of ten, a wilder crowd—a scrum at the ticket window, actually throughout the entire hall. A swarming madness and a madness of noise. When I tried to buy a ticket, it was like trying to enter a disturbed swarm of bees—don't even think about it.

I backed away and observed. This Art Deco building was high ceilinged and felt as much like a fortress on the inside as it had looked on the outside. But inside it was a huge echo chamber. The noise roiled up and over again and again till it seemed to fill my entire body. All this from what must have been a core of nearly a hundred people in the swarm. I couldn't believe my ears or my eyes. In a disturbed awe, I watched.

Everybody impatiently struggling toward one ticket window...

A boiling cluster of people strained in at the window sized for only one at a time...

At the window itself at least four people were forcing their heads through and screaming at the ticket seller...

And that was just the front row...

Eight more people were shouldering in on that first group...

Some looked rural, others looked urban, some in hooded robes, others in suits, all were men...

All were reaching over, shoving and shouting at the poor fellow selling tickets.

Behind the men, groups of women with children were all huddling in obvious, uneasy, uncertainty...

There was no air space between people...

Everyone was passionately contributing to the amplified echoes of a roaring guttural staccato.

People, having bought tickets, jostled to get from the ticket window to the platform. The disturbance increased in volume and intensity as the crowd squeezed, one by one, through the narrow ticket-checking gate out to the platform. The entire scene was more furious than any National Hockey League bitter grudge match brawl after both benches emptied out on the ice. Everyone was clustered together, everyone was bursting energy, everyone was pushing and shoving against someone else.

What was I seeing? Just people behaving badly... or was this normal here? What non-stop intensity of noise and physical pushing! What a welcome to Morocco! I took a moment to try to think it through.

Between this and the street scene, I was more than troubled. From my preparation reading, I had learned that people around the Strait of Gibraltar had always been a seething social pot with four cultural taproots struggling for firm foothold—Berber, Arab, African and European. I had thought it was hyperbole, but now, it wasn't theory and history, it had become real—visceral, personal and complicated. I had experienced some kind of strange sociological storm. I did not understand any of it. This was to become my life in Morocco? I had to get past this tangled mess.

I missed the early morning train because the crowd was so hot.

But I had to get to Meknes, to find and talk with Herb Striet. Then slowly an idea formed in my head as I watched the crowd inside the train station dissipate as soon as the train left. I went to the ticket window and bought a first class reserved seat for the next train. There was a 10% surcharge for the "early advance" ticket. What the hell. Small price to pay.

When, still well before noon, the next train came in and emptied of the passengers, they opened the boarding gate. I was the first to climb aboard. The swarm was just getting started. Forty-five minutes later, my train departed. I was sitting quietly and peacefully. The drizzly rain had stopped and the clouds had begun to clear.

On the way to Meknes, nobody troubled me. A porter came by and asked if I'd like petit déjeuner or déjeuner, breakfast or lunch? I asked for breakfast and for $15 he served a small glass of freshly squeezed orange juice, a cup of black coffee and a croissant with apricot jam and butter.

My first food of the day. The black coffee woke me up. The orange juice refreshed me. And the apricot jam? Never had it before. A delight. Fresh-looking color. Sweet but not too sweet.

It came from a small jar labelled "*Produit du Meknes*". And that's where I was going. I was feeling better, actually quite good as the train headed south and then inland.

I watched the rolling hills of a broad river plain, a rich agricultural countryside—lots of cultivation. I saw no irrigation system hardware. I concluded that, like the rain of the last days, nature provided the farmers with adequate water. Plants looked healthy. I truly relaxed. Finally. Having calmed inside, I noticed that the gnawing madness had disappeared. Thank God.

I took out Herb Striet's three-month-old letter in which he had enclosed a passport-size photo of himself and a Meknes map to get me from the Ville Nouvelle train station to his apartment. I hoped he would clue me in on my unsettling arrival experiences in Tangier. Was this what I was going to have every day for my six-month study? I certainly hoped not; but I was cautious if not downright worried that I might meet a Tangier-like greeting as I arrived.

At the Meknes Ville Nouvelle train station only a small number of passengers disembarked with me. The large numbers remaining must have been going on another 60km, to the final stop, Fes.

As I exited the single platform at the station, I noted a guard, again with machine gun. No "helpers", either. What a relief. I pulled out Herb Striet's map one more time—right or left from the station? As I looked at the map, I heard a soft but clear voice, "*Besoin de quelque chose, m'sieur?*"

No pressure, just a quiet question. It was a "helper". He was short, in his twenties and as close to a gentleman in his sport shirt and neat trousers appearance as anyone I'd seen yet in Morocco.

He continued, "*Je m'appelle Hameed. Moi et mon cousin restons au Café Cyber Club de l'autre cote, au coin. Si t'as besoin de quelque chose, viens nous voir n'importe quel temps.*"

"Thank you." I said.

"*M'asalama*," Hameed said.

That was all. As he walked away, I thought, that was easy. No pressure, he just asked if I needed anything and then told me where I could find him. Also, I was surprised that my French, so long dormant, handled his words.

After only a ten-minute walk from the train station, I found Herb Striet's apartment building, the Beau Séjour. Along the way, nobody troubled me on the street—no swarms of "helpers"—so different from Tangier.

***

Beau Séjour

The Beau Séjour, with its pleasantly balanced building masses and curving corner details, was another Art Deco themed building. I found especially delightful the playful geometric design on its front door. Overall, it had three floors, ground floor and two floors above.

Judging from the floor massing, I figured three proper apartments on each of the two lower floors and four studios on the top floor. I climbed a flight of stairs to Herb Striet's floor. I knocked once. No answer.

His was the only apartment with all the wood shutters closed. I knocked again, more forcefully, many times. Still no answer. Not a sound. What? No, I thought, it can't be. I dreaded what might be. Disappointment already darkening me. Then I thought maybe he was out shopping or something. So, I looked around the rest of the building.

On the ground floor of the Beau Séjour, I found a 30-something American, Tom, lean and looking knowledgeable. I learned from him that he and his wife managed the apartments. He, also a Midwest American, listened to my story and predicament. Then he warmly invited me into his place and introduced me to his wife, Marcela.

They knew Striet, that's how they called him. They told me that he had always been coming and going; but this time he had terminated his lease—moved out last month and was now in Tangier. Tangier?! I thought—okay—something ironic in there somewhere?! So, no Herb Striet... when I was already needing his help.

I explained to Tom and Marcela more details of Herb Striet's role in my study, and my first 24 unsettling hours in Tangier. Fortunately, both Tom and his wife took sympathy on me. They offered me, at no charge, a furnished top-floor studio flat in the Beau Séjour while I sorted out what to do. Additionally, they suggested, if I wanted to make Meknes my study centre, they could let me stay in a furnished apartment in their building at a discounted 'student price', $200/month.

I told them I wanted to be on the Med and Tangier had become my preference.

"What's the difference between Tangier and Meknes?" I asked.

Tom snorted. "Tangier is Europe—in a historically dirty morality way—dirty in more ways than one; and Meknes? Well, Meknes is an agricultural and quiet town. No pollution here. Your choice—moral pollution of Tangier or agricultural richness of Meknes."

"It's more than that," Marcela added, "sure you have your Med climate in Tangier... but here... CJ you're from the Midwest, right..."

"Yeah, that's where I went to university..."

"Well, here we get cold winters, I'm sure that would make you feel at home... but the summers... we get what we call *shergee...*"

"*Shergee?*"

"From the Sahara, we get hot, dry, dusty winds all day and all night, 24 hrs/day, sometimes for as long as a week... everyone calls that wind, that weather, Shergee," Marcela said. "Impossible to breathe. I can't stand it. If you care about your health, you won't like it. And the summer is just starting."

"Can't make any decision yet... got to get my study set up. That's why I need to find and talk with Herb Striet."

They told me Striet left no forwarding address. But there had always been rumors that he kept a small place in Tangier. And they'd heard that for most of his daytime hours there, he might be found at the Café de Paris.

No Herb Striet?! I had to repeat it to myself over and over. I had hoped he would be my anchor for the study. Someone to

49

get me through the unknowns and disturbing cross-cultural weirdness. His absence was a blow.

Tom and Marcela were all that were giving me any balance. As he marked up a small tourist map showing me how to get from the Tangier Port train station to the Café de Paris, Tom said, "If you need to find Striet in Tangier, here is how you can start."

That was helpful, but overall, things were going downhill. My first 24 hours in Morocco, in Tangier, had shocked me into some new cross-cultural reality that was nothing at all like I remembered back when I was here with my mom. And my last night and day were, when compared to my recent road trip of landscape sites in Europe, dissonant centuries apart. I was off-balance to say the least.

There was a knock on Tom's door. Marcela welcomed a man who looked like a sporty professional administrator. She introduced Justin to me as Tom's older brother. He was lean like Tom, but taller and looking to be in his late 40s, balding just starting to eat at his full head of hair. Tom introduced him further to me by saying that Justin was fluent in both the classical Arabic of the Koran and the regional Arabic dialect *Darija*.

I needed some background and Justin provided it. Outlining his local history, he said, "It had all started for me in Morocco in the Peace Corps... I came in the early years, the 70s... and now I am with the United States Agency for International Development (USAID) English Language Centres as Morocco National Director."

Through continued conversation I learned Justin knew Morocco in depth. He kept a personal research centre in a bolt-hole apartment here at the Beau Séjour and regularly traveled to all the USAID Language Centres around the country.

Over dinner, he gave a short history of the bled Berbers, the hill and mountain people native to this country. He explained that there were three different Berber tribe roots and languages—one in the Rif, another in the Middle Atlas and the third in the High Atlas.

And here is what was new for me. Justin made clear that each of the three original Berber languages were incomprehensible to the others. I thought how confusing and wondered, from where do the roots of Moroccan culture come? This was the question that lodged itself deep inside me. I wanted to understand the strangeness I was experiencing here in Morocco. I must have been too young to perceive anything strange when I was here with my mom 20 years ago. I wondered where did it come from? And what was it?

Before I could ask my questions Justin added, "Meknes was originally all about the Meknassi Middle Atlas Berbers and the plentiful river, Oued Boufekrane, draining the Moyenne Atlas mountains." He summarized the coming and passing of the Romans, the Middle East Arabs, the Moorish dynasties, then the Euros at the beginning of the 20th century—and finally liberation in 1956.

Then, believe it or not, came even weirder stuff I had never heard about. Justin and Tom went into disturbing detail about how, during the 1956 revolution for independence from the French, Westerners were beheaded. Not only beheadings, but their heads were displayed on long stakes in the main square of the Meknes medina, the Place El Hedim.

I recalled my recent talks with Don Rafael in Granada—about the 15th Century Abencerrajes and the Alhambra beheadings. Between those and these 20th century beheadings, I wondered, is that how these guys solve their serious misunderstandings?

Cutting heads off?! Meknes? Only 50 years ago?

Maybe that was why my mom gave me that Hand of Fatima good luck charm. Maybe she saw what I was too young to see.

I'd heard enough. I needed a good night's sleep. I needed to think through what I had felt and heard in my first couple days, because none of it was positive for my term abroad design study.

Tom and Marcela led me to a furnished studio on the top floor. Tom even invited me for breakfast, made me feel comfortable—almost like home. I was thankful for meeting these expatriate Americans. Because of them, I felt relaxed as I washed up before taking rest.

When I laid down, I thought, aside from the hospitality of

Tom and Marcela, it seemed like I'd just been through 48 hours of non-stop nightmares. I crashed—needed the sleep.

4-Meknes Deeper

Ville Nouvelle

After an excellent night's sleep, I woke to a sunny summer morning. Over coffee I told Justin, Tom and Marcela more about my study. I was frank. I told them I really wanted to be on the Med.

"But if I had to do my study here in Meknes... tell me more about the climate and other differences between Tangier and Meknes?"

"Mild, as you probably already know, Tangier is mild compared to here. We have climatic extremes not experienced in Tangier."

"We can get snow in winter and in the summer like Marcela said last night, we get those *shergees*."

"Tell me more about the *shergees*."

"...weather systems influenced by the Sahara... the temperature stays above 30° all day and all night. Everybody hunkers down inside. Few people on the streets."

"Marcela was right... it is dry, very dry and hazy. The haziness is from fines in the air..."

"Fines?"

"The fines are the finest desert sand and dust particles whipped up by the *shergee* winds from the Sahara. In fact, if you look at the Meknes medina, you will see it has that yellow *shergee* stain. Centuries of Sahara fines have been deposited on the walls."

"Powerful, eh?"

"Definitely, powerful enough to push across the Middle and High Atlas mountains and still strong enough to cause days of hardship for people in this region," Justin added.

"Nobody comes here for a suntan," said Marcela.

"That's Tangier... they used to have a Club Med up there," added Tom.

"If you want mild and suntan, then the best place north of Essaouira is Tangier."

"I hear you. That was my plan. I'll stick with that plan; but I'm starved. Tell me about your typical breakfast, do you buy cereal, milk or do you eat eggs and I understand no bacon, no pork sausage..."

"That's right, can't find pork anywhere in the market, though there is a black market if you look hard enough... but stay away from anything black market, anything contrary to Islamic culture."

"We have plenty of fresh food options... eggs, bread, butter, cheese, fruits... a lot of agricultural holdovers from the 50-year French occupation."

They talked about food and asked if I liked donuts. I was surprised—hadn't expected something that reminded me of home.

"Sure thing," I said.

"Here they are called *sfinj*," Marcela said, "and they are made fresh on certain street corners here in the Ville Nouvelle."

I had a "fastfood" thing with chocolate and peanuts—M&Ms, the most popular. Some people call them "junkfood".

Three months earlier, when I left the US for my bike trip in Europe, I brought some with me for snacking on the road. In addition to their enjoyable taste, I found even in Europe on my road trip, those chocolate covered peanuts felt like a comfortable cultural tether to the US.

But, gradually, I evolved, first with Belgian chocolate and hazelnuts, then *pain au chocolat* in France, then a step further with fried churros and hot chocolate in Spain. So now, with no chocolate, it might be *sfinj*—Moroccan donuts—would they become my fastfood favorite? Would they become an ersatz cultural tether—some kind of link back home?

They told me there was a guy on a street corner two blocks away, making *sfinj* to order every morning. Marcela sent out her Moroccan maid, who brought back a dozen donuts. Maid? I wondered... their life style was only middle class in appearance... nothing extravagant... tending rather to the austere. Only later did I learn they were saving money for their future.

Marcela sprinkled the donuts with coarsely granulated sugar and served them still warm, with Nescafe and Nido (powdered milk)—no chocolate, but an enjoyable breakfast, anyhow.

I had already spent the dirhams I got from Lazló, so, after breakfast, Justin and Tom took me to a local bank.

As we left the Beau Séjour, they pointed out, next door, the small local grocery store, called a *bakal*. It looked like a hole-in-the-wall. I remembered those hole-in-the-wall grocery stores from my earlier visit to Morocco with my mom—dreamy places.

"Do you want to step inside?" Tom asked. "Marcela was planning to pick some things up here on her way back home—maybe she can get them now."

I was all for it. Marcela went to the counter and spoke with a short, thin worker guy there while we waited at the door.

The inside was just as I remembered it—always smelled of cumin, small as an oversized closet, everything stacked floor to ceiling, even hanging from the ceiling, no space unused and poorly lighted. Dreamy? I was in the dream!

As Marcela walked out she said, "Anything you'd need in a pinch, but the best quality fresh fruits and veg are in the Marché, just up the street about three blocks. I'm headed there now."

We walked with Marcela to the Ville Nouvelle Marché. There we split—she for her fresh fruit and veg shopping, us to the bank.

At the bank, I changed an American Express traveler's check into dirhams. Tom warned me to keep my wallet, my money, anything of value out of my back pockets. Secure everything of value, he said, in my front pockets or inside in a money belt. We left the bank and started a casual stroll around what I would call downtown in this urban agricultural centre the Meknes Ville Nouvelle.

I was interested to find out more about the town.

"You guys talk about medina and Ville Nouvelle, tell me more about them. I'm into urban landscape."

"Villes Nouvelles are the new towns the French built after they occupied Morocco at the beginning of the 20th Century—all roads are wide, sized for motor vehicles, buildings flavored by Art Deco." Justin said, "Medinas are the old parts of town, some 5 or more centuries old, that were built after the Middle East Arabs arrived 700 years ago—all paths are narrow, sized for pedestrians."

"These medinas..." he continued, "have been respected as world cultural landmarks by the UN. So most of the large cities of Morocco have two parts that are geographically separated by one or two kilometers. In essence then you have two very distinctly different towns in each major city that the French occupied. Before the medinas, there were only the people of the bled, the country, the Berbers. And most of the Berbers are still country folk."

We went to look for Marcela. As we arrived at the Ville Nouvelle Marché, I examined the scene. A one-story building from the outside but inside a high ceiling, open air, partially-covered courtyard with the open air end having a small rectangular undecorated water basin, around which cut-flower vendors sold their goods.

The rest of the vendors, all Moroccans—maybe 25 of them, sold fresh fruits and vegetables, some from open crates, others from carefully arranged pyramidal stacks. The courtyard smelled of fresh produce and sounded like hawkers' paradise—everybody doing business—each vendor asking us to taste their sweet fruits. It didn't take too long before we bumped into Marcela. She had her panier overflowing with greens—lettuces, beans, tomatoes.

Nobody was in my face. There was room to move around. The entire scene—colorful, vibrant, aromatic, exciting. This was more as I remembered from my visit to Morocco almost 20 years ago. I liked this market. From the donkey carts parked outside I concluded that the produce from agricultural field to market to home all happened in less than one day. That was what I called fresh.

The most attractive I saw were the mounds of oranges. Most vendors had four or five different types of oranges, many with the fresh green leaves still attached. Marcela showed me some small bins of orange flowers that were being sold primarily, she said, for giving added aroma to mint tea.

The vendor made sure I smelled the orange blossoms. Orange blossoms have always been magic. Their magic starts with a beautiful invitation—their clean and tidy, velvety white, small flower petals. Then their fragrance kicks in—a heavenly fragrance. They yield an essential oil, neroli—and before I knew it their magic captured my mind—memories flowed.

My girlfriend Sachy absolutely had to have neroli in her hair. Again I inhaled deeply the orange blossoms—my head was completely taken into a real but distant world filled with pleasant memories of Sachy. Internally, I swooned and committed myself to do whatever it would take to complete my design study and be home with Sachy for Christmas.

***

Meknes Medina

Then Tom and Justin shook me back to reality.

"C'mon, let us show you the Meknes medina now. Marcela has to go back home."

"To get to the medina from here," Justin added, "we have either a 30 minute walk or a five minute Petit Taxi ride. Petit Taxis are your friends. Take these little Renaults anywhere in town anytime of the day. Just make sure to agree the price before you climb in. They are cheap by American standard."

We took the Petit Taxi.

In the Meknes medina, culture shock continued. I was glad to have walked with people from my own culture, but that was only mental. Everything else around me bombarded my senses with intense unfamiliarity. Once again, all was in my face. I had no private space. My personal distance from strangers around me was zero. I could not generate any perspective.

I was jammed with people pushing up against each other—and up against me everywhere, like I saw in the Tangier train station yesterday. Couldn't take a step anywhere in the medina without being touched by at least three other people, at the same time!

The medina crowds were all men, mostly wearing strange, pointy-toed, bright yellow leather slippers (*babouches*) and hooded robes (*djellabas*)—long-sleeved, single pieced, summer weight cotton, colored in a variety of pastel shades. Weird! Cartoon weird—but not a laughing matter.

And as if that wasn't enough. Almost everyone had their heads hidden inside their *djellaba* hoods. At least they weren't trying to sell me anything, or trying to be my friend. So many hoods—no faces. A sea of mysterious strangers.

As constant as the dense body-against-body uncomfortable crowds of strangers were, so too was the din of impassioned human voice cacophony that hurt my ears. Everybody was shouting. Shouting at each other or across the crowd. Deep guttural shouting. Not a language of whispers.

Half the time I thought they might have been shouting at me. That's how the shouts felt. All directed toward me. My companions assured me otherwise. Tom chuckled and said, "Welcome to the medina, my friend." The pathways were unpredictably narrow—never more than 2 meters wide—and roughly and irregularly paved. We were closed in on both sides by tall, leaning, strangely yellowed buildings that looked centuries old. I had no awareness of sky above. And each building frontage—10 meters or less—had a ground floor vendor hawking his goods to the crowd, at the top of his voice.

For me, it was strangers' aggressive, guttural utterances non-stop! The only thing that changed that arhythmic aural threat was someone shouting even louder, warning that an overloaded, heavily beaten, fur-bare donkey was squeezing through the crowds, while at the same time dropping poop out the rear.

I had sandals and no socks.

Couldn't help stepping in it.

Couldn't see the ground.

Felt my foot sink into the warm, soft stuff.

Life goes on.

The crowd never stops.

What was driving this strangeness? Something inside me or something in them? Lots of thoughts. No answers. Yellow babouches, loud guttural Arabic—I remembered that from when I visited years ago with my mom. This time I was overwhelmed with an indescribable strangeness. What was it? Why the difference?

For the rest of the day, Justin and Tom led me around the medina. Different souks—souk was like a district or a section where all the different vendors, cheek by jowl, sold the same goods—veg here, fruit there, leather over there, etc. No all-in-one stores. The medina definitely had a 19th Century pre-industrialization Budgett Meakin vibe, just like Lazló described. The souks revitalized my memories—good memories of an intriguing, mysterious urban landscape—this was a real downtown—such were my memories.

I was getting just a bit hopeful. I only needed to... what... get accustomed to verbal assaults—to being jostled in public every time I was in the medina? That was never described by travel writers as anything more than locals being pushy—definitely understated.

The spice souk—strong aromas—huge pyramids of spices—so colorful—so enticing—cumin, turmeric—vendors were busy—no glass containers—nothing prepackaged. They used pieces of old newspapers that they fashioned into hand sized cones for each customer.

Then the olive souk—more huge pyramids—olives displayed like the spices—black olives—purple olives—small olives—large olives—ruby olives—green olives—olives mixed with peppers and pimentos—olives mixed with cut lemons—amazing variety—amazing olive aura. Each vendor shouted and offered tasting. Justin told me they all had families to support. They needed sales. That I understood.

Then prayer call echoed through the souks and all the vendors covered over their wares as they went to the nearest mosque for about 30 minutes. I really did like the feel of this market place—the medina souks of Meknes. It was just as attractive as described in all the contemporary travel websites and books. Even more so to me because it resonated with my pleasant memories of my time with my mom here 20 years ago.

I tried to put on my landscape architect's hat to analyze what I had just seen in this medina urban landscape. The Meknes medina was an unbelievable pedestrian network of public ways and places filled with hooded people, packed tightly as sardines in a can, but moving—continuously flowing. Streets? None! Cars? None! Medina was truly pedestrian only—especially because of the very narrow dimensions of the pathways.

Call them as you wish—alleys, alleyways, passageways, pathways, byways—all narrow—making the slivers of sunlight blinding, and the shade darker than night. These public rights of way in the medina, the main pathways, never uniform or straight, always narrow, always twisting and turning. Unpredictable.

The pathways were an inextricable confusion of men and donkeys, all too close, all bellowing, in tone all complaining. Wonder what Edward T. Hall, author of *The Hidden Dimension*, one of the books at the academic basis of my design study, would have made of this? Talk about an urban landscape! And I hadn't seen a tree or plant yet.

To my disappointment, we saw two no-longer-functioning public water fountains. That was a blow, a low blow on top of everything else going on around me.

"Is this it? Have we seen all the public water fountains of the Meknes medina?"

"No, there are a few more; but far from here. We'll take you to see them, but not today," said Tom.

Justin followed, "According to my memory most of the public water fountains in the Meknes medina are not working or under repair. We'll find out tomorrow."

This was really bad news! My head was spinning, then I asked, "Is this the case for all the medinas in Morocco?"

"Not sure, but possible. CJ, let's take it one step at a time. We'll show you some classics tomorrow," Justin said.

But I was already worried about my design study. It was sinking. In a strange way, it was disappearing before my very eyes. And I wondered about Herb Striet. Where was he? And if that wasn't enough, the medina mood of shouting, in-your-face passion was bumming me, big time. We continued shouldering our way through the medina.

***

Medina Disappointment

Tom and Justin took me through a souk of leather book binders, not very many. That reminded me of my study. The study final report hard copy the guys from my school originally did here in Morocco had been bound in red Moroccan leather by a Moroccan bookbinder. It had been inspirationally beautiful and I wanted to make my final hard copy bound in leather at least as nice as theirs.

So I went inside a book binder shop with Tom and Justin. First thing I noticed was the quiet. I briefly luxuriated in my quiet respite from the medina crowd. When I looked around I saw some fine tooling and gilting skills. That was a good discovery. I took note.

Then we moved on. Not far away, in another souk, was Damasquinerie, metalwork being noisily hammered out by craftsmen originally from Spain. Finely worked designs reminded me of the Alhambra architectural details. At another souk, I saw decorative boxes like the one my mom had. Thuja inlay boxes from Essaouira. A pleasure to see their skilled handwork. Amazing variety—some fine craftsmanship; but the street scene in the public realm—very disturbing.

And my study focus on traditional medina public water fountains? From what I had seen today, I couldn't do it here because those fountains were no longer functioning here in the Meknes medina. Definitely a low blow. Maybe the fountains we will see tomorrow will still be functioning. I did still have hope.

Tom, Marcela and Justin's introduction to expatriate life in Meknes had been helpful, but it oddly didn't sink in. I felt detached from their explanations. I felt unusually isolated. It was something basic. Like trying to fit a square peg into a round hole, I was unable to process what I was seeing and hearing.

On one hand, I was hearing an American expatriate delivering a Meknes intro to 21st century Morocco. On the other hand, and at the same time, I heard it as an intro to 19th century Morocco. I had to conclude that my crossing the Strait of Gibraltar had been an experience... but not time travel as Lazló had suggested... for me, the experience was more about an involuntary shape shifting.

Believe me. When I looked deeply into the shadowy light of the Meknes medina, and listened carefully to my inner ear receptions, that place in the ear—somewhere between where I hear thoughts and where I hear ringing—I strangely found myself displaced from what I call the real world.

I was so out of balance, I didn't know if I was in the 19th or the 21st century and if either would be more helpful than the other. Linear-time, cyclical-time... it was all a mish-mash of confusion. I had to focus my thoughts.

"How do you guys get by day-to-day? How do you guys fit in? Any serious street problems?"

"No beheadings since '56." Tom chuckled, then added, "In town, we all wear non-descript, blend-in, beige hooded robes, cotton in the summer, wool in the winter, the *djellabas*. We wear them most of the time, though Western dress works okay for men—and in Tangier, anything goes."

"But Western ladies need to, how do they say it now, keep their assets under cover—wearing hooded *djellabas* or the more modern, hoodless *kaftans*," Justin added.

Tom said, "Not to worry, once the people recognize you as a regular, a resident, they ignore you."

I thought that is good for you guys to say, having been here for years, but I'm only going to be here six months.

Tom added, "...except for those beggars who are 'managed'."

"Managed?" I asked.

Justin said, "Few people talk about it, but it's a sad part of life."

Then Tom added, "You see what appears to be unfortunate

mothers with driveling, snotty nosed, young babies in their arms..."

"What?!" I was astounded.

"I always like to help out poor people—and I saw no women with babies in Tangier—but poor mothers with babies in arms? You're telling me they are managed?!"

"Managed and unfortunate," said Justin. "There usually is a man, like a prostitute's pimp, who manages them, taking their daily collections—we might call it a protection racket or worse."

"Is it legal; and what do you do?"

"Not legal—here is where it gets culturally and socially complicated. Without going into detail, give if you want; but be warned, once you give it is like you have established a personal connection with the beggar and they stick like fly paper. If you stare or even just look, they still will stick like fly paper. If you don't give, just ignore 100%."

Flypaper? I felt, uh, not sure how I felt—as if someone had just ripped out my multi-cultural compassionate wisdom teeth—all four at once. From 30,000 feet, identity politics had sounded plausible; but down here face to face on the ground, "multi-culti, diversity-is-good" did not work.

I was fighting off a huge case of the nerves. Culturally uncomfortable things aside, my Morocco design study had begun to fall apart. The medina public water fountains, at least the ondes I had seen today in Meknes, were no longer informal daily social gathering points. Heck, they weren't even functioning. And my in-country professional advisor, Herb Striet, was AWOL.

I didn't have a "Plan B". And I was not particularly comfortable to "go with the flow". Not this time. I was off-balance and I did not know why or how to stabilize. Maybe I was just being a "nervous-Nellie", but ever since my turbulent ferry crossing of the strait, my head felt like one of those Sahara *shergees* had filled it with desert fines.

***

Café Cyber Club

That afternoon after returning to the Beau Séjour, I needed to try to put my imbalance into an understandable stability. I focused on my study requirements. That usually put me into a working space I could understand.

For my study, I needed to examine local digital options. And I was also curious about the urban landscape of the Ville Nouvelle, so that afternoon after washing up, I went out again and looked for the Cyber Club that the "helper" Hameed had mentioned the day I arrived in Meknes. I walked up the street toward the train station. The street was lined on both sides with dark green broadleaf evergreen trees that looked like orange trees. Orange trees? Nobody plants fruit trees in pavements as urban street trees—messy fruits on pavements.

I stopped in front of the train station and looked across the street for the Cyber Club. Both sides of the street were chockablock with three- and four-story buildings in that 1920-30s cheap Art Deco look. Definitely small-town downtown. Dark shade from the trees made it hard to see detail on the shops and store fronts. The Ville Nouvelle was not bustling like in the medina. Vehicle traffic looked like agricultural town. Slow moving. Pickup trucks. Donkey carts with agricultural goods.

I crossed the street. No Cyber Club; but I noticed a little alley and turned in. First door on the left, Cyber Club sign with an arrow pointing down stairs. Really felt like the neglected back of house, poor finishing, old paint, filthy walls. Had that dirty alley feel.

Went downstairs and through the door. The sound of modem dial-up connections. Small room, low lights, five terminals and a desk. On the wall was a poster. Netscape, See the World. All the terminals were Wintel machines. Nothing fancy. I half expected to hear the Rolling Stones singing "Start Me Up", advertising Windows 95. Slow speed dial-up modems and five year old equipment would not be useful for me. I'd always been a latest release Apple guy; and as I was chuckling to myself, Hameed, whose back had been to me because he was working at a terminal, greeted me.

I asked, "*Que faites-vous?* What are you doing?"

"*Je cherche du travail à la Corse* (Corsica)."

"What kind of work?" I asked in my best street French.

"*Carreaux, couche de carreaux. A la cuisine, aux salles de bain, comme ça.*"

"*Avez vous de la chance,* any luck?"

"*Peut être, insha allah. J'attends leur réponse.*"

When he said tile work, my eyes widened as I imagined he might be doing that traditional Alhambra-like Islamic tile work. No such luck. Kitchens and bathrooms—a bog standard tile laborer. I had other questions for him: the street trees, oranges? He said they were amer orange, bitter orange, not for eating. Hmm... I thought even though they make a mess on the pavement, shade trees on the street are good. I'd seen no trees in the medina.

In the background, over the loudspeaker, I kept hearing Arabic songs emotionally sung by a throaty deep voiced lady. I asked, "*Qui est la chantesse,* who is the singer?"

Hameed's eyes went glassy when he, with a fanboy reverence, said, "Om Khaltoum."

Meant nothing to me. But her voice had something in it. Something deep. Deep roots?

I asked Hameed how much to use the Internet. He said, "*Rien du tout,*" as he pointed to the older guy behind the desk in the back, because it was his older brother who ran the place. Hameed said, "*Y'allah, allons au café pour un thé à la menthe.*"

He took me through the back door, past a filthy toilet and up one flight of rickety stairs.

5-Speaking the Unspoken

Keef

As soon as we passed through a door at the top of the stairs, I looked around. Definitely a low budget tea room. The tea room was bright, sunlit on one end with large glass windows onto another Nouvelle Ville street complete with street trees.

Immediately on my right, I saw a small tea making area—gas canister feeding a single burner sitting on a meter-square wooden table next to a sink that was filled with tea glasses in various stages of washing. A one guy, low budget operation. The sink had only one simple faucet and above it were two shelves. One with clean tea glasses and the second with boxes of black tea and bags of sugar. On the floor under the sink was a huge batch of fresh green mint stuffed into a re-purposed, old 10-liter safflower oil tin. Hameed said the mint was cut this morning. The smell of the mint was invigorating.

But this was the back of a much larger unfinished room full of plastic tables and chairs. Square tables with two, three or four chairs at each. A men-only place. On the table next to the sink was a ghetto-blaster size audio cassette player loudly playing that same deep, throaty woman's voice singing, as Hameed told me, songs of love.

Most of the tables were occupied primarily with older men smoking long wooden pipes. A cloud of smoke hung over the tables. The room had an unmistakably sweet smell—marijuana. Hameed called it *keef.* A young guy came up to us and Hameed introduced him as his cousin, Marwan. Marwan said *keef* was a mixture of marijuana flowers and tobacco, both finely cut.

I saw the old men smoking it in small, thimble sized, clay bowls through the long, nicely carved and painted wooden pipe stems, 20-25cm long. Marwan called the pipes *sebsi*. I asked if it was legal. Hameed said no; but the police tolerate old men smoking it. Felt a bit awkward being the only Westerner in the place.

Marwan reached into his *djellaba* and pulled out a couple small, palm-size newspaper cones. He opened one and showed me the *keef*, saying for ten dirhams I could buy it. I told him no. Hameed said it was illegal to sell but Marwan made money selling the cones mostly to the older men.

I found the old men smoking to be intriguing but I didn't want to be around anything illegal. Last thing I needed was to get caught involved in illegal activities. I'd already felt my study slipping away; and I needed this for graduation.

In what I came to understand as typical Moroccan hospitality, Hameed said I must have some mint tea. I said next time, and as I excused myself, I had to say I was sorry over and over before Hameed let me loose. With a certain relief, I walked, by myself, back to my Beau Séjour apartment.

***

Sfinj

The next morning I went to Tom and Marcela's again for breakfast. After I thanked them for their hospitality, they asked me if I'd like to get a dozen fresh warm donuts for our breakfast. The cost? Two donuts one dirham (five cents apiece). Sounded like fun. Told me how to find the donut guy. I borrowed Tom's bike.

In less than three minutes, I found the donut guy, under a shady tree on a Ville Nouvelle residential neighborhood street corner. He was older, thin, wiry and sitting cross legged on the back of a flat four-wheeled wooden trailer, his donkey tied to another tree close by. The guy was cooking the donuts in a broad, large wok-like pan of boiling safflower oil, over gas canister fed fire, everything within arm's reach on his wooden trailer.

He kept his batch of dough next to him in a deep aluminum pot covered by a cloth. I ordered a dozen, gave him the six dirhams. I waited and watched. He reached into the batch, tore him off some, and one by one, opened a centre hole then dropped each piece into the bubbling oil. He laid out a ring of twelve doughnuts. He had a recycled home-made L-shaped thin metal stick that he used to turn them while they cooked in the hot oil, flipping them over and over, until they were ready. Then he pulled them out onto a wire rack.

Next was a Moroccan version of take-out. From a stack of palm fronds, he took one and stripped off four or so individual short and narrow palm frondlets, which he knotted together into two long pieces. Then he strung six donuts to each before tying the frondlet ends into convenient to carry loops, and handed me the dozen, still very warm. Donuts ready to go.

As I got back on Tom's bike, I scraped my ankle on the curb. An abrasion, didn't bleed, but I should have worn socks.

Back at breakfast over doughnuts with Marcela, Tom and Justin, we talked about my immediate plans. I had a couple things on my mind. First I needed to see those other fountains in the medina. Justin said we would go after breakfast. Then, I needed a trip to Rabat to sort out my bank affairs, set up accounts while in Morocco. Justin suggested I stop at the United States Peace Corps (PC) office in Rabat because the PC Director used to be in charge of architects and urbanists years ago and maybe he'd have insights on my study or info on Striet. That was a sparkle of hope. I needed that.

Justin marked up a map for me that showed the Peace Corps and bank were in the same downtown Rabat neighborhood.

After a full and satisfying breakfast, I went back to my room. Before getting ready to go to the medina, I analyzed what my first couple days in Tangier and Meknes had taught me. I felt, on the good days, I was gradually moving into Moroccan culture; though it was a superficial movement at best. Superficial? Unfortunately, because the reality I faced in the Meknes medina had been dominated always by strangers, always too close for comfort.

Not like Tangier, where everyone wanted to have my ear. No, here nobody was talking to me; rather it was the intensity that pushed me. And that intensity impaired my thinking in real time. As if I was being swept up into an unrelenting storm. What I was hearing fully occupied my thoughts—I couldn't shake the obsessive overbearing that internally pained me. Sounds without meaning but carrying high decibel emotive powers.

My ears were being abused by agitated people sounds harsher than I had ever before heard from the mouths of humans. Very similar to the furor I had witnessed at the Tangier train station. High decibels. Screaming. But this time the sharp guttural exclamations actually pained my ears, specifically, deep inside, like my inner ears had been bitch-slapped. You'd have to hear it to believe how deeply disturbing it was.

The cross-cultural negativity kept cranking up, as if I was under the sway of... something... what?

***

Meknes Medina Deep

There was more downside.

Later that morning Tom, Justin and I finally took a Petit Taxi to the medina specifically to look at what Justin called the best of Meknes medina public water fountains. Off the edge of Place el Hedim, we looked at a long and beautifully tiled public water fountain—like many I had seen illustrated in the earlier student study; but it was filled with wind-blown paper, bio-trash and god knows what else. The wall spigots were crusty and dry as a bone.

Was that my study?

We started down another medina alley. Squatting at the side of the alley was an older woman, a study in black clothes head to foot. Head, hair, arms, legs and feet all covered in black, only her eyes showing through the narrowest of slits above her black veil. She was rocking back and forth, repeatedly shouting in a shrill high pitched Arabic voice.

Justin translated, and as I listened, I was shocked at her extremely loud volume and sickeningly venomous tone.

"God's curse be upon your religion! Curses—curses on you!"

Justin and Tom sped up and Tom said something about evileye. We kept moving.

Next, they showed me another public fountain, beautiful proportions and inspirational tile patterns. Its strong presence made it suitable for a local landmark, but no longer working. I felt a certain sadness looking at this fountain that time had passed by. Sad? Yeah, sad as I would be if someone who still had nous had been retired too soon. I felt sorry, gravely disappointed, that the retirement of these fountains meant my study was not doable, at least here in Meknes.

The beautiful fountains that had been documented by student studies fifteen years ago were in disrepair. The fountains were no longer used, and falling apart. Modern infrastructure had superseded them. The basis for my study, the use of public water fountains, had, at least in Meknes, disappeared.

My careful planning for this last design course was dissolving. There would be no easy design study for me. I tried to keep a brave face. I was going to make it happen. Maybe there would be working fountains in Tangier—at least that was my hope. Med beaches and working fountains—the game was not over yet.

But today was a real bummer. The outlook for working fountains in general had taken a massive hit in Meknes. I went to sleep that night in a bad mood.

***

Justin Dishes

I woke up late and unsettled. In the apartment below mine I saw the window open and Justin working inside. I knocked and asked to come in. He said he was busy. I told him I needed more info on fountains and local culture—really, I needed bucking up. He suggested that we take a walk in the afternoon.

I met Justin at 2 o'clock in front of the Beau Séjour. He grabbed a Petit Taxi and we rode north to the edge of town. We stopped at the end of another treelined Ville Nouvelle boulevard. This one had a wide grass central median with a double row of shade trees. Sidewalks and additional shade tree rows on both sides gave this boulevard a ceremonial feel. But at its end, it just died. And that was where Justin told the Petit Taxi driver to drop us.

After leaving the taxi, we walked a further one hundred meters before encountering ancient and wide fortifications, or I should say, their remnants. Justin said this wall was built in the 17th Century when Meknes was an Imperial city, the home of Moulay Ismael.

We stood on top of the ramparts and looked out into the distance. It was the north eastern edge of town. Beyond where we could actually see but in the same direction, Justin said, were the remnants of the Roman town known as Volubulis; and not far from it was the town, Moulay Idris, founded almost a thousand years ago by the first Muslims coming from Arabia.

Then Justin said, "The history is deep and intense; but, CJ, I must share with you the modern forces at play in Morocco, because they have old roots and you might find them impacting your study in not only a serious but dangerous way. In the 19th century was a time of the Barbary pirate kidnapping European ladies from boats and selling them as white slaves, concubines. Islam has always treated its nonbelievers as slaves—and it still happens today. There is a market for young white Christian women—trafficking, we call it now. And the Peace Corps has from time to time lost one or another of its young female teachers. Never found, never publicly acknowledged."

"I don't understand. Why are you telling me this?"

"Listen, a whole lot of young Americans come to Morocco in a cocoon of idealism. They come to live out some kind of freedom dream that has nothing to do with reality here. This place is not a Disneyland exhibit. History tells the truth about Islam and North Africa. And modern technology now has facilitated the illegal movement of people, drugs and big money. Needless to say, crime abounds. You may find yourself on the idealistic edge of contemporary human trafficking. And your profession, landscape architecture, is at the front edge of international real estate development, sometimes under fraudulent conditions. Should I tell you more?"

"I don't need more to worry about; but I am listening."

"There has always been a trade of *bakshish* money to buy favors associated with the ruling people. Today's government has similar issues and especially in Tangier and Marrakesh where modern real estate developers from Arabia are trying to 'work' their way into North African riches—I can only warn you to keep your nose clean." Justin paused and, without speaking, we looked out on the quiet agricultural landscape between Meknes and in the near distance, the Zerhoun mountains.

Then Justin continued, "And speaking of keeping your nose clean, marijuana and hasheesh used to be small stuff but now they are big business from here to Europe, the Middle East, North America—again keep clear if you want easy-in easy-out for your study."

I was speechless. My head spun with these warnings. Justin could see it in my eyes and said, "Look, enjoy the Mediterranean sun, fresh produce and laid-back, fatalist spirit. Let all the rest of the complications just flow around you. Do your study and stay focused. Enjoy the fresh air. But don't forget, you are a *nazrani*, a Christian in a Muslim country. You will begin each day with that disadvantage."

No sooner had Justin finished speaking, than we saw at the base of this old 17th Century thick fortification wall below us, somebody, who didn't see us, squatting down about 25 meters away and dropping a deuce.

"Stay away from the stinky stuff," Justin said.

We chuckled and as we walked back to the boulevard to find a Petit Taxi, Justin had one more practical piece of advice for when I would head back to Tangier.

He said, "Remind me back at the apartment and, on Tom's map of Tangier, I'll mark the path to the Old American Legation. There, ask for Erik, he's the Director. He knows Tangier. He might know something about Herb Striet."

***

The Police Arrive

There was still plenty of summer daylight when we got back to the Beau Séjour. I was getting restless. I had to move on—so much bad news. I went to the train station to buy my ticket to Rabat in advance, an early-advance ticket, like I did in Tangier. I wasn't going to take any chances. Bought my first-class seat for 2 July.

Then, on my way out of the station, I bumped into Hameed. He asked me to have that mint tea with him. I agreed. Nothing else to do; besides, I relished the chance to speak with a Moroccan youth about local youth and street culture. I was a bit concerned that I would be going to a place where keef was smoked, but I thought what's the harm, we were only going to drink the national pastime—mint tea. We sat near the back, next to where the tea was being made. Something energizing about the smell of fresh mint. I liked it.

When the tea came to the table, Hameed asked in Arabic for something and the guy brought over a scoopful of fresh orange blossoms. The mint tea was in an inexpensive, clear. 6oz. glass. The glass was already full of a light yellowish tea with a small amount of black tea. But that was not all—the glass was jam full of fresh green mint leaves. The guy, following Hameed's request, sprinkled fresh orange blossoms on top of the already stuffed glass.

The tea was finger burning hot—I grabbed the glass with my thumb and forefinger on its very top edge—and it still was burning hot. But its fragrance was strong. The mint and orange blossoms were, alone by their smell, intoxicating. I blew on the top two or three times before I sipped. Oh, it was sweet, very sweet—but just right. I relaxed with Hameed as we took a couple more sips. Then all hell broke loose.

Two men in suits burst through the front door and, at the same time, two men in police uniforms burst in through the back door. The four converged on... they converged on Marwan, who was near the front.

"What's happening?" I asked Hameed. He shushed me.

I asked, "Should we help Marwan?"

Marwan was being roughly treated and handcuffs were placed.

Hameed said, "Don't do or say anything. Let the police work. If we interfere they will take us too."

"What happened?" I asked again.

"Marwan sells *keef* to Westerners and the police do not tolerate it," Hameed said.

In 10 minutes the ruckus was over as all four police took Marwan away in a van.

"What's going to happen, Hameed?"

"Only Allah knows."

I was trying to work back through all that I had just seen, when... the two plain clothes policemen came back and walked directly to our table. They noted we were only drinking, not smoking, then asked to see my papers.

Fortunately, I had my passport with me. They asked me what I was doing here. I told them I was making a student project. They examined my visa, which did indeed say I was in Morocco for university studies.

While handing my passport back, one of them said, in quite clear English, to me, "It is against the law to buy and sell drugs in Morocco. That includes marijuana, *keef* and hasheesh."

The other added, "If you visit these *keef* cafes regularly, you may be suspect and arrested. This is your warning. Your passport details have been recorded."

What? I was both shaken and stirred. I had thought about keeping the incident to myself; but upon returning to the Beau Séjour, when I saw Justin's light on in his apartment, I decided to tell him what happened. As I told him, he stood up and his eyes hardened.

He said, "Didn't you listen to what I said about keeping your nose clean?"

"Hey, look, these were just a bunch of old geezers passing time... what we used to call nickel-bag stuff... not big time like you were talking about. Besides, we were only drinking mint tea."

"CJ, anytime the police are involved there is danger. Don't mess with it. If you break the law and get taken to jail you are on your own. US government will not intercede; and the conditions inside? You'll be lucky to get one meal a day; and as an infidel it will be your worst nightmare! If you are as serious about your study and professional career as you said, stay away from the Moroccan drug scene."

I went to bed that night thinking I was damn lucky to walk away from that scene in the *keef* parlour today. Lucky. First time lucky.

***

Aragon

The next morning, I rode Tom's bike again to buy breakfast donuts from the same *sfinj* vendor. Back in my room, I noticed my ankle abrasion had not healed yet. It had been a couple days since that superficial abrasion—hardly more than broken surface skin—so I went to Tom and Marcela's apartment to see if they had first aid stuff.

Marcela was home alone. She brought some first aid antiseptic and gauze bandages. I had wondered about how she liked living in Morocco, in Meknes. So I asked her while she was cleaning my scraped ankle. She told me that the fruit and veg markets were fantastic. That the agricultural roots of the Meknes area had a certain attractive flavor. She wasn't really a city girl. She taught in a local private girls' school and it was fun—mostly kids from expatriate French agricultural specialists. She told me she did not mind wearing a *djelleba* or *kaftan* in town. And nobody bothered her on the streets.

She finished wrapping and securing the gauze. I thought it was a little more than necessary, but why complain. Then she asked if I had any questions that Tom and Justin had not answered. At first, I said no, not really, but then I remembered that screaming and ranting lady in black in the medina the other day.

I said to Marcela that I found it strange, almost superstitious, the way that Tom and Justin hurried by her and didn't want to talk about her. They did say something about evileye.

"Marcela, what is that all about?"

She asked me if I had some time. I did; my train to Rabat

86

did not leave until the afternoon. She went into the kitchen to prepare Nescafe. When she returned, we sat down with the Nescafe, some *Petit Beurre* cookies, and she commenced.

"You know I am Spanish, right?"

"Yeah, Tom told me."

"Well," she went on, "my family is from the north, Aragon, and when I was a child, all around me I had aunts and great aunts. They told many stories about the south of Spain, *Al Andalus*. That is how I first heard of the evileye. It was something the Moor brought from Africa. That is the story. Here's how I remember it being told. The evileye is like a heavy ground fog. It puts everyone under its influence. And those under its influence do not, after a while, even know they are affected. At the edges of this ground fog are ragged mists swirling out, like witches' fingers, looking to get hold of people not already under the influence of the evileye. But I had one great-great uncle, he has since passed away... and I really shouldn't talk about this."

"What's this?"

"This is all so subtle and powerful."

"Powerful?"

"...but not in any sense we normally talk about these days..."

"Tell me, I came here to learn."

"My great-great uncle was very old, spoke rarely. As a young man, he was the black sheep of the family, subject of many stories among the women... he might have even been a teenager when he had to go to the sea... he was a seaman... but he didn't like to tell stories... especially about his years along the ports of West Africa, Dahomey and others... but one day... after my aunts had been going on with their speculative stories about the evileye... they had taken a break for siesta... and my great-great uncle, he stirred and said quietly to me, 'It is not fog, it is sound, a sound that has organic roots that move silently like fog, roots that attach to the human inner ear and live on the essence of human.'" Marcela went quiet.

"What's the matter?" I asked.

"We shouldn't talk about this. We are too close to its West African home."

Marcela sat quietly for the longest while. We both finished our Nescafe and cookies. Then she looked at me with sympathy and hope in her eyes. She spoke as if to save me.

"My aunts used to warn me to go to church, for the Lord Jesus, Mary and the Holy Ghost with the angel hosts would protect me, if I was sincere; and, thank God, I've been sincere all my life."

"What about living here?"

"Well, there are so many charms and spells people here use for protection—especially in the medina—you can see them and hear them everywhere."

"But you, Marcela?"

"Like I said, I am a sincere believer. I feel protected. And in two years, Tom and I will move either to northern Spain or Canada to raise a family. We will not do that here."

"What about my time here, my six months?"

"You are Christian, right? Keep your faith strong—there is no room for atheism, agnosticism or secularism. Without your faith in God, you are bait, waiting to be gobbled up in the fog."

What could I say? I was speechless. I thanked Marcela for her hospitality and help. I had to get ready to catch the train to Rabat. Her Nescafe, cookies and ankle cleaning were nothing compared to her evileye story. Was that real? Was I already enveloped in some kind of Moorish fog? She had told the story as if a Joseph Conrad acolyte. Nah, nothing in it. I said to myself, forget it—get on with the details of the study and living here for the short six months.

Time to move on to Rabat—make sure my finances will work here and hopefully find out more stuff about Herb Striet and the doability of my study.

6-Rabat

The Capital City

My dad taught me to be financially savvy and secure. That has always been helpful. Fewer things to get in the way of daily life. He tried to instruct me about the long-term picture. In his own life, my dad had been a pushy go-getter. He wanted me to be the same.

That's why he had arranged for me, on the front end of my Moroccan design study, to make potential international business connections by taking the two-month European road trip on bicycles, with four other university students from his high school alma mater, the International School of Brussels. After my exhausting design studio efforts at university, the trip with those guys had been not only interesting, but a much-needed, relaxing change of pace.

Now, on my own in Morocco, I had some business to take care of. Out of financial necessity, I had to go to an international bank in Rabat to arrange and secure access to my funds. That, I hoped, would come together without any problems. I needed some success. Especially now, since my study was ominously coming apart. I could, while in Rabat, also meet, from Justin's recommendation, the Peace Corps Director, a long-time resident and urban planner/architect, who likely had insight into the status of Moroccan medina public domain water fountains. In fact, he might even know something about my in-country professional advisor, the AWOL Herb Striet.

So, I was hopeful about my trip to Rabat. In Meknes, on the afternoon of 2 July, Tom walked me to the train station. Departure was easy, no mad crowds like Tangier. Ride was smooth, not much more than two hours. Landscape, not agricultural or forest, more hilly, scrubby and wild, looked dried out from summer.

Arrived in Rabat and used Justin's map to find the bank—walking distance from the train station. Met the responsible people and started the paperwork to assure access to funds in Morocco. Spent an hour and a half at the bank, sorted almost everything. Relief.

While Meknes was definitely an agricultural, slow moving town, Rabat Nouvelle Ville, the capital, had that special, busier, downright bustling feeling—less hooded *djellabas*, more European suits. Felt like a smaller European downtown—no "helpers". Used Justin's map again and after about ten minutes undisturbed walk, found the Peace Corps office.

***

Peace Corps

Met the Peace Corps In-country Director, Rick, a Southern Cal architecture-urbanism graduate, from back in the late 60s. I knew nothing about the Peace Corps, so I asked him. He told me that the Peace Corps was there to help Moroccans wherever they needed help.

"Back when I was a PC Volunteer," he said, "the help was often in very practical tasks associated with water supply, forest management and urban planning—and the volunteers more often were people who had already worked post graduation.

"In recent years," he said, "our implementation has evolved. We call our efforts 'Community and Positive Youth Development'. We have a larger focus on youth education and the family. And the volunteers are predominantly fresh graduates in education."

Then he asked, "Tell me what brings you, a landscape architecture student, to Morocco."

I told him about my design study, assessing medina public water fountains—and the problem in Meknes where those fountains were no longer working.

"That's interesting... we are seeing more and more students from American university programs coming to Morocco for term abroad studies... and you know what they have in common?"

"Tell me, what?"

"It is not unusual for students to identify a study topic in the US, then come here to find local conditions demand redefining the topic. Because of the confusion this often causes, most undergrad students come in groups. You are by yourself? How's that?"

I told him the whole story about how I convinced my advisor that I could do it by myself—embed myself in the culture. But then I admitted that what I saw on the streets of Tangier and in the Meknes medina had put me off.

"How exactly?" he asked.

"I felt awkward, off-balance, unsure of my perceptions and reactions," I tried to clarify.

Rick asked if I had a contact back home. I pulled out my wallet and said my contact was my girlfriend of six years and she was studying to teach art and music at primary schools. I looked at Sachy's photo and I could feel I was already missing her. I showed her photo to Rick.

He did not try to hide his "interest". "She's a real looker. Have the two of you ever thought about helping poor people in foreign countries? The Peace Corps needs people like you."

I didn't know what to make of Rick's comments. I wondered, does the Peace Corps officially prefer female volunteers who are "real lookers"? Not my interest, so I continued to explain the context of my study.

"I have fixed myself on becoming a landscape architect and this term abroad design study is all I need for graduation. I'm focused on that. I'm supposed to have a contact here in Morocco, an in-country advisor. His name is Herb Striet, and he's supposed to be in Tangier; but I don't know exactly where. Maybe you know him?"

"Herb Striet, yeah, Herb and I did some projects here a long time ago. Haven't talked to him in years." Then, Rick dug into my study.

"If you have time, I'd be glad to show you around the Rabat medina and that should help you develop your study ideas," he offered.

"Perfect, I'd like that. When can you do it?"

"Let me check my schedule." While checking his appointments, he added, "You might be interested to meet some of our Peace Corps Volunteers. All of our Moroccan volunteers (PCVs) will be here in Rabat the day after tomorrow

94

for our annual 4th of July party."

I thought it would be good for me to talk with other young Americans about how they were finding Moroccan street culture.

"CJ, why don't you come home with me tonight. You can spend the night in my place, I've got plenty of room... we can talk more about your study..."

"That's good, I'd be glad to... if I'm not putting you out?"

"Not at all."

Rick then shifted back to my study. "Most of the public water fountains have fallen into disrepair and will, in the next couple years, undergo refurbishment."

Not at all encouraging.

"The Kasbah of the Udayas, here in Rabat, might have some fountains operating by the end of the year; but the schedule is not guaranteed. Tomorrow, let's plan to walk the Rabat medina and Kasbah of the Udayas," he suggested.

"Are you saying I won't find public water fountains as social gathering nodes in any of the Moroccan medinas?'

"Maybe you might find, in some medinas, the odd fountain still functioning as social infrastructure, but that's now a rarity."

He recommended I might want to re-focus my study. Not what I wanted to hear.

Rick told me he had appointments the rest of the day and walked me downstairs to the Peace Corps library, in particular the section on New Town Planning and the work of Marshal Lyautey—the French guy responsible for preserving the historically rich medinas and building the Villes Nouvelles.

For the rest of the afternoon, I stayed in the Peace Corps library, where I read about the history of French 20th century urban planning in Morocco. That was interesting background that basically reinforced what I thought was the social value of those traditional, absolutely beautiful medina public realm water fountains where people drew water for household use— amazing social hubs.

At the end of the business day, Rick, a bachelor, looking to be in good shape even though pushing his 50s, drove me to his home in the Ville Nouvelle. In a neighborhood of single-family, two-story villas, Rick's villa was large enough for a family of five or six. His Moroccan maid/cook had dinner already prepared.

Maid? That was twice in rapid succession that I encountered Americans with maids. I knew well-off people in the US, like Sachy's parents, had maids, but people, on "get-by" salaries, helping poor people? Didn't seem to add up. Certainly, there was nothing middle-class American about a maid.

I listened to justifications for Moroccan maids and, if I was to generalize, maids were justified as a means of cultural integration. I didn't understand that at all. Not understanding the local culture? For me, this was an uncomfortable regular occurrence. I didn't want to think about it. I was hungry and happy to be distracted when Rick's maid entered the room and served dinner.

After she left, we ate. During dinner, Rick reinforced the real problem I was facing—no functioning water fountains in the medinas. He said, "Morocco is modernizing."

I didn't want to hear it. I wanted to stick with my plan. I was hoping to find one of the remaining functioning fountains.

Then Rick told me the plans for 4th of July, the night after tomorrow when all the Moroccan PCVs would be in town. Rick said he would make other sleeping arrangements for me because he needed my room for that night.

"There are single room sleeping accommodations in government facilities for the PC Volunteers arriving from all over Morocco. You can have your own room there. And by attending the party and staying the night with them, you will have the chance to get a feel for the Peace Corps," he said.

Peace Corps? My study was on my mind. After dinner, Rick showed my room, bathroom and shower. I took advantage and showered. Under a stream of hot water, I thought about my study.

My design study was not starting easily. My local contact was missing. The focus of my study, water fountains in the medina public realm, were for the most part, no longer functioning. Interesting challenges. Solvable, I hope. But as I went to sleep, my persistent unsettlement began taking even firmer root.

The next day, Rick took me to the Rabat medina and Kasbah of the Udayas. It was all a bummer. Medina jam packed with hooded people shouting at donkeys and each other. Filthy walls along all the medina byways—same as the Meknes medina. No working public water fountains anywhere. My worst nightmare come true. But I had to trust my plan and that meant getting to find my in-country advisor in Tangier.

That afternoon, when Rick went back to work, I finished my business with the bank. Then, in the Peace Corps library until the end of the day, I read more 20th Century Moroccan historical background. We ate dinner again at his place like the night before. I was looking forward to the all-day 4th of July party the next day. I needed some relaxation.

***

Born in the USA

US Independence Day, the Fourth of July.

My short time in Morocco had been a lot like the pop music tune, *Born in the USA*, by Bruce Springsteen. For years, many thought it was an anthem in support of the July 4th Independence Day, when in reality it was an anti-USA war statement. Upside down. The song and its meaning were upside down. And that was how I was seeing Morocco, upside down... or inside out... I really wasn't sure, yet. The street culture continued perplexing me.

Since Rick, as Peace Corps Director, had responsibilities to comfort and strengthen particularly stressed volunteers throughout the day and evening of the party, all the rooms in his villa would be in use. He kindly arranged for me to spend the night with the Peace Corps Volunteers at the English Language Schools Annex (ELSA) near the Embassy.

ELSA was a contracted compound, controlled by the Embassy's Public Affairs Section. The ELSA annex had all the bells and whistles: Olympic sized swimming pool, beach volleyball sand pits, dormitory accommodation, large all-purpose meeting rooms, smaller team size classrooms, dining facilities—a taste of American-style higher education.

It was used regularly for Moroccan student extensive English language training programs. At the Peace Corps hospitality induction table, I signed into the dormitory accommodation. They assigned to me a lockable storage cubicle and a dormitory style bed in a single room. Each pair of rooms shared a toilet and shower. Stowed and locked my stuff. Went out to meet the volunteers.

Turned out to be one crazy day—another view into that cross-cultural looking glass. There were well over a hundred Americans, mostly young, recent college graduates. All had made their own way from every corner of Morocco to Rabat, just for this party.

***

The Party

The party? I can't deny it, I felt like I was at some kind of American university "Greek Rush Week" open house. Large open spaces abuzz with noisy American chatter. I could understand every word I heard, like it or not. It was a real change from my medina experiences.

Lots of girls, few guys, maybe a ratio of 8:1. To my eyes it was obvious that they all missed each other and were gloriously happy to be with people of their own culture once again. I met a lot of distressed volunteers—quite a few free-wheeling and looking for action.

First girl I met was by herself, drinking up a storm of Budweiser. "Four fuckin' months without alcohol, buddy," her words exactly on introduction.

"What do you mean no booze," I retorted, "I've only been here two weeks and I have seen beer and wine in every *bakal* in Meknes and Rabat."

"You ain't seen the boonies yet—the small Berber villages in the mountains—dry as a bone."

Then she started talking about her Moroccan boyfriend. How she was being persecuted by the neighbors, the kids, everyone. She was just being herself, she pleaded. I listened to her sexist ravings about Moroccans—ravings, ravings, and more ravings—non-stop. This girl was stressed, her diatribe so intense she could not listen; I couldn't listen either. I excused myself. I needed fresh air.

I walked around the open air, Olympic size pool. Some were playing volleyball in the pool; lots were swimming widths.

Took a lounge chair poolside.

Another girl sat down next to me and we talked. She, too, was culturally shell-shocked. These volunteers were shell-shocked by cultural realities hitting them directly in their faces and upside their heads, over and over. That's what I thought after having sat with two volunteers.

These were people who had undergone "careful screening" back in the USA, psych profiling, then three months of in-country language and culture training in the homes of volunteer Moroccan locals. And these kids had now been on their "jobs" maybe six months already. Overall, damn near twelve months of Moroccan reality under their belts.

I listened to her experiences and, just like the first girl, she was upset because of all the strange day-in, day-out cross-cultural realities. I suggested we get up and inspect the all-day-buffet table. She welcomed the change of subject. We walked over and took inventory.

Iced down coolers of pop and beer.

Candy bars.

Cotton candy.

Corn on the cob.

Hot dogs, hamburgers.

Tacos, burritos, potato chips—all flavors.

Pizzas.

All the great American summer 4th of July party food.

Even *muesli* and vegetarian stuff.

She told me none of this was available in stores here. And I certainly hadn't seen anything like this for sale in Meknes or Rabat. I went right into the candy and picked up five bags of M&M peanuts—red, white and blue.

We watched a beach volleyball game in the sand pit—looked just like Venice Beach, Southern California to me. But there were no Moroccans. No Moroccans. Service was by Peace Corps and Embassy office volunteers.

This girl I was talking with, Brandi, she respected the cultural values here, dressed properly in public, behaved properly in public; but she felt alone, culturally isolated under a strange stress that turned her only shelter, her apartment, into what she called... a prison.

"Prison? Why?"

"First of all, I came here to help people. But WTF! The street scene with men is intolerable. Sexist comments without rest. Just have to ignore and walk on. Too much!"

"How do you get by? Do you have a friend or someone from back home?"

Brandi looked at me like I had just opened a door that she normally kept closed. But she let loose. She walked through the open door, saying, "If only. No brothers, no sisters. Mom and Dad divorced."

"I hear you."

She said, "Not just divorced but living lives that have nothing for me. I'm on my own. So I joined the Peace Corps to help out some other poor souls—and this is what I find?! I'm going over to Rick's place tomorrow. He understands. He has his ways. But the local Moroccan guys, they are just a quick night's work. What about you?"

She was looking me over, up and down. I could see in her face the heat. I knew what was about to happen. I reached for some M&M peanuts and said nothing.

She liked what she saw and continued, "You free? Need a buddy, a BFF?"

I now understood why everyone had a single room. I felt like I almost had a duty to relieve her sexual tension—take one or even four or five for the team—you know, so they could get back in the ring, get back on the job with renewed energy. Too much! Took all my empathetic skills to walk away without making a bad situation worse.

Went inside where they had game consoles and fast, wide-band terminals. Had to get in line to go online with a 15-minute limit. I learned from those next to me that nobody could get fat pipes on the public connections. That jived with the dial up modems I saw at the Cyber Club in Meknes.

This was party time for all. What I saw was a great group of American youth under stress—drinking deeply from their own cultural water well, a refreshment that could not exist outside these walls.

Wondered if I, amongst these other young Americans, was seeing my near-term fate. My own fragility in the next six months? Now that my study scope was coming apart, would I get my study done? Was I to become like these, culturally stressed to some ill-defined breaking point?

Wandered around. Talked with lots of girls; looking for buddies, they were. Culturally shell-shocked, no doubt about it, definitely unhealthy anxiety.

Finally, I talked with a guy who wasn't wrapped up with a girl. This guy was a thinker—he was trying to figure out this cross-cultural shell-shocked situation.

He said he was under stress and accordingly modified his public appearance, his philosophy, everything. Was an atheist— now pretended to be a Christian. In his own words, he tried his multi-culti, politically correct hardest, bent over backwards twice over to "fit in". It wasn't working.

He said he felt like the sharp end of a spear on a 21st century imperialistic psych battleground. His dilemma was, in his words, a "Catch 22".

He explained, "Do I do things my way, the American way, knowing that they'll actually get done and be done the way that I want them to? Or, do I do things the Moroccan way, relying on locals to get things done, even if they're not done correctly or done on time?"

He went on, "It's not about black or white, my-way-or-your-way work process. I'm trying to find a balance... a cultural balance... but it feels like it is all one way... how to fit in? How to make a contribution?"

I listened as he tried to reason it out. He concluded, "Honestly, I'm still trying to figure out the answer to this question." I wished him luck and strength, then took off for another beer.

It wasn't the beer that made me dizzy. This culture thing— strange—I couldn't take any more of American Western culture sloshing up against and over Moroccan culture— appeared to be injurious on multiple levels. Time to go— enough party.

Had to see Rick to thank him. It was crowded. I wandered

among the crowd at poolside. I was still looking for Rick when a girl grabbed my arm and asked, "You the landscape architect?"

"Yes," and I started to explain.

As I spoke, she pushed her breasts into my arm and interrupted, saying, "If you're a landscape architect, I have a garden that's just itching to have a tree planted." She began rubbing her breasts back and forth on my arm as she spoke. Her other hand squeezed my back side and was moving to my front.

I took her hand in mine and brought it to my lips, kissed it and said, "As much as I love to plant trees, Rick, the Director, who personally invited me here, was expecting me, so please let me excuse myself."

That was the magic. She released.

I turned and saw Rick making sure that PCV girls who needed attention got the appropriate attention. No wonder he needed his guest rooms empty for tonight. Worked my way over to him and thanked him for the assistance. Said my goodbyes and headed back to my room.

Somebody put ZZ Top on the throbbing sound system and everyone started rocking. Not going to hear any prayer calls at this party. A good party? Not really. Relaxing never happened.

I went to my bunk alone that night. I scrubbed the M&M peanuts out of my teeth and lay down to review what my first two weeks in Morocco had taught me. I might have to redo my design study statement because the public domain water fountains no longer functioned. My in-country advisor was nowhere to be found. And the street culture was so strikingly different from America that during my short six-month term abroad design study, I might never settle in. At least that is what I learned today from these stressed out, yet well educated, carefully selected and in-country trained Peace Corps Volunteers.

Were there any good points? One. Herb Striet may be in Tangier. Two. Maybe there might be a functioning water fountain in a medina somewhere. Two too many maybes. What and where was my design study? The box ticking, easy effort study had disappeared. And some kind of ill-defined cross-cultural cloud was hovering over me. Sleep, anxious sleep.

7-Tangier

Diving In

I had read in the Peace Corps library that in the early 20th Century, during French occupation of Morocco, not only did Marshal Lyautey protect the ancient medinas and build new towns, he also established the national rail network, now all electrified—much of the electricity supplied by massive dams in the Atlas mountains.

My train rides had been problem free. This time again the train ticketing, boarding and ride were all smooth. I left Rabat on my way back to my original nightmare. In less than four hours, I would be back in Tangier; and, more than tinged with dread from the last time, I mustered hope for a better reception.

That hope was contagious. Hope... I hoped I would find Herb Striet. I hoped I would find a functioning public water fountain in the Tangier medina. Hope was all I had.

Before the train arrived in Tangier, my morning coffee wore off. Becoming drowsier, I put on my MP3 player—Tom Petty lulled me into an unsettled snooze. I nodded off with his words repeating in my ear... I feel something creeping in....

From Tangier train station to the Almohades Hotel, just like before, I ran a gauntlet of guys. Tom called them teeps, after the French, *les tips*. Helpers, the teeps, descended on me like flies to fresh meat. Same as before.

Did my best to ignore their appeals to show me the town, to show me a better, a cheaper hotel, to sell me souvenirs, to sell me girls, boys and drugs. I was already losing my multi-culti tolerance for these invasive teeps. Always pushy and tasteless.

A relief once again to enter the Almohades. At the hotel, a minor victory, I had the same room. Off the street and in the relative peace of my hotel room, I said to myself, here I am on the Med, with a broad, sweeping sand beach outside my window. But I was not peaceful. I wondered, what kind of culture, what kind of neighborhood had I dropped myself into? And my study?

I figured I had one primary task. I'd hang out at the Café de Paris—hoping to find Herb Striet. I'd stick with my plan, my approved study until I spoke with him. My early evening dinner was at the Almohades—hamburger and Coke in the hotel restaurant again—I paid the price. Then upstairs and early rest.

In the morning, I followed Tom and Justin's map. Worked, and I mean worked, my way uphill from the port, seeking the Café de Paris. It wasn't a steep hill, just a confusion of teeps, non-stop. Did I hear "*nazrani* go home"?

I barely had breathing space along the narrow, busy-with-taxis one-way street, walled in by tightly packed old, three- and four-story hotels with ground floor shops, their vendors hawking their wares on the sidewalks. Mixed in with the teeps, little kids tugged at my arms. Were these the "managed" beggars that Justin had described? With sad faces and tearful eyes, they begged, most dutifully, for "*un dirham s'il vous plait*" and "*donnez moi quelque chose.*"

At the top of the hill, on a prominent corner of a traffic circle, I found the Café de Paris, a single-story Art Deco building, modern in the 1930s, now aged, without change or much maintenance since then. Tight against the outside edge of the curving glass front, interrupting the busy sidewalk pedestrian flow, was a single row of helter-skelter tables.

The tables? Definitely Art Deco—decorative wrought iron base with marble tops—each occupied with at least two men, facing the street traffic—"sitting on the corner watching all the girls go by". The teeps fell away as I stepped through the Café de Paris door.

From the filled tables, I concluded it was a popular place. Men were dressed mostly in sporty European style, though by skin and eye color, I guessed their roots were North African.

Drinking? All nursing either mint tea or coffee. The café was smokey, crowded and noisy, smelled mostly of tobacco with occasional aromatic drifts of freshly brewed coffee and mint tea. Nobody paid me much attention as I wound around the full tables.

I found a small empty table on a narrow, raised platform in a back corner. From there, I could watch all the café. I could watch all the conversations. I could watch all the comings and goings. I could see the tourists and teeps passing by on the sidewalk. I was set to find Herb Striet.

The view from my seat also enabled me to assess from a distance the traffic circle, its use, its overall function and esthetics. It was a petite traffic circle—small but busy with a too dainty, undersized, decorative water fountain in its centre.

The traffic circle kept my interest. Even indoors, all the noisy, stuttering, horn beeping, automobiles working around that small traffic circle dominated my hearing. Traffic bristled just like Rabat, impatient and pushy, more like big city Europe.

Then I looked at Tom and Justin's map. Justin's notes said the Café de Paris was smack on the Place de la France. That's where I was. And to my right, across the street, was the French Embassy.

I focused on the indoor café crowd. Few tourists seemed to stop. Inside, the tables were filled with men only. I saw that a couple tables, not far from me, were occupied by older Western men. Maybe one was Herb Striet? I took out a letter from him and looked at his photo—no such luck. He wasn't at either of those tables.

I ordered a glass of just-squeezed orange juice. In the Med, the taste of fresh squeezed orange juice? Magic. Made me forget about the smokiness of the café. Orange juice, nice— refreshing, pushed my thoughts. Oranges, orange trees, orange blossoms—healthy tastes and smells. I hoped I'd never forget the simplicity of those pleasures.

Over the next hour or so, as I settled in, it seemed like everyone was just sitting there all morning. Working? Not working? Could not tell. The crowd seemed not to change.

Nobody, not even the waiter, bothered me. I relished that lack of imposition from strangers.

I was alert for Herb Striet. In my last communication, I had told him I was arriving in Meknes the middle of July. He didn't know I'd be looking for him in Tangier. Plenty of room for error there. Had to improve my chances of meeting him, had to take Justin's recommendation, check at the Old American Legation to see if someone there might have contact with him.

Around one in the afternoon, the café was still a busy place, but no Herb Striet. Took out Justin's map of Tangier again, to see how to get from the Café de Paris to the Old American Legation. Figured I would take the walk and try to find it. Looked like ten minutes away, into the medina.

The path I had to take turned out to be the main connector between the modern Tangier and the medina. That main connector felt like a path in a plantless, urban maze. No plants, no trees, but overcrowded with pedestrians.

Along the main path there were many side passages, each one looking like it could be the path to the Old American Legation. No signs. Couldn't be sure since each path quickly curved away and disappeared.

Each of those side paths was also filled with pedestrians, who, when I paused to look, immediately began speaking to me in broken English along with at least seven other languages. They always had one thing in common—a deal for me that I must accept. I could only take so much of that.

When I buried my head in the map, it was like a dog whistle for the teeps. Each one knew the best way for me to go, even though they had no idea where I wanted to go.

This was one strange place.

As youngsters, weren't we all told by our parents not to trust strangers? The medina passages were filled with strangers demanding my trust. Not comfortable. Didn't work for me.

I walked, not ten, but a struggling twenty minutes until, on a tight, very narrow, hardly more than a meter wide byway, I found myself at an ageless, heavy wooden door. This time there was a sign—the Old American Legation. I knocked, rang and waited. A lean, 60s something, Westerner, of average height, in a thin, moth eaten sweater answered the door—turned out to be the Director, Erik.

He told me he had a meeting in 30 minutes but he invited me in for a brief exchange in the privacy of the vestibule. He asked what brought me to the Old American Legation.

I told him about USAID English Language Centre Director Justin's recommendation and gave him a brief summary of my intended design study. Erik was friendly, helpful; but he knew nothing about the guy I was trying to contact, Herb Striet.

He asked for more about my study. I told him about the problem I was having finding public water fountains used traditionally in the medina. He said, "Maybe ten years ago in some neighborhoods; but these days modern infrastructure has taken over. There might be one here or there still functioning. But most people in the medina receive potable water piped directly into their homes."

"Even in Tangier?" I asked.

"For the most part," he said.

More disappointment. Then I asked him about how to address the troublesome street culture I was encountering everywhere.

"There always looms over everything the shady historical reputation of Tangier." He then suggested, "Try to keep in mind the Islamic street greeting exchanged between all people one to another. '*Salam alaykum.*' '*Alaykum salam.*' Peace be with you. Keep your mood like that, and you might find a calming on the street."

That was about all we had time for.

***

Petit Socco

As the days slowly passed, I came to understand the Café de Paris as having an inherent strong social and geographic presence. It was an invisible gateway that no one could see, but a landmark that everyone knew.

Any tourists, staying in hotels in the modern European part of town, passed this café on the way to the medina and Kasbah. Additionally, most social and cultural activities in the European part of town happened within 500 meters of the café.

Sitting on the Place de la France, it had been "the" gathering spot since Tangier became an official International Zone in the 1920s. It had been everything Rick's Café was in the movie *Casablanca*—and more so, though it had started to look a bit sleepy—busy, but sleepy, and no live music.

It was, nevertheless, the landmark for all directions. It was Paul Bowles' public hangout. And for me, I used it as my home base in the beginning while looking for Herb Striet; but afterwards, it was too close to the dark tourist hustle that I sought to avoid.

Every morning, on my way to the Café de Paris, it was the same when I walked out the Almohades hotel door—helpers, teeps—sometimes the same guys, sometimes new guys.

Pushing, touching.

In my face.

I show you, my friend.

Come with me, my friend.

My friend, my friend—they all said it; and I had never met any of them.

I saw them as all about hassling the tourists. Day in, day out. Like mosquitoes. Even the buzzing disturbed me. Could not let them land—they might bite, suck blood. For me, each day in the public realm, I was truly distracted until I arrived at the café. There, I always felt relief! No teeps allowed.

Café de Paris started to feel like my hangout. I passed entire days at the café—no Herb Striet. What if he didn't turn up? He was supposed to be the in-country professional advisor for my study and I needed some professional advice. Study, what study? Hadn't found a single operating fountain, yet.

The days at the café started to drag. Only so many times could I review my proposed study documents and my folder of Striet's communications. The crowd at the tables started to look the same every day, like mannequins in slow motion.

A certain tedium built up parallel to my frustration of no Herb Striet. One day at the café, I decided to explore further into the medina, maybe even find one of those "illusive" traditional public water fountains. As a landscape architecture student, I had always been attracted to pedestrian districts in towns. Those were places where all the cars and trucks were left behind—a natural domain for urban landscape architecture planning and design.

As pedestrian districts, the medinas were fantastic, amazing! Their narrow pathways, or byways, were not only the primary, they were the only transportation corridors. They functioned extremely well as a non-mechanized network in the pedestrian public realm—though I did wonder about fire equipment, ambulances and trash removal—major modern urban scale bugaboos in the Western world's "pedestrian" districts. In theory the Moroccan medinas contained the ideal pedestrian byways described frequently as eminently desirable for an urbane public life by William Whyte and Edward Hall, the two primary academic resources for my design study.

The Moroccan medinas were humming with the humans that make the human scale. They were not mechanically disrupted in any way—dimensions, sound, pollution, safety—none of these impacts from motorized vehicles impeded pedestrian life. That, I could live with! But the behavior of the people on the street—no way!

That morning, I walked all the way, according to my map, to the Petit Socco, in what I thought might be the heart of the medina, a cluster of small shops, cafés and "night" places around a very small open space without trees. I tried, while shooing away the teeps, to investigate all the little paths leading out of the Petit Socco. Petit Socco—heart of the medina? For sure there must have been a traditional public water fountain nearby.

Such a warren of twisty, turning, narrow, bumpy, cobbled paths I had never imagined—more like a carnival funhouse— easy to lose my way and impossible to mark my path. And again I was always being pestered by "my friends", strangers. And this time I was on my own—no knowledgeable Western expatriate to "hold my hand" as in Meknes and Rabat. Too much!

There were no empty lots, no fountains, no trees, no plants. But every pathway was lined with two-, three- and four-story buildings that forbade direct sunlight. And each building had a ground floor shop, often with frontage barely wider than the width of one door.

I found it impossible to figure out what was being sold in those myriad shops. Maybe that was on purpose? Something always prohibited me from achieving understanding of what was around me. Was it the pushy teeps? Was it that Moorish fog Marcela had described? I had no idea.

But I had ventured into this medina on my own—maybe I had begun developing some kind of hybrid aural/moral callouses. The teeps were still all around me. I hated that.

On foot in the medina, I had trouble analyzing, even with forming thoughts... but the Tangier medina... it had... what... its own history... its own fog... and strangely... its own perverse magnetism. Did I like it? No! But maybe it had something to offer.

This was the third medina I had visited in my three weeks in Morocco. All were jam packed with pedestrian activity. All were cacophonic with human and animal noise. But only Tangier had the teeps, the non-stop aggressive helpers. And most disheartening, none of the medinas I visited had functioning traditional public water fountains.

Finally, somewhat out of disappointment and frustration, I turned around and retraced my footsteps toward the European part of town.

***

Striet

I wormed my way back through the medina. Ignoring the teeps with all their pushy pleadings—still nightmarish—not my nature to ignore people trying to talk to me. Happy to get back to the Place de la France and the Café de Paris.

I was safe inside the café again when I saw a guy that I recognized—had to be Herb Striet! He was sitting down, eating by himself. I opened my folder of his letters and checked his photo. It was him!

He looked just like his photo—mid 50s, dark hair, medium length, no gray, dark eyes... short of sleep?... grizzled beard on the rough side of fashionable. Sitting at a table, he looked shorter than me—comfortable in his couple-days-old clothes—as if he had spent the last three days walking the medina—not flash at all—but for what I had become accustomed to in the café, he was Tangier presentable.

He was eating what I learned later he called breakfast—*cafe solo y dos tostados con mantequilla,* black coffee and toast with butter. I walked up to his table and, without even introducing myself, started.

"I've been looking for you in Meknes. They told me I might find you here. Am I glad to see you!"

He paused his chewing and looked me up and down.

"So you're Janus."

"Everyone calls me CJ."

"Welcome to the rim of Africa, my name is Striet, Herb Striet. Everyone calls me Striet." He put out his hand and we shared a firm handshake. He continued with hardly a breath,

"But don't think you can walk all over me just because of my name."

Then, obviously pleased with his play on words, he looked smugly into my eyes. As he continued to look me over, Striet spoke to me out loud. "You have that outdoorsy look in an American way with your longish blond hair, blue eyes." He paused, looked me up and down again.

"You're what, 5 foot 11, thinnish, not muscular, but firm, wiry, agile. Blue jeans, American style, well worn from use rather than by design. You have well broken-in sports shoes with a touch of design in your belt—wide, hand-tooled, New Mexican leather—engraved silver buckle—turquoise accents. Long story short, you have 'MARK' written all over you."

I was speechless.

He continued, "From your letters, I was convinced that you, like many Americans, were naive about the larger world; but you had a spark. You were an independent doer. I figured you'd sort out Morocco and your study in your own time."

He paused again, took a drink of his coffee. "I still think that. Let's talk. Sit down. Order something to drink. Glad you made it," he said, "a bit early but it works—welcome to *le Maroc.*"

Striet didn't say Morocco. He said *le Maroc.* It took me a while to figure out what he meant; but I finally gained the insight. What's the difference between Morocco and *le Maroc?* First of all, Morocco is genderless and *le Maroc* is 100% masculine.

Le Maroc begins with an entanglement of popular cultural roots from contemporary continental France. Then you must add deeper cultural influences from older roots like the French Foreign Legion and Edith Piaf. Stir all of that into the mix. Add *keef.* That gives a "taste" of *le Maroc.* Morocco, on the other hand, is simply an exhibit, a tourist-passing-through thing.

I came to learn that for nearly a decade, Striet had been barely getting by in Tangier, taking his relief, from time to time, in Meknes. He had been in a dark funk when I first contacted him by snail mail. Nevertheless, he had agreed to help. He felt an obligation to help students of landscape architecture get to know the "real world", the world outside the university ivory towers.

In the Café de Paris, we were finally face to face. I looked at him as if I had just met someone I thought I'd never ever see. I thought he was my savior. He acted like it was just another day.

He chomped through his afternoon "breakfast". I lingered over my Coke. Finally, he paused with his chewing and said, "I have a rooftop flat that I am using. You can stay there for your design study. The lease is good for another three years... I'm off to Arabia, and... if you can take care of plants, it's yours."

He looked me in the eyes, saw a glimmer of possibility and continued, "I'll show it to you."

***

Tangier Penthouse

We paid our food bills and Striet led the way. He hailed a Petit Taxi and off we went to his apartment. I can't forget that ride. Old car, maybe Renault Dauphine from the 60s, robin's egg blue, worn out back seat uncomfortably crowded with just Striet and me. The taxi sped through traffic circles and turns, rocking like a single car carnival fun ride. Tried to track the directions. Couldn't.

Disoriented, I could hardly think. The car windows were open—wind noise and constant horn beeping from the traffic around us. From inside the car, my ears struggled with the taxi driver's favorite Arabic woman singer, and her emotional intensity at high volume. I was in a daze. Striet sat relaxed as if all was normal.

Everything was happening so fast. Couldn't speak. Thoughts spun in my head. My study. My in-country advisor. Would Striet know about traditional public water fountains in the Tangier medina? How did Striet get around here with all the preying teeps? My head was swimming—questions—the ride—what next.

"Here we are," Striet announced.

As we got out of the taxi, he pointed to a nearby rank of Petit Taxis just around the corner from his building and said, "You can always get a Petit Taxi here any day, any time."

Finally, with my feet now on solid ground, I turned toward Striet and said, "We've got to talk."

He didn't pause, spoke over his shoulder, "We can talk upstairs."

His building looked 1930-ish—six or seven stories of apartments—an Art Deco feel, very European, nothing Islamic in its architecture. I was feeling a bit more normal. My observation skills returned.

Key in front door—elevator out of order—elliptical staircase with Art Deco wrought iron railing. Striet told me the elevator would be fixed soon. We walked up—three apartments per floor—six floors. Finally the roof.

Striet told me there were two rooftop apartments, his two rooms and a larger one with three rooms belonging to a friend of his, an American, an ethnobotany freak who doesn't keep plants, who, he said, mysteriously came and went rather irregularly.

We went inside Striet's apartment, a place disheveled, but clean. Took me outdoors onto his large terrace with a view, as Striet described, over the Bay of Tangier to Cape Malabata and beyond over the strait to Spain and Gibraltar. More than the large terrace and expansive view, the first thing I noticed on this roof top was the fresh air—the fresh Med and Atlantic air—clean air—the breeze felt beautifully healthy. Draughted deeply. Filled my lungs twice with it. Hadn't been able to do that since I arrived in Tangier. And his place, his terrace, was quiet.

"These are the plants, do you know them? Some have been here more than 10 years..."

I didn't hear the details because I had been overwhelmed, absorbed in the intoxicating Med ambiance of the airs, the roof top terrace and the view where the Atlantic Ocean and Mediterranean Sea jostled each other.

He continued, "...and that date palm? Got it in Kuwait as a baby from a guy doing tissue culture research. Pay attention!"

"What were you saying?" I asked.

"You came here to learn, right?"

Surprised by his sharp tone, I looked carefully at him. He was right. He did call a spade a spade and I had been drifting into a Med dream.

He went on. "This date palm is a *Barhi* and the dates are best when eaten half ripe. Do you know these plants?"

"These plants? Yeah, I know them. I worked with them two years ago during my internship in Southern California." I looked more closely at them. A couple tall, stately, single trunk palms—the taller, with the thinner trunk had the long silver gray feathers of *Phoenix dactylifera*, the shorter of the two with stouter trunk and happy green long feathers was a *Phoenix canariensis*, and a spectacular multi-trunk, 1.5 meter high clump—it actually looked like a bouquet bursting with innumerable clusters of the short, green fans typical of *Chamaerops humilis*. Each of these three had its own large container. Under them I saw—must have been a dozen—*Agave americanas* and variegated *Agave americanas*—both with bluish-gray, spikey, swordlike sheaths nearly a meter long.

And beneath all the above was a carpet of pots, small pots—lots of them, filled with every imaginable color. These were the classic matted succulents—*Carpobrotus, Delospermum, Lampranthus, Drosanthemum*. When I looked even closer, I saw among them, popping up here and there, some *Osteospermum* varieties.

Plant names came back from my internship in Southern California. Came back like my street French came back. Like muscles partially atrophied from non-use and happily in use again.

"You listening? The plants..." Striet blurted.

This time I interrupted him, "Could I take care of this garden, you wondered?"

Striet stood there watching me marvel. "Well?" he asked.

"Sure, I'll take care. My pleasure!" Striet's terrace garden and its view had, there was no other way to say it, in retrospect, seduced me. The terrace was quiet, filled with beautiful plants, a view over the Med, and there were no teeps tugging at me. No wonder I felt positively overwhelmed and relaxed at the same time. He led me back inside.

Showed me around his kitchen which was simple with the basics only. Mini-fridge, two burner stove, gas tank, sink and drainage board, one cabinet with dishes and food.

We went back out on the terrace—sunny and partly cloudy—what a view over the Strait of Gibraltar! He had two large, cheap, but comfortable, wicker chairs outdoors. As he offered me a seat, he said, "You wanted to talk?"

Then he asked, "Like red wine?"

"Yeah."

He went inside and I saw him rinse out two bog-standard 6oz. glasses that had been in his sink. He wiped them dry, grabbed a bottle from his cupboard, came out, sat down and poured two glasses.

"Some good red wines here. You'll like this. You can get it for a fair price in the Souss brothers' *bakal* downstairs—I'll introduce you to them tomorrow." He spoke like we already had a done deal.

He handed me a full glass, and we toasted. It was good. Then we started serious talking.

Asked him about my study falling apart, "Why didn't you tell me the medina's traditional public water fountains were out of service? I have not yet found one that is functioning, here, in Meknes or in Rabat. Do you know of any?"

"All these ideas you young US guys have—they turn to dust as soon as you get here—as soon as those ideas confront reality."

He looked me square in the eye and said, "You're either gonna make it or fail. That's the challenge. That's the game. It's just like life, you either figure it out and succeed, or you whine and fail."

He let his words sink in before he added, "I figured if you had the balls to come here on your own, you're a winner—so, you gonna work on this mystery? You gonna solve this puzzle? You gonna go wherever it takes? What are you gonna be in real life—a winner or a whiner?"

He had some strange power in those words. They made sense. But, really, I had no choice. I had to make this design study happen. And I was already here with a "helpful" advisor. Did not need to think long and hard.

So I said, "I'm here, let's do it."

"I'll make you an offer. I've paid my rent, including all utilities, in advance; and, in a couple days, I'm on my way back to the Middle East. You'll have the place to yourself. Cost you, say, a token $100 per month. How long will you be here, six months? Say $600—the place is yours."

I was gobsmacked.

"You will take care of the plants, right? All these sons-a-bitches are tough—don't over water them."

"Yeah, I can handle that."

I was in, I would make it work. A Tangier "penthouse" apartment, on the Med, was mine.

And my study? Still needed some details from Striet.

"Bring your stuff over tomorrow. You can stay on the banquette till I split."

Strange guy, Herb Striet—liked to use the snail mail—*poste restante*—no computer—no phone—definitely a luddite. Asked him about digital connectivity. Told me he didn't like all that electronic kit in his place. Liked it quiet.

He said, "But next door, the American, StoneSteve, he has all the electronics stuff. Short wave, satellite dish, security cameras—a digital and communications freak. He went to the same university as you. Not a bad guy—but, he is out there, somewhere. You'll meet him. In fact, if I am not around, just give him my keys, or give them to the *shaoush*, the apartment building caretaker, when you leave, when you've finished. When do you figure that'll be, again?"

"I'm out of here in about six months, the end of the year. Back at school in January for graduation."

Done.

"I've got more questions about Tangier and my study." I needed his help.

As if it was no big deal, he said, "Talk to me later."

We said goodnight and I took a Petit Taxi, without incident, back to the hotel. My last night in the Almohades. Thank God.

8-Tangier Spine

Pro Tips

The next day I brought my stuff over to Striet's and set it in the corner of the living room. Striet was moving about, packing his own things. I took my time—looked around his two-room apartment—good room with a view.

Hey, this was a Tangier penthouse—slightly down market, but spectacular geography in a world famous city—a rooftop penthouse with terrace garden for only $100 a month!

Striet, still bustling, told me he would show me around the neighborhood and the city. He took my map and marked up what he called the "spine of the medina". He marked the only two starting points I needed to know, the Grand Socco and the Place de la France.

"Now I'll show you how those two nodes relate to what I call the Tangier medina spine."

Then he took me on his Tangier medina spine walk. First, fifteen minutes on foot, from his place to the Grand Socco node. It was a huge open-space traffic circle with a pedestrianized seating area in the centre. I never could understand what sense there was to have a pedestrian park in the middle of a busy traffic circle—non stop conflicts between pedestrians and vehicles—19th century meeting the 21st century?

The traffic circle itself was filled with cars, trucks, busses, donkey carts—all helter-skelter and noisy with horns and shouting. He pointed to the shaded entry to what he called the Moroccan supermarket, a huge, covered outdoor market with everything I'd ever need to eat—none of it in packages— all fresh, or thereabouts. Reminded me of the Meknes Ville

Nouvelle marché.

"Grand Socco?" I asked.

"Souk, main souk," he said. I guessed that.

Suddenly, we left all motorized traffic behind and went through a huge Moorish archway into the medina, along a heavily traveled, main pedestrian path, toward the Petit Socco. I recognized this part. I had been on it a couple times already; but we were going further into unknown territory. Striet just kept pushing on.

At the far edge of the Petit Socco, marked as a node on his map, we made a left. The path became steep. We walked up, up, up. We labored uphill through the medina on a twisting byway, closed in by tightly packed, very old, two-, three- and four-story plaster-faced buildings of unpredictable frontage, colors varying between dirty yellow and dirty white. They were noteworthy for their plaster having an utterly filthy condition irregularly tracking hand height above uneven cobbled paving.

I noticed for the first time that the exteriors of these buildings had no decoration. The only breaks in the surface were for the doors—which were always heavy, wooden, secure looking, but often crudely constructed—and windows—none on the ground floor unless there was a merchant. Otherwise the windows were few and well above street level. The windows were invariably covered with wrought iron grills—everyone eye catching with tightly woven geometric patterns.

This path was thick with hooded, *djellaba*'d pedestrians, and led us to the Place Mechoir in the Kasbah. We paused for a moment as Striet told me that this node was the elevational high point of Tangier, the centre of centuries of cannon defense for the city.

"Kasbah means fortress or castle, something like that," he said. To me it all looked like the same medina.

Then we headed back the exact same way we had come. Striet didn't have trouble with teeps. Waved his hand or something, and they just flowed right by him. I stayed close and observed.

On our return to the Grand Socco he went left and took me to the Place de la France node and the Café de Paris. Told me anything in the modern town, the European Quarter, could be

130

found starting here. I was getting the picture. We had a coffee together. I was glad to be off of the teep thoroughfares and sitting quietly.

Sometimes Striet was just stubbornly silent; but he did have a clear understanding of this town. I was glad that he shared it. I had lots of questions.

"What is that waving thing you do when the teeps approach you?" I asked.

"You'll learn it. It's a timing thing; but the most important is to give zero energy with your eyes. Don't let them connect with your eyes. Then they will get the message when they see your hand flick like brushing away a fly. They understand you know what you are doing and they don't have any way to connect."

"Not sure I follow."

"In other words, ignore."

Striet sat, without speaking. He had made his point. Nothing more to say.

I tried to put it all together. I had just been through the entire Tangier medina and to the Kasbah for the first time. This town's medina was a pulsating labyrinth—a labyrinth densely packed with moving humans. It had intertwining, flowing layers of the most intense human emotions—almost sucking my air out—almost suffocating me. Emotional flows that were suffocating me? Something strange there—so much I didn't understand.

And the noise... the guttural noise... so similar to Meknes and Rabat medina noise. It had an over the top effect. These paths were filled with so much human and animal noise that thought and real-time analysis just didn't happen—I felt hampered. Hampered? And my study? More questions.

Asked him about other Americans or Westerners living in Tangier—people who might have insights for my study. He mentioned three. First was his neighbor, Steve.

"Everyone knows him as StoneSteve," he said. I looked quizzically.

"You can figure that out," Striet continued, "he's a retired Morocco Peace Corps Volunteer from a long time ago, an American, and keeps his apartment here as a bolt hole—knows the forests of Morocco and the ways of getting things done, in a timely fashion. Might be a resource if you have to change your design study. Remember, I told you he went to your school— well, he's got a Natural Resources Management degree."

"My university?"

"Yeah, you guys might become chums," he said chuckling.

I was getting a whole lot of input and before I could ask or say anything...

"Next," he said, "David, also American, he's another retired Morocco Peace Corps Volunteer from a long time ago—an architect—really into Africa. Never left Tangier, he owns a *riad*, that's a medina house that has an internal courtyard garden. Deep in the Kasbah. Renovated it. I never go there much.

"Third are a couple of guys living in a sprawling villa, outside of town to the west, on La Montagne. Couple of weirdos—it's one of the Tangier rabbit holes. Those guys are into plants—a forest of strange trees—they redid all the gardens around the villa. The two of them been there about twenty-five years. I visited once. They speak English, but they aren't American. Europeans, maybe Brits, can't remember... oh yeah, a Brit and a Rooskie. But if you're into flowers, they have a world class collection of hibiscus—everyone calls their place Hibiscus House."

This time Striet paid the bill, both his and mine, and we left the Café de Paris.

***

Striet Holds My Hand

Leaving the Café de Paris, Striet led me on a short walk to Rue de Mexique. Showed me Brahim's Sandwich Shop. Brahim was there and Striet introduced me. Brahim was in his 40s—tattooed up both arms.

Striet said, "Brahim is the guy who can tell all you need to know about telecom and digital in Morocco." That was just what I needed.

That would be useful for my final report hard copy. But it was Brahim's sandwich shop that interested me—a buzzing centre of activity all its own—about five guys working behind the counter, eight tables with shisha, fifteen counter seats inside, ten more small tables outside, another two guys handling the shisha pipes and coals.

Whole place had a fast service vibe with the feel of long-lasting community comfort. We grabbed a sandwich. Striet insisted on takeout. While we were watching the sandwich preparation, I asked Striet, "Can I get animal head sandwiches in Tangier?"

Crunching up his face, he looked at me and asked, "Where you coming from?!"

Told him about the animal head vendor in the Rabat medina where I saw, up close and in my face, a place that had multiple rows of dead and skinned animal heads displayed in the front of the shop to attract customers—or so I figured.

"If you are not sure about anything here, just ask. Like you did; but, if you can't stand ambiguous answers, best to go back home now, back to the US. Save you trouble."

Yeah, Striet was strange, but straight.

He told it like it was—as he saw it.

His mind was obviously on something else. He had things to do—getting ready to head to the Middle East.

We took a Petit Taxi back to his apartment. He explained the differences between Petit Taxis, local go-anywhere-in-town-anytime, small, old Renaults, and the grand taxis, very old large Peugeots and Citroens that would often be used as custom bus service, with six to ten people sharing, for longer between-town trips. And just as Justin in Meknes had already told me, Striet said, "Always agree the price before climbing in." I was getting the picture.

Stayed up late—Striet talked, no, he ranted about how Morocco had changed in the last thirty years. In the old days as he called it, the country, the rural landscape began 500 meters from the edge of town. The town had only two clear parts—the medina and the European Quarter. "In the countryside," he called it the *bled*, just like Justin, "no traffic.

"No inhabitants other than farmers, the Berbers, and they keep to themselves.

"Once in a while a bus would come by—nothing else—no mechanical noise.

"Quiet countryside.

"Peaceful landscape."

I liked that. Striet and I had some things in common.

"Now," he said, "what used to be *bled* has become places crammed with unfinished new construction—breeding grounds of dystopia—cars, people, dirt—noise—hubbub. Sickening urbanization. All looks like a made-to-order landfill—no effing redeeming qualities—a real bummer!"

I interrupted his rant. "Six months ago, when I read your letter bad-mouthing Tangier," I said, "I thought you exaggerated. But now that I'm here, I see you had accurately described the day to day Tangier reality. And that reality, along with the fact that I have not yet found a traditional water fountain functioning in the public realm, really bums me out. Study looks to be impossible. Do you have any advice for me?"

Striet said nothing while he put on a CD, lit up his small

hash pipe, inhaled three times, and by then, Tom Petty was singing *Runnin' Down a Dream.*

Striet offered the pipe. I said, "No."

"Unless you want it," he said, "I'll smoke the rest of it before I split."

I told him, "I'm staying away from that."

Even without the hash, I easily got into the music—dreams... it was about dreams. Dreams are supposed to be nice, aren't they? ...helpful with positivity? But not so far here in Tangier—still chock full of nightmares—both real and, I guessed, imagined—wasn't sure. And that very uncertainty had become its own nightmare.

Asked Striet again about my public water fountain study. No answer. He offered me his hash pipe. Again I declined. He took the hits. Looked at me and said, "Your study? Just do it."

He shut down his CD player and stayed silent. He went to his bedroom. The flat remained quiet—nice. Sofa was comfortable. I slept like a baby. I had unsettled dreams—but who ever knows the future?

The next morning, Striet was making noise, getting ready to go and he woke me up, saying, "C'mon, I'll introduce you to the *shaoush* and the guys running the *bakal,* the local grocery store. Then I'm splitting."

I pulled out my map and asked, "Anything else to show me?"

He marked up my Tangier street map showing Hibiscus House with a circle and said, "The place with the Brit and Rooskie? It's in this part of the La Montagne area."

Then he said, "The architect's upgraded *riad* in the Kasbah... I don't know where it is exactly but it should be somewhere not too far from the Place Mechoir. He has tarted it up, the outside is quite clean and crisp so you should be able to see it—not musty, dingey and dirty like normal public walls."

Lastly, he marked with an "x" exactly where we got the sandwiches from Brahim and handed the map to me saying, "That's all... that should get you through six months."

Then he added, "One more little thing. You know downstairs that Petit Taxi stand I showed you?"

"Yeah?"

"Well right around the corner from it is a drug store—an *apothéque*—should you ever have any health question—open around the clock, every day, all year. And that's it. That covers all the basics."

"That's all?"

***

Off to Arabia

Striet paused for a couple moments, carefully looking me over as if seeing me for the first time, before he said, "Tangier is a town of rabbit holes. Choose carefully what you explore. Cute little baby bunnies don't nest with snakes. In Tangier expect every rabbit hole to have snakes. If you've come here hoping for bunnies, you're a tourist and you've taken the wrong door. The medina, the Kasbah, la Montagne—all warrens of rabbit holes. Mind yourself. And like I said, I've given you all you need to get through your six-month study. Stay alert."

I stood numb like a statue after his last words. This wasn't the first or last time I was stupefied, speechless by what I heard or experienced here in Tangier.

"Come on, let's go meet the locals," he said.

Took me downstairs and across the street to a *bakal*, a local hole-in-the-wall grocery store about the size of a walk-in closet plus a room in back, similar to the *bakal* I had seen in Meknes, next to Tom and Marcela's. Striet pointed out how this place catered in a Moroccan way to Western European expats—every basic—handy, convenient, right next door. Bread, milk, butter, cheese, eggs, wine, fruit and veg, everything except fresh fish and meat. Inside the *bakal*, every inch of space was used—cans, boxes and bottles on shelves stacked floor to ceiling.

"You can get *baguettes* here every morning—and they always have fresh butter," said Striet as he pointed to a huge block, a cube of butter 18" on a side, sitting on the counter where one of the guys was slicing off a chunk for another customer.

Striet used a combination of French and English to talk with the *bakal* guys. On the way out, Striet told me, "They are from the Souss Berber tribe, way the hell down south. All the *bakal* operators all over the country are Souss Berbers—you figure it out."

"Why do you keep saying I should figure it out? I've got my own study to do. I need to focus on that."

"Okay, okay, point taken—but this is kind of interesting. You've heard of the mystery of Atlantis, right?"

"Yes..."

"Well some archeologists and other explorers say that Atlantis was not under water—that it was south of Marrakesh in a region called Souss Massa—and that is how the Souss grocery keepers throughout the country had the innate commercial skills—still a mystery—so I said, 'You figure it out'. But you do have to get into problem solving here if you want to succeed. Notice that door in the back corner? It leads to a very small back room, that's where they sleep. They are open every day from 7AM to 11PM. Dependable."

Striet, in his own way, was helpful. Took me back to his apartment building at a ground floor apartment where he knocked on the door frame of an open door. Introduced me to a person, the likes of whom I had never seen. Could only really think of him/her as a Spanish *shaoush* lady, 50-ish, 5'4", rotund, clean. Hair, graying, a bit thinning, up in a top knot held tightly by a net. Clothes seemed old, worn but acceptable material, just getting by.

Not my world—the *shaoush* was a man who had lived his life as a woman for other men, a queen—now past "her" prime. She had the appearance of an old cleaning lady; but she was a man even though her voice was soft and feminine. An old queen, having a mix of Moorish, Spanish and Jewish blood with a story yet to be revealed. Seemed so much like the Cervantes' character Sidi Hamete, to me that was who she was.

She took kindly to me. Asked me, "Need cooked meals?"

I thanked her and said, "Let me settle in first, and let me find my way around, okay?"

She wasn't talkative; but whenever I saw her, she always

asked, *olà ça va?* That was all, that was it. I never saw her in the doorway of her ground floor flat; but the door was always open and she was always slowly busy in a housedress and work apron. Nevertheless, she always stopped and looked my way when she said, *olà ça va?* Then before I could answer, she always had turned and carried on with her chores.

She locked the building at 1AM and unlocked it at 5AM. Never answered the ringing door in the middle of that four-hour night. She looked like a type that had a lifetime of secrets wrapped up tightly in her little round ball of a body and nobody else would ever know or guess what they were. She was protective.

After the *shaoush* introduction, Striet and I stepped out into the street. Suitcase in one hand, Striet handed me the keys to the apartment—said goodbye—then took off. I watched him walk around the corner.

I was in the European Quarter of Tangier. I looked up and down the quiet, short street lined with, actually covered over in, an arcade of flowering trees—*Jacaranda mimosifolia*—floating umbrellas of pale blue, hazy purple flowers. What a place! I took a deep breath.

Now I was on my own.

And, despite the dreamy beauty of my situation, I was beginning to understand Tangier was a place to be on guard. Relaxing, that which young Americans do so well, does not work for Western newbies in Tangier. And I was a prime example. I had a lot of work to do. I had a lot of learning to do.

But here I was on the Med for six months... I doubted that a suntan was on the cards.

***

Erik's Tangier

Some days later, still looking for functioning traditional public water fountains in the medina while facing head-on non-stop intervening street culture teeps, I went to the old American Legation again to see Erik. He had been welcoming and helpful on my first visit. Bringing him up to date, I told him that I had found Herb Striet and I was going to do my study here in Tangier.

Erik told me he had an open space for the *Darija* one-week immersion language stage in Casablanca the last week that month. I would have to make my own way to Casablanca, but the housing and classes would not cost anything. I was definitely interested; anything that might help relieve the daily street culture anxiety which had been getting in the way of my hunt for a functioning water fountain in the medina public realm.

"Since you are studying landscape architecture," Erik said, "do you know about *riads*...?" He thought from my eyes this might have been new to me, so he continued without pause, "...the urban houses unique to medinas?"

"Striet defined them once to me but I'd welcome more."

"Medina houses are all cheek by jowl, having three of their four exterior walls in common with neighbors—only the exterior wall with the door to the street is open, allowing only one wall where sunlight can penetrate into the houses through windows.

"The houses, medina *riads*, are two, three and four stories tall with a central, often postage-stamp-sized courtyard open to the sky. This courtyard is how light and fresh air are distributed to all the rest of the *riad* rooms because they are all facing on the open courtyard. The well-off merchants have larger courtyards and grow gardens there."

"What do people do with the courtyards if not for gardens?"

"They do chores, laundry, kitchen preparations—they may have one or two plants in pots—plants for health, fragrance or flowers—very simple."

Erik then offered, "Perhaps you might like to see the entire Legation. It is unusual because it is a complex series of interlinked *riads* of various sizes resulting in an unpredictable sequence of surprise courtyard gardens."

"I'd love to..." But before we could start, Erik had to step away. He left me with one of his Moroccan assistants to show me around.

And so, I began a labyrinthine *riad* garden tour—courtyard after courtyard—I should have been dropping bread crumbs because without a guide I could have never found my way back out. But I was having fun.

In one small 10 meter by 10 meter courtyard, divided by narrow flagstone footpaths into quarters, each quarter had a mature Norfolk Island pine. That made four *Araucaria excelsa* in that one garden—each sporting red bark, beautifully checked and flecked. The four huge 50cm diameter trunks supported interwoven foliage crowns.

Those crowns in turn were creating a trellis-like structure of overlapping branches whose fine textured evergreen needles gently filtered the sunlight. The courtyard's delicately blended dapple of shade and sun... well, it took my breath away with its aura of peaceful beauty. The Norfolk Island pine trunks stretched to well above the three-floor building, their first trellis-like branching high above the second floor. Strong health and spectacular beauty!

Then the strangeness began. The fellow showing me around said I could take photos if I wanted. I had not planned to take photos but I did because I found the movement from the dark inside the buildings to the light of the courtyards an integral part of its magic. Light and what I call luminosity became a big theme for me on my bike trip south through Europe—Monet at

Giverny and the Musée de l'Orangerie in Paris, Frank Gehry's Guggenheim in Bilbao, and then the exhilarating juxtaposition of architecture and courtyard gardens in the Alhambra. I had become fascinated by the inherent drama to be had with the manipulation of light and dark. Now I was face to face with it again. I had to try to capture it in photos.

I was in the midst of taking a series of photos from the bright light of one courtyard in sequence into the dark of an adjacent large stairwell. As I snapped the photo of the dark stairwell, all of a sudden a guy, whom I had not seen in that stairwell, started shouting and screaming in Arabic at the guy who was showing me around. An incredible scene of shouting and pushing began and carried on for at least fifteen minutes. There was running and chasing everywhere, upstairs, downstairs, throughout the entire Legation. It was an all-out level 10 shouting match—all in Arabic. I figured a fist fight was on any minute.

I stood to the side; I was watching a strange movie. Didn't know the characters or the story line. A tragedy in the making? Big time cross-cultural something—gap, crevasse, cliff—I was speechless. A roaring staccato storm of shouting. Didn't know what was going on. Finally, Erik ran in, told me to step aside, and calmed the whole thing down.

Apparently, according to Erik, the Muslim Moroccan guy in the stairwell was making his prayers and took offense at having his photo taken during prayer. That was his simple explanation. I was not so sure. There was some kind of cloud of negativity hovering over the whole scene; but like all my cross-cultural vagaries, I could not easily understand what was actually going on.

Erik apologized for the incident, but warned me about taking pictures in public without securing permission in advance. He repeated it a couple times. I got it. Keep my camera out of public.

But the scene! What can I say, a life might have been taken if either of those guys, both Moroccan, both Muslim, had a knife. It was that violent and aggressive. I hadn't really understood any of it.

After the fight and in the quiet privacy of his office, Erik explained, "The mad guy was a *Shia* and my assistant, a *Sunni*—a thousand-year-old conflict—animosities rooted deeply. Don't even try to get into that. But this next bit will impact you.

"Some younger Moroccans are in a frenzy because Western and other foreign influences are undermining their Islamic life, breaking down families and tempting Moroccans with huge amounts of money, especially fraudulent real estate schemes. Be careful whom you associate with. It is easy to become a target. Some won't think twice about taking advantage of a Westerner, to say the least. I must repeat, be careful who you hang around."

I remembered that Justin had told me something about real estate fraud, so I asked, "Real estate, what do you mean, Erik?"

"Let me try to make what I am saying clearer. There are a couple things that together agitate a fair number of Moroccans... when I say Moroccans you can assume I am talking about Muslims. For decades Moroccans have lived with Westerners; recently that tolerance has decreased. Real estate issues bother a lot of them. Look at the unfinished housing complexes everywhere. The Middle East oil money uses Western architects, planners, landscape architects, engineers as their front men. They become too often targets for the unrest."

"Well, how can anybody see me as anything but a tourist?"

"The questions you ask... the people you hang out with... you can stand out like a sore thumb even if you wear a wool *djelleba* and yellow *babouches*."

Felt like a punch to the mid-section; but he had not yet finished with his warnings. Erik spoke about the "itch" that Peace Corps Volunteers bring here to make Morocco a better place according to the popular young American view of free sex, as long as it is healthy, which here has led to a rise in strange cultural conflicts.

He continued, "This place had traditionally strong families even before Islam, and traditionally strong families during Islam. But Peace Corps Volunteers are now saying through their health, safety and community development courses, in essence, that families are optional. Women's freedom should be more important than family tradition."

I volunteered, "I was just at the Peace Corps 4th of July Party in Rabat and I met quite a number of young female volunteers under stress because they were face to face with the cutting edge of this cultural conflict you have just described. Many were disturbed, just trying to get by."

Erik said, "For the most part these young volunteers have little idea that they are on the front line of what some people have called an imperialistic psyop. And you should not be surprised to learn as I have found out that very strange times are brewing. Certain Muslims are very upset by this kind of cultural intrusion."

I thought, hell, I just wanted to do my study, and then I said, "I don't want any part of these cultural wars or any other nefarious activities."

"You're an American," Erik emphasized, "in a North African, predominately Muslim country. You will always be suspect. And, as I said, especially with this amenable Mediterranean climate, landscape architecture is the fancy foreplay of real estate development and voila—again you will be suspect. Best if you keep a low profile, stay out of trouble and work around, instead of through, all the cultural ambiguities."

Once again my head spun with these warnings about the dangerous world into which I had just naively stepped. Seemed like every person I met who knew well about Morocco was warning me. Erik saw perplexity in my face and concluded, "Don't go into it."

Asked him a bit more about the local culture on the street. Told him I found the local street culture was intense but my few words of street French had been useful. He suggested if, in addition to the *Darija* classes he had mentioned, I was interested in learning more about cultural interactions here in Tangier, I should go to the Piliers Culturels, a respectable bookstore in the city. I concluded to go there.

He told me that language was key, plus a firm understanding of right and wrong in cultures; but it could be confusing because there was an ongoing dynamic mixing pot of cultures at play: American, Islamic, European, Berber, West African—

144

each having their own evolving hybrids and off-shoots.

Hearing Erik's succinct explanation of how the turbulent street culture came to be was one thing. Understanding how to adapt to it was another and making my study happen was another still. Quandaries were an easy way for me to describe what had filled my day after day.

Striet had told me about an American architect in the Kasbah. Maybe... maybe he would have some helpful insights I could use to resolve my varied and continuing quandaries.

9-Kasbah

Kasbah Teep Nightmares

I was trying to find David the architect's place in the Kasbah. Striet told me it was close to Place Mechoir—well, close on a map did not translate easily to real life on the street in the Kasbah. And no map of the Kasbah was ever 100% accurate.

I thought about it. From a movie set it was Peter Lorre, "come with me to the Kasbah". But in real life it was a dozen teeps, "you want see Kasbah, my friend—I show you—come with me, my friend". Craziness never relented.

Many times, many teeps, every turn I took, they were all over me, each flogging the best ways in the Kasbah. I hadn't mastered Striet's flick of the hand yet. Whenever I turned a corner, I got lost. Each passageway looked the same. All the front doors looked the same. On top of everything else in the Kasbah, the sameness was disorienting. My sense of direction was like 2+2=5.

As I constantly encountered multiple teeps, I felt continuous awkward waves of off-putting emotional excess and exponential increases in stress. My entire body pounded with physical and emotional reverberations. No exaggeration. Never felt anything like that.

Where was it coming from? Couldn't figure it out; but it was non-stop. It undermined my study efforts because it, along with the crowded conditions, the animals, the shouting—altogether short-circuited my access to reason. Nothing about this hunt in the Kasbah was easy. Each day was like this. I couldn't find his place. Teeps relentlessly in my face, grabbing my arm— pushing, coaxing. It felt threatening.

Then one day when frustration and exasperation were maxing out, I found in the Kasbah, by chance, the Café on the Sea. Looked up a short, side passageway—saw a teahouse window at the end. Through that window, I saw the strait and Spain on the horizon, so I brushed off the teeps and went inside. Ordered a freshly squeezed orange juice and sat outside on their quiet cliffside terrace. That was Cadiz, Spain on the other side of the strait. I found some tranquility—nobody bothering me—looking out over the blue waters of the strait.

Once I left the teahouse and stepped out on the byways, cultural fatigue set in again. One teep too many? Give up, let the hustler take me? Soft sell... hard sell... always the sell. Always on guard. I understood how those Peace Corps Volunteers got so stressed out. And I did not want my apartment to become a prison of safety.

Then I found myself thinking in teep street language, "You don't know nothing, my friend." It was happening. Day after day in the medina had taken its toll on me. And now the Kasbah.

This Kasbah adventure had turned into everyone's bad dream—a pumping heart of a nightmare—enter by mistake—can't find the way out. Look, if you were not born in the Kasbah, it will be your nightmare. You will get lost. You will be confronted with people who will pretend to be your friend and then use you, cheat you, steal from you and worse... you want this to be your neighborhood? Your home?

I had enough of the Kasbah. I was sure I would find a traditional public water fountain somewhere in the medina, like between the Grand Socco and Petit Socco. I tried something different. In retrospect, this was a day when my multi-culti training got the better of me—gave these guys, these teeps a chance. So, as I got ready to explore for fountains, I grabbed a couple tangerines for casual refreshment and headed out to do battle. On an offshoot from Striet's medina spine, I started into a yet unexplored area.

Looked down the smaller alleyways, off the sides, for water fountains. Nothing.

I was trying to keep my bearings, moving uphill in the

direction of the Kasbah, but I got lost. Pulled out my map. I'm sure I even looked like I was lost. I was clearly giving off the signal for the helpers, the teeps to descend on me. Drugs? Hotels? Souvenirs?

Let me show you the medina, my friend. So I thought, what the hell. Another teep came up and said, "I help you, my friend."

"Okay," I said.

"What you want, my friend?"

"I want to see some water fountains, the fancy ones with pretty Moorish tiles."

"Come with me, my friend, I show you."

Walked and walked. Saw no water fountain. Carried on broken conversation in street French and pidgin English. Lots of gaps in understanding. Then he asked for money. Then he said he had nothing to eat. Again he asked for money. I stopped and pulled a tangerine from my pocket.

I offered it to him for his hunger. His eyes darkened. He took the tangerine and started to walk away. Then he began shouting in Arabic over his shoulder. Before I knew it, he fired the tangerine at me, then spat at me. Strange kind of quasi confrontation. I just stood there for a moment. Then he took off. Disappeared around a corner.

I had to think about what just happened. Guy got mad. Threw something. Spat. That's all. Not really any danger. Would have had more trouble in the wrong neighborhoods of LA or any other big city in the US. So maybe things weren't so bad here in Tangier.

I was in a strange place, off the beaten track, somewhere deep in the medina. Dead end pathways every way I turned. I recovered my thoughts. I was lost; but my knowledge of topography helped me to get to the Kasbah and Place Mechoir where I began to retrace Striet's Tangier medina spine back through the medina and home.

I was beat and I was feeling like my ankle wasn't right. But I returned safely without further incident. No fountains yet. I had to talk with that architect in the Kasbah. Like I said, getting to the Kasbah was never easy, despite lots of teep offers.

Teep, as I learned from Tom in Meknes, is a transliteration from the French tips: *les gars que l'on trouve sur les rues au Maroc.* In Tangier, they were the people who grabbed my sleeve every day. They demanded entry.

Teeps were like the bacteria flowing through our blood system. They attacked at will anywhere. The hurt was physical, emotional, psychological. It was warfare, believe me. Defenses always had to be alert. There were the low level teeps, the first generation, representing the in-your-face cross-cultural reality that is most uncomfortable to the Western visitor.

But there was more. There were iterative second and third level teeps that had more and more powers. They came better disguised as your friend. These weaponized teeps could not be seen in advance but they were out there and their powers came from the roots of cultures for which we, of the West, have no understanding. In my days in Tangier, in Morocco, I confronted all of them.

I don't think I conquered them. Tangier's uncertainty has always stuck with me. But they taught me a lesson. I learned that lesson. And what is that lesson?

Multi-culturalism and its ugly sister, diversity, are not inherently good. Self defense is essential. Go to Tangier. Find out for yourself.

And my ankle? As I was resting safely back at my flat, my ankle still bothered me. Believe it or not, the scrape from Meknes had not yet healed after three weeks of bandages and the antiseptic that Marcela had given me. I had used up all her supplies—now it was time for some outside help. I went to visit the local *Farmacia.*

The guy at the *Farmacia* asked to see my ankle. Gave me a cleaning solution, an antiseptic salve and special wraps for changing every other day for the next two weeks. Told me if it did not show improvement, I should see a doctor. I hoped that wouldn't be necessary. Headed home, did the cleanup and wrapping. Wrap was stiff. Made me limp—but it felt better.

And I was off to the Kasbah again. Had to find David's place. Had to learn my way around. Had to make my study happen. Had to seek shelter from medina and Kasbah teeps. Revisited the Café by the Sea almost every day.

Later that week, first thing in the morning, I cleaned and bandaged my ankle. Then I walked Striet's Tangier spine. I was going to find that architect's place in the Kasbah. But along the way? Distractions, an understatement. Non-stop human noise. Like looped recordings. Pleading whinings from teeps. Grating mashups from men.

The medina was chaos—an urban landscape of chaos, chaos of sound, chaos of dimension, chaos of wayfinding, chaos of cultural dissonance. I couldn't find my way and I was losing myself.

I pushed on. Started for the nth time at Place Mechoir. Wandered. Wandered more through the crazy tangle of spaghetti-like public ways, my study drove me. With unbelievable luck, I finally found David's place. Along the narrow passageway, it was not noteworthy, except the door looked better crafted, sturdier fittings, rich with patina, but fresh looking, clean, not abused. That was what Striet had told me to look for.

It had taken me days and days. I found it, half by graft half by fortune. Weary from teep impositions and walking too much, I decided not to knock; too fatigued to meet someone new. I needed respite. With what remaining energy I could muster, I made sure to mark my way back to Place Mechoir where I grabbed a Petit Taxi back to my apartment.

***

David's Riad

The next day, refreshed and feeling stronger, I took a Petit Taxi to Place Mechoir and walked back to David's place. Knocked on his door. He answered. I introduced myself and, in outline, my design study. David looked to be on the young side of 50, tallish, with a healthy start on corpulence—reminded me of the Sydney Greenstreet character in the movie, *Casablanca.*

I asked, "Do you have time to talk—can you share professional local background in relation to my landscape architecture study?"

Still at the door, he said, "You know I'm an architect, don't you? I also figure a couple things about landscape architects—like you guys really wanted to be architects but had to settle for something less." He chuckled, while I thought, nothing new here—when I did my internship with a large international landscape architecture firm in Fort Lauderdale, I ran into a lot of architects and civil engineers—same story—they, too, thought landscape architects were just glorified gardeners—trying to elbow into their professional turf.

Then his face became serious as he looked me up and down while apparently absorbing the scope of my proposed design study. Finally, he extended his hand, inviting me in and added, "I take my work seriously; and, all kidding aside, it sounds like you do, too."

Inside, he began with technical summary about how Tangier was currently entering a planning and development period. But I was distracted.

My eyes had been overwhelmed by his home, with its *riad*—two and a half or three stories tall, small central courtyard open to the sky, narrow rooms distributed around the perimeter—a typical *riad* as Erik had once described. As I examined it, I found was much more. Walls looked like hand finished mud in a natural reddish/beigey brown color. I called it modern minimalist with traditional materials.

I felt balm to the depths of my soul. His *riad* was quiet, green and full of oxygenated air. That I understood. But there was something else—real magic.

I'd been in a lot of gardens, walked lots of landscapes—but never this—never like this. The Alhambra overwhelmed me for many reasons. But I never felt plants overcome me like my first visit to David's *riad* in the Tangier Kasbah.

The small courtyard (30 by 60 feet) was filled, dominated with palms. Not just any palms and not the drought-toughened Phoenix. There were two luxuriant palms—luxuriant as only kentia palms can be. Kentias, *Howea foresteriana*—two languorously curving, graceful tall single trunks growing out of the courtyard floor tiles. One of those kentias reached nearly to the top of the building, maybe twenty-five feet of trunk while the second kentia had a shorter trunk, fifteen feet tall.

Their airy crowns of relaxed, spreading umbrella-like fronds were the roof of the open courtyard. Their long, fine textured, healthy green feathery frondlets made a gentle sun shade. They gave me the feeling of well-established health and wealth. They made me want to sit down underneath them and read my favorite book. Classy, to say the least. Classy and quiet.

And my eyes had just gotten started!

Under the fine textured kentia overstory, I saw a feathery layer of *Dicksonia antarctica*, those always exotic tree ferns. I counted them—four. Each had a two meter diameter head. As these gentle tree ferns go, their heads stretched out like a friendly ball of delicately soft fireworks in all directions on top of single trunks. It was easy to walk under them, having trunks each about ten to twelve feet tall. They were growing out of a mossy groundcover in large 48" clay pots—beige clay pots. The low-fired pots had a design of their own—covered with decorative arabesque scraffito.

But there was more! I saw another almost groundcover-like layer of pots—movable furnishings—about ten or fifteen 18-24" pots with small, very young, baby kentias. Any bare soil in those pots was covered with what looked like dwarf ferns, maybe *Dryopteris*. Result was a courtyard with character—very light, very airy—in feel. Impossibly elegant.

The plants gave the courtyard an aura—an aura from plants that were healthy and fulsome. Could I say titillating? Such graceful curving of the stems. It was a seductive presence—I had never felt that effect from plants before. It felt like a modern spirit, a modern take on what Lorca wrote about Andalusian gardens.

At the edges of the courtyard against the walls were a couple low, backless, armless sofas (*banquettes*) with wool coverings—broad, bold horizontal stripes—black, sandalwood brown and cream.

The floor tiles—two tones—light beige and medium beige were hand formed and mud-like—square about 4" a side. They had been laid in a light beige field—set on a 45 degree bias to the courtyard walls, which at the edges had a quadruple-wide medium beige border.

I couldn't help myself. This garden courtyard impelled my analysis.

The centre of the courtyard floor had a couple of high-back woven wicker chairs and a family of three, tall, teardrop-shaped, floriate arabesque brass lamps. The lamps? The tallest about two meters high, the shortest about one meter, and the arabesques were done as cutouts, very small. In the cutout openings it looked like semiprecious stones—all colors, while probably colored glass, they were nevertheless—dazzling—all sizes—each piece different.

The midday sun, its narrow beams twinkling through the kentia fronds and tree ferns, caused the arabesque glass pieces to sparkle and vibrate—carried their colors onto the floor—dappled sparkles. And it was quiet. Quiet, so rarely quiet.

The courtyard perimeter walls had eye level niches in them—

no tiles, all in that hand finished, smooth, mud reddish/beigey brown color. The unframed niches were in shade—but they were individually lighted internally from hidden sources—softened LED backlights.

Each niche featured individual smallish glass bottles of oriental shapes I had never before seen—almost floating—each filled with variously colored shades of amber liquids. The backlighted glass and liquid gave off unusual waves of colors—thick, rich, full. From each niche I received auras mesmerizingly unique.

My eyes? They had been hypnotized by the delicate transparencies of green overstory—feathery palms—lacey ferns. And there was animation! Points and beams of color. Everywhere was animated by jewel-like, flickering points of color from the lamps. Through the entire scene I encountered broad throbbing beams of color from the niches in unmistakably voluptuous rhythms.

I heard nothing. I only saw. My imagination and reality had become one. I had become entranced by a bejeweled garden in the midst of the bedeviled cross-cultural hell of Tangier.

I could have sat quietly there, forever. Such shelter from a simple garden. This garden was both peaceful and inspirational—made me think about the purpose of landscape architecture—really did not hear a word David said.

Next I knew, David had opened two bottles of Coca Cola; one he offered to me. Seemed so out of place for what I had just seen—any kind of exotic spirits might have been more appropriate.

I accepted the bottle of Coca Cola. I had returned to normal. David drank Coca Cola with me and told me that the niches held a collection of perfume bottles with attars mainly from Egypt and the Arabian Peninsula—oud, amber, sandalwood. That explained their voluptuous, oriental aura.

The courtyard? It had seduced me. Me? I was just learning.

***

David's Advice

David handed me his business card. I looked at it. It had all his contact details; on it he called himself an International Development Consultant.

Then he said, "You are looking for assistance?"

I talked about local culture shock—he was not surprised.

"The *Magreb* was originally the land of the Zemours. And they were fanatics, robbers, murderers," he said.

"Zemours?"

"You've heard of the Barbary brothels and their pirates?" I nodded my head in agreement, and he continued, "They were Zemours; and those with Rifian Berber roots are the toughest... even if you go back to the Tangier founders, the Phoenicians, 2,000 years ago... they too were known as pirates."

"What about Islam, wasn't that supposed to be peaceful?" I asked.

He laughed long and hard from deep in his belly—a laugh so full I could not remember ever having heard quite such a hearty "Sydney Greenstreet" laugh. He wiped tears from his eyes, took a drink from his Coca Cola and started with his summary of Islam.

"Basically," he seemed to be talking down his nose at me, "every inquiring and academic Muslim takes apart the Koran and by word jugglery—sophistry—explains it to justify his earthly desires while still remaining on the path to heaven."

After a short pause for a swallow of Coca Cola, he continued, "There are an infinite number of schools of interpretation from East to West across the entire geography of Islam. One

158

takes each word of the Koran as pure, as the exact word of God. Another uses abrogation and says that what Mohamed, Peace be unto Him, says later is more important or replaces what is said earlier. It is all the ultimate in confusing philosophic labyrinths for most Muslims on the street.

"The easiest way is to just make sure you support your family and follow the five requirements.

"*Shahadah*: belief in God and his prophet Mohamed.

"*Salat*: prayer five times a day;

"*Zakat*: donation to poor and needy;

"*Sawm*: fasting during the Ramadan month; and,

"*Hajj*: making pilgrimage to Mecca once in your lifetime."

David paused and looked directly into my eyes. I was listening and he concluded, "The rest is nothing but selfish politics—confusion and word jugglery."

He asked, "You are what, here in the *Magreb* for six months?"

When I nodded agreement, he cautioned, "Stay away from the details of Islam. But you should know that Islam came from Arabia; and, Morocco, the *Magreb*, is more a part of Africa than of Arabia. That is real. That is how this place starts to have some resonance.

"Your study... somebody gave you bad information if you thought that public water fountains were still the heartbeat of community life here. There might be one or two still around; but times have changed. Modern technology has removed the Moroccans' traditional care in using water resources. It might be better for you to make an historic study on how the local people used to be sensible about water use and how the modern technology has now made them profligate water users."

That shocked me. My plan, I wanted to stick to the plan; but everything here on the ground told me otherwise.

Then David, cautioned me to listen carefully as he said, "Moroccans say we are all sons of Adam, but don't cross them, they will get their own way, especially with the infidels. And never forget, you, my *nazrani* friend, are an infidel."

"What? That's interesting but I am trying to figure out how to get around daily in the medina."

"That is like talking about playing baseball. To learn it,

you have to play it. But, I suppose, if you want to read about it, you can do no better than Mme Zsófia's bookstore, Piliers Culturels. You know the Café de Paris?"

"Yeah, Place de la France traffic circle?"

"That's right. The bookstore's not far from there. If you have a map I'll mark the location. She's been here nearly 50 years and specializes in making cross-cultural connections."

That was the second time that bookstore had been recommended to me. I made a "must visit" note. David had just downloaded to me a slew of contemporary and historical cultural context. Then he said he had to leave to do some business, and invited me to stop over when he had more time. In the meantime, he suggested once again I might reconsider my public water fountains as social gathering nodes study subject because it just wasn't part of life anymore.

I thanked him.

He noticed I was limping and suggested a short walk to the nearest Petit Taxi stand. Took the Petit Taxi home. My visit to David's Kasbah *riad* sat in the back of my mind like an amorphous dream that I really never did experience; but I did and his Tangier garden was real—real landscape architecture dominated by plants—as pleasurable as a pleasant dream. And I really needed something pleasurable.

I gathered some food supplies from the Souss brothers' *bakal*, and headed back up the stairs to my apartment. Glad to get back. My shelter. Quiet. Places of no intrusion—few and far between for me in Tangier. My terrace, its view over old Tangier across the strait with Spain and Gibraltar in the distance. I relaxed; but my study kept bubbling up in my mind. I had nothing, except the hope that maybe there still existed one or two public water fountains in the Tangier medina.

The next day, I kept after my study—had to find a functioning fountain in the public realm. Despite the regular cleaning, ankle wound was still slowing me down. Struggled while walking Striet's Tangier spine. Again, my ears hurt... assailed by the usual vociferous, wretched wailing sounds from people on the medina streets. Headed back to my flat to eat lunch and relax.

Convinced that David had a good grasp of Tangier, I decided to stop by his Kasbah *riad* that afternoon to question him about additional design study options. In an attempt to minimize teep grief and medina noise, I took a Petit Taxi to Place Mechoir and from there walked to David's. Along with my study questions, I really wanted to enjoy his courtyard as dusk settled in.

Knocked on the door, rang the bell—couple times.

Finally, a lady, cautiously and partially opened the door—hiding herself behind the door, questioningly said, "Yes?"

I asked, "David there?"

Then only her head peeked around from behind the door. I saw her skin, glowing smooth-as-honey—a lustrous mocha/butterscotch. I saw her hair, shimmering brunette. Soft brunette eyebrows with sunlight blue eyes. Long dark lashes. I tried to focus on my purpose, my study. Then I heard her soft, silky smooth and throaty voice invite me.

"No, David not here. But please do come in."

10-Riad Anomalies

Zainab

Anomalies? I had thought David's Kasbah *riad* garden was a pleasant, peaceful, and undoubtedly seductive garden... until it, too, like the streets of Tangier, became populated by strangers of unclear purpose. But these strangers were different, very different.

Late in the afternoon, I had re-entered the hidden Kasbah world of private gardens, David's *riad*. This time his *riad* offered more than a seductive garden. In that garden, I made one step beyond into a world never spoken of in any landscape architecture class.

A female aura emerged. If I had to describe my experience... she was the essence of female... the essence of everything attractive in a female. I asked myself, over and over, who was this lady?

Except for her mysteriously shy yet alluring face, she was still hidden behind the door; but her scent invited. It was fresh, youthful yet nostalgic, sophisticated, figgy, maybe some sandalwood, and coconut. She had the allure of shade on a hot, sunny day.

She spoke. "Please come in and sit down. Rest yourself after your travel. My name is Zainab."

I entered and sat myself down in the same wicker chair as I had in my last visit with David. The courtyard had all the genteel elegance I remembered. The wall niches were warming and attractive. The floriate arabesque brass lights were sparkling from a soft internal light and Zainab, with her face of beauty and ever so inviting eyes, fit in perfectly.

Before I could see her fully, she disappeared.

She soon returned with an 8oz. bottle of Coca Cola and a plate of small bite-size chocolate cookies—*majoun*, she called them. I couldn't turn them down. As she stood in front of me, she became the garden's elegant centre piece.

She was dressed in finest transparent long silk wraps, pastels—cerulean, coral, sea green, amaranth, salmon and jonquil. The colorful transparencies took my breath away. Everything in seductive layers climaxing with a large clasp of chased silver and precious stones. All entrancingly graceful as were her movements.

I was not only breathless but captivated beyond thought at her genteel fluidity in placing the refreshments in front of me. Her every movement was part of an inviting dance. When her eyes met mine as she bowed bending toward me—her eyes spoke to me. She offered herself to me as her silks parted ever so slightly and revealed her nubile beauty. My breath had not only returned but quickened when our eyes met. Then she smiled and stood up, turning slightly so I could take in her full, womanly profile. She began a pirouette and a dance in the courtyard, around and through the palms and ferns.

There was no music, but I heard, or I saw, music in her every motion. My brief glimpse of her fulsomeness kept my eyes searching her movements—only to meet her eyes, her smile, her wordless offers to me. I was fully absorbed. We were in a metaphysical dance, in the first stages of sharing the timeless root of deepest pleasure known to humans.

As she danced, I drank my Coca Cola and tasted her chocolate cookies, two or three times. She was a fountain of promised favors, sensual satisfactions. Again she came floating, in front of me, ever so close. Attractive? An understatement.

I noticed something unusual. She had a tattoo on her breast plate—the tattooed tip of a sword touched her throat. The blade and grip stretched down toward her breasts. The base of the ornate grip had what appeared to be the eye of Horus, all of which sat on a lotus flower that had its stem and foliage growing from her breasts. My eyes were full. My chest was heavy. My breaths were deep and fast as again she slowly

166

bent toward me. Then she pirouetted behind and whispered in my ear a question, "Can you see truth?"

Truth?

I was fixated with her beauty.

Then she quietly arrived at my other ear and whispered, "Do you have thirst?" The aspirated "s" felt like a hot tongue gently on my outer ear. And that began reverberations. Those reverberations stirred a greater heat in my head that became a passion... shut down what remained of my intelligence... and I swam. My temples pounded.

I finally yielded and said, "I have thirst."

I turned to meet her head, which was still hovering over my ear. She whispered, "Come to me. I give pleasure and protection. I can save you."

Those words meant nothing as my passion rose. What breath I still had was taken away and before I could recover, she looked me in the eyes, and melted me when she said, "My service is your desire."

At the same time, her teasingly fresh aroma of moist coconut and sandalwood took over my nostrils—my sense of smell—a dizziness of beauty overwhelmed me.

She had wrapped me in her powers. I wanted to wrap her in my arms. I stood up, and barely conscious, unsteadily walked a step or two—turned and looked—she was nowhere to be found.

She had metaphysically unlatched a hidden garden door, and I had entered. She gave me a fleeting peek into a realm of mysterious discoveries that she would lovingly lavish upon me. And this all happened in a garden?

Was it a dream?

Had I become entranced?

Was it Lorca magic?

Or was this what gardens always had been about? She had become an integral part of the seductive beauty in this garden. Was I just a part of how humans behave when they are one with the garden? Was that transfiguration or just the most enjoyable sexual tease I had ever experienced?

On the other hand, maybe I had tripped over a cross-cultural gap? Or a cliff over which, if I tumbled, I might not wake up until I was under the sheltering sky in the middle of the Sahara with no memory of my study, my graduation, my Sachy...

Zainab was powerful. Her beauty. Her presence. Language leaving me. Thoughts leaving me. Like my head had been grasped and gently, yet forcibly, turned in a direction I had never before imagined.

And she said so many strange things. Pleasure? Protection? Were these dark pleasures? Or my future? This was no dime-a-dance romance. None of it made sense. Confusion grew like a thunderstorm.

Blinded by desire, I didn't understand anything. I could not analyze in perspective. Magic mocha woman? I had to get out. While Zainab was no longer in sight, I, with some remainder of will power, opened the front door and let myself out of the *riad*. Struggling with unsteadiness afoot, I left David's *riad*.

Out on the street in the Kasbah, I felt I had been under that odalisque's power for days when I had only been there not even thirty minutes. That woman—she, Zainab—must have been an odalisque. Was she some kind of black magic woman? Nah, that's a fantasy... but isn't that where I was?

Black magic and gardens? I thought gardens should weave their way into people's heads just like that odalisque did mine. She and that *riad* garden were a perfect match.

My unsteadiness was either my ankle wound or a full flow of unrequited passion that had just been stirred throughout my entire bodily core. As my breathing steadied, I wove my way on foot, brushing off the usual teeps along the way. I made it to Place Mechoir and took a Petit Taxi to my apartment.

Along the way, in the relative safety of the taxi back seat, questions flowed through my head. Was she a personification of an exquisite garden? Or was she just giving me a message? What was that she said, truth? Thirst? Mixed messages? Thirsting for truth or thirsting for sex? Was I missing something? This had to be more than gardens and sex? Or did it? My thoughts were spinning like a too fast merry-go-round.

I tried to clear my head. But Zainab was in there, big time. Was that sex talking to me in all caps? I couldn't be sure. There must have been something I was missing. I had that feeling.

The sex thing was so strong, so attractive, yet... sex... beauty... there must have been something more.

My reactions were so unusual. Unexpected. Was there something I missed? Was it a stage show? No, couldn't have been. It was all too real—the garden—too sensual—too sexual—too beautiful—the dancing, her grace, her beauty, her studied revealing of her assets. Was she telling a story? An allegory? Allegory... about what?

Wait a minute. What about my study? I had to cut the distractions. I needed to stick with the study plan—it would work out, or was the truth that I had to give up the study plan? Wait a minute? Had I just been in a magic garden? Should I do a study of that magic garden? What was I afraid of? Afraid of not sticking to my plan? Afraid of Zainab?

Maybe I should have chased Zainab. Maybe she was the door to my success? Then why turn away? Was she truth or illusion? Whatever, she was powerful. I needed to talk with David again.

***

What Happened?

The next morning, I was still trying to work through it. Strange thoughts crossed my mind, even stranger connections came together—could one actually lust for truth? Lust for truth? Such a moral contradiction; but if I was not mistaken that was what actually occurred when I was in Zainab's presence in David's Kasbah *riad*.

Nothing in my experiences here in Tangier matched my previous experiences in life. I had no roots from which I could stabilize myself. I wasn't floating, I was being battered by strange cultural realities. I didn't like it. Hurt. Off balance. Off balance from what? Was lying and cheating covering me with a smothering blanket? A blanket that smothered reason? That stunted my ability to analyze through to conclusion? Had I been in some kind of deep dream? Nothing was making sense.

From where came my fear of beauty? Beauty is supposed to attract not repulse. Truth is beautiful. Why was I wanting to get away from truth? Did I not see truth? Was I afraid of truth? Was truth the fallacy of multi-culti diversity and I did not want to admit it? What was going on? Why the confusion?

Was it the garden? Was it Zainab? Or was it something else? I was confused. My study was not happening. And all the input I was receiving deepened and broadened my confusion.

I was a typical middle-class American youth, with, as Striet observed, provincial naivety. But, stepping away from beauty such as Zainab? Her beauty had physically and mentally overwhelmed me. Stepping away from fear of beauty? I could not measure that experience. Maybe I was not naive—maybe I

170

was but a human who had been to the brink of the "real world" and, with reasoned intelligence, stepped back.

Around midday, the sun broke through. I sat on the terrace and rested my ankle. I imagined that I could almost feel my ankle healing. Not surprisingly, the summer heat built up quickly.

I stayed out on the terrace. Could not help thinking about Zainab last night at David's—like a dream it was—a beautiful dream that had just a quizzically deep, dark danger behind the beautifully floating layers of colorfully languid silks. But I still had study questions.

The afternoon heat broke and I went out. Took a Petit Taxi to the Kasbah again. Had to double check—dream? Unruly imagination? Had to be sure. This time David, apparently by himself, answered the door and invited me in.

As I started my story of yesterday's adventure in his *riad* garden, he interrupted, "You must have met Irene, but everyone calls her Zainab." David explained he had met her, years ago, when he was giving lectures and a course at the Architecture Department of the American University in Beirut, Lebanon.

"Beautiful, isn't she? She has many roots—from Gibraltar— from Asia—originally from Nubia. Did she dance for you? Did she tell her story of how her two little mosquito bites grew into two large juicy mangoes?" His laugh was so jolly, then he continued, "Did she offer fruit for your pleasure?"

I was speechless.

Before I could talk, David continued, "She is the best servant. I trust she offered you some of her own homemade *majoun*. Nobody makes them like she does. She uses *bouhachem*, a terribly attractive Moroccan honey. She blends it with imported Yemeni honey. Then uses a mixture of chocolate and crushed cashews. She puts that coating over a pistachio marzipan core, then she rolls these small treats in crushed pine nuts.

"Anyone who eats these small balls will have enjoyed a night worthy of... big balls.

"Her secret is the control of moisture, enabling her to serve *majoun* as bite size chocolate cookies. Did you enjoy them?"

"Honestly, I've never tasted anything like them before—

majoun?" I said.

"Right, you just got here. The base of the chocolate coating on the cookies is a hasheesh oil from the Rif mountains," David explained.

"That's why I felt woozy."

Woozy was an understatement. My thoughts from last night about truth, beauty, sex and gardens came flooding back. Now though, I had just learned that I was also under the influence of hasheesh last night. What was real? What was truth? What was imagination? My thoughts were under water. David brought me back to reality when he asked, "You have some questions?"

"I have many questions about Zainab and my study."

"Fire away."

"Your garden, your *riad*, your courtyard garden... I struggled getting words out..."

"Yes? You wanted to know how I built it? You never thought an architect could design and build a garden?"

He was a bit sharp with his tone of voice. And I was still struggling for words. He continued, "I had help from a couple gardeners who had training at a large villa at La Montagne, a place called the Hibiscus House..."

Just then I came out of the daze that had paralyzed my words and thoughts. I had some brief clarity, remembering that the most important for me was graduation and this study. I had just started asking him about the water fountain I had discovered in the Grand Socco market when somebody knocked at the door.

David excused himself; and I could hear talking at the door—sounded almost like a lady, a cultured lady. And then immediately began a bouncy, sweet, yet, melancholy piccolo tune—I almost recognized it.

***

172

Harlequin

I could hardly tell... anything... what happened to my clarity? Was I in a haze, a daze or what? Was it the African fog Marcela had described? But this was not subtle. The cultural roots of Morocco kept nudging, shoving into me, they were all aggressive—now it would be West Africa and its stories.

Into the room walked a big, blue-black, bald headed African—in the prime of his life, the size of an American professional football player, a defensive lineman. He had been, surprisingly, the one playing that piccolo tune. He played it as if it was his theme song. I finally recognized it, *Tears of a Clown*. But as he finished his tune, he spoke. Never expected a young lady's voice, but his clothes—he looked like he had just come from Venice, in fancy dress—a Renaissance harlequin.

A harlequin?!

And then, believe it or not, David introduced him to me as Harlequin, originally from West Africa. David reminded me, "Recall when I told you that Tangier and Morocco were as much about Africa as they were the Muslim Middle East? Well, Harlequin's roots are deep in the Equatorial African jungle and Tangier is now his home. You might be advised to take him seriously because you most certainly will need to restructure your design study; and he has so many stories growing from the West African landscape—they might inspire you." I listened but I heard only what I wanted to hear because I had hoped to stick with my approved design study plan.

As soon as David finished speaking, Harlequin reached out his hand toward me. We shook hands and this six foot three inch huge man had a handshake like a limp dead fish. In what I hoped was a friendly manner, Harlequin bored in on me with his eyes. Meanwhile, David set out bottles of Coca Cola and a plate of *majoun*. They both tucked in. I only drank the Coke this time, wasn't going to touch that hasheesh nut fudge.

Harlequin read my mind immediately. Before I could speak, he explained every part of him upon which my eyes fell and how he came to be like he was.

"Yes," he said, "I am wearing a scimitar in a rhino hilt attached to my silk belt, holding up my scarlet and black diamond patterned trousers. In Senegal, as a child, I, with my twin brother, walking home from my uncle's house, was playing in the jungle along the way when I encountered a djinn-like magician. I was separated from my brother and spirited away. I suffered an horrendous physical trauma and disappeared from home and family for fifteen years."

He paused to let it all sink in, then he continued his story, "During that time as I grew up, travelling Europe in the Cirque Medrano, a savant in Vienna gave me shelter and taught me the lessons of life. In time, I became popular in certain segments of the Viennese social scene for my abilities both in the magical arts and the reading of personalities by auras.

"Mandrake of Vienna, that was my name. My deep roots come from southeastern Senegal, before the Christ, before written history, way, way back among the deepest roots of the griot—the griot—serving *nourriture* flowing from deep in the animist black West African heartland. I tell stories. People listen."

I was totally out of it, spellbound by his words as much as by his soprano voice.

Topics of discussion spun round and round like the animated harlequin patterns—starting with eunuchs and finally focusing on the ancient history of tribal Africa. When Harlequin spoke a story, everything disappeared, except the story. His words came from some kind of deep root—so deep that even I felt... a hard-wired connection to my ears.

He talked about humans, the things people like me only think about when we are alone. Man and woman, love, sex—

engrossing stories with unprintable details. I listened to all that, and finally said, "This can't be so."

I looked at David and asked, "He is weaving a tale, isn't he?"

They looked at each other and said nothing.

I tried to put things into perspective, gain some hold on my thoughts, turn them toward something I knew was real—my design study, my impending graduation—I wondered about landscape and people, plants and people—then my thoughts veered into his stories and their content—manhood and people, manhood and gardens.

David offered me *majoun* again. I declined. Said I needed to go back to get my study in order. Harlequin sat there smiling.

I got up to leave. My head was woozy. Had I just heard West African history in a nutshell? Or did I just have my leg pulled?

I said to David, "Maybe I can ask my design study questions another time."

"As you wish," he said.

I excused myself, saying goodnight to them both. Out of habit, I started walking home on Striet's Tangier medina spine, slowly downhill out of the Kasbah toward the Petit Socco. My head was spinning... Africa... Morocco... Tangier... was this all some kind of deep dream?

It was 10PM, the medina cafes and byways were busy. The teeps wanted to sell me girls, boys, hasheesh. Nothing new there, that was the story of the Tangier medina at night—girls, boys and hasheesh. A guy in a *djelleba*, couldn't see his face inside his *djellaba* hood, partially exposed a clear plastic bag from his *djelleba* pocket. Cupping it cautiously in his hand, he showed me about 25 grams of white powder, whispering, "Cocaine, my friend, cocaine for you?"

Striet called me naive; but even I knew better than to give the time of day in the middle of the night in the medina to a hooded guy flashing a bag of white powder at me. I ignored.

Pushed on through the Grand Socco up to the Place de la France where I started feeling pain in my ankle. Then I finally reached Brahim's, busy, hopping with the night time crowd. Grabbed a takeout sandwich. Walking had become difficult, on top of which I was still in some kind of daze. I was bumbling.

175

Had to get home. Somehow found a Petit Taxi.

Next thing I remembered, I was collapsed on my apartment stairway and Sidi Hamete was by my side, trying to help me. She had a cooling cloth she used to daub my forehead. Strength gradually filled my legs and I slowly moved up the stairs. Inside my apartment, I looked at my ankle—wound was open. Cleaned it up, redressed it. Then I sat outside on the terrace, where even eating my sandwich was a huge effort.

I had eaten no *majoun* tonight, but I was still dizzy with it all. I knew I had to have a clear talk with David. Between Moroccan street culture, Oriental odalisques and African history, such intensity! Everything seemed to push me further away from my study. I could only eat a couple bites from my sandwich, then I struggled to my *banquette* and bam—out cold.

That night, I had the strangest dream—a dream that occurred just as I began to wake.

In the dream, Sidi Hamete was next to me on the apartment stairs, she used one hand to hold my head down and with her other hand she reached deep inside my ear.

Her hand was pulling on something—whatever it was, she was struggling with it in my ear.

Sidi Hamete was grunting and chanting words—verses— not Arabic, not French, not Spanish, but over and over, she repeated strange words louder and louder until she pulled something out of my ear and rushed back into her apartment.

She returned with some kind of cooling, herbal potion-soaked cloth that, as soon as it touched my forehead, woke me from the dream.

My eyes opened. The dream was over. I was alone on my *banquette* in my apartment and saw morning light just hinting at the eastern horizon.

For me, after one month in Tangier, Morocco, Africa, I could get no relief. Impossible to be tolerant of that which confused me. Unfortunately, this wasn't the first time since I'd set foot here that my multi-cultural indoctrination failed a real-life test. And my thinking needed to be focused on my design study. But now these inexplicable, intolerable cultural waves were drowning my thinking.

I was, however, clear about one thing—though even that was complicated. As much as I liked the garden courtyard of David's *riad*, I decided I would never go back there again. Something strange was embedded there. Enough said.

I needed to review, to try to understand these last 36 hours. Harlequin told stories. Stories with roots deep into West Africa. Stories as an idea intrigued me—kind of like small special purpose gardens. But concept of stories aside, it was the Harlequin story content that undid me. For me, his stories were not a cross-cultural gap; they were a bottomless cross-cultural crevasse!

First the Oriental odalisque, Zainab, then Harlequin. Huge batches of Asia, huge batches of Africa, crawling all over my body, my psyche... even, I felt... grappling with my soul.

Look, I am a Christian. I come from the inland US. We are conservative, all having escaped from European religious persecution not too many generations ago... but... but here in Zainab and Harlequin, it was like a huge Cat 5 hurricane in the process of uprooting, of eroding, of breaking away all my previously well rooted cultural values.

Or were Harlequin's stories, those experiences he related, just old-time traditional stereotypes, post-progressively being reintroduced? They couldn't be true—could they?

Wild?! All I came up with was that if all I have heard is true, then what nonsense is this progressive premise that we are all one, all materially equal? Impossible. And then in my more reflective moments, I asked, if we are progressively bound and determined to save every plant, every animal as unique genetically, why are we so hell-bent on saying that all people are equal, the same?!

Somebody get me a BS-meter because this stuff did not add up!

OK, the cultural stuff was swirling and wild. But I wanted to do my study and this cultural stuff kept getting in my way. Phew. Had to find a way through it.

177

11-Bookstore Backroom

Mme Zsófia

As tense as my cross-cultural experiences in Morocco had become, I decided, on David's and Erik's recommendations, to seek out Mme Zsófia at the local bookstore for what I hoped would be some cross-cultural clarity.

I went there... Piliers Culturels. It was not surprising that I looked to a bookstore for some shelter. And there I found some much-needed relief... most of the time.

At university, I had started in literature because that was what I knew best. During my two years as a Lit major, I kept frequently turning to contemporary writers who had bents to landscapes, to gardens, to plants.

Of course, the writings of J.B. Jackson and Aldo Leopold influenced my thoughts; but other writers seemed to draw my attention again and again to the landscape. One was Jorge Luis Borges. Borges' stories always seemed to have gripping landscape components that drove me into strange physical and metaphysical conflicts.

For example, in Borges' *Garden of Forking Paths*, I, even before my change from literature into landscape architecture, was challenged and asked myself, "space without time, what is that?" And, "a labyrinth that folds in on itself in perpetuity... you never exit... it continues infinitely, what is that?" Questions from garden allegories that had no answer, but I enjoyed the hunt.

There was more from Borges, more puzzles: "In a riddle whose answer is chess, what is the only prohibited word?" I spun

Borges' riddles around in my head. Actually, I was overcome by the perception that I was living a riddle but I could just not put my finger on it. I could not formulate the question. I worked on it and it always came to the same conundrum... how many times could I turn myself inside out, before... before... what, before what? When there was no more meaning to anything? That started to sound like Morocco.

So when I walked into Piliers Culturals I was already a bibliophile. But that didn't half prepare me for my meeting Mme Zsófia.

There are some women who wear their age with fashion, with comfort, exuding confidence and knowledge, with just a touch of mystery. Respect beyond reproach. A beauty that transcends the need for the makeup of internal or external uncertainty. That was Mme Zsófia. She was a person I might never find in the USA.

A post WW2 Eastern European escapee via Paris, who became a Tangerine, Mme Zsófia was the kind, helpful and knowledgeable librarian you always hoped to find. But she was much more. I found her as a Tangier character, a quiet player, organizing cultural events, connecting cultural threads across generations—she was a pillar of cultural credibility. She shared light whenever light was required. She was perhaps what my schoolteaching purveyors of multi-culturalism assumed we all should become.

I liked talking with her. She was personification of the most intriguing of Western art and culture, tastefully wrapped in the filigreed aura of Magrebian art and culture. It was perfect and understandable. The idealization of cultural blending. And in a bookstore that was the centre of the art community in a town with two thousand years of artifacts, two thousand years of roots reaching down into Black Africa, into the Mediterranean Basin all the way to the Moyenne Orient and back up, into Europe from the Dark Ages onward.

She was the melting pot. Ageing and attractive. But around the edges, I felt an ever so faint sensual mist hiding that which is never said. And what was that?

What do you think? Nobody would say. Nobody would be so

classless to say or to ask. Nobody knows. Or do they?

What I do know is that walking into her shop was a guarantee of a discovery of something unique—something with admirable cultural resonance. She was approachable; but she also stood apart. She had her own distance.

She spoke excellent English, Spanish, Arabic and French—embarrassed my street French. Told her I was interested in language and culture books. She selected a used book—English translation of *Morocco* by Pierre Loti. She also brought out a second book, about a Berber explorer from the 14th Century.

His name was Ibn Battuta, a name I had seen in my prep reading. He spent 25 years sailing to the Middle and Far East. She thought I might like to understand some local roots because he came from Tangier. According to her, he was a world explorer and a Tangerine whose scientific thirst for geography was exceptional. A little too far afield for me. I bought the Loti book.

Then she talked about contemporary culture here. She said, "I and some of my friends go to Madame Porte's on Sunday afternoons for tea and pastries—gives a bit of Western culture feel—little pleasures you know—all that are needed sometimes."

She told me that last year the bookstore had organized an art and culture conference, focusing on Moroccan ethnobotany—sponsored by two old-time Tangerines from La Montagne—one British, the other Russian. At that conference, the bookstore hosted two eminent Moroccans—one a parfumier par excellence and another whose fieldwork in the bled had been published and brought to public attention. He published that work under the title, *Moroccan plants for herbalist and pharmacological use.*

Mme Zsófia suggested I talk with the two sponsors on La Montagne. I was hearing about these guys again—Striet had remarked that they might be useful.

"Can you tell me more about them?"

She told me a couple things, "They are reclusive, and—off the record—under some financial strain."

"If I want to meet them, will I need an introduction?"

"Reclusive but accessible—just go to their villa and ring the bell."

Seemed a bit too far off my immediate public water fountain design study focus, so, I filed all that for use later. We said our goodbyes and I headed back to my flat eager to read Pierre Loti's descriptions of the North African landscape.

***

Backroom Stories

It was almost the end of July when I visited Piliers Culturels again. I was preparing to go to Casablanca for the *Darija* Stage—a one-week intensive course on local Arabic language basics—primarily for Peace Corps volunteers, but Erik had kindly given me a place. Looking for a basic *Darija* book, I stopped in to talk with Mme Zsófia. While there, I talked more about my landscape design study. She took an interest in my landscape architecture focus and invited me to sit, take tea and talk with her in the bookstore back room.

The room was small, no window, and books stacked higgledy-piggledy from floor to ceiling everywhere. There were two chairs and she offered me one and excused herself for a moment. I was quietly looking around when I heard some rustling behind a couple book stacks.

"Hello?" I said.

"*Hallo, qui est-ce,*" replied an older woman's voice in a heavy Eastern European accent.

"*Parlez vous Anglais?*" I asked.

She wormed her way through the stacks to see who she was speaking with. The heavyset 60ish woman with stringy grey hair looked like she had been 24 hours straight researching her way through this jumble of books.

She asked me in English who I was and I repeated all about landscape architecture and my university design study.

"Landscape architecture? Not many around here. What brings you to this store?"

"Looking for books on language and local culture."

"Local culture? What do you want to know?"

"Why is the mood of the medina so intense and why are the youths on the street so aggressive?"

"You do get right to the core of it with that question. First you should know that my name is Olga and I am a longtime Tangerine friend of Mme Zsófia. We arrived here in the early 50s and have been part of local culture since."

I told her my name was Christopher Janus.

"Pleased to meet you," she said. Then she sat down and carried on. She talked about how the two of them shared times in the 50s at Merkala Beach Café, with fascinating stories of *keef*, drink and rough life, with names like Lachen and Idir.

I liked hearing her perspectives on Tangier. She talked about the International Zone and relationships with strict Muslims.

She said, "The Zone had a reputation for diversity of culture and religion, which concerned the pious Moroccan population who saw it as 'a plague zone as much infested with cockroaches as infested, nay, infected by infidels'. But it has its own ways to 'clean' itself."

"What do you mean by 'clean' itself?" I was perplexed.

She began, "It is difficult to define... the cleansing... some people like to call it a superstition... some like to call it a curse. It is both and more. Here you can find it as a disease, bad dream and misfortune in daily life. It is a storm cloud, it is a bad taste and it is a burdensome possession. All are here. You can't control it. I can't control it. We can't control it. Maybe you can say it is like bad weather or an earthquake or hurricane. But for some it lasts their entire life, every day and every night."

I hesitated before asking, "It sounds like you are talking about the evileye or something?" She said nothing.

Then, after taking a sip of tea, Mme Olga said, "Let me tell you a cleansing story."

She paused, before beginning, "There was a guy in the early 1960s—lots of guys trying to get attention of Paul Bowles. This guy was American. Not like you. He was very big, bolshie and beautiful. Emphasis on the bolshie. This guy had hubris. There wasn't a pretty girl or pretty boy that he didn't think was his.

You could see it in his eyes. He was around for a couple weeks and we could all see what was going on. The *Magreb* does not tolerate such a fool running loose.

"He had a thing against camels—always talking about camel jockeys. One day, he was after a beautiful, but tender, brother and sister—orphans—for his own pleasure as was his normal way. These young kids lived on a farm just past the edge of town, toward Cap Malabata. They kept camels for tourist rides. The bolshie American followed them home, planning to have his way with them. They, offering shelter to the *kaffir*, invited him in.

"But his attitude gave him away when he, making sex eyes at both of them, demanded a drink. Well, they gave him a drink and he fell into a stupor. That area had an unusual Marabout, an absolute rock pile of a shelter, filled with scorpions and the boy and girl tied him down and left him there for days.

"Somehow he managed to free himself and was last seen being led around by a donkey and offering donkey rides for tourists. His sexual fantasy became satisfied only with the donkeys. Everybody thought he had met his due. But there was more.

"He had a couple American relatives who came looking for him, cousins or something. Just like him. They also fell under the donkey spell; and as the story goes all three Americans were given 'shelter' by a Pasha from the Levant, never to be seen again."

I listened to it all, then said, "This story sounds a lot like stories I heard from a strange West African guy..."

Mme Olga interrupted, "Not a story! This happened. I knew the neighbors. They told me."

"Is this about human enviousness or evileye?" I asked.

Mme Zsófia returned to the room, listened, said nothing, looking like she did not want any part of this conversation.

Mme Olga said, "Okay, my friend, there is and there isn't. We are on the African continent—a landscape of hidden power. That is life here."

We heard a customer enter the store. Mme Zsófia excused herself and left the back room to serve the new customer.

Then Olga and I sat quietly alone, saying nothing. I thought, she said "that is life here". I've heard something like this before at David's in the Kasbah. What is this "evileye" stuff? Misfortune? Bad karma? Or the influence of the devil himself? Everybody was oh so cautious when speaking of it. Could it explain all my misfortunes to this point? Could it explain the dream I had when Sidi Hamete pulled "something" out of my ear? Will I have this evileye cloud around me for the rest of my study time here? Study? I still didn't have my study going yet!

My anxiety was raising my pulse. Sweat was forming on my forehead.

***

Socco Curios

I looked at Mme Olga; and she was looking at me as if she was anticipating a question. My mind was spinning through everything that had happened to me since I arrived in Tangier, especially with her story which for the first time seemed to tie everything together in a strange knot. But I wasn't clear, I was tangled. Trying to gain control of myself, I paused before a simple question came to mind. "When did you arrive... what was Tangier like then?"

"You don't expect me to give you any specific date, I hope. I can say it was before Independence. And I found work in a small shop just off the Socco Chico. The shop was run by a very old lady who took a fancy to me... rather she showed sympathy to me. You know, giving me a proper job. I was a shop assistant— actually I ran the shop out front. The shop was smaller than a *bakal* but it had lots of shelves. She had a back room like we have here; and she told me to take care of everything out front, unless a customer asked a strange question."

"Strange question?"

"It was a shop of curios... maybe you call it a second-hand shop. The things on the shelves in that small shop... many looked as old as Tangier itself."

We could hear Mme Zsófia bustling about with the customer.

Mme Olga continued, "Every day, the same young boy came into the shop—always rummaging through the crowded shelves and always asking me questions I could not answer. He was young, his voice had not yet changed but his questions were always phrased like those of a *sadhu*. And every time the owner heard him, she came out and invited him for tea in the back room."

"Why is this important, or rather, why do you tell me this?"

"Be patient, young man."

Then Mme Olga paused a long time before continuing, "I asked the shop owner that same question and her answer... well, I will share it with you. It was an answer that was not an answer... but a clue to Morocco... to Tangier... to northwest Africa."

Mme Olga went silent again. We heard Mme Zsófia still helping the particular client.

Then, after what I thought was the required patient pause, I said, "And?"

Mme Olga looked at me with eyes that betrayed her taking an inner deep breath before she said one word, "*Anquietas.*"

The back room was pin-drop silent for immeasurable seconds that seemed like minutes before she continued, "That was what she told me then and ever more."

"What's that? Is '*Anquietas*' something I should know about?" I asked.

Just then Mme Zsófia returned and having heard my question she spoke. "Is Olga resurrecting old mysteries again? Don't pay any attention to her. Everybody, at least the oldest of the Tangerines, talks about the ancients and their so-called 'special powers'." She gave Mme Olga a hard look. Me, I didn't know what to make of it.

I tried to push all that "historical" stuff aside and asked Mme Zsófia about the *Darija* book. She gave Olga another stern look before leading me back into the bookstore.

Before I left, I found a good used book on *Darija* to prepare for my stage in Casablanca. But as I went to bed that night, I could not help turning over all that had happened to me since the evening I crossed the strait, plus the Aragon stories of Marcela, the Malabata story of Mme Olga, the *Anquietas*, Zainab and the strange stories of Harlequin. There was death, torture, a lack of logic and a lack of civil dependability.

Was this the environment for my study? I shivered. A sickly aura of fearful uncertainty began metastasizing around the edges of my thoughts, suffocating my hopes. It took hours for me to fall asleep.

As soon as I awoke, I went to the train station and bought an early advance ticket to Casablanca good for 48 hours. Spent the rest of the day with my Darija book. The next day I took a late morning train to Casablanca, arrived mid afternoon. Then a Petit Taxi to the Peace Corps Arabic Language Annex where I checked in for the *Darija* stage.

12-Casablanca

Kerfluffle

As if the cross-cultural intensity from the West African Harlequin at David's riad in the Tangier Kasbah didn't throw me completely off balance, what would happen in Casablanca definitely did. West African roots sprouted big time in Casablanca.

Casablanca?

This was not Rick's Place. Not like that movie set.

The real Casablanca, a city of multi millions, is on the immigration route from sub-Saharan Africa to Europe. A continuous flow of West Africans through the city. That was one overwhelming thing I learned while I was there. It brought home to me how the French West Africa scene—how black African cultural roots work their way north, along the West African coast through Casablanca. I saw them. I felt them. I interacted with them.

From the outset, the *Darija* stage didn't go smoothly. Things were screwed up—no room in the Peace Corps Language Annex dormitory for myself and two girls, primary school teachers.

So the Peace Corps Language personnel assigned the three of us to a hotel a couple blocks away. I had never met these girls before. The two of them could not have been more different from each other. One stood out like a neon light advertisement in the medina. The other would attract no attention in the medina.

We had to wait while the annex arranged a driver to take us to the hotel. I looked more carefully at the teachers and introduced myself. Both were new Peace Corps volunteers.

The neon light advertisement was Bree, from Massachusetts, toting a large suitcase wheely. Her hair was short, red and wildly unkempt, styled like Johnny Rotten. She was cute like a sorority girl but her sex pistol aura took her over the top.

Her look? ...well endowed, emphasized by being a bit advantageously overweight, wore a silky sleeveless blouse that was one size too small with one button too many open at top, wearing skin tight jeans with designer tears in the knees. I wondered—showing her ample assets and having trousers worn out at the knees—is that some kind of new style? Lewinski style? How did she become a Peace Corps volunteer in Morocco?

The other girl? Chalk and cheese. Eileen carried a reasonably sized black sport bag over her shoulder—sport bag, which had a noteworthy huge brass padlock. She was tall. I'm 5-11 and she was almost eye to eye with me. She was lithe, with a build, as I guessed, like a distance swimmer, mousy brown short hair that she wore like it was a helmet rather than a fashion accessory.

She was a Texan—plus size cowgirl shirt down to mid thigh— almost like a mid length kaftan, dark blue denim with light blue cowboy embroidery—though she didn't need it—the plus size hid her assets—black capris, black, heavy-duty athletic shoes—she dressed to disappear.

While we waited for our driver, we talked. Eileen taught middle school back in Texas and her hobby was jogging, hiking, physical fitness. She came to Morocco to teach sports to girls, boys, whichever. Bree seemed right out of a sorority house; at least, that dominated her opinions. She was here just to help poor people; and her hobby was plants. At first glance, not my kind of girl, but plants as a hobby? That interested me.

The driver arrived and in five minutes we were at the hotel. Driver said he would pick us up at 7:45 tomorrow morning. Hotel was a disaster. Old, 1920s—must have been cheap construction even back then. Interiors poorly lighted, ceilings were high, no AC, few windows—so horribly dirty—only dim light entered.

In the lobby, the walls were covered with dusty, dark red velveteen. The only lights were bare fluorescent tubes. The few chairs in the lobby were, this evening, the centre of loud, animated conversations among bluish-black, young West African men, dressed as if on their way for a night of clubbing. As soon as they saw the two girls they became quiet as they stared. After a long moment, they started up again with loud, animated conversation.

When we checked in, the hotel gave us rooms on the same floor. Then they told us no rooms with toilets—one common toilet each floor. My single room and the girls' double room both had wash basins only and French doors to a balcony. The balconies were not private—they were connected outdoors continuously to every other room on the floor. No locks on the balcony doors. Anybody in another room on this floor could walk into your room—anytime.

For cheap security, I planned to use my shoe laces and my room chair to secure my French doors to the balcony—and keep my Swiss Army knife under my pillow.

***

197

West African Events

At about 10PM, there was a knock on my door. It was Eileen. She asked if she could come in and speak privately. I said sure; but I had no idea what was going on.

She said she and Bree couldn't use the communal toilet at the end of the hall, because every time they tried, other guests using loud, shrill, clipped French, kept opening the unlockable toilet door.

She said, "These guys are over the edge and Bree is in tears. She has been sobbing for the last half hour. You need to help us."

"Ok," I said, "You gotta plan?"

"That's why I am here. We should work out something together. Something that these guys can understand without this situation getting worse."

"I'm not quite in the picture yet."

"When Bree went out to the toilet they asked her what are you doing here. She told them she just wanted to help poor people in Africa. Well these guys are out there, bare chested in soccer shorts and bare feet acting like they own the place, and the guy that speaks a little English says to her, as he grabbed his crotch, 'Help this! You want real African cock? Come and get it honey. I give it all to you.' Then Bree said he started to pull his pants down. She ran back to the room and has been sobbing ever since."

"Where is she now?'

"In the room calming a bit. We secured the balcony door

and she won't open the hall door, unless it's me."

Then Eileen said, "Listen to me, CJ..." as she opened the lowest button on her plus sized shirt, revealing at the top of her black capris, a magnificent set of taught wash board abs—didn't know what to expect—then just on the top edge of her capris, she reached into a wide black elastic band.

"What's that?"

"I call it a belly band but what's more important is what it holds!"

"What?" Before I blinked she held a gun in her hand. And just as quickly she ejected the magazine in one hand and just as smoothly emptied a bullet from the chamber, did some other mechanical noise things with the gun and showed me it was empty. I didn't know what to say. "Whooooaa..."

"M9, I don't go anywhere in this country without it. I don't go for it unless to use it. And I shouldn't need to use it here with these guys. But it is an insurance policy if things go unexpectedly south."

Then she proceeded to tell me more about herself and her father. All her life, at least as far back as she could remember, her dad was Master Gunnery Sergeant, in the Marine Corps Embassy Security Group. While growing up, she travelled the world with him. He taught her gun safety and gun use from her youngest days. She grew up with an M9.

"But wait a minute, where did it come from? How did you get it in here?"

"Here's the quick and dirty. Dad has connections at State. I flew in here on a charter from Langley."

I stared. Speechless.

She said, "We have to do something. You cool?"

She continued, "I don't want to use it but these guys are a problem, they are wildings just out of West Africa. This should not be a life or death issue. But I need your help. I think we can defuse this thing. I figure if you go out there while we are using the toilet you can tell those guys that we are your women. But you must be forceful. Can you do that?"

"Then what?"

"Come back to the room with us and spend the night with

us. We have a sofa you can sleep on."

"What about Bree?"

"I can talk her into it. We have to calm her down and put these guys in their place. No hotel people. No police. Just us."

"I'm in. Give me 15 minutes to get my stuff together in my backpack." Half hour later Eileen and Bree knocked on my door. Bree had been crying—had make up running down her cheeks. They asked me to guard the public toilet as they used it before bed.

While the girls used the toilet, I did toilet door guard duty.

In the red velveteen wallpaper-covered hall, I talked with the guys, who, up here on this warm summer night, were, as Eileen had described, barefoot, shirtless and in baggy football shorts—their well toned, dark, blue-black skin seemed electrically charged and vibrating in the flickering fluorescent tube hallway lights.

Their room doors open, they were relaxed, their boom box blasted a strange mix of hip-hop/reggae—a couple of them were practicing their dance steps and making the hallway their own.

I talked with them. They were from the Ivory Coast—on their way to Europe to find work—to save their lives. *Sauver la vie*, that's what they said. One of them asked me if the American women in the bathroom were mine. I said, "Hell yes!"

The hallway went quiet except for the boom box. Then they all once again got rowdy with laughter.

The most aggressive guy, laughing, in an exaggerated way, grabbed his crotch—and said he knew what free American women liked.

I told them, "No, no, no! We all are American government employees, and they are my women!" I squared up to him and puffed out my chest saying, "Do not touch! My women! No touch!!"

The girls came out of the toilet. I put my arms around both of them and walked them to their room. The guys talked among themselves and continued dancing.

We double locked the door and sighed in relief.

"But let's not get complacent, we have a long night ahead,"

Eileen said.

I looked around their room. We adjusted the sofa and bed to secure the doors and windows. Fortunately, they had a corner room—windows on two walls and a balcony only on one. We closed the shutters and curtains. We made one more furniture move so that the sofa had its back to the girls' bed and wash basin. We all felt secure in the re-arranged room.

"That hallway drama was kind of fun." I said.

Bree looked at me in disbelief and said, "I'm still shaking inside."

Eileen said, "I'm with you, CJ. We pulled it off pretty smoothly. But now I have to wash up and hit the sack. CJ, what are you going to do?"

"I'm going to sit up for a while till all is quiet then I'll take rest on the sofa."

"There's no way I can sleep," Bree said. "CJ, I'll sit up with you."

"Just as long as you guys are quiet..." Eileen said, "No party, okay?"

"No party?!" said Bree. "That's the last thing on my mind. Don't worry."

"Just about forgot that we came here to learn some *Darija* and that begins tomorrow," I said.

It was already after 11. Eileen said, "Bree, do you mind? I'll take the side by the door and you take the side by the wash basin?" Bree nodded agreement.

Eileen continued, "We have to meet the driver at 7:45 tomorrow morning. My alarm is set for 6:30. I'm hitting the sack. See you in the morning." In less than five minutes a soft snoring came from her side of the room.

***

Bree

In their room the only light was a low wattage table lamp on a small table next to the sofa. It was summer, no AC and the room felt not only warm, but stuffy. I had sweat forming on my forehead. So Bree and I quietly opened the two windows on the "safe" wall, the wall without balcony, for the slightest warm breeze. We both felt the subtle relief.

Bree, looking calmer now, reached deep into her wheely, rustled around a bit and emerged with a half liter bottle of red wine. She whispered to me, "Shhhhh... Eileen's a tea total."

"Tea total?"

"That's not all..." she continued whispering, "...her alarm... it's a Toby Keith recording... *Courtesy of the Red, White and Blue.*"

"I don't know it."

"She told me he only sings it when he plays live for the troops—the key line at the end he sings something like—don't mess with the USA or we'll put a boot in your ass, the American way. She wakes up to that! Do you believe it?"

"Never heard it."

"It's not commercially released yet. She recorded it when she was someplace with her father last year. He's a Marine."

"How do you know that's her alarm recording?"

"We shared training together back in Colorado. Hey, believe it or not, I kinda like it... we both love America."

I thought... but these two girls were so different... yet they both loved America. Can two white American girls demonstrate diversity? Too much for me to think about. My Morocco experience had taken all thoughts of America from me. I couldn't figure out what was going on here. I started fading away with my thoughts...

Then Bree brought me out of it when she said, "But here in Morocco, I had to seek out their wine."

"Why? I didn't have you pegged as a wino." We both chuckled a bit, then talked some about our lives back in the US. I talked more about mine and how I was trying to detach myself from home culture at the university. She listened and said little about herself.

Then the conversation revolved back to Morocco when I asked, "Wine? Muslim Morocco? I knew the French had been here, but..."

She told her story, unveiling her horticultural knowledge. "Between WWI and WWII, the French, especially the botanists and horticulturists from Vilmorin and his competitors, used Morocco—between Meknes and Fez—as testing grounds for grapes and other fruits. They cultivated experimental vineyards and made some unusual wines—a few of which are still around. I found some in a *bakal* today."

"So you really are into plants. I thought it was just a line. I'm studying landscape architecture and am doing a study here." I told her the whole story.

When I spoke of the *maquis*, she corrected me, saying, "You must distinguish between *maquis* and *garrique*, the difference between acid and alkaline soils and therefore plant associations." As she was speaking, she opened the wine, tasted it out of the bottle, and offered the bottle to me. She was definitely relaxing.

"No thank you," I said.

I thought—here we were, both sitting on a sofa after a couple intense emotional and sexual cross-cultural social events. I did not need to get shaken all night long by her American thighs. No party. And, what if those guys tried to get into the room? I needed to be alert—Eileen and the gun—I didn't know what Eileen might do.

"The wine is sweet and sharp, you sure? You a tea total, too?" Bree asked.

"No, I just want to keep clear."

"Well, I'm digging in. I've had enough adventure for today."

I had to ask, "How about your red hair and clothes? Isn't it a bit aggressive for Morocco? Is the Peace Corps okay with that?"

"Aggressive!? I'm an American. That's who I am. I came here to share that with the Moroccan girls. They should not be slaves... and the red hair? That's henna. Surely you must know henna, *Lawsonia inermis?*"

Every time Bree paused or finished a sentence, she would take a slug out of the wine bottle. She was hard at it. She was determined to lecture me, not just on the hair dye and skin tattooing properties of henna, but also the herbal. She started her spiel. "Listen, I minored in and did a Masters in hort. My thesis was on the Mediterranean biomes."

There was more to Bree than met the eye. She was some kind of quicksilver girl. Then she laid into me, in her own gentle way. "I heard about you landscape architects and your one-dimensional aesthetic approach to plants."

"Hold on! I've seen you science types before when I interned two years ago in SoCal. There they were environmental 'scientists' rewriting municipal regulations requiring more native plants in parks and residential subdivisions."

"So?"

"So?! The result was coyote habitat in human yards and mountain lions in parks. Their 'well-intentioned' regulations increased proximity of death for kids, for everyone. Now I don't want to say you're like them but I do have worries when people who aren't landscape architects start meddling."

She assured me she was just into plants.

And I emphasized, "Don't lump me in—I'm into plants, too; and I would have never guessed you were into plants by the style of your clothes and hair."

"Okay, you get a point. Now, let me tell you about *Lawsonia inermis*—native throughout the Mediterranean."

She went on and on about its bark, seeds and leaves, the variety of ways that it gives benefit to human health. She knew her hort and botany stuff. Then after one more deep draft of wine she started on the Ayurvedic uses.

Before she finished the benefits of its floral fragrance, she drained the bottle, and reached into her wheelie again, saying, "I really shouldn't do this but I am having a good time." She brought out a second half liter of wine and opened it.

***

Bree Unleashed

"Man," she said, "it is warm in here."

"It's July—mid summer and we are South of the Med, not far from the Sahara, which makes the southern and eastern edges of this country. Summertime here means hot," I said.

She asked, "Are you sure you don't want any? This is a special wine. C'mon, share this with me." I thought what harm one glass.

"Okay, one glass." She poured it for me. The room was hot and I was thirsty. The first taste was refreshing—made me take an immediate second swallow—two swallows and my head started feeling light but happy.

Bree said, "I'm too sweaty, been too tied up all day. Mind if I take my bra off?"

The wine had surprisingly already softened me. I said, "Make yourself comfortable, I'll turn away." Which I did.

She continued talking. "My bra is more like a sports bra—straps me down like an elastic straight jacket—I just have to open my blouse to slip it off." After a brief rustling of cloth, I heard her give a sigh of relief. I started to turn around and saw her fully bare breasted.

"Sorry, thought you had finished."

"Not to worry, I'm proud of my breasts. They are double G and they are real." She affectionately held them in her hands for me to admire. I gasped.

She continued, "They like to be free. If it embarrasses you, turn away again and I'll tell you when my blouse is all buttoned up." I turned away again.

She was not at all shy. "My breasts need air—it is almost like they are extensions of my lungs. I feel stifled when I have the bra on—I wear it when I am out in public here. In private I like to let them breathe. When they breathe, I breathe as deeply as they are full and free. Just a couple more buttons. There. Ready." She added, "Let's share the rest of the wine."

I looked at her. She looked altogether different. She had a peaceful, yet powerful, moon glow about her. Her luminous bosom emanated the moonlike glow, filling her face. And she didn't look even the slightest overweight now. Her healthy breasts, pushing out more than ever from her sleeveless, silk blouse, had relaxedly filled out. Her overall impression and her proportions were classic. She was in her prime and ripe— like a fresh piece of fruit begging to be tasted.

And her previously dreary henna red hair now reminded me of an "anything goes", electrically charged, ginger-haired Celtic Rhiannon. And what before looked like a bad Johnny Rotten haircut now had a flowing freedom as if designed by the blowing wind itself—amazing. She generated an aura of electric sexual energy like a Tesla coil that had just been fired up. I was captivated. As she raised the bottle to her lips, I also drank the remainder from my glass. The night had just begun.

"Really now, tell me, how did you ever come to join the Peace Corps? In the last month, I've met scads of volunteers and you just seem so different? Tell me the story."

She took another hit from the bottle, paused and said, "This is complicated... are you ready for a long story?"

"Let's do it... I've got all night."

***

Other Realms

Bree was just getting started.

"My parents died in an auto accident when I was young. No brothers or sisters. No near relatives. Foster care—went through a bunch of so-called homes. High school was horrible; but I had some smarts and got into a great university on a scholarship.

"I joined a fancy sorority, I guess, still hoping for a family. Didn't work out. No lasting friendships—to say the least. Read a lot of Eastern religion and concluded that service is what I had to do in life—service to other humans in need. So after my education and hort degrees, I joined the Peace Corps.

"And as I see it, in the past years they have become more open minded, more tolerant of ... how can I say it... volunteers who don't look like the 1950s. So with me, what you see is what you get."

I could feel her heat. This was not the time or place.

She said straight out, as if she had read my mind, "I feel your heat, too. We have no obligation to come together. I'm sure your girlfriend would appreciate that restraint. And I would, too. A man's restraint is admirable. It is strength."

There was nothing I could say. And looking at this attractive woman demanded all my will power to restrain those instincts from time immemorial.

"Tell me more about your master's thesis studies of the Mediterranean biomes—did you study only the European side or also the Asian and African sides?" I asked.

She sat quietly as if contemplating an answer to my simple

question. My question wasn't complicated—just a yes or no.

"If I say I can trust you, I have said too much. Trust is more than words. I have already trusted you so many times tonight. So trust is not a concern. What I am about to tell you is serious and not to be taken lightly. Please remember that as I answer your question."

She had my full attention. I had no idea what was coming.

"I researched biomes around the entire Med basin—all three continents, and all that historical research took me into archaeology, anthropology, philology and now we cross a line—into the realms within and above." She paused, looking long into my face and deeply into my eyes. I asked myself, did she just say realms within and above?

"What realms? What are you talking about? Are you telling me a story?" I asked.

She continued, "As long as there has been human populations in all three continents around the Med, there have been, call them what you will, stories, legends—about another world of life forms inhabiting this region. I call those other life forms as living in the Faerie Realm. Before I say any more about that, I will tell you it is my own intimate, personal story, separate, yet part of my Peace Corps work. I do want to help people who are being kept down but I also want to hear their stories that they learned from their grandparents about unusual things in the landscape, in the forests and deserts, that nobody learns about from books." She tilted the bottle to her lips again.

Now my thoughts kicked in. What did I just hear? This Peace Corps volunteer had a hobby and that hobby was to understand the life forces behind the landscape. In other words, she had done her own landscape study. Maybe, if I believed her, her study might give me some landscape insights should I need to change my study plan. The least I could do was listen.

As landscape questions started rolling through my mind, I could not help thinking, is she serious? Faerie Realm? Then I remembered the story Marcela had told, from her great-great uncle, about the evileye. I thought which is more believable or unbelievable, fairies or the evileye?

After a pause in my thinking, I spoke. "Mythology. I am not

joking, but most people when they hear the word fairy, they think of the illustrations in the Lang books or the flower fairy work of Cicely Barker; but... what are you saying?"

She started, "I've always had unusual experiences in certain landscapes. Sometimes I even feel possessed by them. I didn't know what to think until someone pointed me to Tolkien. Tolkien's writings *On Fairy-Stories* convinced me—it all fit together—I accepted, became at ease with it all. And to doubters, he wrote that modern languages are a disease of mythology—that there is something more than we can write using modern language.

"The Faerie Realm is wide, deep and high. Its very richness and strangeness tie the tongue of anyone who would speak of them. Listen to me carefully, CJ. While anyone is in the realm, it is dangerous to ask too many questions lest the gates should be shut and the keys be lost." Then she paused.

I was in another world, I thought maybe the wine... gates, keys, what was she saying.

She continued, "Faerie itself may be most nearly translated by magic—but it is magic of a peculiar mood and power, nothing at all like those people we call magicians today."

I interrupted. "...but, but..."

"There is nothing silly here. This is not about what plants should be in your garden to attract fairies. Tolkien did not call this the 'Perilous Realm' for nothing. I can't reiterate everything I learned from Tolkien and others, but just think of the power of our mind. The speed of mind. What is its purpose? How did it begin? These are unanswerable questions that used to be dealt with in the Middle Ages by people we called alchemists. Their work is unfortunately out of favor like last year's shoe styles. But that does not reduce their authentic inquiries."

I was sleepy. She kept on about the Greek nymphs and how they were so diverse and so many of them. I listened but my attention waned until I heard her say, "...countless foliage on trees of tales carpeting the forest of days..."

"This is way too deep for me. Philosophy is beyond me. I just want to design and build gardens."

I took a deep breath and remembered the awkward hotel situation while she smiled and drained what was left in the second bottle.

She said, "You're right... too much talk..." Her eyes closed, she held the empty bottle in her lap and fell asleep sitting across from me in that old, upholstered chair. She really was sweet. But her naivety might get her into trouble here in Morocco. In my mind, I wished her well—she was due some good luck.

13-Co-Ca Co-La

Perilous Thoughts

I got my sleeping bag out and laid down on the floor next to the balcony doors. Before I went to sleep, I reviewed the uncertain hotel situation and thought about Eileen and her gun. I recalled something else I'd read by Borges.

In *The Aleph*, Borges revealed a secret commandment: "thus fought the heroes, tranquil their admirable hearts, violent their swords, resigned to kill and to die." I had puzzled over these words, how strange they were. Fighting was bad, death was bad, that was what I had learned in my dreamland schools. Even though I had been embalmed with that schoolroom totalitarian progressivism, I somehow sensed that without the willingness to kill, there could be no social, no civilized peace in the public realm. Yeah, I was alright with the use of force for defense. I went to sleep.

I'd like to say I slept soundly till morning; but that was not the case. All night I fought off cockroaches. When I was finally awakened by their crawling on my face, I looked around and I must have seen twenty or so. Bree had already moved from the sofa to the bed, so I shook out my sleeping bag and resettled on the sofa.

Before I fell back to sleep, I ran through my head the weird cross-cultural events of the past evening in relation to all I had been experiencing here since I crossed the Strait of Gibraltar.

It was as if I was riding on a strange carousel, where everything was in constant, unsettling change. I felt something tonight. In the hallway talking with those guys from West Africa. Same thing I felt on the streets of Meknes, Rabat and

Tangier. Same thing I felt when I was with Harlequin.

As long as there has been Africa, there has been a North Africa and a West Africa. That is a geographical reality. But if I tried to identify a geographical line that separates the cultures of West Africa and North Africa, that was impossible. At best that line might be a wide buffer that varies in its width.

A buffer, like in an ecological biome between the territories of two species. The division is vague and changeable over time. But the force I felt was similar. I have heard this force described as djinns and as the evileye. But what is common is these both are labels of the unknown. No more to be said. But I took personal shelter of the Lord's Prayer while I was in North Africa.

And those talks with Bree about her Faerie Realm interpretation of the Med Basin? Another horse on the carousel—interesting but couldn't give it much credence—just something else to keep me off balance. I finally drifted off to sleep.

Next, I heard Eileen's alarm, the soft country sound of Toby Keith. All went smoothly in the morning. Toilet with no disturbances. We met the driver and he took us to the Annex for classes. What can I say? That night had been disaster on so many levels—but we lived to tell about it.

***

The Darija Stage

First thing at the *Darija* Stage Annex, we went to the Program Manager. She promised us, starting that night, space in the dormitory for the rest of the stage.

After the room fiasco was sorted, the week-long *Darija* lessons started to fall into place. I received an introduction packet and set up in my assigned room. The class schedule was six days solid. Each day, mornings 9-12, afternoons 2-5, evenings 7-9—absolute immersion.

Busy, busy, busy all week with classes. Memorizing poems, songs, stories—all in *Darija*. Classes were taught by Moroccans. Only ten in the class—seven girls, including Bree and Eileen, the only ones just arrived in country, two other guys and me. During the class breaks, I heard from the others stuff like Morocco is an increasingly hysterical place to live.

One girl said, "I used to get frustrated with it all; but now I mostly just laugh—I love it here, I really do, but for God's sake, some things just crack me up."

Another confided in me, "I am blessed to have many kind hearted Muslim men in my life. I am cursed to be surrounded by so many young Arab men who do not practice what they preach." She gave me what she called a typical street dialogue.

"Are you Muslim?"

"Yes, of course."

"Then why did you touch me when Allah tells you not to touch me?" ...blank stare.

Then one night after class, at the Argana Café, one of the students said, "As far as safety goes, I don't fear for my life here at all—I know it's just a bunch of sexually frustrated idiotic boys who have nothing better to do than bother us girls; however, that doesn't dismiss its effects." She continued, "The harassment has led me to take anti-anxiety medication, has made me more skeptical of everybody's motives, and has made me more of a homebody than I would like."

More than one of the students agreed that in the larger cities in Morocco, the eligible Moroccan girls were liberal bunga-bunga—partying all week at work in the big cities, but at home on the weekends, in their small villages—they were conservative full burka.

One of the primary school teachers told me about her all-girl health development classes—how the girls were so eager—but yet when she was out in the community, their parents would not acknowledge her in the slightest.

Even the guys concluded that there were certain things about Morocco they would never be able to grasp—the horrible street harassment being one of them—not just in Tangier. The girls all said they had to deal with it every single day unless they didn't leave their houses, which happened too often.

I had wanted only to study the language and find inroads to my design study; but the West African night in the hotel had unsettled me and my co-students in the class were so wound up about Morocco. The whole thing kept me dizzy.

On the next to last day, we all got together again at the Argana Café. Bree was there with all the others, except Eileen. Eileen never went out with us as a group in town. Discussion was intense at the café. I could only listen so long.

I moved over next to Bree and said, "I've been meaning to ask you since that first night in the West African hotel."

"Yeah? What's that?"

"You really got into that Toby Keith red, white and blue song—that's all about soldiers, right—and you're in the Peace Corps—how do you fit all that together?"

Bree said, "There is war, which I don't like. And there are soldiers committed to defending the homeland. That I like. It's the mentality of doing everything you can for your country and being proud of it. I'm proud of the USA, land of the free.

I've got a first class education in all the subjects that I chose; and now I have work to help poor people in hardship; and I will do my best for it while I'm here."

"I hear that; but don't these hardship stories from other volunteers get you down?"

"Yeah... a bit... nobody ever told me that local people might be against our trying to help them... that is a bummer. But this is a battle. I'm in it to win." We both stopped talking and listened to the others.

My heart was breaking, listening to these other girls' stories. Something about the Peace Corps was totally out of balance—training, expectations, political correctness, cultural imperialism? The US Government spent a lot of time and money in training; yet... yet, results were wrong. These volunteers were not settled. Something not right about the whole picture! What a bummer.

***

Bree's Landscape

I looked at Bree; she was pretty. She did have a lightness about her. I recalled her explanations of Med mythology; and even though she had objected to my choice of words, I did find her presentation intriguing, if not even a bit frightening. I thought now was a good time to share some landscape talk. When I suggested this to her, she said she did not want to talk about that mythology stuff around her colleagues.

So, we left our colleagues, to sit alone in another part of the café. We ordered coffee and I said, "Fairies and the Med landscape, Bree, tell me more."

"CJ, if I spoke your landscape architecture language, I would speak of ethnobotany. And that only comes close. Do not speak of fairies—that is not proper—to use Tolkien—we are speaking of a perilous realm when humans happen upon it and its inhabitants. I do not speak of fairies or fairy stories. I speak of the Realm of Faery."

"What? Your words are dancing in my ears—I don't understand—but your doors and keys to unlock doors had some resonance. But with all respect, what really brought this realm into such focus for you?"

"Well, I am talking about the nature of that Perilous Realm—I took one year for field research in the Med Basin—no, it wasn't a vacation for suntans. All my research on all three continents comprising the Med Basin, deep research into archeology, anthropology and comparative philology took me to stories about life forms in the landscape."

She continued, "Let me try to make this short but sweet for

you—I spent a lot of days and nights on foot and sleeping in the Med Basin landscape. I heard things. Rarely modern words, but things. They entered my inner ear—that's how I describe it."

I could understand what she said about the special receptors of the inner ear; at least, I thought I did. As personal experience, I only had my dream about Sidi Hamete reaching into my inner ear. But I had plenty of interest in the subject of "taking a ride on music" as some kind of mystical inner ear working.

She was on a roll—this was clearly her thing—continuing, "In summary, on the European side from the *maquis* and *garrique* I continuously heard mournful moaning. Loss of the rich forests and sub forests, but among the *maquis* I felt patient hope within the mournful. The *garrique*, though, while sharing an impatient mourning, wanted revenge—warlike intensity.

"On the African and Asian basin edges, there was also a mourning but it was the hopeless dark mourning of already lost in war—depressed—no hopers—but more frightful than that... and I'm not really sure how to put this into words... I felt that those two continental basin edges embodied a certain undercurrent—a satisfaction—a pleasure—a job well done—in respect to the failing richesse of the biomes.

"But this was nothing compared to the sands of the Sahara, where two conditions repeatedly surfaced. There was a screeching—a highly pitched, extreme wailing riding on waves of unbearable pain—pain for me to hear! I feared it! I dreaded it!

"But other sand desert places revealed absolute silence—like nothing I can describe or even imagine. I could not hear the wind. I could not hear my breathing. I could not feel my heart beat. I could not hear my voice. I could not hear my thoughts! In retrospect—I became temporarily insane!

"These were my experiences, gathered following a year of field research—make of them what you want—they are not made of the composite material of contemporary landscape architecture."

I was spellbound. Silent. She drank her coffee. I didn't move.

She continued, "Between you and me? I have grown to see the bottom line. I see the existential forces behind those things I heard, I felt... I sensed a time frame of centuries if not millennia. And in the end, I did reach one crystal clear conclusion—I had witnessed a huge intercontinental battle between forces of good vs forces of evil.

"And then, when those guys roughly challenged me in the hotel hallway that night, I was faced by my worst fears from that most Perilous Realm—I was in that battle—I was in that war—I was crushed by the reality of it. Since then, I thought a lot about it and it has removed all doubt that there is an ongoing battle between good and evil in the Realm and it is being manifested in the Mediterranean basin... oh, I see our friends leaving—we should leave with them."

I was still frozen in my seat by her story. She stood up and took my hand. I rose. We walked over to our colleagues and all returned together to the annex.

As I prepared to sleep that night, I turned her story over and over. Was it a possible root for me to use in revising my design study? Na, too far out. But she talked about hearing in the landscape. She talked of strange, perilous realms, insanity. I'm for gardens and beauty and peace. Fell asleep easily.

The next day of classes was our last. We all agreed the *Darija* stage training was useful. I have a great memory of the first time I sounded out a Coca Cola advertisement in Arabic on the street—Co-Ca Co-La! But less happily for me, the West African cultural roots I encountered in Casa added to my Harlequin experience, and what to speak of Bree's revelations—eye opening. This cross-cultural, multi-cultural stuff never showed up on maps.

The day after the lessons finished, I took the train back to Tangier. That was some odd stuff in Casa at the hotel. I figured to just put it away because I had to get something started on my design study.

No unusual incidents on the train; however, Tangier was Tangier. Brushed by, as best I could, the teeps outside the Tangier train station. Took a Petit Taxi direct home. Stopped into Souss brothers' *bakal* and bought food. My ankle was troubling me, so I had to slowly climb upstairs—even still, definitely glad to be home. Glad to be free of that emotional tangle that was the Peace Corps. Had my own problems to sort.

Was trying to graduate and my design study had gone under water. Read some Bowles, listened to MP3s, relaxed. In perspective, concluded that after all I had seen and heard in Casablanca, Rabat and Tangier, just for practicality and safety, I needed to get my own local use SIM. Next day, after conferring with Brahim, I did it.

And my ankle—the *sfinj* accident I had my first week in Meknes. Even with the *Farmacia* wrappings, I had been so active on the trip that it still hadn't healed. Not stinging, just not closing. Not healing. It needed resting.

***

Tangier Writ Large

Even though my ankle was a problem, I still was preoccupied with my study. I was anxious to make it happen. So I slowly walked Striet's Tangier medina spine in the afternoon, all the way to the Kasbah. Walked around the Kasbah and the area along the coast to the East of the Kasbah, still hoping against hope to find a functioning community water fountain in the public realm. But I was tired—ankle sore—needed to rest. Teeps everywhere. Went into the Café on the Sea. No teeps inside. Took the airs at a small table on the cliff face terrace, looking out to Spain. I leisurely drank a freshly squeezed orange juice and recovered. Took a Petit Taxi to Place de la France.

Went by Piliers Culturels and told Mme Zsófia about my *Darija* classes. Told her about the guys from the Ivory Coast and the experiences of the Peace Corps Volunteers.

"Now that you have had a picture of how West Africa affects our region, perhaps it is time to understand how SW Asia affects us," she suggested.

She showed me a small used book, a short story by Arthur Conan Doyle, written in Egypt at the end of the 19th century, *Tragedy of the Korosko*. She said it was a big picture of how Arabia and Africa merge into North Africa. I bought it, took it home and started reading.

I sat on the terrace of my apartment, drinking a homemade orange juice. *Tragedy of the Korosko*—story takes place on the Nile. The Nile is the link, the border, the edge, the beginning of a buffer between Africa and Asia. On one side is the home of Islam for the last 1,300 years. That is Arabia, SW Asia, where they live. Where they started. On the other side is Africa. The Nile touches all. The Nile gives life to all.

But they? Who are they? They always battle the West.

From personal experience, I was understanding how this Morocco was fed by many different cultural roots. Berbers, Black Africans, Europeans... and the Muslims from the *Moyenne Orient*. The last an influence from where Asia meets Africa—always friction—read about the history of slavery.

But what intrigued me most from this Arthur Conan Doyle story about Europeans on a trip in Egypt in the 1890s was the aggressive behavior of the Muslims in their fight against other cultures which would not adapt to their Arabia-based *Sharia* way of life.

What does their book (*Koran*) say about this never-ending fight to convert? In preparation for this study, I did some reading. Nothing by Doyle. I read about the Crusades. The Western Christians went to recover lands that had been taken by the Muslims. Christians had been there first. And Istanbul. Istanbul was Constantinople. Christians had been there first and then the Muslims fought to take it.

And the Muslim occupation of Spain for five hundred years. Christians had been there first. And the foreigner's heads on stakes in the main city plazas here in Morocco in the 1950s? It is not a pleasant history—far from a religion of peace.

This was some weird stuff. Never spoke, thought or heard about these realities before. This was the foreign culture subtext weaving through all my daily interactions in Morocco. Just weirdly uncomfortable. Like that day in the American Legation when a young Muslim guy, praying, went berserk because my camera was aimed in his direction. Like I said above, this was weird stuff.

Freedom of religion—how is that defined? No big deal if it doesn't get in the way of my study. My study—had its own problems.

But I couldn't recover from my trip to Casablanca—the West Africans and the Peace Corps Volunteers. At the 4 July Independence Day Party in Rabat, I worried that I was seeing, in their overwrought anxiety, my near-term unsettled future. After this past week with many of these same tension-filled PC Volunteers, I became convinced. Convinced I would never find the peace I needed for my design study here in Morocco.

I went inside and squeezed a second glass of orange juice. This time when I walked back out on the terrace, I stood at the railing. I took a deep breath and gazed out at the strait, the place where the Med meets the Atlantic, the place where Africa meets Europe. Always turbulence—water—air—emotions. Where was my peace?

Took it easy next morning. Cleaned out my ankle, a month and it was still open—but looking like it might be getting better. I still had optimism about the ankle healing. I stayed home and rested it.

Read Meakin's description of the small things in life here long ago, in the 1800s. Seemed the same as the 21st Century— getting a bit cynical about what this place offered. What have they lost? What have they gained? Was my optimism wavering? It was too often hard to tell if I was coming or going.

Six weeks in Morocco laid heavily upon me. Peace and my design study. Both were AWOL. But... but... my talks with Bree about her research, though on a back burner, were reaching a slow boil. Landscape—landscape culture—so much more complex than I had ever imagined—and it was suffocating my study efforts—maybe I could turn it around—maybe I could use it to restructure my study... I was upset... mental indigestion... sleep slowly came.

14-Safely Home

StoneSteve

As I had laid down to sleep that night, I was worried about my study, confused about my cross-cultural experiences... just unsettled. Landscape had always been my friend—my passion—but something here in Morocco had upset my certainties.

I had just about fallen asleep when the wall of my bedroom started thumping with a base beat, then a rhythm guitar. I recognized *Straight On* by Heart—long-time favorite of mine. What the heck?!

Then I could hear the lyrics. Yup, that was me—been "sittin' it out". Have to do something about my study. Just sat and listened to the lyrics. I've got to get straight on to my study—somehow, I'll find some active public water fountains in the medina—just have to brush away the teeps.

Certainly, *Straight On* by Heart was somebody else's favorite, too. Played repeatedly about four or five times. Then came a medley of Dire Straits from *Brothers in Arms*.

Got up and went out on the terrace. Saw all the lights were on next door. Must be the neighbor, StoneSteve, had turned up. Striet called him mysterious—said he was American—likely so with his choice of loud music. I closed the bedroom door and went into the living room, which had no shared walls with the neighbor. It was quiet. I went to sleep.

The next morning, after eating a late breakfast on the terrace—plants looking okay—I went next door and noted mini-cameras above and beside the door. Knocked, rang, knocked again. Finally someone spoke through the door, "Who's there?"

I explained.

He opened the door. He looked to be fit, outdoorsy, and in his 50s. Talked for a moment about why I was there. Shook hands. He apologized for the noisy music last night and invited me in.

As I walked in, I was face to face with *Blues Brothers On a Mission from God*—a huge poster of Dan Aykroyd and John Belushi. My mom loved that movie. Poster was attached to a makeshift room divider that prohibited people seeing into his place from the front door.

Sat down on Steve's backless sofa—I said it looked just like Striet's sofa. Steve explained, "Maybe Striet didn't tell you... but what you just called a sofa is a piece of Moroccan-made furniture that everyone here calls a *banquette*."

"Oh? ... thanks... I am in the picture. Just speaking American."

"You comfortable? Settling in alright?"

"Yeah, pretty good..."

"Listen CJ, I know what it's like to be dropped into this country, especially Tangier, without in depth understanding of context. How long you here for?"

"About six months, hope to be home for Christmas—I'm still getting my feet on the ground. Striet did tell me that you and I went to the same university, is that right?"

"Yeah, long time ago—undergrad in civil engineering and masters in natural resources—doesn't mean a whole lot now—but we do have that campus in common. Beautiful landscape there, eh?"

"That's for sure."

"Six months you're going to be here? Not very long. Things can be tough, if you need anything or any help, let me know, okay?"

"Appreciate that. There is one question."

"Yeah?"

"Internet connectivity... I saw here in Tangier and also in Meknes that the only connectivity was... what I would call... Internet cafés... right?"

"Yeah..."

"Well, I will have to do research for my project and make weekly email reports... how can I get... at least a dial-up connection to my flat?"

Steve shook his head slowly, "Little chance of that—the national system is not well developed... but... I have a router, 56k modem and wifi that I can let you get access, password and everything, 24-7... text stuff only... no graphics... if that will work for you?"

"That'd be great."

"But that's just between you and I—alums, got it?"

"Guaranteed—no problem."

Steve then asked, "How long is your visa good for, three months? That's a typical tourist visa—I can help you with that."

"No, I have a special six-month visa for student studies."

"Well, let me know if you need to extend it, I can fly you out to Gibraltar and back the same day for quick turnaround."

"I'm hoping to get my study done within my scheduled time, thanks anyway."

"Here, take my phone number and call me if you are ever in trouble."

"...trouble?"

"You never know here in Morocco. Anyhow, this apartment building is good. And you will be safe up here."

Couldn't tell if he was scaring me or just being practical—time would tell. Looked around and saw on the back of the Blues Brothers room divider, this quote from the Bible, Genesis 1:29, "I have given you all the seed-bearing plants and herbs to use." ...or was it a quote from Cypress Hill? I wondered, is this guy a Jesus freak or a doper?

Relaxed on the *banquette* and continued looking around. He had been eating breakfast when I knocked. Offered me a bowl of Frosties in milk. I thought—ok... Frosties... most likely a doper. As I looked around, I was convinced.

On his living room walls were more framed posters, prints of comic covers from Robert Crumb, Gilbert Shelton and an engraved quote from Shelton, "Dope will get you through times of no money better than money will get you through times of no dope".

231

And on his living room table, there was a huge transparent glass jar filled with multicolored glass beads. StoneSteve said that they were Venetian glass beads that he collected from the gateway to the Sahara, near the Tropic of Cancer, a place called Goulimine—he called them magic beads—each one unique and each one telling its own story of beauty. He said he had a friend who asks people to pick a favorite bead and then his friend tells their fortune—reads their future from the unique beauty of the selected bead—magic.

They reminded me of the Hesse paperback my mom gave me for this trip, *The Glass Bead Game*, a story also about beauty. I said nothing, just kept looking around.

Next to his magic glass beads were two huge water pipes—*narghiles*, he called them—Paşabahçe glass from Turkey, beautiful swirling, colored glass. The business ends of those pipes were well used.

He said Striet had told him I might be staying in his place. Asked me again how I was settling in.

"You sure everything's okay? The *shaoush* told me you have had a rough time."

***

The Ankle

Told Steve I had a problem on my ankle—the whole Meknes *sfinj* story. He looked at it and said he'd seen things like that go south real fast. Said we needed to do something and suggested a visit to the local *Farmacia*.

"I've already been there," I said.

"If it is not getting better, you should see a doctor. I know a dependable one. Let me know and I'll take you to see him."

"I still have another ten days' worth of antiseptic and wrappings, I'll get back to you," I said.

Then one afternoon, a couple days later, after one too many bad experiences with teeps and no water fountains, I needed to talk to a Westerner. Stopped in to talk with StoneSteve again at his apartment. I had to talk about local culture—this place was weird. The street culture—everything in the urban landscape—had turned me upside down. I felt like everyone out there was trying to use me. The conversation started like this about Tangier, drugs and the Peace Corps in the 1970s.

"Hey, I'm just a nice, get-along kind of guy—what's going on?" I said.

StoneSteve said, "Weird it is—the Peace Corps makes it even weirder. They tell you to get in touch with local culture—then they tell you no contact with drugs. And the local culture, youth culture, is all about drugs—especially here in Tangier— but all the large towns are the same—youth and drugs is local culture—not hidden at all—in your face 24/7/365—and that hasn't changed at all over the past thirty years."

He continued, "That's not the only stuff the Peace Corps

233

never tells newbies about—evileye culture. Evileye is always beneath the surface but when you know the signs, you will see everyone protecting themselves, everywhere, all the time."

Steve offered another two bits. "Look, here's the short story—if you can work through this, you'll make it here. Nothing is black and white. Nothing is straightforward. All in colors. All in shades. All in transparencies. All in layers of varying transparencies. It will seem like that in the beginning and each time you begin to think you understand—the layers change, the transparencies change... and everything confuses.

"Can you live with that?" he asked.

I listened. I looked at him. I had six months of design study to do before graduation—I thought, so what if I'm confused?

"I've got no choice. But there is something about drugs here in Morocco that has continued to confuse me," I said.

"Fire away."

"Well, they are against the law, but they are everywhere on the streets. And Striet smoked in his place and you have these trusty looking water pipes—what's up?"

"On the street, don't touch, don't ask—you never know who is undercover police and here in Tangier there are so many trying to get your money—cheating is rampant."

"Yeah but I've been in a couple cafes where keef is openly smoked... and what about you?"

"The cops won't bust you in a cafe unless you are dealing. And up here, like I told you it is safe. Relax, if you want to get into it just say so and we can get down."

"Thanks, Steve, can't start that. I got to get into my study. But the cross-cultural stuff still has me stymied. When I'm on the street, I just can't seem to get my stuff together."

"Hey, don't get uptight—that's what this place is."

I looked quizzically at him.

***

234

Trying To Get By

Steve went to his CD player and he said, "Listen to this... this will start you from the ground up on local landscape culture."

He put on a Rolling Stones CD and played a cut called *Continental Drift*. He said, "It was the Stones' Western culture attempt to use music to link up with Morocco—the Joujouka, people from a Berber village just south of here, inspired them. Listen to the music—some people call it a music obsessed with madness—others call it obsessed with healing."

After the CD, Steve said, "The BBC did an interview with Mick Jagger about the Stones' visit for this song—watch it yourself sometime. I think the BBC has it online."

Then he told me, "Even when you go with the flow, you will choke sometimes. Take care. This is a place for adults—not kids."

I heard it all—it meant nothing—I had to do a landscape design study—that Stones' music was too far out.

I came to know StoneSteve's apartment rules and abilities. He made sure I knew that this roof was a no-maid-zone.

He told me that the *shaoush* was okay.

"You mean Sidi Hamete? That's the name I have given her."

"No big deal, I never use any names with the *shaoush*. *Shaoush* is trustworthy, but no one else up here, got it?"

That was clear.

StoneSteve had stamped and sealed letters of introduction from the US and Moroccan governments—Agriculture and Defense Departments, allowing access anywhere to take landscape photos. Otherwise, he, as Erik had done, told me not to mess with photos or videos—because between cops and older teeps everywhere, pretending to be cops, cameras could get you tied up for months of trouble—wasted time.

Steve asked me to talk about my school study. Told him about my no longer existing social medina water fountains. Steve told me about his forestry and water resources background and said he would be glad to help if I needed anything.

Striet had described StoneSteve as a "don't-you-know-I'm-loco" type; but StoneSteve looked straight. He had a natural ability to talk one minute like a Furry Freak brother, then shift back and forth between freak and government-bureaucrat-speak. I figured StoneSteve would be my security and insurance policy. If I got into any trouble, StoneSteve would be my go-to-guy. To me, he was some kind of undercover guy who had a very practical understanding of this place—something I had not mastered myself.

The next day, after a rough and fruitless morning in the medina, I came back to my apartment. I needed some Western culture, so I went next door to talk with StoneSteve again.

"How's your ankle?" he asked.

"It hasn't changed. I'm still pushing on trying to make my study work; but the teeps got to me today... I need relief..."

He butted in, "I've got just the ticket."

"What do you mean?"

"C'mon, we'll take a taxi—I've got something that'll help you."

StoneSteve introduced me to his idea of relief. The mid afternoon heat was at its Tangier height when we took a Petit Taxi there—a place called Heinie's Keller.

Steve said, "Heinie's used to be called Number One—a dive in the old days."

Now it was a nondescript place, hardly noticeable along a dirty side-alley. Entry was downstairs between Boulevard Pasteur and Rue de Mexique. Paused at the door.

Steve showed me the array of mini-cameras used by Heinie to I.D. people trying to enter. From the outside, it was impossible to know there was an old-fashioned bar down those stairs. Steve waved to a camera—the door opened.

Dark, quiet bar—welcoming in an American Western culture way. Reminded me of a place my dad used to take me—a place in Detroit where he, my grandfather and their friends hung out.

Heinie's Keller, a cool, quiet place with cold beer on tap. The owner, Heinie, had a classic collection of vinyl long playing blues records; and his favorites were by Janis Joplin. Heinie's easily became a shelter for me, where, after another day of struggling around the medina trying to bring life to my design study, I could discriminate, reflect.

Reflection was important, because out on the street, the teeps were always on me—reflection impossible on the street. I went to Heinie's for blues music, cold beer and seriously peaceful thinking.

***

Heinies

Two days later and after having had another day of searching in the medina, I woke up and dressed my ankle—stiff, sore, wound open, still weeping, still not scabbing—it did look larger. I needed to buy some food. Prepared to go out. Walked slowly down the six flights of stairs.

As I carried my food from the Souss brothers' *bakal* back to the apartment building I saw Sidi Hamete, unusually waiting at the bottom of the stairs. She pointed to my dressed ankle and told me she would bring to my apartment door a hot *tajine* of paella every Sunday evening. Her sincerity and practicality overwhelmed me. How could I say no? Said yes, and thanked her whole heartedly.

On one particular morning, I was putting off my walk in the medina to find a working water fountain. Instead as I got up, I cleaned and rewrapped the ankle—then had breakfast next door at Steve's. Saw a book there, Hopkins' *Tangier Buzzless Flies*; buzzless flies—I thought, that wasn't Tangier! The teeps are buzzing flies, no, buzzing wasps—every day, all day and all night—it was the noise of the Tangier medina that shocked me—so "buzzless flies"? I was intrigued... borrowed it to read and went home—tried to read, but fell asleep.

I woke up feeling guilty about no progress on my study. But my ankle was troubling. So, in the late afternoon, I made a half hearted attempt—just to go out. I took a Petit Taxi over to Heinie's and he introduced me to his version of pleasure—Austrian monastery draft beer, Seagrams Seven Crown—boilermakers—shot and beer for others like my father and grandfather in the old days—smooth and rocking. Good idea. I did two and then ordered another. Heinies was feeling like a safe cocoon.

I became absorbed in the minimal decoration of Heinies. Noticed a picture and frame behind the bar and asked Heinie. He said, "That one? That's St Augustine of Hippo, Augustinian monk, patron saint of brewers."

Heinie quietly added, "St Augustine of Hippo was in this area three hundred years before Islam—mind you, this, these places, these people would be much happier under Christian religion."

Interesting bit of history but I didn't want any part of that discussion. I was getting tired of trying to figure out every "effing" thing. This was supposed to be a simple study on the Med. Cold draft beer was relief and the Seagrams made it last. Turned my attention to the Boilermakers and said to Heinie to keep them coming, and went to sit by myself.

Forgot about my study—had nothing anyway—after a month of searching and researching, could only dream about the no-longer public medina water fountains—zero—another, please. Knocked down three or four more Boilermakers—can't remember—just sat in the back, in the dark, by myself. Listened to Janis Joplin sing the blues. Last I remember was thinking this cross-cultural thing had me weighed down like a ball and chain.

***

The Blues

Another time, maybe more often than I realized, after a hot day struggling with teeps and the turbulent commotion in the medina, it was only appropriate that I visited my cultural priest-hole, Heinie's. There we had a discussion of blues music that ever so briefly turned my despair into a glimmer of hope. Heinie said, "Humans do share struggles in life," and he looked straight at me, before continuing, "...and humans do find shelter from those struggles in music."

"Is that why you feature blues singers like Janis Joplin and Annie Lennox... music about struggles and fears... shared by all, no matter which culture?" I asked.

"Something like that... but it is just so sweet... yet sad—everyone gets it—that's the bottom line in life. You must have heard this quote from Janis about her music, 'When I'm there, I'm not here... I can't talk about my singing; I'm inside it.' How can you describe something you're inside of?"

Heinie had a point. Even though blues singers tell sad stories, I always come away feeling better. Heinie then asked me a direct but strange question, "CJ, do you believe there is magic in the music?"

"Magic? Well, I never thought much about it... well I have thought about it... music does take me away..."

"That's my point... how does it take you away... and where does it take you..."

I emptied my beer, and asked Heinie for one more boilermaker. Then I said, "You're right, there is magic in music—maybe somewhere in between the ears and mind…" I chugged the Seagrams.

The more I thought about it, music sits in unique cultural envelopes. Those envelopes do not dissolve easily. And they are real. People fight and die for them because they are so central in their lives. Those cultural envelopes, I was beginning to see, are organic—like large-scale cocoons made out of the rootlets growing from deep cultural taproots.

Magic, music, culture—culture was just as weird and inexplicable as the magic in the music. How much music could be in a cultural envelope? And it was funny how music sometimes could provide a cross-cultural linkage. Funny? Strange? Magical? How does that happen? It is a rich area waiting to be explored.

The more I thought about the isolation of those cultural envelopes, the more I realized that I most likely would not penetrate this indefinable culture that surrounded me in Tangier. Music would not solve my cultural problems; rather it gave me a way to forget them. And that made me wonder where the hell could I find the threads, the rootlets to restructure my design study. Restructure? Where did that come from? I had a study plan… or did I? Maybe I did need to think about what restructuring would mean?

I sat there in confusion, in uncertainty. Then I got overtaken in my thoughts by my memories of school, high school and university, where we were culturally indoctrinated. Every day in every class we were fed the continuous, politically-motivated, multi-cultural pressures on speech and behavior.

What pressures? These were the oft unwritten pressures that we had to respect all the different cultures as long as ours was at the top of the heap—the one that made all the definitions that everyone "had" to accept. That stuff was so repetitive, so tedious that it gradually wore every one of us down.

Tangier, northwest Africa—that's real life. I looked back on those school times and intentions as naive dreams at best. Somebody was seeking to universalize a cultural base— or how can I say it—make everyone wear the same clothes? Impossible. Cultural differences are the real world. Those strange differences have a certain beauty in their own right. I still thought the "golden rule" had it all covered already, "Do unto others as you would have them do unto you". But here... hadn't worked.

I knew there is magic in music, like Heinie had described in that quote from Janis Joplin. And I knew from personal experience there was a "magic" in plants, gardens and landscapes. Leave the cultural roots untouched. Do not uproot. Plants on the edges of ecotypes gradually adjust to their changing environment. The key phrase is "gradual adjustment". Humans don't need government declarations for thought and speech change. Humans don't need governmental cultural manipulations. Cultural stuff—cultural roots—are deeper and darker than the oceans of this world. But was the magic in music going to make any of that clearer?

My time in Morocco, with its millennia of diverse cultural mixes, made me think two things. Cultures have such deep roots that they will never be killed. And... or... here in north west Africa there was something in the air... in the water... in the landscape that prohibited smooth cultural integration. Even in Heinie's, I was bound by uncertainty.

When I was still in the US at university, the guys I hung with, my friends in our landscape architecture program, were beer drinkers, and we all turned away from identity politics—superficial categorizing of humans based on "the clothes they wear". Don't judge a book by its cover.

We marvelled at the freedom and diversity shown by humans. And that was part of the fun of life. I think it was because we all realized how diverse were the plants and animals, insects and microbes and their geology, climatology, natural and social components of the landscape. Only logical that humans should mimic that natural diversity—no need for politically expedient, pre-defined boxes—male and female were clear enough. In that binary definition, I found a needed clarity—a clarity I could not find in the Moroccan landscape.

I had my own cultural roots. Some of them I could identify. At university after we all worked brutally long hours in our landscape design studio projects, we'd cut loose on Friday afternoons and take a bunch of beer to a local park. We'd have a good time drinking and complaining about our workload. Boys having fun.

No big thing for me because my dad, too, was a beer drinker. When I was a little kid, during our visits to Detroit, my dad and I used to hang out at a corner bar with my grampa. That small bar was a dark, cool place where men, like my father and grandfather, played euchre, drank beer and talked.

Men only, no girls ever. I think that was why I felt like a regular at Heinie's Keller in Tangier. It was just like I remembered my grampa's place in Detroit. I was glad StoneSteve introduced me to it. That was helpful but unfortunately, StoneSteve was about to open a door to even more intoxication. And intoxication was already becoming my shelter since my design study was one step beyond atrophy.

Well, back at school, though we were beer drinkers, everybody had tried marijuana. Heck, it was the 1990s. We tried everything. But we just liked the joviality of drinking beer together.

My landscape architecture design study in Tangier? I wasn't getting there. This town was weird. Medinas did not have parks, or street trees or gardens. They were without public green. My original study had been to examine how something as basic as water functioned as a social gathering node in the medina public realm—until I found that the water fountains were no longer functioning. I struggled looking to find an old water fountain still functioning as a traditional community gathering node. No water, no green—what kinds of cities were these medinas?

All I did find were too many bad experiences with teeps who were "trying to help" me. Was I getting confused by the "clothes" these guys were wearing? Nope—I tried to be "understanding". Didn't work. Zeroes everywhere. What to do?

I knew what to do. I grabbed a Petit Taxi back to my flat, gimped up the stairs. Before I crashed, I thought about good books. Good music and good books were similar. They take us away to strange, to different places. Exploring a book was like exploring a garden. A garden taking us to strange and different places like a book, like music. Then I crashed.

15-Hakim ben Wais

Preparations

Late the next morning, I heard noise next door... conversation. I went over and knocked. Found StoneSteve there, with two friends of his from Amsterdam, Arjan and Ruud. Steve said they were planning to split for someplace off the beaten track in the Rif mountains, as Arjan said, "...to see some country folk... where people make their own smoke."

Told them I thought it might be time to see that doctor in La Montagne because of my ankle. Steve looked at my ankle and said it looked better than the first time. Arjan and Ruud both looked and thought it was looking like it was healing.

Ankle "taken care of", the next order became relaxing in the Med on a summer afternoon. StoneSteve started the party. We all got into homemade boilermakers, mixed in with a couple drags on the narghiles for variety—couldn't say no this time—I really needed to forget my frustrations—my uncertainties. They put on a Hank Williams Jr CD real loud and sang along with *Country Folks Can Survive.*

I forgot about my design study, the street stuff and even my ankle—beers, Seagrams, smoke—out cold. They carried me back to my flat. It was a couple days later when I saw StoneSteve and his friends returned. I was worried about my ankle again. I was sure the open wound was growing in diameter. This time, upon checking my ankle, they agreed that healing was not apparent. This time they said it was time to go see the Hakim on La Montagne. Steve said he would drive me there if I could go right then. I went back to my apartment to get ready.

Steve and his guests, Arjan and Ruud, were in the final

preparations for their next excursion to the Rif, a follow up *Cannabis* landrace research trip. Arjan and Ruud had already left Steve's apartment and were downstairs packing their Land Rover. Finally, after cleaning and wrapping my ankle abrasion, I hobbled down the stairs. As they finished loading up the Land Rover, in front of the apartment building, Steve told me more about Hakim ben Wais.

"Since World War II, here in Tangier, the Hakim has been a private practicing family physician. On health and medicine, the Hakim knows his way around—can fix anything—it'll work out—not to worry."

I just listened. I was glad to be going to a proper doctor.

I remembered that much earlier, Erik had told me the same, that I should go see Dr. Benways. That was how I heard it. But Steve called him Hakim ben Wais. *Hakim* is Arabic for doctor. Wais is his family name. 'ben' means he is of the Wais family. Transliterated into the Western, Benways, Dr. Benways to some. That *Darija* stage had been helpful.

Even that explanation revealed the breadth of seemingly minor cross-cultural challenges. Each one offering a potential trip, a potential fall—a failure to communicate.

The doctors I had as I grew up had long ago left behind the concept of a single, small office family physician. The insurance companies had already made it big business, complex forms, permissions for specialists.

While we were driving over, Steve continued, "Hakim ben Wais is an old-school family physician. He has access to everything in his office. Everything he needs for most normal problems—medicine—equipment. He has two assistants who work the reception desk and in his surgery as needed."

I was comforted by those descriptions. My ankle was an uncertainty that had contributed in no small amount to the dark cloud of despair that nagged me. Hakim ben Wais? Sounded like healing was his only purpose. And that was what I needed.

This was my first visit to this famous part of Tangier. It was exciting to see how it fit into the region. It was uphill from and west of the medina. La Montagne—place of Westerners and well sited villas. It was the place to live for the affluent. It was a district of Tangier that was part of everyone's conversation.

The geography was amenable in many ways. All villas were sheltered from prevailing westerly winds off the Atlantic Ocean. They all had extensive gardens, privacy and great views over the city, over the Kasbah, over the medina, across the Bay of Tangier to the Strait of Gibraltar. La Montagne was a place of slopes, blanketed with floriferous *Bougainvillea species and hybrids*—reds and purples everywhere—flowing over walls—flowing across pergolas—the bougainvilleas owned this landscape.

With one exception.

On the way, Steve pointed to a well-situated villa. "Hibiscus House," he said, "...look at that weird place..."

Couldn't miss it. He was right—I saw a forest of mature *Dracaena draco* between the road and the front of the villa. I had seen one once in Southern California, dragon's blood tree. That common name was the result of two things, red sap and the age-old belief that its sap could cure virtually anything internally amiss in humans.

Before I could satisfy my eyes with that astounding forest of dragon's blood trees, we arrived at the doctor's. They dropped me there. StoneSteve walked me to the front door. At the front door I found a name plaque for Hakim ben Wais with an arrow pointing the direction to his Surgery entry. The Surgery entry was close. StoneSteve waited as I rang the bell. When a Moroccan servant answered, and began to lead me in, Steve motioned to Arjan and Ruud. They all came in with me.

***

Medicaments

Inside the Hakim's surgery, the servant led us to the waiting room, offered us a seat and said it would be just a moment. He knocked and entered what I figured was Hakim ben Wais' inner office. After a moment, the servant showed me in—no formalities—no informalities—no paperwork.

Doctor Benways asked the history of the wound, he unwrapped it, did a preliminary cleaning around the edges, then carefully examined the wound. Told me it was a *Streptococus* infection and fortunately in the very early stage—but it could become a necrotizing fasciitis and the ankle, in order to facilitate healing, had to be put in a cast.

I was more than surprised at the diagnosis. I was shocked. Before I could say anything... Steve knocked on the door and the Hakim told him the details, including that I would be with him another hour or so for the cleaning and cast.

Steve said, "CJ, the Amsterdammers and I have to leave..."

"No problems, there is a Petit Taxis stand only 50 meters from here," the Hakim said.

Then Steve and the guys left for the Rif. And the Hakim got down to business.

He looked at it again, then cleaned the entire 3cm diameter wound—damn that thing had grown—used some kind of strong-smelling antiseptic and a scouring pad! Wow! Pain! Then he wrapped it and put the cast on it.

Needed to stay off it for two weeks and then return for inspection. Warned me about atrophy of muscles during the cast and healing. Told me to do simple leg lifts everyday—but put no turning or strain on the ankle.

Gave me a Penicillin shot and Penicillin pills, crutches and pain pills—pain pills just in case, he said. Pain pills? Now the surprises continued. Tramadol—ten 50mg capsules as needed, Oxycodone—fourteen 30mg pills if I needed more pain control and finally, he said, should the need not to move around cause me increased anxiety, Diazepam—twenty-one 10mg pills and last but not least, a bottle of Paracetamol.

He gave me his phone number and told me to call or stop in anytime if the medicines needed adjustment. Told me not to worry about paying until the healing was accomplished. Scheduled a return appointment on 22 Aug.

Then he sized up my crutches and asked me to practice with them. I'd had crutches before, in high school so I had a familiarity. After he saw me moving around on the crutches with reasonable balance, he saw me to the front door and pointed the direction to the Petit Taxis.

This was something I had to do—ankle had gotten out of control—I understood what and why. But it was Hakim ben Wais' medicine cabinets I had never seen the like of. Walked out of there with morphine as if it was aspirin! At first the crutches were awkward, not impossible but awkward. Slowly, I made my way to the Petit Taxis around the corner.

When I got back to my apartment building, before going upstairs, I stopped into the Souss bros. *bakal.* I arranged a standing order for basic foodstuffs to be delivered to my apartment via Sidi Hamete every other day—no problem. But I did encounter a real problem—six flights, 72 stairs—repetitively using new muscles. The higher I climbed, the slower I went. I worked hard with the crutches up to my rooftop flat. I was beat.

16-Roller Coaster

I Succumbed—Big Time

That same night after the Hakim had scrubbed the wound and set my ankle cast, I took one of each of the pain pills—just to make sure I'd not be kept awake by the pain. Not surprisingly, I slept deeply and woke up the next morning—late, very late. I grabbed my crutches and hobbled into the kitchen.

On top of the mini fridge, I found three fifths of Seagrams 7 Crown and what must have been an ounce each of four different types of Cannabis plus a half dozen different chunks of hasheesh, each about 10 grams, plus a small water pipe, a Gandalf pipe and a box of wooden matches. With a note from Steve—a "Welcome to Morocco" house warming from StoneSteve and the Amsterdammers. That was their idea of help for my coming times of immobility... plus a PS from Steve where he suggested I'd better change my apartment front door lock if I wanted privacy.

In a cast. Off my feet. Stuck in my flat. Bummed. I thought, what has happened? What was going on? What brought me back to this place? What keeps me here? Beach? Sun? Study? Or something else? Was it just pleasant childhood memories that brought me back to northwest Africa? And what was keeping me attracted to all the uncomfortable strangeness— the pain of it all?

I had no answers.

I cracked open a bottle of Seagrams, mixed in some water and collapsed on the banquette. Took a long drink. Slowly downed the whole glass. Meant to be... I guessed. Crutched around the house and on the terrace... what to do... not sure.

Then I remembered the *bakal* standing order—today, the first day. Crutched to the front door, looked and found my *bakal* standing order sitting outside my apartment door.

Ate my late breakfast—baguette, butter, jam, fruit and coffee—on the terrace.

In my own little world, I had culturally adapted. I put my foot up and reflected. I had wanted to stay clean from any drugs. But I had had enough of the teeps, the medina chaos and worrying about my nonexistent study.

The following morning, after having taken once again one-of-each of the pain pills the night before, I felt a little bit cloudy. The potpourri of pain pills I had taken definitely had part of me under their influence. Cloudy? Pain pills? Morphine? Morocco? As I was thinking about intoxication, memories took over. I remembered my mom; and I began reliving twenty years ago jumbled with my recent arrival in Tangier. Unsettled uncertainty mixed with the comfort of my 20 year old memories. The good memories were winning.

I can't say Herb Striet didn't warn me. My mom and I had discussed that one warning letter from him. She just tossed it off. She told me that she remembered she was respected on the street everywhere we went because she was a mother and she was with her young son—but she did slip me that silver hand of Fatima key chain for "good luck". Never thought much about that—but... now... this time...

I spent the next couple days taking advantage of the Seagrams but staying away from the smoke. I quickly descended into a kind of deep funk... then late one morning.

I heard StoneSteve and the guys returning from their trip to the Rif. It was about noon when I crutched next door. I thanked them for their gifts—then I threw caution to the wind.

Right then, I joined StoneSteve and the Amsterdammers in a good smoke-up. Under the influence, I felt free of everything that had been bothering me. Even though I had long ago, with a clear head, concluded that serious intoxication was not a tried and true path to success. On the day, that conclusion got lost in smoke. That was the beginning.

***

My Roots

On the contrary, this was the real beginning.

My mom, Kate... I was an only child. My dad, Sam, an international businessman, was a driven "Gordon Gekko" character, forever into beer and whiskey. And my mom, before her marriage, she was a "Janis Joplin" character, into pills and natural psychoactives. You can imagine the household conflicts.

What more can be added to having a mom like Janis Joplin? Actually, a lot. Janis Joplin describes my mom's era, her approach to life then. In the 1960s, she went out to San Francisco and became a Janis Joplin groupie, somehow survived and returned to go to the University of Florida where she met and married my dad. My mom was a good-looking American girl, blond hair, blue eyes and an Olympic swimming star. She was a Southwest Florida native, grew up in Bokeelia. She still called that home, though La Belle was actually where she was born.

A Gemini, she was restless, though responsive, curious, and caring, maybe caring to a fault. She home-schooled me for a year, around the time of the divorce. Divorce? Yeah, it happened when I was six.

Home schooling? No complex classes, she made sure I could read, write and do math. But even when I was a baby, she constantly read to me. She bathed me in literature, kids' books and classics. No surprise that I naturally liked books, naturally liked reading.

After the divorce, as she put her life back together, she took me on a one year road trip to Europe and North Africa. Home schooling continued. When my mom and I were touring Europe, she showed me the highlights of Western civilization. I had been too young to remember all the details. But as I grew up, I had a thirst for culture and the arts. Those interests spurred my first university major in literature.

After Europe, my mom had taken me to North Africa, Morocco. The two of us had lived out of her VW camper van on the beaches of Essaouira for about three months. I guessed it was memories of those beaches that were the seeds of my desire for more Moroccan Mediterranean experiences. That and all the long design studio hours made my design topic study decision easy. A study that would have let me sit in the sunshine, and watch people gather water while I took notes in my journal, in other words, an excuse for relaxation and easy Med suntan.

When I was planning my term abroad landscape design study, my mom and I both fondly recalled our time, our closeness, our adventures in Europe. Focusing on our three months in Morocco and my natural ability with street-wise foreign languages, I used that twelve month experience in Europe with my mom as the basis for getting an exemption from the team requirement on the term study abroad projects. I stubbornly fought my Academic Advisor and Department administration to get my single status on the study in Morocco.

I succeeded. But actually, I did not really remember too much more about Morocco from my original trip except no chocolate in the shops and those noisy prayer calls before sunrise.

I can't talk about my mom without bringing my girlfriend Sachy into the picture. Sachy? She was a star. She had the well-endowed beauty that made guys who shared lectures with her forget what lecture they were listening to. For her first year at university, every guy who spoke with her was interested only in bedding her. That was not her style. She was Laura Ashley all the way—a rural landscape feel with natural materials in subtle combinations that embodied her mood of chastity. When we met, we became friends quite easily.

And we grew together over six university years. In the beginning, we were both Fine Arts majors. Two years of literature and music courses brought us together. While I switched to Landscape Architecture for the last four years, she earned her BFA and now was doing a Masters Program in Fine Arts Education.

On a physical level, I had already learned from experience that sex and social life at university simply detracted from the energy available to study and learn. I took a detached approach to what I called the "magic gristle". Neither did I get involved at all anymore in the time-consuming game of "pole in the hole". This worked for both of us because our relationship was built on discovering diamonds, not on traipsing over broken glass.

We focused on emotional stability. We investigated intellectual and spiritual patterns in the relationships between humans and the elements of landscape. Sachy called these efforts activities in the mode of goodness. It worked for us. And I have tremendous respect for her fine arts knowledge, human insights and cultural opinions.

I never imagined that my term abroad for six months would highlight how important were my true cultural roots back home. Without those roots? I didn't even know I missed them. The smoke took their place.

***

Everglades Landscape

It became too easy to fire up my new Gandalf pipe and work through the grass and hash as an adjunct to my pain pills. That put me in the mood to question culture, cross-cultural, multi-cultural, cultural roots and landscape roots. That was all dark stuff that I never had the philosophical propensity to examine. So I used the smoke.

Back when I was at university... on spring break... my girlfriend, Sachy and I went to SW Florida from time to time to visit my mom. I didn't know it when I was in the Florida Everglades, but in those days, cultural roots grew quickly. And they grew strong. I had never even considered that cultural roots had anything to do with the landscape. My time in northwest Africa cut... damaged my cultural roots from back home. But they were not lost forever.

It was my mom who helped Sachy and me grow closer through the landscape. Early in her life, Kate had ventured into the Western Everglades and had become friends with Clyde Butcher and his wife. My mom, in turn, introduced me to Clyde's photography. Clyde Butcher became, for me, the Ansel Adams of the Florida Everglades. Clyde's images were of a landscape perpetually recovering from a Category 5 hurricane every thirty years. His black and white photos captured all the plants in those swamp forests that had been "vegematic-cut-and-sliced" by the recurring hurricanes or scorched and burnt by lightning fires. These were landscapes that survived nature's most destructive forces.

Mature trees were rare, yet the life force of a recovering

landscape was impressive, overwhelming, hopeful. I loved my vacations to see my mom in Southwest Florida.

One time I will never forget. Sachy, my mom, and I boated overnight from Bokeelia slowly south, Useppa, Captiva, Sanibel, Estero Bay, Naples, Rookery Bay, Cape Romano before putting in finally at Everglades City. Kate had a friend there, an ethnobotanical specialist in "square grouper", a marijuana habit she never kicked. We rented a camper and drove across the Western Everglades, that sub-tropical water wilderness of South Florida, where we spent two days at Clyde Butcher's Big Cypress Gallery. We loaded our stuff into his Swamp Bungalow accommodation.

We sat with Clyde and he told the story of how his black and white photography was linked to the unfortunate death, some years ago, of his teenage son. Clyde only recovered out in the swamps, where, in that ever-so-still-quiet, he stopped seeing color and began photography in black and white. A mystical healing occurred which enabled him to see all as shades of gray where death was simply a gradual, transitional part of life's cycle. He got through the hard times and felt a resonant inspiration every time he walked and waded the swamplands. I was mesmerized by the story of a landscape that healed a hurt human.

I said, "Landscape has always been a richness of colors for me—colors beyond identification—millions of colors. Yet, when I look at your work... when I look at Ansel Adams' work—both of you have captured something special in black and white—a worshipable feeling in the landscape. It's humbling. Tell me, how do you describe it?"

"Black and white reveals in each aspect of the landscape a oneness, a belonging, a union that everything shares. An interconnectedness. We all share it."

Clyde continued, "To understand, you have to get into the swamp. It's about quiet. Human quiet. Are you interested?"

I listened and thought, it was the "quiet". How he talked about the "quiet"—struck a deep root. It resonated.

Clyde waited. Looking at my mom and Sachy, both softly smiling, I said, "Am I interested? Is the Pope Catholic?"

"Good, I'll come to your bungalow at 8 tomorrow morning and we'll take it from there," Clyde said.

So began our walk through the Big Cypress National Preserve, more generally known as Florida Everglades swampland. Explaining the mosaics of habitat, he took us to one of his favorite places, Fakahatchee Strand. He talked about the death of his teenage son and how it had bothered him so deeply. Yet now, each time he sets out in the swamp, the quietness recharges him. He feels the interconnectedness. And the sadness of his loss becomes clean, fresh and healthy, like a fully healed wound. But it was the quietness of the Strand that struck me.

It's about hearing; I came to believe there was something magical about how hearing and the ear work on the human psyche.

We stopped talking and walked knee deep through the swamp for another hour. Paused, exchanged observations. Then returned without further talking.

That night, after dinner, I built a fire in the outdoor pit. We all shared "square grouper" over that campfire as the last of the sunset yielded without pause to the full moon. We talked and listened until well after midnight. After my mom went to bed, Sachy and I sat on a glider in the screened porch and talked more. How can anyone measure the peacefulness two lovers share in quiet talks under a full moon?

Roots were growing.

***

Stuck in Smoke

SW Florida? Everglades landscape? Wow!

I had just taken a mental trip—I had just left Tangier—for how long? I spent that time with people I loved. They were my true roots. I missed them. I looked around. I was in Tangier, in Morocco. My foot was in a cast. And I had a Gandalf pipe in my hand. My real world? My study? I was in prison.

Then and there I decided to test each and every one of the varieties of hasheesh gifts. I figured if I smoked enough hasheesh, I might understand the culture that had turned the streets of Tangier into ugly... might even discover a path toward a new design study. I was on the path. The path? Right or wrong, I was on the path.

What was I seeing around me? I couldn't make sense of any of it. The questions themselves were too ugly to ask so I took shelter in my flat. Took shelter—smoke, drugs, alcohol—my MP3 player was cultural mainlining. I lived in a cultural cocoon. Don't ask don't tell had a new meaning. The questions stopped forming because they were so ugly—and I had no answers—it was all horribly dark and existentially noisy—threatening—fearful thoughts bred fearful sounds. In my imagination or reality? I never knew.

As I worked through the different varieties of hash, I had brief views of clarity. For instance, I recalled Marcela's story about her great-great uncle, the seaman who spent his life sailing the West African coast and his strange description of the evileye. Marcela warned me to hold on to my Christianity for protection. Then I remembered Mme Olga's story about how northwest Africa protects itself from the evileye. What is that thing called the evileye?

And Bree, God bless her, I didn't put much stock in her Faeryland but what she said about what she heard in the Med landscape—the battle between good and evil? All those things were trying to line up in my head. Then I recalled a blues number... *John the Revelator*... yeah, there was something Biblical about my variety of deep root north west African landscape insights.

I had one more variety of hash to try. Broke off a big chunk—put it in my Gandalf and fired it up—took four hits to smoke it all. More questions emerged... teeps, medina, pedestrian precincts... was this 21st century Viet Nam? Were these guys upset because we were undermining their culture—by we I mean the Peace Corps and its western culture tentacles? And then I lost track, too much smoke, fell asleep.

When I woke up, my ankle was aching, so I took extra pain medication—slept the rest of the day.

Next day. Took medication. Smoked medication. Tried my best to stay off my feet all day. Recalled my thoughts from last night and wondered if this strange landscape of north west Africa actually infused the people with an evil influence—the people were under the spell of the landscape. The landscape was a medium to transmit evil into the people... naw... that was goofy... that was fantasy... I crutched out to the terrace and took the Med/Atlantic 78° airs—deep breaths many times. The landscape and the cross-cultural behavior of Tangier people in the medina? Couldn't make them work together.

Back inside, I got more into sampling Amsterdammers' goods and listening to MP3s than my design study. And so the day went.

I had to send SitReps to my Academic Advisor every Friday. Last week in my first SitRep, I told my Academic Advisor, Neil, that I had arrived safely and found a good place to stay in Tangier.

My next SitRep was due. Didn't know what to write—that everything was coming apart?—couldn't write that! I didn't email anything.

Medication and smoke, reading and MP3s, sleepy, drowsy, quiet, stayed inside. Made toasted cheese sandwiches for lunch. I thought about my study. I was sure I was not going to find functioning water fountains in the medina. So, there I was, stuck in a cast in my flat for at least two weeks, maybe that will be helpful—maybe my design study needed to rebirth itself from my imagination.

Tried the water pipe—nice mixtures of marijuana and hasheesh—and before long, I found myself in the medina when I was not really in the medina.

Questions came. Was the flow of pedestrians just the chaotic flow of life—a jumble—no time to think—then I thought about back home and how my life, our lives were all about being in a container—cars—separated from other people—here it was visceral beyond viscerality—human life brushing against human life so impassioned and so without intimacy—a current of human activity in unceasing flow regardless of birth, death, infirmity—we all just keep moving and why... Why do I seek this solitary—this peace that doesn't exist in public? I can't pause out there undisturbed, and ask those questions. Too much noise. Too much flow.

Something about the medina flow that is nothing less than the immutable force of eternal time. I felt that but I could not understand that. Here I am surrounded by humans and their noise that does not let me in but repels me and I have no place to hide in public. Same as always—no fresh insight.

Tried to read. Browsed the remainder of Pierre Loti's *Au Maroc* and Hopkins' *Buzzless Flies*. Both were depressing pictures of Tangier—of Morocco. Hard to find beauty or inspiration in them. I had to get away. Took some pain pills, some smoke... the path spoke or was it the smoke? I heard that if I just smoked a bit further... the answer would appear. MP3s, sleep.

***

Chosen Profession

The next day—oh, the tedium. I'd been in Tangier for two months and how the time was dragging. Dragging but I had to get moving. I felt mired—mired in uncertainty, packaged in worry. I needed to do my study—my study? Disjointed.

Medication, smoke, reading and MP3s. In my drowsiness, my design study thoughts became an inspection of design—noun or verb? All the same. University had put me off design. Each instructor had favorites. That was the game. Figure out the favorites and get good grades. And design? Anyone could search the internet for the elements and principles of design. My thoughts were racing. I poured a glass of Seagrams and drank it like water.

Yeah, anyone could learn design just like handwriting. Practice and repetition. Drills. But who wanted assembly line repetitive work? With vigor, like I was onto something, I stuffed the water pipe with grass and hash. Took a couple hits. What is landscape architecture—we analyze, plan, design, manage—I took another hit—and we nurture the built and natural environments. I must have memorized that in my beginning LA101 class.

My internships saved me—real world projects. We move people from building to building—from A to B. That's straight line stuff. Then we repair the landscape over a bunch of other straight line stuff, called utilities. On top of that we spread grasses, ground covers, shrubs and trees like butter creme frosting on a cake. Where was the design? Baked in? No, it has

266

to be more than that, doesn't it?

I put together another batch of marijuana and hash for the water pipe. Grabbed a couple tangerines, peeled them. Then took a few drags on the pipe. Washed my throat with the tangerines. I thought a design study topic surely would emerge. When I woke up it was mid morning. There were no notes. Nothing from my smoke fest the day before.

***

Nights in Spanish Gardens

S o the next day began. Another sleepy, drowsy, quiet day.
I was intent on resting my ankle. Kept my weight off that
leg. I worked through all the MP3s I had brought with
me and I was feeling melancholy until... I got to one of Don
Rafael's Spanish tunes that I hadn't listened to yet—Manuel de
Falla *Nights in Spanish Gardens.* Orchestra became the swirling
mists of all garden influences. Piano became my discovery of
unique garden features.

Heard a haunting uncertainty with a strong yet
unrecognizable beat that I now call African influence—not
Moorish, not Islamic. I heard a strange sensual knotting of
Arabian and African—a stark, jarring, repetitive imbalance
relieved by the sparkling, well focused promise of the piano.
But the piano's clarity kept getting lost in a pining melancholic
haze—a melancholy from fear of having lost something... that
something was not Arabian or African... was it from the West?
I felt a sad uncertainty that only de Falla's piano could relieve.
I listened to *Nights in Spanish Gardens* over and over.

De Falla let me ride on the theme—very smooth—then
interjected something to change my focus from overview to
detail, and before I could grasp the detail, he forced me back
into the overarching theme. And that happened again and
again.

Like here in Tangier and its shape-shifting culture, de
Falla's music shape-shifted and though entrancing, it left me
with nothing in the end. Things are not what they seem. ...
*Danza del terror... El circulo magico...*or are they?

But I was attracted. Maybe there was something. It was not the first time I took a ride on music. A ride on music? My sense of hearing taking me on a ride? But it was a strange ride. On that ride was the first time that the music paralleled the cultural experiences I was having here in northwest Africa. How did it fit together? Where was the clarity? Was it hidden by confusion? What was I doing in this place?

The more I thought about it, the less I understood. Maybe it was simpler? Maybe I was making it too complicated? The less I understood, the more I smoked. Boring days, troublesome days had set in and my diary started to be repetitious. Took medication. Smoked medication. Stretched leg muscles by simple leg lifts. Hardly thought at all about my design study. More medication and smoke. MP3s distracted me.

**

Nyx

I wanted to explore, discover—my design study and cross-cultural displacement overlapped each other in a heavy cloud that hindered my vision. I didn't want my tethers to the past; but I felt I needed them. I needed them but didn't want them. Confusion non-stop. Took more smoke—to bring clarity? But instead I got sleepy, drowsy, quiet. Came to, later.

Hunger. A couple oranges, a couple fresh figs. Another day and night of rest. But I needed something more. I needed a breakthrough. It wasn't coming; but maybe it was just around the corner.

But all I got was more of the same, reading and smoke. Kept my foot up. No progress on design study ideas. "Medication" made me sleep like a log. Hints of the downward smell of death around here—wisps of depression. What's that saying? It's always darkest just before the dawn?

Then Sidi Hamete brought up the warm paella *tajine*. Put it on the floor outside my door, then knocked. By the time I crutched to the door, she was halfway down the stairs back to her place. Paella was marvelous—better than medicine.

And then another day, reading, medication and smoke. Tended Striet's plants on the terrace—a little water is all they ever needed—felt better knowing they were refreshed.

But I felt impatience setting in. Had to get out into the medina, but shouldn't stress my ankle. Had to make progress on my design study. Looking for options. Needed fresh vision—tucked into some hash. My head got thick with hasheesh. Nothing happening... until... I took rest.

The hasheesh put me slowly to sleep. Then something happened—a dream, I thought, but not sure. I had gotten out of my apartment and was on my way to walk Striet's Tangier medina spine. I was in the midst of a run-in with the tattoo-faced Rif ladies selling white cheese wrapped in *Washingtonia* fronds on the edge of the Grand Socco. I was just admiring the textures and colors of the cheese and palm fronds when one of them stood up and addressed me by name.

She said, "Janus, my name is Nyx. If you want to know about bled landscape, come back to see me here, tonight. After the color from the sunset has given way to the dark sky, meet me here. If you have a strong constitution, I will give you the key to the secrets of the bled landscape."

I returned after dark to the same spot, only to find no one but a gang or rather a nest of teeps that descended on me with passionate vampirish thirst. The moment that my fear reached its peak... my eyes opened. I was soaked in sweat in my apartment bed.

I went outside, and sat on the terrace amid the plants with a gentle midnight Med breeze refreshing me. Fell asleep in my wicker chair until morning.

The next day, I brushed off the dream as a dream. Nothing more, nothing less. Just part of my tedium.

***

Searching for a Thread

Endless days, no results, no ideas... I was feeling desperate about my design study, having been in Morocco more than two months and nothing to show for it. Went out for a bit, thought if my ankle felt alright, I would try to visit the Tangier people and plants I had heard about at Hibiscus House. Maybe it would be an alternative for my no longer viable design study.

Too much strain on my ankle—lucky to get down the stairs—didn't even get to the neighborhood Petit Taxi stand—struggled big time going back upstairs—not going out again.

Let me try to summarize. Africa. Morocco. Islam. Tangier street culture. Harlequin and Zainab in the Kasbah palm and fern *riad*. Fresh fruit and veg markets. The Mediterranean. Can't summarize—still confused by swirling, omnipresent dissonance. I just didn't get it.

I thought more about the year I spent preparing for this study. It was a year of maps. Hell, I'd been looking at maps of Europe, Africa, Morocco, the tropics, the Equator for years. What are maps? What had I been seeing? What had I not been seeing?

I could never truly understand that cartographic dimension called scale when I tried to compare it with real life. There was something peaceful when I looked at the Strait of Gibraltar on a map—the narrow piece between Africa and Europe—between Tangier and Algeciras. But in real life on the medina ways of Tangier there was a human emotional force, a power that no map ever portrayed. Why has that been hidden?

And the tourist brochures, they hid it, too—at best they describe it as pleasant, or fun. Such mysteries in the landscape—never even discussed back in my university classes but slapping me in the face big time in real life. Ominous? It had all been ominous since I crossed the strait that fateful night. On one level or another—everything troubled me.

Couldn't take it—I was lost in a maze I couldn't define. I thought, what the hell; and loaded up the Gandalf pipe with my favorite variety of hash. Maybe I could find my way out with the smoke. Didn't work. Just another maze. Not sure.

Okay—I scribbled here and there... smoked here and there—came out with stories, music, gardens, plants, other worldly experiences.... But why come all the way to Morocco? Stories—stories from Africa? Maybe something was forming... design study? What was forming? What was missing from the maps? Sound. Sounds. My hearing had been assaulted—day in, day out. My ears hurt when I was out on the street. My ankle hurt all the time.

More medication for the pain. More smoke. Sleepy, drowsy, quiet.

Couldn't tell one day from another. Today—a dreary day, until I remembered the Souss brothers' *bakal* delivery. With excitement and pleasure, I found my standing order from the *bakal* outside my hallway door. Fresh fruit, fresh bread, butter—simple pleasures well enjoyed.

I ate on the terrace. Striet's plants looked okay. Thoughts emerged about Mediterranean plants—orange trees, Canary Island palms, date palms, prickly pears, pink geranium lierre, red geraniums, pomegranates, figs, climbing roses, bougainvilleas, olives, aloes, acanthus... simple pleasures for me. More a gardening travel diary entry than a design study core.

From my rooftop terrace I could hear across the city below prayer calls from multiple mosques, each with loudspeakers five times a day—every day. I dwelled on it for a bit.

After two months struggling with the intense emotional flows among the roiling confusion of the medina pathways, I began to think that the prayer calls, five times per day on loudspeakers from each mosque, were to remind the maddening crowds that there was a God, that they were servants, and, that peace could be found only within the sheltering walls of the mosque. Maybe I was right. Maybe I was wrong... maybe there was something in my prayer call observation that could be a seed for a new design study. Sounds? Absence of sounds?

I went back to reading. Dr Leared... Mrabet... Bowles... Meakin... Loti... Hopkins.... The reading led not to design study ideas, but to more frustration. All those guys said the same thing about this country, this landscape—not comprehensible. My study confused...

I put down those quasi-sociological, quasi-anthropological, travel adventure books and dug more into landscape as the universal domain upon which all people must do, must act in real life.

My restructured design study must somehow rise from the indisputable fact that all people manage their lives in the landscape—no exception. And somehow I then found myself in a mental and intellectual cul-de-sac. What to do? Then I remembered what Mme Zsófia had mentioned.

Hibiscus House... but I hadn't forgotten... it was the smoke. What was Hibiscus House? According to what I had heard from many sources—botany, horticulture and gardens. Far away from my university education but... too close to landscape architecture for me to ignore. Maybe I could get access to them.

I wasn't getting design study access any other way here in Morocco. None of the teeps ever said come see my fine collection of plants, my friend, or come see my beautiful gardens, my friend, or come see these spectacular landscape views, my friend. Every idea that crossed my mind always ended with a depressing twist.

Medication and smoke. And again. Nothing.

Out on the terrace, wind blowing up a storm. Palm fronds rasped, shouted. The smaller plants hunkered down. Clouds formed above my head. Could almost touch them—then they disintegrated before they crossed the Bay of Tangier.

I went back inside. Sleepy. Drowsy. More ankle pain. More medication. More smoke. Quiet.

***

Rock'n'Roll

It was Lyum Jm'a, mosque Friday, and I had to email a SitRep to Neil.

18 Aug 2000

Dear Neil,
Settling into apartment; analyzing real life conditions here versus design study plan.
C   J

That SitRep had a nice generic bit of truthful misinformation. In reality, I was struggling with my design study.

Got an email from Neil—said he was glad I got to Morocco early and was settling in. Told me he would arrive for a visit 29 and 30 Aug. Asked me to make a hotel reservation for those nights at a reasonably priced place. I wasn't sure whether his visit would be a good or bad thing. Maybe my cast would be off by then.

Okay, I tried to get with it. Anthropological facts are cross-cultural interpretations... observed as exchanges across the boundaries of the cultures involved... otherness. What is that? A sense of not belonging where one is? Crazy. Or reality for me in Tangier?

My thoughts carried me to past readings about Aldo Leopold. He thought it was important for humans to get closer to the complexities of something other than human, otherness, the natural environment—to study those complexities.

No, that didn't work for me. Here I was embedded in the human communities trying to understand a subset of humans that were making my daily life impossible. I felt more empathy with Darwin's survival of the fittest. Then my thoughts banged up against some mental dead end. I had but one choice—medication and smoke.

When I came to the next day I concluded I had but one door open to me—patience—only patience. But patience was not my strong point. So, I was spinning again with uncertainty.

Ah, then Sidi Hamete delivered the warm paella *tajine*. Hope restored. Great meal.

Had some tasks to do. Made reservation by phone for Neil and emailed him.

20 Aug 2000

Dear Neil,
Room reserved at the Almohades Hotel in your name here in Tangier, for the nights of 29 and 30 Aug.
CJ

Tasks complete, I relaxed into my regular disciplines—medication, smoke... and again... more of the same. This time the words of JB Jackson bubbled up in my thoughts.

Jackson knew there was something unusual buried very deep in the landscape. He thought that thing would be useful to human culture; but he could never put his finger on it. And he gave up his Judeo-Christian roots for pan-theism. Pan-theism.

Essentially he saw good, some might say he saw God in the landscape—not just landscape but also in gardens and plants. Gardens and plants? They were subsets of the landscape that I could not find in the public ways of the medina. With those thoughts I drifted into a deep sleep.

My return appointment with Hakim ben Wais arrived. Ankle did feel better. Moved with eagerness, but carefully down the stairs. Took a Petit Taxi to my appointment with the Hakim.

276

Hoped all was well.

He opened the cast—the ankle did look less inflamed. There was new skin for the first time—healing had begun. He scrubbed the unhealed area—painful, even though he scrubbed gently. He dressed the wound and he put it in another cast. Told me to take it easy, to move as little as possible.

I was supposed to come back in two and a half weeks, when he figured all should be well. Almost three more weeks! Couldn't be! I'd still be in a cast for Neil's visit!

The Hakim continued professionally, asking me about the pain pills. I told him all the Tramadol and Oxycodone were finished. Still had some Diazepam. Told him I had desk work to do and preferred to be active. Gave me a bottle of Phentermine—50x30mg capsules that would help me carry on with my limited activities. Topped up both the Tramadol and Oxycodone. Doctor scheduled my followup for 7 September. Crutched to the Petit Taxi stand.

All these events aside, the bottom line in my life was I got my ankle properly seen by a doctor, that was good; but now I had been gifted hasheesh and cannabis plus all the psychotropic meds. It was an invitation to trouble. And I had taken that path. Drugs galore and stuck in my flat, downhill I continued. Nothing stopped me. Not even my Academic Advisor's visit in seven days.

And the next week passed strangely—like a flash. Every morning was a drag. And every night I hardly noticed the day had passed so quickly.

Rest... reading... medication... smoke...

Received email from Neil—thanked me for setting up hotel and asked what was going on with my design study. He wrote that my SitRep emails had not been satisfactory in regularity or content—asked if everything was okay.

I emailed back that I was changing my design study statement due to local conditions and looked forward to reviewing all with him when he arrived—I was pushing my luck—I had nothing of substance as an alternative design study.

Smoke... Seagrams... sleep.

I was in dire Tangier, Morocco circumstances. I was down,

imprisoned on crutches, beaten up by local culture, taking "shelter" of intoxication, unable to see a doable direction for my design study. Now, my Academic Advisor was on his way to meet me. Nervous time.

17-Neil

Guilt

Back at university, Neil was my instructor and Academic Advisor in Landscape Architecture. He had been there some twenty-odd years and had initiated the term-abroad design study program. I busted his chops to allow me to do the study without a team. I did not want a package trip.

I did not want to bring the US university culture with me. I did not want to live in that dormitory, fraternity or Friday/Sat night "party-and-get-laid" culture. Could you blame me?

I had my eyes set on getting out of school with my degree and going to work in a landscape architecture office on real world projects. I wanted to build the things I designed. In this, my last class before graduation, I did not want any "home-culture" distractions.

Neil had argued strongly against my solo study. Anyhow, he caved and let me do the term abroad by myself. Maybe he shouldn't have. Tangier, the teeps, the "modernization" of Morocco, all have worked against my design study which I thought would be easy-in, easy-out.

I carried some guilt as I prepared for his visit. I had that desire to show him a face that implied I was still in the game. I wanted to show that I had not misinterpreted my strength and direction.

In preparation for his visit, I was at sixes, I was underwater. I had kernels of hope but could find no way forward, so I had followed the path of least resistance.

Then I remembered. It was mosque Friday again. Had nothing new to send to Neil. No SitRep sent.

And before long, another day had gone by with more of the same—rest, reading, medication, smoke. And more smoke... was a good idea forming?

A good idea for my design study? This was where I might find it—like encountering a huge antique carved and inlaid wood chest of cabinets and drawers. Open the outer doors and there are too many smaller drawers and hidden doors inside—more than can be counted—each containing valuable surprises to discover. And always just one more special thing hidden. Then, behind the hidden thing would be... something glorious. Yes, doesn't that sound like what a garden should be for anyone's exploration? Yeah but here I couldn't even find the chest; and if I did, the teeps wouldn't let me near it.

The following morning, nerves set in regarding Neil's arrival. Passed my day with the usual—rest, reading, medication and smoke...

Received email from Neil. Asked me to meet him at the Tangier airport at 10AM, 29 Aug. Emailed back—will do. Well, Neil is coming to visit and my study is nothing, nowhere—bit upsetting.

Took some smoke, some medication... Will work it out somehow.

Felt edgy until the highlight of my week—just around sunset—Sidi Hamete brought up her warm paella *tajine*. Quiet evening. Heat had broken. Ate slowly on the terrace.

Struggling with my design study—why don't I see any Mediterranean gardens in the medina? So what is a Mediterranean garden if there are none in this Mediterranean country?

Smoke, Seagrams. Academic Advisor coming tomorrow.

***

The Visit

Finished cleaning apartment for Neil's visit—arrival scheduled for 10AM at airport. Downstairs for the first time in days. Ankle stiff, but no pain—crutches good, ankle good. Met Neil at the airport. He was shocked to see me on crutches.

Told him the whole story. Added that I thought the worst was over and the cast would likely be off before the end of next couple weeks. Via Petit Taxi, I took him on a mini tour of the nodes of Tangier. Place de Mechoir, Grand Socco, Place de la France. Finished the tour via a sandwich at Brahim's and a draft beer at Heinie's Keller—blew Neil away. Finally, to his hotel, the Almohades. Gave Neil my address and challenged him to take a Petit Taxi to my apartment the next morning.

Got back to my place. Beat. Up the stairs. Soreness in ankle. Took pain medication. Quickly asleep.

Alarm got me up early. Neil's coming to my place for breakfast. Took medication. Cleaned up the apartment big-time that morning, that is, hid all the smoke paraphernalia, Seagrams bottles, the wide range of medications—all out of sight.

Picked up *bakal* order in the hallway. Yeah, good timing. Set up a little breakfast buffet service for Neil—Nescafe, fresh figs, selection of dates, orange sections, cheese board, bread and butter.

Neil arrived, he walked up to my apartment on his own. He said, "Six flights of stairs and crutches? How do you do it?"

Told him the elevator was supposed to be fixed soon. Small

talk and small talk. Quality of life, my health.

We both lingered over breakfast—an excellent mélange of fresh grains and fruits. Though he enjoyed the breakfast buffet, Neil was shocked with my living conditions—mini fridge, gas tank, two table-top gas burners, a small flash water heater and only a shower. Clothes washing in the kitchen sink. Told him I forgot about hot baths and washing machines. He almost smiled; then our conversation turned abruptly into a splash of ice-cold water in my face.

He said to me, "Okay, let's cut the bullshit, and have an honest talk. We both know you are in over your head. I tried to warn you not to come by yourself, but you had to be a tough know-it-all. If you had it together, your SitReps would be on time and full of useful info. Instead, they are unpredictable and filled with nothing. So, tell me, what's really going on here?!"

Taken aback to say the least, I looked at him and, not knowing what to say, smiled nervously. My silence felt guilty.

He asked, "You into drugs, I've heard everyone here is?"

"How could I not? Being on the street, getting into local culture meant being into local marijuana, no big deal, I am doing the work. No problem."

Neil said, "Bullshit, I can smell it, but we'll get into that later."

He chastised the weaknesses of my SitRep emails again as if he had a grudge to pay back.

"Okay, Neil, let me level with you about the impact of the culture. I've done everything I could to get a grasp of it; but it has been slippery and difficult. Being out on the street—the public realm is aggressive and off-putting. I can hardly think straight when I'm in the medina. And as I did tell you there are no more functioning water fountains in the medinas in any towns."

Neil said, "This morning, there were so many guys trying to get my attention outside the Almohades Hotel—I know what you are going through—you just gotta work through it. And need I remind you, you asked for it. It's your test. Your design study. Your graduation."

He continued, "Look CJ, I've been running these term-abroad design studies for twenty years. Get a hold of yourself. Grab your inner strength and determination. Listen, you are in a position that many others have found themselves in. These overseas design studies in foreign cultures often require a complete revision of their basic scope. And that's what you ought to do. It was a good thing you arrived here a month early."

We talked for a while longer about culture, landscape architecture and possible design study topics. He asked, "What was the most notable landscape observation you have made?"

I had nothing.

He asked, "In the medina, anything noteworthy?"

"Oh yeah, water fountains not used."

"Other stuff?"

"There is that inescapable cross-cultural din."

He prodded me for more. I said, "Green space—no public green space—not even plants."

"Let's take that apart in the spirit of Frederick Law Olmsted. For example, how many people in the medina? What is the density? Where is the closest green to let off steam?" he said. He was working with me.

We chewed that over and, for the first time, I saw something for my study—simple and clear. Absence of green space and presence of human friction.

I said, "I'll map the medina for public green space and measure how many people have to walk more than five or ten minutes to see a plant-dominated green space."

He said, "Formalize that. Have you read *Writings on City Landscapes*, a compilation of Frederick Law Olmsted's writings by S.B. Sutton—that could be the basis of your revised design study?"

I hadn't read it; but I grasped the principle. He said he'd send me a pdf of the book for my reference.

"That works for me."

He asked, "But how can you get maps and population data?"

"I have some contacts."

"Contacts?"

"I've been lucky to meet a bunch of older retired Peace

285

Corps Volunteers who have stayed in Morocco. They have contacts and they know how the systems work."

"So you think you have something you can do?"

"That is interesting in many ways, I'll look into it as soon as my cast is off."

He asked me to strengthen my weekly SitReps, then he explored my cross-cultural gaps.

"Have you been in contact with anybody from your family? And what about Sachy? She always was your bright spot."

I reminded him my original plan had been to absorb myself in local culture.

He continued, "I remember the last couple years whenever Sachy visited you in the design studio—you two were close and she had a spell on you. She always was a beauty. She brought out honesty and ambition in you. You and she were all about graduating and working professionally. Now, however, when I read your SitReps and hear your explanations, I see a fish flopping out of water. You are missing those admirable qualities now and frankly, back at school, her eyes have not been the same the last couple months. She has stopped altogether coming by the department. I am missing her glorious and shapely presence."

"Okay, Neil, let's stop it right there. I miss her in more ways than one."

Neil then asked, "Maybe it's time to re-think not having a home cultural linkage?"

Internally, I took his comments about Sachy as a challenge and for her sake, I would email her soon. But the culture observations from Neil, not so much—then, with a little too much collegial intonation, I said, "Maybe I do need a cultural hand-hold?"

"Give it serious consideration," he said.

And until he approved a revised design study, he wanted me to call him every Saturday to assure my timely progress and to talk about my overall local culture comfort level.

I listened.

As we finished breakfast, we kicked around his restructured design study ideas. He helped me to see a way to rejuvenate my design study topic. Good stuff. My metamorphosis? For the first time, his snarky comments about Sachy aside, I had found Neil helpful.

I thanked him and wished him well as he went on to visit the two other design study groups in Europe, before returning to the US. I called for a Petit Taxi. He went down the stairs without me, met the taxi and returned to the hotel by himself.

Woke up mid morning the next day. Neil's visit hadn't been so bad after all. Knocked on Steve's door. He opened and let me in. He was packing to go somewhere. Chatted about my guest and asked Steve if he had any more books on Moroccan culture.

He went to his back room and came out with two. One by Rabinow, an anthropologist in Morocco in the 1960s, and another by Westermarck, a sociologist passing years in Morocco during the early 1900s. Original research, Steve said. More sociologists—I was not impressed.

Borrowed the books anyway. Always a chance for an insight or something to relate to the absence of green in the medinas. I said thanks for the help, goodbye, and returned to my place—put my feet up, read and healed.

The remainder of the day, I lazily paged through the new books. Sociologists, anthropologists, in Morocco they are just like me trying to figure it out. Some have cleverness and some are tediously academic; but all of them finish their efforts with unanswered questions. No help.

And I thought, north west Africa? The battle between good and evil? Couldn't get those stories from Bree out of my mind. Who would have imagined that the landscape, especially the urban landscape, was in that battle—but anyone with their feet on the ground was in contact with the landscape and... no, nothing—this was fruitless conjecture.

I didn't think that was the meat or even an idea for my six-month term abroad design study. And what did that have to do with what Neil and I had just talked about?

So where was I? Not real clear on moving the topic of my design study into a statement—content and form—not sure.

Took more medication... Wrapped up the night with a good

smoke... The smell of death?... or is it just an overburden of anxiety and uncertainty, rising like a mist, thickening like a fog.

18-Muhendis Abdulwahab

Seeping In

Next day, I made an effort to clear my study thoughts. It worked... for a while. Thanks to Neil's visit and help, I finally had the kernel of a revised design study; but I had to work hard, and even then... As the first days of September passed, I was still searching for doable content, structure and form. I still had to work through the haze; but even still I could see lots of questions to answer and lots of processes to figure out.

I took the medina green space idea and tried to formalize a design study statement. Seemed like when Neil left, so did my clear thinking—like I suddenly was no longer sure how to approach my new design study—uncertainty everywhere. Metamorphosis stymied.

My Tangier habits returned. Working again with Seagrams towards the end of the afternoon... c'mon study, c'mon design study... more Seagrams fuel... kept resting the ankle.

Who could supply Tangier medina population data? David? Where could I get a digital map? Tourist office hard copy and scan at Brahims? Kept up the "medication".

And complexity—what complexity? I felt it had to do with abnormal relationships in the regional landscape—relationships between natural landscape and the social landscape—the intensity of those relationships, those connections. Hell, I could not even define those connections. And another day slipped by.

So, I needed to get a map of the Tangier medina, needed to get population data, needed to support the disorienting cross-cultural realities... needed to chase these... as soon as the cast was off.

Reading, medication and smoke. And another day slipped by; but my day to see the Hakim drew closer.

Received an email from Neil's assistant with attached pdf—Sutton's studies of Olmsted writings. Okay, my revised study statement will draw from Olmsted's studies before Central Park—the 1850s, during his time in the UK. A path forward?

Rest and patience; but I'm anxious and still uncertain. I'm starting from scratch on this design study even though I've been here on site for over two months—not sure how I can finish.

Wondered if David had maps and data or connections at Tangier Municipality. Hakim ben Wais day after tomorrow. Rest—I must have patience.

Finally, 7 September. Crutched down the stairs and grabbed a Petit Taxi. Reported to Hakim ben Wais. He took the cast off, examined and pronounced it healed. The wound had healed over—the new skin was strong.

Should be able to walk without a problem now. The Hakim told me to take it easy for a couple days.

Asked me if I needed more pain pills or otherwise. Asked him why? He said you can never be sure as you regain normal activities. Asked him for something stronger than Phentermin. He gave me 24 Dexedrine and scheduled a follow-up 7 October

Walked... walked out—that felt nice! Carried my crutches just in case, like the pain pills, just in case. Took a Petit Taxi back home.

Cast was off—I was free—things were cooking! Stopped to tell Souss Bros *bakal* guys and they were all smiles. I ended the home delivery standing order and pulled out my wallet. Spent twenty minutes settling up what was due. Haggled to show my appreciation. Thanked them profusely.

Crossed the street and entered my apartment building. Stopped at Sidi Hamete's door and told her the good news. She walked to the door this time and, with a smile, noted that instead of using the crutches, I was carrying them under my arm.

Told her that her Sunday paellas had been an important part of my healing—they kept me focused and upbeat. I told her I hoped they would continue. She looked me in the eyes, smiled again, but said nothing.

Then I carried on carefully climbing the six flights of stairs—first time in more than a month without crutches—elevator still had not been repaired.

Felt good. Grabbed some celebratory smoke... Went out on the terrace into the sun, took off my sock, put my foot up on a chair, felt the sun work its magic. Inhaled, and let the smoke work its magic.

Beautiful sunset, gradually revealing the moon glow...

The Strait of Gibraltar.

The Med.

Spain.

The Rif.

Morocco.

I'd get to the design study later.

Then it was Friday, mosque Friday, *Lyum Jm'a*, and following was my SitRep email to Neil:

8 Sep 2000

Dear Neil,

Cast is off and ankle healed—much better and more active now. Working on new scope for design study that would be a medina green space map with population density and green space access buffers. Plan to have an annex of examples of cross-cultural realities that impact design. Need to contact local people for mapping and data. Will do that this next week.

Glad to have seen you. Thank you for your understanding and support.

Phone call to you tomorrow, 10AM, your time, is that okay?

Please confirm by email, ASAP, so I can arrange the international call.

CJ

Data were first on my to-do list. I went to visit StoneSteve first because he was in town and supposedly could get anything done here. He pursed his lips and through them took a deep noisy inhale of air, then said, "You want aerial photos, maps and data about Tangier?"

He said, "Let me tell you some history. In the 1970s, there was an attempt to assassinate King Mohamed V. Moroccan Air Force jets tried to shoot the king's plane out of the sky. It all happened above the Tangier region and the pilots were native to Tangier. Deaths were the penalty for failure and even to this day, any government information from this region is heavily protected. My best sources are national. Try that guy, the retired Peace Corps Volunteer, David, in the Kasbah, he always has got something going on with municipal planners and engineers."

I knew that; but going to David's *riad* in the Kasbah—always filled with strangeness.

The next day after steady smoke and Seagrams, I came to some 'clarity' such that the revised design study, maps and examples of cross-cultural realities that impact design was going to focus on plants and the human need for plants.

I had to contact David for Tangier data access as soon as I could get Neil's approval of my new topic statement.

9 Sep 2000

Dear Neil,

Confirming our phone call today at 10AM your time, right? Please re-confirm by email.

To get our call discussion started, here is my revised Design Study Statement:

International design requires understanding cross-cultural impacts on design. I will address how to identify these and how to implement them into design.

In the study, I will specifically assess the relationship of open space

294

access to medina population density. Then, via a documented series of cross-cultural experiences (regarding the interplay of culture and design), I will demonstrate how, even though cultures may be substantially different, the lack of urban access to green is a negative factor in quality of life.

My recovery schedule tasks:

Task 1: Gather base maps and population data.

Task 2: Redraw maps to incorporate data.

Task 3: Document cross-cultural experiences.

Talk with you later,

CJ

After a long phone call with Neil, where he pushed me to be very specific with Task 3, I got his approval.

Now I had two channels of work to achieve. The maps and data from Tangier Municipality and Task 3, the collection of cross-cultural and green experiences. I focused first on the cross-cultural—I had a ton of those.

Called David about access to the Tangier Municipality maps and data. He said he would help. Asked me to keep Saturday, 16 September free all day, and he would get back to me.

That had a good sound!

***

Chief Engineer

On 16 September, a phone call from David woke me at 8AM. Told me to meet him in front of my apartment at 10 to go to the Tangier Municipality with him to meet Muhendis Abdulwahab.

We rode in a Petit Taxi to the Tangier Municipality—I still cannot get used to every bank and every government office building having at least one military man in front, guarding with a machine gun—same thing here today. We met Muhendis Abdulwahab in a first-floor conference room. I learned he was the Chief Civil Engineer.

He received us warmly, had tea served and we sat with him from 11 to 12. He had worked with David many times before. David explained my student study needs for Tangier medina population and map details. Abdulwahab agreed to see if he could assist me.

Asked me to return Monday, 18 September at noon when he would report what he found. He said it was not necessary for David to return and he looked forward to seeing me Monday. We shook hands with Muhendis Abdulwahab and left the Municipality.

On the 18th, after breakfast and some writing, I took a Petit Taxi to Tangier Municipality for my noon appointment with Muhendis Abdulwahab. He was out.

An assistant met me and told me he had no documents. I asked if Muhendis Abdulwahab had found anything for me? He said, there was *oualu*, nothing.

The whole exchange was one of those weird communication

things—like every other word fell through a different cross-cultural gap—like language was a real time mutating virus. I asked when I could see Muhendis Abdulwahab. The assistant gave me a phone number and told me to call next week—I was getting a strange feeling, as if I had confronted an office of super-empowered teeps.

Amidst a flurry of *insha-allahs*, I quickly found myself out of the building and on the street—major cross-cultural haze. All I knew is that I had nothing but the thinnest of hope and a phone number. Grabbed the first Petit Taxi, went home and emailed status to Neil.

18 Sep 2000

Dear Neil,

Progress is happening. Access to Tangier Municipality maps and data has been slow starting but it is moving.

Thank you for your support.

CJ

At the very beginning of the next week, I called the telephone number at Tangier Municipality—didn't recognize the voice. My French didn't work. My *Darija* didn't work. It was a dead-end phone call. I had nothing.

I called David. He said it sounded to him like a blind tunnel with no exit—a cross-cultural thing that said essentially for some reason Muhendis Abdulwahab was not going to help—even though nobody would use those exact words. David apologized.

I dug out Rick's number at his Peace Corps Rabat office. I got him and told the story. He told me once the Chief Engineer says no, no political pressure except from the Royal Family will change his mind.

He asked me if I had met Steve. I asked carefully, you mean, StoneSteve? Rick said, indeed. Told Rick I lived next door to him. Rick said talk to him. And that was the end of our conversation.

In my mind, I said, been there, done that. The maps and population data part of my study might not happen. The cross-cultural stuff fogged over the whole effort. No path forward. No daylight. All slow motion at best.

I was stymied once again. Went to Heinie's Keller for beer, blues, then home for smoke and an update to Neil:

23 Sep 2000

Dear Neil,

Working on cross-cultural content.

But the maps and data gathering have faltered. The Tangier Municipality has not shared anything. Sounds like another cross-cultural thing. Big time disappointment. Tried all my contacts without result.

CJ

I wrote that email but it bothered me. I was not happy with my failure to get maps and data. I was sure there had to be another way. I decided not to send the email. After too much smoke and Seagrams, I said enough is enough. There had to be some collegiality between professionals and students. I decided to go find out for myself what was going on at the Municipality office of Muhendis Abdulwahab.

The next morning, I headed to Municipality, up to the third floor, and asked the secretary if I could see the Chief Engineer. At the same moment, Muhendis Abdulwahab walked in.

He vigorously shook my hand and asked how I was, while leading me into his office and asking me if I would like coffee or tea. I asked for coffee and he shouted to the secretary "*zjouzj kaowa u jib Ianus dosya*". I understood him to ask for two coffees and bring the Janus dossier. His office was large, with expansive windows overlooking the Bay of Tangier. His desk, I should say his grand desk because of its size, and five chairs were on one side. The other side of the room had two large banquettes and a low table. We sat there. On the wall was a civil engineer's map of greater Tangier along with enlarged black and white photos of old Tangier.

No sooner had I gotten comfortable on one of the banquettes when in came the coffees and a large binder, the dossier, I figured. The Muhendis, instead of taking the dossier to share with me, told his secretary to put the dossier on his desk. We sat on the banquettes and sipped coffee as the Muhendis asked me how was my study progressing. I was about to begin my story and plea for assistance when his secretary, in a frenzy, entered and loudly interrupted about a special visitor in the outer office. Abdulwahab excused himself to me many times and left the office in a hurry.

My mind raced. What could be in the Janus dossier on the Muhendis' desk? Didn't have to think twice. I got up, walked over to Abdulwahab's desk. Heard a lot of talk far away in the outer office and thought now or never. I opened the dossier, looking for digital files, file format info or hard copy of Tangier maps and population data.

Couldn't figure out what I was seeing. Then I heard Abdulwahab's maddened voice as the office door slammed open, "What are you doing at my desk? Stealing information? Spying?" He yelled at his secretary and in 10 seconds there were three military guards, one with machine gun, in the room. They grabbed my arms. Abdulwahab asked for my passport.

I told him I didn't have it. He told the guards to lock me in a conference room downstairs until he called for me. In the locked conference room, my mind could not stop racing. My girlfriend Sachy, my parents... was this going to be a Moroccan version of the disturbing torture during the Turkish interrogation of Lawrence of Arabia? Couldn't think straight.

An hour passed before Abdulwahab and David unlocked the conference room and entered. David told me that Abdulwahab had made charges of attempted theft against me and if my papers were not in order, spying would be added. I asked David to remind I was a student just doing a university project. David said, "I told him that, but it is your word against the Chief Engineer and you are in trouble. He will, however, be understanding and let you make a phone call to retrieve your passport which better be in order and valid. Otherwise, you will spend tonight in jail and who knows after that."

I had a number for StoneSteve and fortunately he was at his flat. I told him what had happened and where to find my passport. He said he would bring it right over.

The next two hours were the longest of my life. Then Steve arrived in his diplomatic best. He was searched by the three guards before he was allowed to speak. He stood before me with David, Abdulwahab and the three uniformed military. Steve carried his own dossier binder. First he pulled out my passport, which confirmed I was a student and that I had a valid student visa. He handed it to the impatient Chief Engineer. As Abdulwahab scoured through my passport, Steve spoke *Darija* to him. As best I could understand, Steve said I was working with him on a landscape project, as he brought out of his binder an oversized document with a lot of florid Arabic writing and a large red wax seal. The document confirmed the most powerful, non-politically-aligned Sidi Ahmed Cherif had given StoneSteve a sealed letter of permission for him and his staff to collect photos, maps and information of the landscape in the Tangier-Tetouan Region.

And before I knew it, Abdulwahab said to me I was fortunate to have the Cherif's approval because my unlawful searching of documents on his private desk was normally inexcusable. He said I should not expect any further help from him or his department beyond my being freed from any criminal charges. The Chief Engineer made it clear that it would be in my best interest to leave this country at my earliest convenience. He would not shake my hand but exchanged kind words in *Darija* with Steve then asked Steve to take me out of his sight and out of his building.

This was the first event after my ankle cast was off. I was shaken and I had gained no maps or data for the main part of my revised design study. Steve said it was a good time for me to drop under the Tangier radar. I didn't need any more convincing; but I needed to make this study happen. I had just

300

blown out the revised design study that Neil had helped me start. My next imperative—clear my head.

19-Zerhoun Sufi

Escape

Landscapes had always refreshed me. They fed my life. I needed them. And after my altercation with the Municipality's Chief Engineer... I say altercation; but he did put a new kind of fear into my life... I definitely needed large landscape fresh air. Immediately! Meknes-style!

And without the cast, I was free to walk, to roam. But first I had to arrange my things before going into temporary hiding, getting out of Tangier. Emailed the disappointment story, without all the details, to Neil. Arranged with Sidi Hamete to hold my Sunday paella *tajines* until I returned.

Confirmed with Tom and Marcela my arrival and week in Meknes to firm up the leather craftsman artisan work for my design study required hard copy. I wanted the hard copy to be bound with tooled leather, having gold gilt detailing. I had been impressed by the craftsmanship, color and intricately carved details I had seen at the Alhambra. In fact, when Justin had originally shown me the leather workers and book binders in the Meknes medina, I was impressed with their high quality workmanship.

Interestingly, I had not seen such care in workmanship and maintenance in the medina public realm—craftsmanship appeared to be popular but declining in quality. It was high quality that I sought for the cover and binding of my final report—but, hell, my study was now... because of the Tangier Municipality... non-existent.

Meknes was quiet, solid—a chance to think through what had happened since I arrived in Morocco, especially the last couple weeks—the visit from Neil—the ankle cast and its removal—and that "small matter" at the Tangier Municipality.

Bought my ticket a day in advance. Made sure to take my first-class seat early. All went well—safely out of town. Meknes—six hours on the train. Thought the quiet of the agricultural landscape would help my design study thinking. And it did, or did it?

As the train rolled across the fertile north west of Morocco, I recalled Pierre Loti's description of the Moroccan landscape when he made the trip from Tangier to Fes in the late 19th Century—an agricultural scene diametrically opposed to the Tangier medina's seething urban scene. Same as today.

I fell into a daze where Loti's images mixed with my emotions and academic imperatives—stifling crowds in the medina—urban landscape—tensions—urban public realm—no relief—fresh breezes in the agricultural landscape—fruit, vegetables, grains—nourishment. If Jackson, Leopold and Olmsted had so much respect for the essential landscape but not one of them could actually define measurable connections between the landscape and humans—how could I totally disregard Bree's Faeryland, the *djinns* of Morocco or the roots of darkest West Africa?

As distant rain clouds were building up, I saw the end of dry summer landscape browns. I felt big relief in the wide, open horizons. The mental cleansing, the relaxing feeling I got watching the big landscape out the train window reminded me of how the quiet largeness of the Florida Everglades calmed and healed Clyde Butcher's emotional disturbance.

And then... as the train slowed to a stop, Meknes. Relief. An easy walk to the Beau Séjour. More relief.

***

Agricultural Landscape

Justin was in town, too. It was a pleasure to see and talk with all of them again. I briefed them on the pluses and minuses of my study and my cross-cultural life in Tangier. Tom and Marcela had an empty room ready for me. It was a studio on the top floor. The top floor apartments were single loaded, on a covered but open corridor, with a mini terrace view to the north east where I could see miles of agricultural land falling off the Meknes plateau—backed up in the near distance by the Zerhoun massif.

Meknes was a country city with no hint of industrialization—and that prospect over the Zerhoun country beckoned.

The next morning, I woke up late-morning—ate some leftover cheese and bread—weather was calm, partly cloudy, nicely sunny—had to go outside. I left a note to Tom and Marcela, then grabbed two small bottles of drinking water from a nearby *bakal* and started to walk—and walk—and walk. I forgot about my ankle, the Hakim had done his work well.

I started by climbing down and around the 17th Century Moulay Ismael wall fortification on the edge of town. Then, across the grain of the landscape, I trekked up and down the ages-old drainage rivulets. Yeah, that landscape, free from closeness, free from teeps, filled with aromas from a growing and rejuvenating earth, grabbed my soul and massaged away my inner tensions. I did well. I crossed dry creeks. Then I climbed up on the raised fingers of the Meknes plateau.

Olive trees.

Fig trees.

Fallow wheat fields, waiting for sowing. Agriculture meets landscape—humans working the land for daily food and drink—something calming about hard work for food from the earth. Walking this landscape gave me time to think, to reflect. I found clarity in my thinking, especially Neil's comments about my condition—cultural and Sachy.

Neil brought up Sachy and that had lit an internal fire. I had to talk to LittleWing—LittleWing?—one of my nicknames for Sachy—about metamorphosis. I had to undergo some kind of metamorphosis if I was going to make my design study happen. Or was I tiptoeing on the edges of Moroccan madness that Paul Bowles describes so well? I had some groups of ideas that just wouldn't fit together—despite inspirational insights. Awkward.

I cannot definitively explain the cross-cultural gap experiences. I dearly wanted to leave my Western culture behind for this design study. But what actually happened as I immersed myself into the street life and culture here, especially in Tangier, was that without my Western culture tethers, I gradually became paralyzed.

I was not the first person to be trapped in gaps between two different cultures. It's been going on for centuries.

My dad told me one time—he was always trying to make sure I was well prepared for life.

He warned me that if I don't learn from history, I will be condemned to failures that humans had already encountered. This was one of those.

But in response to my dad, I decided I could read my entire life (nothing but reading every day and night) about human behavior from the Greeks to modern day—but what would I have experienced? I decided I'd just get on with life and read bits as I encountered specific problems. And as life would have it, here I was—entrapped.

My time with Neil showed me how withered, how atrophied my own cultural root had become. I really was trapped.

Cross-culture? Mysteries never solved.

I wasn't metamorphosizing anything—more like something bad inside was metastasizing—had to work through these cross-cultural hurdles—barriers—gaps—crevasses. It was the smell of death. And that was the Tangier landscape and me—all rolled into one. But on that very day, with Meknes disappearing behind me and the Zerhoun massif in front and growing larger, I was somewhere else... walking the open agricultural landscape... it freed my mind.

**

LittleWing

Yup, no doubt. Had to talk with LittleWing.

LittleWing? Just how did we build our relationship on shared cultural roots? At university, one of my major influences was my girlfriend, Sachy Sitwell, whom I called affectionately LittleWing. We were both admirers of the ballads of Jimi Hendrix, of which *Little Wing* was a favorite for both of us and became her nickname. Nice thoughts. Pleasant memories. We had some great times.

I remembered how our relationship grew deeper. I became absorbed in memories. LittleWing brought me to visit her parents in Buckhead, just outside of Atlanta and her grandparents on her father's side, in Beacon Hill, Boston. These were duties for me: formal dinners, drawing room chats. But, on the plus side in those times, we needed breaks from the university routine.

When in Boston, we visited the Arnold Arboretum and the Isabella Stewart Gardner Museum. We had a memorable conversation one afternoon at the museum.

LittleWing had been looking at an exhibit of drawings from an Arabic translation of Dioscorides, *De Material Medica*. Nearby, I had been absorbed in the plant details done in metallic luster and polychrome on centuries-old pottery from Anatolia and Persia, when I said, "I'd hoped my chosen profession of landscape architecture was leading the way to bring plants into the contemporary day-to-day lives of humans... but... even the courtyard garden here in the Gardner Museum... it's almost like plants done by Madame Tussaud! Do not touch. No life.

310

Missing the essence."

LittleWing looked quizzically at me and listened as I continued, "I liked my summer internship in Santa Monica. Making the link between design and construction. Design and horticulture... but in the end... so much with the plants was superficial, flat without depth, like putting paint on a wall. Thousands of people walk by a planted set-back for a commercial, mixed-use building in the urban realm... they walk by... a few plants... nobody interacts with them. Just like here in this courtyard—look, but don't touch."

I went quiet. Closed my eyes. Slumped in the chair.

LittleWing watched my posture change. "You're vexing me," she said.

"What?"

"You're vexing me."

I was surprised. She read my look and continued, "Perhaps you are letting idealism overwhelm practicality? Perhaps you are missing the very thing that you will create?"

She paused. I ignored her comment on idealism. I was unsure.

She said, "Your future. Your future design work as a landscape architect. Is it not up to you to mold that project environment? Is it not up to you to work with your clients and convince them what must be... how the plants, gardens and landscape can be more than a commodity?"

I said nothing.

"That is your future, no?"

I nodded my head in agreement.

"Then where is the difficulty?"

I saw her logic, thought a bit, and said, "Those drawings and the text translation from Dioscorides where the intent was always to embed in the plant name a massive clue where it could be found—I miss that richness of botanical content. Then those details of leaves and flowers in the pottery from Anatolia and Persia... they beg me to examine the plants more closely. My design should be like that—beg people to look more closely—to enjoy the plants—to understand the plants—to discover more..."

With bright enthusiasm, LittleWing said, "And that is it. That is your challenge. The fire is still alive inside you. Don't vex me with your indecision."

I took her hand in mine, looked into her eyes. As our eyes met, I squeezed her hand. I was healed. She was no longer vexed.

Such was the relationship between us, landscape and emotion. Funny how the richness of memories can fully occupy the mind—shutting down all sense input. Yeah, it was time to talk with her, voice to ear.

***

Sufi Revelation

I paused and rested a bit as those memories just about overwhelmed me. Then I looked up ahead toward the Zerhoun. It was close.

If I walked six hours at two miles per hour, then I walked twelve miles—say twenty some kilometers as the crow flies and the afternoon was almost past. My legs, my entire body—tired— but my mind was free—the air had refreshed my thoughts—a great walk. What I had learned from Clyde Butcher applied to and worked for me. Quietness. Rejuvenation. A superb walk, a much needed walk.

The sun, in a partly cloudy sky, just broke through to display, directly in front of me, the brilliant day's-end sunset colors on the slopes of the Zerhoun. I had given my legs a hefty workout. Even with the leg lift exercises I did over the past month, I was bushed!

...and I didn't know where I was going. It didn't make any difference. I was happy to be walking in an agricultural landscape free of teeps.

At the foot of Jbel Zerhoun, I watched a farmer, with his donkey, plowing his last single furrow. He finished for the day and began heading up ahead to a nearby village. I walked with him. Didn't talk much.

Salam alaykum.

Peace be unto you.

Alaykum salam.

Traditional Muslim greetings.

He had an old leather bag over his shoulder, he reached

inside and pulled out two small dried dates. Without words, he offered them to me. I accepted. Said thank you. Put them in my mouth. Hard as rock candy. Gradually they softened.

Enjoyed the first thing I had eaten since my quick breakfast a long time ago.

It was past sunset when we arrived at the small barn where he kept the donkey. There was a loft of hay. He gave me a hard-boiled egg and a blanket. Then showed me the outdoor toilet and water and said goodnight. I slept in the hayloft above the donkey. Peaceful, sound sleep.

The buzzing of children's voices woke me up. Six or seven of them, like munchkins, standing around me. As soon as I stirred and sat up, they all ran away.

In that early morning sunlight, the farmer, in his well-worn field clothes, reappeared with a neatly dressed *djelleba*'d man who was the leader of this small village. These were farmers living the life of old-school farmers. Country folk.

The leader showed me around the village and took me to where their cooperative processed olive oil. All non-industrial. All hand-work. Showed me, in broken French and Arabic, how the olive oil was processed.

A clean, bare headed, sweet-faced young girl, a child, about 12 years old, came up with a bread board on her head. She took it down and removed its cloth covering. Revealed two round loaves of *khobz*—local bread—warm, just from the communal oven.

From one loaf, the leader tore off two pieces, gave one piece to me. We went over to a ground-level vat of olive oil. He showed me I was to dunk my bread in the olive oil, then eat.

I did.

Then he did.

We ate bread simultaneously.

Just baked, warm bread dipped in fresh olive oil. A good appetite for a great taste. Repeated two or three times. Words do not describe that basic pleasure. Don't need no stinking restaurant. Remainder of the *khobz* handed to another man who in turn disappeared with all the kids.

By that time, another person, a young man college age like

314

me, maybe a bit older, came to us and walked with us. Spoke better French and some English. Told him I needed to return to Meknes. He said he would drive me to the nearest town where I could catch a bus to Meknes.

He said he would drive. Don't know what I was thinking—Renault R4 from the 1970s, or something. He came back with a donkey pulling a two wheeled wooden wagon about the same size as the *sfinj* maker's cart in Meknes. He sat in front driving the donkey and I rode in back for thirty minutes on dirt roads to Moussaoua.

Along the way, we talked. What I could understand, I found intriguing, actually revealing. It was mind opening. Talked about beauty, dance, music, poetry, literature. These, he said, were paths of access, portals, that was his word exactly, to a spiritual bliss on earth—in his words, a taste of the God's glory. An Islamic theist version of Hesse's *Glass Bead Game*, I wondered.

***

Zerhoun, Giverny et al.

Multi dimentional approach to beauty—beauty linking music, literature, math and science—the *Glass Bead Game* got me thinking - multi-dimensional approach to beauty—beauty linking music, literature, math and science. My mind was racing. I couldn't stop thinking about the 17th century Meknes wall I climbed over, my walk across the Zerhoun landscape and the Sufi conversation I was having while riding in the back of a donkey cart. My memory started to rumble. The Sufi student had been talking to me about beauty, dance, music, poetry, literature. This was a Moroccan guy talking to me about things that interested me. Unbelievable—fine arts—aesthetics—I hadn't had any discussions like that since... the Orangerie in Paris—a couple months ago.

Yup, it was after my visit to Monet's waterlily garden in Giverny—back when I was still on the bike trip from Brussels, the month before I crossed the Strait of Gibraltar to Morocco. Seemed like years ago but only months. Giverny got me thinking about light in the landscape—so I headed to Paris to see Monet's paintings at the gallery in the Orangerie. I was alone in the gallery, early morning, looking at the paintings, thinking about light, landscape and beauty.

In the gallery my eyes saw Monet's *Waterlilies*, while my ears were hearing over the gallery sound system the piano of Debussy from *Lent, doux et melancholique*—a gentle piano light as a feather on the senses, but swirling with the mists of deep emotions.

Music and paintings overlapped each other. My emotions,

316

my mood shifted from the eyes to the ears, from the canvas to the music. First I was dancing with joy, then I fell into the melancholy of something missing.

On that day, I had experienced great artistic works living and interacting with each other. I'd always liked the moodiness of music—especially the classics. But I'd rarely felt that emotional connection to paintings. Was I sensing something special about hearing and sound? And how could hearing and sound be part of design, be it garden or landscape?

What had I been looking for? Something that had to do with light, wind, water and plants or maybe just light—sun light. Or had I been seeking something grander? My landscape architecture version of the *Glass Bead Game?*

We carried on our conversations. He told me that stories were relief valves for the human condition. That didn't settle in immediately. Then we reached Moussaoua. He arranged my ticket. I thanked him, telling him how much I learned from his talks. While waiting to board the bus, we continued talking. He told me he was a follower of the Sufi Master, Darqawi. I made note. The bus was ready to depart. I took the hour and a half ride from Moussaoua to Meknes, Place El Hedim.

The bus was full with farmers of all sorts, some with chickens—full of agricultural noise. I was surrounded by all things agricultural. But internally I was surprised. Surprised? Definitely. From my two hours with a Sufi student, the Moroccan farmer's son, I felt an awakening. I felt inspiration threaded through his words... design study inspiration. Later, that same day after I had returned to Meknes, the events of the day started sinking in.

First view I had of Islam that was not encumbered by sexism towards women, or pestering on the street, or super level teep behavior as I had experienced in the Tangier Municipality offices. I meditated on that substantial realization as I prepared and ate my dinner

After I finished cleaning up the kitchen, I sat down to make my diary entries from the day's activities. My "discussions" with the Sufi student had dominated my thoughts. But the more I tried to remember other similar discussions about the arts and beauty, the more I kept returning to... what was his name... Ian. Ian was the quiet guy who came into the Monet water lily gallery in the Orangerie the morning I was there. He was the only other person in the gallery. He seemed a quiet, introspective sort and after about 10 minutes, our paths crossed.

Ian was in his early to mid 30s. English, he was physically and with a personality a cross between Rowan Atkinson and Michael Palin—opinionated, humorous yet sincere. I learned he was born, bred and still living in the Lake District, a region some say of the most attractive, the most mellow landscape in the United Kingdom.

On that day we exchanged some observations about light, emotions, gardens. He had landscape in his blood. He asked, and this stood out in my memories, he asked me, "Do you ever wonder why the landscape beauties so richly brought to our attention by great artists, writers, musicians never become mainstream in our lives?"

He continued without pause, "The museum bunf writes 'Monet hoped his work would make the visitor forget the outside world'.

"That is the 'magic'! How an artist inspired by sunlight, plants and water could create something that makes people forget about *le monde extérieur*!"

And why did I remember Ian's words so clearly? Because his question addressed something that had bothered me through all my art history and landscape architecture classes.

His passion, cloaked with an English coolness, caused in me the re-emergence of thoughts from university—thoughts about what was missing from our landscape architecture education. We, as budding landscape architects, were indeed working with materials that had immense power. Why was that power kept under wraps at university—the power of true and strong inspiration—the power in the landscape?

This was the fire deep inside me. The landscape ties together, as Ian from the Lake District so reminded me. Wordsworth, Coleridge, Byron, Monet, de Maupassant, Debussy, Turner—too many to name—poets, novelists, philosophers, musicians—creative people from the eras Baroque, Romantic, Impressionist, even contemporaries—I couldn't carry the jock straps of those greats already inspired by the landscape.

I was looking for my own path—I thought these different means of expression needed to have direct linkage, direct binding to my profession, landscape architecture.

In the quiet of my flat it was all coming back to me. Ian and I got into a conversation about Monet, his use of light, his intent, his station in life—and before we knew it the gallery was swarming with busloads of tourists. We agreed to carry on our discussions outside the gallery at a mutually agreeable café where we might have wine and a light lunch. So off we went.

Ian said he had a friend working as a waiter across the river walking distance to the neighborhood of the Musée d'Orsay.

Along the way we passed through a neighborhood of art galleries, one of which was displaying landscape art by Claude and Constable. Ian challenged, "What have we been seeing and talking about today?" I figured a rhetorical question. I was right; he continued.

"Somehow, with the Enlightenment and the Industrial age, the 'smart' people threw the baby out with the bathwater! And it became the duty of people inspired by the landscape to remind other people overly anxious about the external world, where their peace and pleasure could be freely discovered. Can't you see that?"

That was Ian's question then in Paris. And today I had just traversed the Zerhoun landscape which had done two things to me. It erased my Tangier Municipality anxieties. And it inspired, reignited my design study direction.

And what had that Sufi student said about stories—I liked it—I thought it had something I could run with—yeah—relief valves. And I always thought stories were vehicles of travel—like I hoped gardens could be.

My experiences in the outskirts of Meknes in the bled, the countryside, convinced me that stories should be the real core of my study—for my annex of cross-cultural experiences. I was inspired by what the Sufi student had to say about stories as relief valves—relief valves that made readers relax, allowing discoveries to more easily occur. Discoveries? Discoveries of ...? Didn't have it all together yet.

Later in the evening when I lay down to sleep, I remembered more about the day I spent with Ian at the Tuileries and on the left bank; some of it was very strange. I had rejected it out of hand as tin foil hat conspiracy speculation.

For most of the afternoon, we had been lazily sipping red wine on the sidewalk café table near the Musée d'Orsay when Ian broke into a monologue following on from his earlier rhetorical question about why we don't see more landscape inspiration quality in our daily lives even though it has demonstrably fuelled the inspirations of historically great artists.

Fair question. But his hypothesized answer went, in my opinion, way off the rails. It went something like this.

Ian thought, said, and this is my summary, that extraterrestrials—*extraterrestrials?!*—were creating false dualities that kept humans in anxiety, thus creating a human "worry energy" that the extraterrestrials lived off of. Now that was some weird stuff.

I thought at the time that the French wine must have been getting to Ian. He told me about some guy named David Icke, a Brit, who had carefully looked into it, as had an American named Alex Jones. Never heard of either of those guys; but the story? That was enough for me—way off the beaten track and nowhere near my design study needs.

I was beat, closed my eyes and fell asleep thinking about... landscape stories... relief valves.

20-Making It Work

New Discoveries

The next day, after unloading my Zerhoun experiences on Tom and Marcela, Tom and I headed to the Meknes medina where I could begin to arrange the leather work and binding for the required hard copy of my final design study. I was planning ahead because I knew from experience that waiting till the last minute to produce hard copy of anything was risky. What is the saying, "stitch in time saves nine"? Visited a number of shops and we settled on a certain leather book binder, Maalem Hamid, based on his high quality detailing.

There, over time, I finally entered the world of "normal Arabo-Muslim family life". Maalem Hamid was a craftsman (*maalem*) making a living, supporting a family. He had a day-to-day routine and he appeared faithful to his religion.

He was respected in his Meknes medina community. Maalem Hamid taught younger people his craft by example. To me, he and his family were gracious hosts.

He would bind and leather-cover the final hard copy of my study in a fashion that represented the best of book binding craftsmanship, embodying centuries of tradition. Now, I just had to do the study so I could give him something to bind.

Later that same afternoon, I stopped by Justin's bolt hole and found him in. That was timely. My discussions in the Zerhoun with the Darqawi disciple built my enthusiasm for stories as integral to my design study. That growing interest prompted me to ask Justin some questions about Darqawi. Justin talked to me about Sufism in Morocco and Titus Burckhardt, a Swiss guy, a follower of Darqawi who translated many of Darqawi's writings into English. Burckhardt had since passed away, but his translations are well respected.

Justin had one of Burckhardt's books on his Meknes bookshelf. I was eager to read it.

He let me borrow the book and over the next days I read quite a bit from Burckhardt. In the introduction, I read that Darqawi's writing provided insight into what Burckhardt called "timeless metaphysical truths". I interpreted that phrase as Burckhardt's conclusion that Darqawi's writing provided an opportunity for one to move from a worldly to a spiritual experience.

I sensed that this was a timeless path that might apply to plants, gardens and landscapes. That thought, though briefly intriguing to me, did not lodge firmly. I was joyful simply to be in the open landscape, experiencing a free flow of fresh thoughts.

This trip to Meknes and my excursion into the countryside provided me an alternative and long missing cross-cultural "balance" that, surprisingly, got no support from Justin. Regardless, I had to press on with my revised design study. I had to extract North African data of value and push forward.

There were some very interesting quotes I picked up from Burckhardt's translations of Shaikh Darqawi's work, including: "From every word, each letter is a precious gem of wisdom, an indispensable key to open certain doors which stand before every traveler upon the Path." I interpreted that as an indication of the potencies of well-written, well-told stories.

I could not help but visualize in that quote, a garden, a landscape analogy where each plant—no!—where each part of a plant was a precious gem, an indispensable key to open certain doors along landscape and garden paths.

On his bookshelves, Justin also had a translation from nearly a millennium earlier, a short text by Ghazzalli titled, *The Alchemy of Happiness*.

Ghazzalli summarized in his introduction by stating the four elements in the metamorphosis that turns an average person "from an animal into an angel". I latched onto the word metamorphosis because I sensed that gardens were places that provided humans opportunities for their own metamorphosis. After all, I sensed that I, myself, was undergoing some kind of metamorphosis as I tried to restructure my design study.

I wondered, maybe all humans knew that they needed to do something to adjust an internal reality... I asked myself, could plants and gardens be part of that human need to undergo metamorphosis?

It was clear that Ghazzalli, Darqawi and Burckhardt were all into the effort of gnosis—knowledge of spiritual mysteries. Something had always attracted me to "spiritual mysteries"; and that Zerhoun Sufi experience showed me mystic and spiritual facets of Islam which I might be able to weave, as subtle themes, through a collection of stories. I came to think of developing my study as a Sufi version of Hesse's *Glass Bead Game*.

And I was seeing how the delicate craftsmanship, the gilt designs on leather by Maalem Hamid, had that certain refinement of a spiritual mystery being revealed... or at least providing a door or window through which one could enjoyably inspect said spiritual mystery.

***

Walk-through Stories

And as far as my design study was concerned, I became convinced that stories were non-different from gardens. A personal metamorphosis was occurring. It was beautiful. I truly felt the internal growth of kernels of inspiration. I saw the all-encompassing trance of a story become the all-encompassing trance of a walk through a garden. Short stories as dalliances in a garden.

It was then I saw my design study shape up for the first time as a walk through a garden of short stories. Short stories about gardens, plants and their importance to humans. For the reader, each story could be like pausing to inspect a leaf or a flower on a different plant in a walk through a garden.

The collection would have to grow beyond the garden, because the cross-cultural reality in Morocco demanded its own stories. I saw twin challenges in cross-cultural and ethnobotanical themes. And that was the nebulous nub from which the stories began to emerge. But true progress did not begin immediately. And it did not begin without further struggles.

In the afternoon, I went to see Maalem Hamid again at his medina bookbinding and leather shop. With Justin and his language skills, we talked through the production process in detail. We realized it would happen during Ramadan.

Justin explained the Ramadan impact at the end of the year would make it a very difficult time to rush any kind of work. I needed to think that one through.

***

326

More Troubles

But something else was bubbling up—Sachy and my home culture. My bubbling up realization was that my immersion in this African, this North African culture had taught me clearly that I was of another culture. Over these last three months, I learned these cultures did not automatically, did not easily blend. In fact, they don't blend.

I had uncovered fragments from this strange culture that I would somehow have to try to patch into my own cultural background. I needed to reboot. And things in Tangier had, without stop, been strangely difficult.

Something else was troubling me, I had taken David's "Islam for Dummies" description as pretty well defining my negative experiences in Tangier. My time with the Zerhoun Sufi had shown me another facet of Islam. So, the night of the same day Justin and I had been talking with Maalem Hamid, I got together again with Justin, to take advantage of his fluent linguistic and broad cultural experiences, he having been a resident of Morocco for well over a decade. We sat down over a bottle of Morocco-grown red wine and had this conversation.

"Justin, do you know David from the Kasbah in Tangier, that retired Peace Corps Volunteer Architect?"

"Yeah, I met him a long time ago—good architect."

"Well he told me some stuff—his opinions on Islam, and it worked for me seeing what I have in Tangier. But... up in the Zerhoun and Darqawi and Burckhardt, they are showing me something else—something useful, something positive."

"What's on your mind, CJ?"

I paused to gather my thoughts, then started. "See, I arrived here in Morocco thinking that Islam was peaceful, yet there was nothing peaceful about my experiences with the teeps of Tangier. David explained that as two things—the roots of the Zemour tribes and that Moroccans always get their way with the infidels, the non-believers arriving from Europe. Yet... my last days in the Zerhoun and reading about Sufis have been a rather peaceful experience—what am I missing?"

Justin said, "Some sects are into exploring the material world to find spiritual connections—that is your Zerhoun Sufism—but a bit more disconcerting, and I think that David may have alluded to it—the other side of the coin from jihad—Muslims will do what they can to attract non-believers—then you have to layer on top of that the Koranic and Hadith positions known as 'taqqiya' which some translate as the authorization to distort the truth if the goal is to spread Islam—if you mix all of that together in a Moroccan 'tajine', you will find a huge amount of uncertainty that you will never be able to sift through."

"So, tell me, Justin, how do you live with that, I mean, how do you work with people day-to-day when truth is not a shared object?"

"CJ, you just have to focus on why you are here and let the drifting fogs of this culture float on by. Ignore them. In your case, just do your study and ignore the cultural ambiguities."

"That's easy for you to say, but I'm the one walking the Tangier medina."

"Well, CJ, Tom and Marcela did offer you the opportunity to stay here in Meknes."

I looked at the floor. The room was silent.

"Look, Justin, I'm going to have to deal with this cross-cultural bullshit in my study because it's been so much a part of my time here. I felt saddened by what I heard from the Peace Corps Volunteers at the 4th of July party in Rabat; and now, here I am, troubled much the same way."

Justin said, "This is Morocco, CJ. Though it won't help, I could quote, oh, so many Koranic verses that justify the unseemly behavior you and the current Peace Corps Volunteers have experienced."

"So?"

"Well, an astute Muslim could find just as many Koranic verses that would show Muslims to be peaceful people. And like I said, this is Morocco. CJ, you going to be alright?"

At first, no answer, only silence. Finally, words came to my lips.

"Yeah, but that's not the way I heard it back at the university. They made me think that Islam was a faith religion like Christianity—everybody just looking for peace on Earth and in the hereafter."

We both took sips of wine. Then Justin continued, "If you look more carefully at the history of Islam, following the life of their prophet, you can see a couple persistent and aggressive threads—warfare to conquer and slavery for non-believers. What you see today as inexplicable are simply the rough, the raw, the unwoven, thready edges of this culture. You've got to take what is useful to your study and work around the other stuff. Can you do that?"

"If I want to graduate, I'll have to." I needed to think through it some more.

I offered the bottle to Justin. He turned it down and I poured the remainder of the wine to fill my glass and drank it all at once. I let the wine work on me, then I had to ask, with a fair mix of cynicism and sincerity.

"Well, Justin, tell me, is there anyone I can trust in Morocco?"

"CJ, it's not that bad. A lot of Moroccans are simple, straight-forward and truthful folks—just trying to earn a living and take care of their families.'

"Is Maalem Hamid like that?" I asked.

"Most likely," Justin said, "but always stay alert. I've been here for fifteen years running the USAID English Language Training Program and I've met all kinds. Many are kind and hopeful... but..."

"But what?" I asked.

"They are Muslim and the Koran is the Koran. Danger always lurks for us, the infidels."

That was unsettling more than calming. Always riddled with confusion, I was—culture vs my design study—never crystal clear. And so ended my trip to Meknes.

***

Breakthrough

On the train back to Tangier, I worked through all of my Meknes visit events one more time. As soon as I got back to my flat, I prepared my SitRep. But I needed some emotional support. I needed to talk with Sachy.

Next morning, I emailed my SitRep to Neil.

1 Oct 2000

Dear Neil,

Sorry I'm late—spent the last week in Meknes and the nearby Zerhoun—learning about some Sufis in the region. It is having a positive impact on my approach to North African experiences of people and plants.

Progressing with study as a collection of stories as the primary task. They focus, as we agreed before, on how international design requires coming to grips with cross-cultural impacts on design. I will address how to implement them into design, woven with local observations on how the lack of urban access to green is a negative factor in quality of life.

I also made arrangements in Meknes for a presentation hard copy of my final design study report. It will be high quality craft from a local bookbinder. Beautiful.

Listen, Neil, the entire study will include only my experiences of North African people and plants. I plan to shape those experiences as short stories. Why, you may ask? Because I've got to drop the mapping and data part. Just can't get the raw data.

I will boost the breadth and number of stories that were experiences in my intended Annex of Tales.

Because of the above-described Sufi breakthrough, I think I can make that happen.

Will you be good with that?

I'm working it the best I can.

CJ

Heard back immediately from Neil.

He shot at me, "Show me something! How many stories are you working? And I don't want to see any weird tales. Otherwise, if you expand your map and data principles into an enlarged introduction to the Annex of Tales, maybe I can approve your reduced scope. And, by the way, aren't we supposed to have a phone call today—let's make it happen!"

I used my recent thoughts on Darqawi's gardens to build up another ten working titles, then rewrote my study statement into an expanded preface for my Annex of Tales. Sent all to Neil. Then headed out to Brahim's for the international telephone call with Neil.

To make a long story short. Neil busted my hump again. He tolerated no excuse for my not having yet contacted Sachy. Then he went through the details of my third restructuring of my design study. I was nervous.

But, thank God, Neil approved. Ha! Needed that good news! He had some conditions; but I finally got a solid night's sleep.

Started the morning emailing Sachy to set up phone call. When her day started we did a friendly quick back and forth exchange. Then, as usual set up my work day with smoke, Seagrams and dex. Worked on story ideas right through the morning and afternoon.

I finally received an email from Sachy confirming phone call time. Headed out to Brahim's for a sandwich, then at his other shop, made the international phone call to Sachy.

21-Dragon's Blood

Reviving Roots

Our short emails had begun to refresh my cultural home link. Contrary to Neil's snarky intonations when he visited, I found that Sachy, in our first emails, sounded normal and helpful.

Many alchemical savants have said that salve from dragon's blood can heal anything—physical, mental, emotional, what have you. I was in the "what have you" category. I needed that salve. I needed its magic curative. I was back in Tangier, with its dark influence immediately shuttering my oh-so-brief Meknes clarity and enthusiasm.

Sachy had always been my support when I wandered off the path. Neil had seen that too. So he suggested I get in contact with her to resolve my current Moroccan cultural instabilities.

Probably should have done it sooner, because when I thought about Sachy, I became absorbed in her multi-dimensional "floating beauty of a butterfly". She was my cure-all.

LittleWing's butterfly beauty had a certain weave in her words that entered my ears and soothed my emotions. Above all, it had been my good fortune that she possessed such an unusual combination to assist me—floating like a butterfly beautiful and stabilizing. She's very special.

We learned together, and were happy together. We were both tech savvy. LittleWing's IRC nickname was Parsec. She was always faster than me, always scored better, always ahead of me. I was muse404, always seeking that which I didn't have, that which I didn't understand. We were close, oh so close, but we were not without emotional upheavals or surprises.

***

The Hurt

My first phone call to her from Morocco, on 2 October, went like this.

"LittleWing? ... LittleWing? You there?"

"I'm here. Must be a time lag over this distance, can you hear me?"

"Yeah, loud and clear, we can make this work. How are you?"

"Worried and upset. It has been six months since you left, six months I haven't heard from you—nothing since you left for Europe—nothing about your European bike trip—some say no news is good news? No way! Then you send a couple strange emails."

"What?!"

"Those emails you sent. Brief, not focused. I could only imagine you had got into drugs?"

"Can't fool you, but we need to talk about my study. I need your help."

"You need my help? I'm the one back here trying to carry on. I'm the one who needs help."

"But like I emailed, Neil said you were looking good; and your emails sounded cool."

"If there was a smile on my face, it was there only to hide my

real feelings—just to look good around your friends. I've been hurting."

"What?!" I said.

"Really I'm sad. It's bad... sadder than sad. Six months since you left... I've been unplugged without you... a light bulb without electricity... nothing. I've been hurting so bad."

I was shocked. "I don't know what to say. It pains me right to the heart to hear you say those things. I'm surprised, 'cause your emails sounded your normal carefree self."

"If I appeared to be carefree, it was only to hide my sadness. Don't let Neil or anything convince you that I've been happy since you went on this study."

"I hate trying to resolve emotions on a telephone."

"You think it's easy for me? You're asking me for some kind of emotional rescue when I'm hurt and you should know that for others I put on a show."

I was confused.

***

The Fix

I was trying to understand—confusion—I always disliked phone calls and their essential detachment.

"Where is this going? I never thought this term abroad would hurt you... and here I am asking you for help when you are already hurt... how do we get through this?"

"Without you, there's no one around. I need you," she said.

"How can I hug you on the telephone?"

"I didn't think it would be like this. We all have doubts from time to time... but this time..."

"And I'm lost, too."

Silence.

"Always lonely, stay in my room." I sensed her weakness.

"That makes two of us."

"Don't mock me."

Hastily, I replied, "Never! You've got me wrong! This is crazy. We're both hurting. There has to be a fix."

"Fix? This is the longest six months I've ever known. I had to ask questions... what is the purpose... why... and endure this to what end... I had to try to understand that there must be something

338

more to life than suffering like this..."

More silence.

Then she said, *"I've read and read... a lot of my Vedanta literature, like Bhagavad Gita and Srimad Bhagavatam, about consciousness... the true essence of life... of human life... and I had a strange realization... I felt, I saw, for the first time a special internal peace that has allowed me to detach, to a certain degree, and in a temporary way, from the hurt... from the sadness... of your total absence from my daily life."*

"I'm not sure I follow."

She, still upset, continued, *"Where have you been? I've had to seek spiritual faith, spiritual understanding, to endure the hurt you have brought. And somehow I have found a transcendental portal through which I have been able to pass... and see... experience the peace of a spiritual refuge. But the underlying hurt that you are not here is still present. I can see that the hurt may indeed be temporary in relation to my transcendental peace; but I still feel the hurt."*

"Transcendental portal? Transcendental peace? What have you seen?"

After a short silence...

I carried on, saying, "You have always had a penchant for Vedic philosophies--sounds like you've found solace there. For me, all I know is my study and how hurt you are. Getting back together will happen—it's October now, and maybe with luck I can be back for Christmas... heck, that's only about 10 weeks away. I have not made any progress on my study—have to do it all in the next two months. But what about you... can you hold on till Christmas? I hear your hurt and I feel it. It hurts me too, so deeply. I don't want to describe my hurt—I can't imagine yours—but we will be together again and pretty soon—home for Christmas—I like that sound. How about you?"

"I can't imagine two more months like the last six—what if we make regular texts and calls? And maybe we can share some deeper understandings to get us both through this together... Christmas does have a nice sound."

"I'll do whatever I can to ease your pain—I wish I could hug you right now—we can make it better."

"Maybe the worst is over. But it's not possible to erase six months of hurt. Talking helps. It has been like salve. We should keep talking. I'm not boiling like before, but we do need to stay in regular contact. That hurt was bad. The not knowing hurt so bad. But deep in my heart I am waiting, just for you. And I have so much I want to share with you."

She paused for a moment, before firmly saying, *"Now, tell me, how are you REALLY doing?"*

"Me? I feel like I'm going down the drain—this place is like a whirlpool and I am strangled, choking, trapped with no control.

"But the strangest thing has been this conversation with you—as I heard your hurt and as I tried to connect with you from my deepest heart—it was, believe it or not, the first time since I arrived here that I didn't feel the horrible negative cross-cultural pressure. I actually felt an internal wholeness, like I was where I should be, listening to you and trying to share emotions with you—even over the phone—I felt a strange kind of healing. I can only hope that you have felt some healing in yourself on this call. Tell me."

"I don't know about healing, but calming, yes. Between this talking and the transcendental shelter I discovered, maybe we are now on a better path. Talk to me about your study."

She sounded almost normal, the Sachy I knew.

***

Moving Forward

This was starting to work—but my words were having difficulties getting formed.

"Don't know where to begin…"

"Just start talking—maybe that will be the magic for both of us."

"This past week, I got approval from Neil for a revised and reduced design study—short stories about plants and people in North Africa."

"What happened to the water fountains?"

"Didn't I email you that none of them are functioning anymore? Then Neil agreed a design study that required data and maps from the local government—but the government people wouldn't cooperate."

"And the cross-cultural stuff?" she asked.

"Nonstop, each day in the medina is a walking nightmare. But I think I might get around it."

"So what is the problem?"

"No plants in the medina, the old town public realm has no green, no public gardens. That's half my problem. I think I may have a solution to that at a villa called Hibiscus House. Now that my cast is off…"

She was shocked, "Whoa! Hang on! Cast? Cast off? What are you talking about!?"

"Didn't I explain in the emails that I was laid up for five weeks with my ankle in a cast?"

"You told me about an infected abrasion, nothing about a cast."

"Long story, but I'm okay now—the ankle is okay but my study is way behind—that's where my trouble is. Now, what my sources have told me about the Brit, the Rooskie and their Hibiscus House..."

"Hold on, hold on! Not so fast. So you have dependable sources or has intoxication fired up your imagination?"

"Sources? I've been lucky there. Met a bunch of current Peace Corps Volunteers but that's another story. My sources are retired Peace Corps Volunteers and government employees who have been living in Morocco for at least 10 years. But there is one lady as old as our grandparents who has been working in a bookstore since the 1950s. She's the only one who seems to have a healthy cultural connection. She told me about the guys at Hibiscus House, their research, their gardens and their connections with international horticulturists."

"So what's holding you up? Is life there as bad as Mr. Striet described in his letters?"

"Life isn't bad—good food—freshly grown—the best of Spain, France and Morocco—and I have a great rooftop apartment."

"C'mon, why did you call—you wanted to do this study on your own. What's up?"

"I need editing help. I've got to write about 30 short stories and I need technical, inspirational and emotional help for the next six weeks to drag me through them."

"Drag you through? I still don't get it. It's just a university exercise, why do you need someone to drag you through and what's the emotional stuff?"

"That's the local and regional culture, the medina nightmare, it really has turned me, I don't know—inside out—upside down—

hard to put words to it."

"I thought you said you could get around it. Try these words—you've got into drugs and everything in your daily life is muddled."

"Too simple. I won't deny drugs, but this is a design study and I'm looking for the magic theme that inspires me to develop the stories. You've got to trust me on this."

"Now, THAT is what I call a crutch—you've got some kind of problem, otherwise you wouldn't have called. I've only one thing to say about that—don't mess with our future.

"Let's get down to business. What's keeping you from writing right now today?"

"I've got plenty of story ideas about people and culture but zero about plants."

"So, why have you not visited the Hibiscus House? Get over there and find out if it's a valid resource because if not, you will have to restructure your design study again and you are running out of time… you need this to graduate, right? Well, get on with it!"

"Gotcha. You're right! I've got to visit Hibiscus House and the guys living there. That's the kind of support I need, Sachy—your focus will make my path clearer."

"My help will have a price. We need to stay in contact on a regular basis, a weekly basis or more frequent by texting. Can you do that?"

Of course, I could.

***

Will This Work?

Our emotionally stabilizing talk carried on for another hour. I was happy to hear Sachy's voice, but hurt that she was sad. Even though she was on my case, she had a clarity of insight and directness that gave me confidence.

But we had not agreed 100% on everything. I kept some things to myself. White lies? Common sense? Or my own disingenuousness? My uncertainty kept bugging me. That's why I needed her clarity.

She had suggested, though, in rather strong terms, that I steer away from intoxication. I thought otherwise. I knew these local drugs would likely be part of the path that, along with her help, could bring alive a unique solution for my design study. So, despite her recommendations, I went deeper and deeper into smoke and Seagrams. Deep explorations. Deeper discovery.

Our phone call had been as emotionally intense as a phone call could have been. As I went to sleep, her words and her hurt returned again and again to my thoughts. Then I dreamt about the early times we shared. I dreamt about when we saw *Sound of Music* together—both of us danced with Julie Andrews in the Alps. That was how we began. We shared the thoughts that hills alive with the sound of music was not a song but a mystical presence that the Alp landscape shares with its initiates—and we, though never having visited the Alps, were true initiates. That was what we both shared in our hearts. Believe it or not, that memory, that was refreshed in my dream, furthered my healing, my cultural healing.

My connections with LittleWing, my home culture, brought me a different perception—our emotional sharing showed me I could detach from the obnoxious persistence of local culture. That local persistence, with its gaps in cross-cultural understanding, was no longer rootlets trying to attach to my Western tap root. It became... noise. Temporary noise while I was here, or so I thought.

I had always been open minded about humans from other cultures. I had always been inquisitive. But in Tangier, I may have met my match. Going out on the street each day and having to do communication battle? Not right. I won't try to change them. And I won't be changed by them.

Through my re-established connection with Sachy, I felt an increase in my strength to focus on my stories. That was really great. And she mentioned that she, while suffocating in deepest misery, had experienced refuge via, and this had to be more than coincidence, a transcendental portal.

It was just a couple days ago that the Sufi student used that word, portal, as a path through the fine arts to experience the glory of God, transcendental glory. And Sachy, someone I loved and trusted, someone with whom I truly shared cultural roots, said something very similar. Portals, gardens, stories. Things were lining up. I began scoping and outlining a series of cross-cultural stories. Finally—to the Hibiscus House—fingers crossed.

22-Hibiscus House

Dracaena draco

The Petit Taxi dropped me roadside next to the dragon's blood trees I had seen on my trips to the Hakim. Couldn't believe my eyes. An entire forest of densely packed dragon's blood trees. I saw one of these, once before, when I did an internship in Southern California and was mesmerized then—did research on it—what a story this tree has in human history! But now, a forest of them! If one tree had mesmerized me, how could I describe the effect of a dense forest of them on me?

These trees—so strange! Abnormal leaves. Unusually found, only at the end of each branch, as solitary clusters. In each cluster, dozens of narrow, 50cm long, gray-green, sword-blade leaves. The unusually uniform thick and straight branches grew with near geometric regularity on the stoutest of nearly one meter diameter trunks. And the so-called bark? Reptilian. The bark over the trunk and branches was silvery grey, leathery and thick. Magic oozed out of that dragon's skin—the historically potent drops of alchemical, blood red sap.

Each individual tree, all greater than 10m tall, was a dome—a regular spreading shape like an umbrella—an umbrella of cheek by jowl clusters of those sword-shaped leaves. The umbrellas overlapped—not like a normal tree—more like a cartoonist's caricature brought to life. Amidst a tightly packed forest of them—so dominant en masse—each so mature in structure and shape, I was stunned, speechless, in a daze of amazement.

I walked ever so slowly uphill along the narrow path that rose up gently through the dragon's blood trees. Finally noticed the ground was covered with drought-tolerant *Sedum*—the lowest of low growing succulent plants, many species and varieties—yellows, greens, grays, bronzes, oranges—weaving and flowing—non-stop.

I started moving again, carefully, very slowly through this sweeping ground cover beneath the pointillistic forest. While still in the midst of the dragon's blood, I came up to a roughly laid, meter and a half tall, fieldstone privacy wall, wrought iron gate and electronic ringer.

Pushed the ringer and waited. While waiting, I noted Art Nouveau wrought iron details on the gate, and also on the frame of a sign on the wall. The gate, the sign and its frame looked very French, very sweet, very Guimard.

The name of the villa—*Loins du Monde Réel*—far away from the real world. Was that where I was? Far away from the real world? ...or... was that where I was going?

I waited for someone to answer. As I waited, I wondered more about the alchemical effects of dragon's blood trees... was I under their influence... I was certainly under their canopy... under their shelter...

A British voice finally answered. I perked up. Asked my business. I explained who I was, then briefly outlined why I came—my Moroccan landscape architecture design study.

The gate electronically opened. I was told to come in and up to the villa entry terrace. I did, continuing through more dragon's blood forest. Definitely under its influence.

Finally, after another slight climb, I saw a low, rambling villa—mostly single story—but with second story construction here and there. The nearest second story looked like a tropical glass house full with plants—that was an exciting prospect. The more plants the better.

***

Toseland

On the front terrace, I saw a mature, shortish, middle aged man, with early stages of balding, watching me arrive. He welcomed me in a friendly, but distant way with a challenging question. "Are you alive?"

Did not know what to answer. So I asked, "Did these magisterial... these mystical dragon's blood trees come from the Canary Islands?"

He answered with the air of someone who knew way more than he let on, "You are looking at trees planted long ago when this villa belonged to the Portuguese Ambassador."

He continued, "The trees? There are two species, *Dracaena draco* from the Azores, and *Dracaena cinnabari* from Socotra."

He had established his superiority with that one sentence. He continued, "And you must know the story of the labors of Hercules, where he slayed the twelve-headed dragon in the Garden of the Hesperides, thus the dragon's blood trees as essential lore of the Western Mediterranean?" He did not let me answer and continued without pause, "And you are Christopher Janus?"

He welcomed me, and said, "Interested in the landscape, you say?"

"Yes."

Stretching out his hand, he said, "My name is Toseland and if you are a landscape novitiate, you are welcome here."

As we exchanged pleasantries at the entry terrace, I noted a raised piece of granite. The granite had an engraving, attributed to Tolkien. But, before I could absorb Tolkien's language, Toseland suggested we go inside the villa.

As we walked in, I asked, "With hundreds of such spectacular mature dragon's blood trees, why do people call this Hibiscus House?"

"Glad you asked, follow me."

We walked through an open floorplan lounge with many sideboards—each one supporting glass bowls filled with water. Each glass bowl displayed a single floating hibiscus flower, each remarkably different and each spectacularly colorful. Must have been six sideboards and a dozen different glass bowls.

I tarried, overwhelmed by the entrancing beauty of all before me. Toseland noticed my interest.

He explained, "Plants in the garden or in the landscape can become some kind of magical four-dimensional mirror, unique to each human looking at or working with them." He paused; I could see he was measuring my reaction. I was interested. Interested? That was an understatement. I was positively intrigued by the respect in his voice as he described the characteristics of plants.

Then he continued, "Those hibiscus flowers you enjoy, they can reflect in their details a unique peculiarity that resonates with the human involved. It is magical because, at any one time, each human only sees one plant facet in the plant mirror, though every other human sees, at the same time, their own unique plant facet in that same plant mirror. They are magic portals, if you will."

There was that word again—portals.

He continued, solemnly adding, "Providing paths to realizations that are simultaneously same but different." That concept intrigued me. I'd heard it before.

"Please allow me to guide you through all of our hibiscus displays."

He proceeded to walk me through three more open plan lounges with numerous sideboards, each displaying on its top, decorative glass bowls, each glass bowl filled with water, each having one floating hibiscus flower as I had seen when I first arrived.

"In case you're not familiar, each flower is unique not only by color but also by parentage, size of bloom, texture of bloom, and symmetrical form."

As we toured the series of display lounges, he matter-of-factly shared the Hibiscus hybrid names and the parentage of each faster than I could follow. Must have looked at forty or fifty different beautiful, floating hibiscus flowers. I understood clearly why everyone called this place the Hibiscus House. This place, with its hibiscus and dragon's blood collections alone, was a show piece, horticultural and botanical.

Began to notice that the glass bowls, holding each Hibiscus flower, were exquisite of themselves.

When I mentioned that, he rolled off the names, "Lalique, Baccarat, Lenox, Wedgewood, Waterford, Orrefors, Kosta, Boda"—only recognized a couple but the others, I figured, were a who's who of glass artists and manufacturers.

Then I noticed the furniture on which sat all the glass bowls and Hibiscus flowers—the sideboards—the side tables—all oak. Beautifully shaped. Beautifully finished. Artisan work with unique elements carved into the legs—gnomes—mice... these couldn't be locally produced. I asked.

Again, he answered as if it was a bit beneath him to address the question. Yet, with grace, he dutifully informed me, "You could find originals by the gnome man, Thomas Whitaker and the mouse man, Robert Thompson."

He suggested we should go sit down for refreshment. Off the hibiscus display entry lounge, he led me into an old fashioned, high ceilinged, large, single room library, saying, "Make yourself comfortable, look around. I'll gather refreshments and return presently."

***

I Was Stoked

The library had, in its centre, a large rectangular table—obviously a layout and work table—with six upright wooden chairs symmetrically arranged. Three of the library walls were covered floor to ceiling with built-in, heavy, solid oak bookcases. All the shelves were full.

Books of all sizes and languages. All neatly arranged—large format books on the lower shelves, medium size on the middle shelves, and the smallest format books on the topmost. Along the top of each wall of shelves was a roller track for a movable ladder to easily access the entire collection.

At the fourth wall were two huge bay windows, each large enough to have, at its base, two well-stuffed oxblood red leather chairs separated by a small table with reading lamp. The oxblood leather chairs were movable—he turned one to face the window and offered it to me. I eased myself into the chair, while he raised the window shade. Then before he disappeared to gather the refreshment, he said, "Help yourself to what you find below the windows."

Looking out the window, I enjoyed an aspect on an oval of bowling green quality lawn. On the inside, beneath the windows, I noted two sets of low bookcases conveniently located for browsing.

Saw a number of titles related to Pharmacology and Ethnobotany. A couple caught my eye. *Doctrine of Signatures*, by Jacob Boehme. Nicholas Culpeper's *English Physician and Complete Herbal*. And a reprint of the five volume set of Dioscorides' *De Materia Medica*.

Among other books, I saw: *Perfumed Garden, Gardens of Cyrus,* Burton's *1001 Arabian Nights* and a selection of horticultural coffee table books from Australia, South America and South Africa.

Covering the top of the low bookcase in front of me was a beautifully detailed antimacassar featuring a swirling paisley print. On top of that an Oriental wood tabletop cabinet decorated with delicate ivory inlays in floral patterns intrigued me. The floral patterns invited. Was this what Toseland had told me to help myself? Didn't think twice. I could not resist. I had to open the cabinet doors. I had to inspect. Discovery.

The interior was subdivided into drawers, each drawer frontispiece having its own ivory inlaid pattern. Each of the drawers had a handwritten label in two languages, English in a gothic style and the second, I think it was Indian, Sanskrit. Looked like something I'd seen before in one of Sachy's books about Krishna.

The cabinet was a pharmacopeia of some sort. Labels on the drawers included. Laudanum, Morpheum, Hasheesh, Cocaine, Hyssop...

Before I could finish, Toseland returned with two large glasses of iced lemonade. He offered me a glass and then sat. Asked me about my visit to Hakim ben Wais. I told him the story and as I finished, he asked if I had interest in the medicine cabinet.

He told me it was for guests and the second language was the Devanagari alphabet of the Vedas. Then Toseland changed the subject. "Now, Christopher, tell me about your landscape studies in Morocco."

I told him the whole story and concluded that I had a desperate need for sources regarding plants, gardens and landscapes in Morocco. I said, "It looks to me like in just this short afternoon, your villa might become my primary source."

"Is that so? How so?"

"Well, when I started seriously looking to re-restructure my design study, I checked the Piliers Culturels for books written by people who had observed the plants and landscapes in Morocco. I already had Pierre Loti's richly descriptive book on

Morocco, but wanted more. I found none at the bookstore; but Mme Zsófia told me about a botanist and geologist, two Brits, Sir Joseph Hooker and John Ball, who, in the 19th century, had written about their time in Morocco. She said there might be a copy in your private library here at the Hibiscus House. If she was indeed right in her suggestion, I will definitely have primary source material on plants."

Toseland looked surprised. "You're in the right place. Let me see." He walked over to a shelf, selected a volume and briefly showed me the Hooker and Ball work.

"But this afternoon, you must excuse me, I have a previously scheduled business appointment. Forgive me for abruptly ending our discussion. But I welcome your use of this library, provided we agree the time in advance."

I politely suggested, "Tomorrow morning or afternoon possible?"

He agreed the afternoon.

I should have visited Hibiscus House a long time ago. Plants were central to everything I saw and heard there; and the mood, it was a healthy mood of on-going discovery—botany, horticulture, craft and design. Exciting!

Made me think about its antithesis, the medina—essentially a depressing, tension-filled non-plant environment. Hibiscus House was light. The medina was dark. Dark?

Dark. I thought of the dark of the medina being like the underground in a forest where every plant's roots fight for food and water—fight for territory. Among the plant roots, there is so much anxiety, so much bolshiness, so much survival of the fittest—plantland style—the fight for iron—it all happens underground. I saw the anxiety and bolshiness in the medina byways as eternal, reverberating reflections of the battle for existential survival as expressed by humans—day in, day out, no smiles, no civility, all encased by dirty, dingey walls. Non-stop anxiety without reprieve.

***

Library

What a pleasure to pass day after day over the next week visiting the Hibiscus House, reading in the library. Usually, Toseland would see me in and ask me questions, often about my landscape architecture university education. After a half hour or so of polite conversation, Toseland would leave me alone. He had placed the entire library at my disposal. I so much appreciated the quiet library—reading Hooker and Ball in addition to anything that caught my fancy.

Surrounded by great horticulture and botany books, I had time to reflect on my university education. Reading Hooker and Ball's Moroccan accounts, I could see there must be something beyond the academic horticulture and scientific environmental definitions of plants, something even beyond the aesthetic mashups advocated by my pop-culture design instructors. I thoroughly enjoyed my quiet times in the Hibiscus House library.

But there were supposed to be two people living in this villa—I hadn't heard a thing or seen the Rooskie. And I had only hearsay about some experimental garden they kept.

I was getting closer to Toseland. While in the library together one day, Toseland educated me on English roots while he put Mahler's *Third Symphony* in the background, on the library sound system.

"You should know this about the Brits, about England. From the earliest times we were a mix of the Norsemen and the Germanic Saxons. Then the arrival of the French in 1066 stirred our Celtic roots. We are as much about mixed genealogies as you young Americans—only a few centuries further along in maturation.

"Like Gustav Mahler, we have no purity in us—just a healthy mix. And Mahler, by the way, listened to plants. Is it not appropriate, therefore, that we listen to his music as we read?"

No argument there. I read deeply—*Hooker and Ball in Morocco.* Then I took a break.

Raised my head and listened as the *Third Symphony* drew to a close. I heard it as a walk through the landscape—a walk through a complex garden. At the climax ending, Mahler brought me to a fantastic realization that I never before imagined. As if I was brought to a door and had the door opened for me. Such was the magic of great music.

That was the kind of garden I'd like to build.

Then, one day, from one of the hibiscus display lounges, Toseland led me through a pair of French doors onto a terrace at the edge of a beautiful garden oval of bowling green quality lawn, perhaps the very same I had seen from the library windows.

"Excuse me, Toseland, what is this?" I pointed to the gardens outside of the French doors.

"This is an entry to our applied research project. We call it the Oval Garden."

I looked more carefully. The oval lawn was neatly edged by a wall of shaped Italian cypress hedges. In front of the hedges, along the edge, I saw trellises here and there, and in the furthest distance, in the sun, a white marble basin with a fountain. A bunch of questions arose in my mind. I couldn't restrain myself.

"Everything is so nicely maintained. I've seen nothing maintained well in the Moroccan public domain. Is it your work? If so, it must take a lot of time."

"We have volunteers—I think you call them interns. We introduce them to our approach, our respect for plants, and they perform all the necessary upkeep."

"Are they Moroccan or foreigners—do you get volunteers from the US or the UK—it sounds like a wonderful opportunity."

"We are particular about selecting volunteers. Loving maintenance is at the centre of our Oval Garden research."

"I like that."

I asked about the irregularly occurring trellises that were disrespecting the oval symmetry in the garden. His reply was, as was becoming usual, curt but informative.

"In the first instance," he said, "we have no trellises in this garden, those you see are gloriettas. You might, in other gardens know them as rondels or pavilions. Here they are gloriettas. The gloriettas support climbing roses and climbing jasmines. They are fragrance foci.

"Secondly, and of significant import," he continued, "gloriettas are shady places to pause at path crossings."

I looked hard. Path crossings? I saw none. I brought to his attention, "The gloriettas I can see occur squarely over the centreline of the linear oval path. And I see no hint of any path crossings."

Toseland dismissed that with a cursory comment about Yanks having limited powers of perception. I ignored that and began that I had California experience with the climbing fragrant jasmine, *Trachelospermum jasminoides* and asked, "Which jasmine do you prefer in the gloriettas?"

He corrected, made clear that I understood the difference between *Trachelospermum species* and *Jasminum species*. Then he summarized the history of climbing and shrub jasmines, concluding that there was only one jasmine that gave the required perfume in flower at the proper time, *Jasminum polyanthum*, and, he said, "We have worked with this plant to facilitate a maximum blooming season."

This was the way most of my visits to Hibiscus House unfolded, a combination of hope, insight and inspiration frequently wrapped in snobbish insults and challenges about my education.

***

Fyodor

I had taken my horticulture classes, my planting design classes at university—requirements for my landscape architecture degree. But they were nothing compared to the library at Hibiscus House, the plants at Hibiscus House and the input I received from Toseland.

It was all about humans and plants—ethnobotany in the broadest sense. Though I had never thought like this back at university, I got it now. The message was plants are not things. Things are mass manufactured without respect for life. Things are numbers on impersonal spreadsheets defining ecosystems.

Here in Hibiscus House, plants were respected visitors, as I was. Strange. It seemed a consciousness shift. And maybe I had sensed it during my schooling and internships as a ghost in the mirror. As something I missed—the essential importance of plants.

Then, a whistling of simple repetitive melody came lightly to my ear. It was familiar... I recognized it... the theme of Shostakovich's *7th*. The simple tune came out of nowhere, from behind my back. Got louder until it was right next to me. I looked up.

And that was where Toseland's partner, Fyodor, entered. Tall, thin, in his fifties, chin carried high. He was bearded and with bejeweled topknot.

For me, Toseland spoke theory. Then I met Fyodor. He applied theory. He was all about communicating with individual plants. He called it "taking a ride" with them. He talked about gateways, portals, and humans moving through them with the assistance of plants. I was on fire. I wanted to hear more.

This was adventure. This was the hope of discovery. Could this be landscape architecture? Could this be my study?

But getting close to these guys was not easy. They both had little respect for my American university education in landscape architecture. Fyodor, like Toseland, seemed to have fun jousting with me. In time, I learned to ignore the boorish words. But some days it was a bit much. On the day I met him, it wasn't long before Fyodor blasted me, a couple times. I tried to turn it around without success.

Fyodor commented to me, "You guys, you American landscape architects, don't know about horticulture or ethnobotany or any esoterica regarding plants. You guys talk about plant materials as if the plants are inanimate. How crude is that?"

I had grown tired of their heckling—I found it taunting, too much to take—though their points were often quite valid. And later, thinking about it, I too, had railed a bit during my internship in Southern California when one of the guys talked about 'cast iron' plants—even then it didn't feel right to me. So, I had a little empathy for Fyodor's spitting out of plant materials. After all, that is how the university taught us. On the day, though, I was more interested to hear Fyodor's take on gateways and portals.

I had told them about my visit to the Zerhoun and recalled the Sufi use of dance, music, poetry to access spiritual bliss... "Portals," I said, "let's call them portals, what about the Sufi portals—might they have anything to do with your work?"

"Beauty," Toseland said, "beauty makes a portal accessible and enables a human to pass through and enter another 'level of consciousness'..."

Fyodor interrupted, "Yes, exactly—a teleportation portal. Zero-point-energy experiments, developing a plant-based container for psychotropic zero-point-energy wherein a human's dependency on time-space constructs is disabled, resolving the 'internal-external' reality conflict."

Much of what I heard was over my head, but I understood the general approach and my interest was honest. I was getting closer to these guys, day by day. I was discovering. I was learning.

The next day, when I was in their library reading, Fyodor entered. He started about the Stargate gateway. "Let me try to help you understand what we are doing by using a pop culture analogy. We are talking about portals or gateways. Passage through gateways in the Stargate movie required two gateways with a strange, ill-defined passage—a wormhole or whatever between those gateways. The gateways were a massive material presence but that was all only fiction."

The key, he maintained, to passing through a gateway or portal was the alignment of complex factors. To crack the cypher to allow portal passage—that was the fictional Stargate story—but Fyodor went further and explained the situation regarding his applied plant research. He said there were other critical physical and environmental factors when considering movement through a plant portal. Temperature, pressure, chemical composition, detached mental state, intellectual focus, spiritual openness—some of what he mentioned. Too much was flowing over my head.

"Wait a minute, wait a minute—I've got to ask about these portals but my question is more based on literature—these portals and their entry to somewhere, something else... are you guys talking about paranormal or magic realism experiences..."

Toseland interrupted, "Don't be silly, it is not about literature or ideas. It is about plants. Plants in real life. Now, kindly let Fyodor proceed."

Fyodor continued, emphasizing, "A person has to comport these gross and subtle environmental factors to the portal. The plants provide the portals. Plants can only have the proper alignment and conditions if they have been nurtured by people who understand these relationships."

He continued, "In most cases, without the correct approach in the human nurturing of plants, the plants' balance of willingness, and thus their ability to become a portal, will be stunted. But please consider this. We have a garden intimately cared for—the Oval Garden—a garden where plants are served, and maintained most lovingly—a development aura that is in

362

continuing evolution."

And this is most important, he said, "This has to be a 50/50 proposition between you and the plants—the Oval Garden plants."

Fyodor looked at Toseland knowingly, and said that some of significant repute, from other cultures around the world, have said: "Once you go plant, you never go back."

Good words, but I still couldn't translate these Hibiscus House experiences into a useful component for my study.

***

The Fixer

I was trying to coax a story out of my Hibiscus House visits. Wasn't working. Even though "portals" kept catching my attention, the unrelenting cultural anomalies (the indecipherable cross-cultural stuff surrounding me) and the "fog" of northwest Africa intervened. I lost my way again. Less than two months before my final deadline and I was descending into a deep funk. I contacted Sachy.

<u>Parsec/muse404 Text Exchange 9 Oct 2000</u>

muse404: You there?

Parsec: Hi, what's up?

muse404: At HH today.

Parsec: And…

muse404: So much plants and landscape input.

Parsec: Yes…

muse404: But I am vexed… vexed.

Parsec: ?

muse404: They have an incredible library and I have found an excellent Hooker and Ball book--but that is from over 100 years ago--for the contemporary stuff necessary for my study… those guys are definitely into plants, gardens and landscape but so deep I can't see how to apply it to my study or even my work after

I graduate.

Parsec: Well, how are you vexed?

muse404: Can't apply it to my stories.

muse404: Hoped they would be the main inspiration and source for plants and landscape.

Parsec: Consider this… it's easy for me to say. Simplify.

Parsec: Maybe you are trying to fit everything into all domains at once.

muse404: What?

Parsec: Take each idea, each image as its own fragment, its own context.

muse404: Yes?

Parsec: Build a separate short story off each fragment.

muse404: Hmmmm, tell me more…

Parsec: Each Hibiscus House fragment is attached to plants, gardens, landscape or humans, right?

muse404: …right…

Parsec: Then let each fragment be its own discrete entity, its own discrete story, will that work?

muse404: …yeah… maybe… yeah, let me think about it.

LittleWing had that knack of getting to the core. We spoke a while longer and gradually my vexation began receding. She offered a simple path whereon I could use the raw material of my Hibiscus House visits as starting points for plant- based short stories.

I reviewed my cross-cultural story notes—my people stories—in that same light. Most of those I put into the category of "cross-cultural anomalies"—experiences that would make impacts on any foreign landscape architect trying to solve a Moroccan landscape problem. But for the plant stories—well—I needed to go back to Hibiscus House for additional observations of plant, garden and landscape fragments. Vexation nearly but not quite gone, I took some smoke, removing the remaining vex, then fell asleep.

23-Portals

Fragments and Portals

The next day, despite a good night's sleep, I still struggled, trying to put my re-restructured design study together. I had some people stories. I'd been to the Hibiscus House, the La Montagne Tangier "mecca" of botany, horticulture and plants. And Sachy had explained how to translate my plant experiences into fragments for story development. But I needed more.

So, using Sachy's suggestions, I reviewed what I had. What did I have? Even in the peaceful privacy of my roof top flat in a European Tangier neighborhood, I wasn't clear. I had to admit that I had felt this lack of clarity since the ferry crossing here from Algeciras... what?... three months ago? Still unclear? Yeah, that's where I was.

Maybe that was why I felt the need for intoxication. If my normal state was unclear—maybe a good dose of smoke would break that.

So I got out the Gandalf pipe and used the grass to "wake me up". Off I went. Okay. I had local plant fragments. I needed stories. What were the fragments? Forest of dragon's blood trees... huge collection of hibiscus flowers... quote from Toseland about plants as mirrors providing paths to "same but different" realizations... and, oh yeah, Fyodor's words about plants "once you go plant, you never go back".

So there I was with a handful of local plant fragments. What kind of yarn was I supposed to spin? How was I mesmerized by the hibiscus and the dragon's blood trees? And what the hell does mesmerization mean? I could have easily entered the

"Twilight Zone". And Toseland's words "plants as mirrors", "same but different"? Again, what did that mean? I had no idea, another trip into the "Twilight Zone"?

I added my favorite "one-hit" hash to the Gandalf—I had to go down a different hole. This time I started with the word "portal". I took out my diary notes—the ones I started with in Brussels. They covered all my biking experiences before I arrived on the Costa del Sol. I searched for "portal". That Brit architectural student Bo—he had talked rather extensively to me about it.

Then in Granada, at the Alhambra, Washington Irving's short story, *Rose of the Alhambra*, was laced with references to transfiguration. Transfiguration? Just another way to describe a portal.

What else did I have? The Zerhoun Sufi was all about portals in the arts. Fyodor himself seemed to be deep into what he called "plant portals". And Sachy, even Sachy, had entered into a spiritual realization—she called a portal—a portal that gave her emotional relief.

Why did I even think that portals had any importance? I for the longest time had been thinking there was something of unusual value in plants—I didn't know what it was—a big unknown.

And that unknown could rather comfortably become the mysterious linkage between spiritual and material, couldn't it?. So I just lumped all my perceptions of unlabeled plant experiences as portal experiences. That was... convenient, but logical? No, intuition. A hunch.

Okay—I had portals and plants; but I still didn't know where I was going. I had to do two things with them. Make them into stories and give them some kind of unity.

***

Portal Confusion

During my years of university education in landscape architecture, the term portal had been used, but only as an architectural device. I felt it was more than that—my head was spinning—I was truly puzzled. A gate? Transfiguration? How could that develop my plant fragments into plant stories?

I needed some kind of design "theme" or arc on which to hang my plant fragments and stories. And I had a hunch that I could find that theme somewhere in the definition of the word, "portal". I hoped "portal" might be my way forward. Portal, not in a purely architectural sense, but in a multidimensional sense, as in one step beyond, as in moving from material to spiritual.

Despite my fruitless attempts to define "portal", it had, nevertheless, over the past six months gradually worked its way into my design vocabulary. I struggled to define it—to understand it—to make it the basis of my re-restructured design study.

Was it material to spiritual? Was it just an "eye opener"? It did have a mystical chime that attracted me; but I could not quite make it work—make the design stories and garden portals fit together. Hell, I was still stuck trying to turn plant fragments into plant stories—could "portal" be the key to unlock that blockage? I still relished a small slice of hope.

I took some more smoke and asked myself some questions... how to cure the uncertainty? I've always been a designer. I was familiar with linking rooms and doors together—with spatial sequences—with plants and people... but, somehow portals? Mysteriously vague. And my first meetings with those Hibiscus House guys left me only with extreme vagueness and an overdose of confusion.

Too much diversity, too many unknowns... no all-encompassing theory.

So this time, was I going a design too far? Had I gone down the wrong rabbit hole? Perhaps I should just have just grunted out the stories and dropped this desire for a designed arc linkage? Nope. Couldn't.

In the following days, I used all my repertoire of medicine, hasheesh and Seagrams in my effort to build a linking arc into my project.

I visited the Hibiscus House again; and Fyodor's continuous references to gateways and portals made me wonder—was he talking oftentimes about plants as active participants in garden portals... I couldn't grasp it.

Back at my flat, I tucked into some hash, small pieces of my favorite "one hit" stuff, mixed it with *keef* in the Gandalf pipe. Once, twice, then washed it down with a shot of Seagrams... now where was I?

I wondered what was this portal thing? It was something powerful, more powerful than any gate or door... but how, and why?

Portal. I tried to break it down again. ...a door... a gate.,, an entry... a passage between A and B... what is A and what is B? If I say a portal is like a door, what is the door? And a door's definition does not include what is happening in the rooms on either side of the door.

Treading the same path, it wasn't happening.

***

Jacob's Ladder

Despite my confusion, I was not ready to give up. I had more material to examine. I dug into my diary entries from the time earlier that year when I was bike riding with the International School of Brussels alumni, in particular my entries from my conversations with Bo. I've known a lot of architects and students of architecture. But Bo was a Brit, studying in London at Bartlett School of Architecture. He was special because of how he wove a good story about architecture, literature and history—about Pugin, about Kenneth Grahame. I learned from him.

At the very beginning of our bike trip, he took me to see Victor Horta's work in Brussels. That was a good adventure in blurring the line between architecture and landscape architecture, between inside and outside.

Art Nouveau, in my university studies, had always been an amorphous wedge of historic time when a certain design style was popular—until Bo took me to a couple Horta townhouse projects in Brussels. I was blown away by the entries alone. I felt as if I had entered private gardens—but there were no plants. Upon closer examination, I concluded that my heightened sensual experience of the architecture and details could have been only if they had been designed in the spirit of a garden. Horta's architectural details—so sweet, so pleasant, so refreshing. A place of refuge from the hectic, non-stop, noisy, mechanical Brussels urban public realm. I asked myself if relief was a portal.

When I examined Horta's work in Brussels I shared my

thoughts with Bo.

"With this quality of decoration... Art Nouveau has become more than a label. It is a real-life place where light, plants, art and architecture, all have become interlinked. Alive! Subtly sometimes, boisterously others."

Bo added, "It's like a 3D *Myst* discovery experience in real life."

I explored Horta's decoration—decoration on the architectural walls of rooms—decorative vertical panels on stairways and balconies. And what did I find in Horta's Art Nouveau architecture? The plants turned into the forms of a woman's body.

My breath was taken away seeing the interlocking of a woman's form with plant growth itself. Graceful twining vines enveloping a seductively posed woman. Yes, Horta had put together into the same composition for observation, for contemplation, the beauty of plants, stems, leaves, flowers and the sexuality of a woman.

Bo brought me to that appreciation. An inspirational garden surprise, indeed. And it had come alive in real life, in Tangier, unbelievably so, at David's Kasbah *riad* garden. But... was there a portal in my understanding of Horta? A portal in my experiences of David's *riad?*

The definition of "portal" still escaped me. Bo talked a lot about transfiguration. I found those transfiguration diary entries.

He was on his way to Ponferrada in Spain. He was going to make a landscape pilgrimage. And it was his talking about that pilgrimage that introduced me for the first time to a portal. These were my memories as they emerged from my drug-infused head.

While on the road in northern France during that bike trip, this is how he told the story in the dark of our tent on a full moon night camping out. We were sitting up that night, after the rest of the guys had crashed. We were knocking off the last of the red wine when he reached deep into his backpack.

He pulled out a waterproofed sleeve from which he extracted something palm size, and handed it to me. I held it up in the moonlight.

I saw a stack of aged teak wood pieces strapped together with coarsely woven strips of hemp and said, "I've seen these before, advertised on the back page of comic books—some kind of old-fashioned magic trick, right?"

"Jacob's Ladder," he said.

He took it from me and demonstrated the optical illusions, explaining, "There is an underlying principle here—simultaneously one and different—but we shan't go into that tonight."

He pointed out the carved scallop shells on both sides of each teak wood block and said, "The shells are the symbol of St. Jacob—St. James as you might know."

"How does this have anything to do with your walk in Spain?"

He silently looked at me before replying, "Didn't they teach you anything in the US schools?"

I said nothing, just smiled.

"Santiago de Compostela is the resting place of the bones of St. James—close disciple of Jesus—first disciple to be martyred." He paused, his eyes measuring my comprehension.

"I'm with you."

He continued, "James was one of only three disciples invited by Jesus for the transfiguration. You do know about the transfiguration?"

"No, tell me."

"Out in the landscape on a mountain, the transfiguration was an event where Jesus linked material nature with eternal life. In the Bible, Jacob's ladder is the link, the path—the stairway for angels to descend to earth. And, if one can decipher the entry, it is the path up to heaven—the stairway to heaven—that's how I understand it. Strange, no?"

Despite being brought up Christian, I had never heard this story.

Bo continued, "Here's how this optical illusion toy works for me in architecture. This little Jacob's Ladder toy, built around an "it's there but it isn't there" concept, says the path is hard to find. It is the portal to the transfiguration. Now, here is the point, CJ, you still with me?"

I was drinking wine. I nodded in his direction, and he continued, "I think that transfiguration—the linking of the material with the spiritual—is the same goal of all great architects and all great artists. So when I make that Santiago de Compostela pilgrimage walk, I will be making a search for a transfigurational portal—a portal both for my career and also for my spirit. It is a portal to a place where there are no longer any surrogates. It is the real real."

He grabbed the wine bottle from me and took a swig. I was thinking about Bo's transfiguration quest because I always had an inkling that there was more to plants, gardens and landscapes than just the five senses and imagination. Portal? Portal to where? Material to spiritual? Religion? Landscape? Plants?

Bo asked if I'd like to finish the wine. I took the bottle from him, drained it and passed out.

That was my first exposure to "portals". And even then, I really didn't get the portal thing. Bo's portal idea—was it religious only? Was it simply like he said, an experiential juxtaposition of the spiritual with the material? Uncertainty. Why does "design" enter into this portal stuff at all? Might it just be about "faith"?

Smoke or no smoke, my head was spinning—I saw no path to making this part of my study move forward. I was beat; but I remembered the Washington Irving transfiguration story. Had to review my diary entries from the Alhambra.

***

Silver Lute

I refilled my Gandalf pipe with grass. I took a couple short drags on the pipe and checked out my diary entries on the story—*Rose of the Alhambra.*

Transfiguration—that was the entire story. In my notes I had called it "a labyrinth of Moorish music and beauty, utilizing a silver lute". The story moved from the lute's filigreed melodies in the Alhambra rose garden to Christian Kings and onward to Italy where the story's music and beauty resurfaced in the violin of Paganini.

I recalled Midori's version of Paganini's *Caprice No. 6.* Sachy had given me all 24 Paganini's solo violin caprices as a gift for my trip. With special clarity, I recalled how Sachy and I listened to and shared a lot of classical music. She had talked to me about Niccolo Paganini. For a while I thought of it as a phase she was going through.

But one day she said to me, "Paganini was a designer who was stretching the limits of his musical instrument and the way it communicated emotions—you might find a little bit of yourself in his music."

I put No.6 on my MP3 player; and I immediately fell into a Federico Lorca *duende.* Oh, what a world I had slipped into. Was it the hasheesh or a portal to time travel... or both?

Strange memories resurfaced. I was sitting in the Torre de Los Infantes in the Alhambra, listening to a lute solo—just the gardens of the Alhambra in my eyes, and the lute in my ears. In the lute I heard all the intricate detail of the architectural craftsmanship in the decorative *mocárabes*—singing, rhythmic and yet so very peaceful—my eyes and ears were in synchronous appreciation—music and garden were weaving something special.

I quietened myself unconsciously, and the music took me off my feet and led me through the gardens—magical liquid for the ears!

Before I knew it, I was dancing through the Alhambra on the strings of Paganini's *Caprice in B minor*—the gardens were no longer burdened with history, with politics, with their religious overtones—they were refined, they were light and bubbly—they were the music, they were the dance. Oh, how to design gardens that would feel like this!

I stood up and walked out onto my terrace. Took a couple deep inhales of Med and Atlantic Ocean air—nice. Tried to clear my thoughts. Maybe too much smoke—but I could still think straight—and there was something soothing about my memories of Irving, Paganini, and the Alhambra. I reloaded my Gandalf and floated once again back to Granada. But portals? Were these portals? The search continued.

***

Eternal Discovery

They still captivated me—my diary notes from the late night I spent at the Alhambra. Rich memories. The search continued. There had to be a clue somewhere in my notes. I absorbed myself in reading, in recalling what happened that night in the Alhambra.

When I made an evening tour of the Alhambra, "portals", or whatever, mystically surrounded me. The experience was so intense—beyond words. I did not realize what those experiences were until much later.

There were rooms, courtyards, gardens in the Alhambra where suddenly, without expectation, I seemed frozen in place, and, with my eyes, began to travel to different depths of the layers of decoration. Within each layer there were independent intertwining depths of geometry or plant-inspired arabesques—all detail scales intertwined—micro to micro—then micro to macro—then macro to macro—then macro back to micro—never break the chain—and, at the end, I had lost where I was, and lost where I had been.

I was dizzy, not knowing where to turn, not knowing upon what to focus my eyes. Had I been standing on the edge of some kind of portal like Bo had described as the beginning, the landing, of Jacob's Ladder? Or like a trance?

Never before had I experienced these effects of architectural decoration! In Brussels, Bo had shown me Horta's architectural details—silky, smooth, languid, sexy—Art Nouveau. But this—this was boringly basic geometry transformed into interlocked iterations of decorative beauty. Each a challenging journey for my eyes.

In those geometric patterns was always something new to discover and the journey was never over. As if I was participating in eternal beauty wherein eternal discovery folded back on itself. Was that transfiguration? And the relationship between plants and architecture... architecture dominated, but I was always discovering plants.

Discovering! Discovery, in and of itself, was a thrill. The combinations of plants and architecture offered something unique, attention grabbing, perhaps it was discovery beyond the sensual.

That evening the walls, the ceilings, the niches of the Alhambra, all filled with the greatest *mocárabe*, blends of architecture, mathematics and art—and cedar wood marquetry craftsmanship, were accented, through clerestory, by moonbeams.

Detail quality equaled awe; and my eyes drank in magnificent beauty—it was awesome! It was not about history. It was about... I could not find words on the night. But craftsmanship, pattern, color, light and absence of light all merged to take me on a voyage that had neither time nor space.

Every time my eyes followed a geometrically linked pattern, I was surprised by an unexpected window, door... or portal? Each a new threshold, like an exciting new character introduced in a novel—surprise—hope. More levels were revealed.

It was more than reading. I felt like I was walking through various rooms of a beautifully crafted puzzle—exploring various layers of that puzzle, entering each new layer cradling the hope of more beauty. Could I ever design gardens and landscapes that generate these experiences for visitors? This must be the sumum bonum of landscape architecture— an ethereal blending of plants and architecture, utilizing subliminal math and geometry. Everything fit together as illusive yet elucidating and entrancing decorative forces.

As I reviewed my notes, I thought that that landscape architecture experience must have been a step toward transfiguration and it must have had something to do with the portal between material and spiritual. I couldn't put my finger on understandable design or design process. Not close to anything from my university education or my internship experiences. A mystery. A mystery of enticing beauty. Left me speechless.

I tried to put everything together—doors, rooms, light, sequences of rooms, decoration... portals? Poured myself a shot of Seagrams, downed it. Let it slowly settle in.

A room was like a scene. A sequence of rooms was like a story. Light was the plot—the goal—discovery. And decoration of the rooms was like the dropping of breadcrumbs along the way—like the ribbons and paper wrapping a package—each package was a room—and the rooms led to a portal. The light shone on the portal. The decorative stuff was almost like a text message—a subliminal code that designers could use to set a sensual experience context. But where do the plants fit in? I stoked up the Gandalf one more time. And this time I was off to never-never land.

I was dreaming or remembering. As if the Alhambra by itself was not enough, while I was in Granada, I had access to the writings of Federico Lorca. I found, in his understanding of culture, landscape, music, people and gardens, a concept that he used to tie them all together. He called it lamé. I saw lamé as a key that might link craftsmanship in the garden to transfiguration.

Lamé properly composed and woven could be a portal, could be the threshold of transfiguration—a combination of sensual, mental and intellectual flows all coming together. Portal? Trance? I struggled with those conclusions because I had no idea how to build them. But there was no denying the exquisite power I experienced that night in the Alhambra.

Great memories... but... none of them were giving me insight for my plant stories. What was prominent in my mind was how my pulse raced when I unexpectedly heard discussions of "portals" in my visits to the Hibiscus House, the villa so aptly named *Loins du Monde Réel*. I had to walk their Oval Garden. I had to search for portals in that garden. I had been tiptoeing around something existentially powerful. It was all too much. I could not let it go.

***

381

Magic Realism

I spent the better part of a week of long nights trying to find a doable path for my plant stories. I looked long and hard at all the portal experiences I had encountered, trying to understand them—trying to get a useful flow forward from them. In the end I thought the answer must be in the Oval Garden. That was where I left it... almost.

I did one more pipe of one hit hash and crashed for the night.

But not quite. I had unsettled dreams... they rattled my head... what was it? Portals? Especially my talks at Hibiscus House—the Hibiscus House villa had a name—translated into English—"far from the real world". Were those guys talking about "portals" to a place or places far from the real world? Portals? Transfiguration? I had to get to the essence of the Hibiscus House Oval Garden. Were Fyodor and Toseland talking about the same "portals" as Bo? Where? What? My dream was more like a university lecture where the professor spoke way too fast.

The dream continued. It was a thought labyrinth. Questions without answers... was there enough of something there to become the core of a design study... one step beyond the real world through a portal... paranormal wizardry... 21st Century magic realism? I was desperate... coarsely stitching together rough-cut ideas into a design study. I was nowhere near a smooth weave... like Lorca's lamé. But I did have "portals"... my study had to be in there... somewhere... but in the dream, I lost the keys... I couldn't get into the library... Toseland was fuming...

he screamed at me, "Christopher, don't you understand this is a liminal journey only alchemists have taken... it is not an American university class... you need to pick up your game..."

Finally, those turbulent dreams, filled with uncertainty, relented. I had peace. I slept deeply.

24-The Oval Garden

Alchemical Prep

I had to go for it. I hoped to discover what might be at the root of these "portals" and transfiguration concepts. Besides, I was still hungry for plant, garden and landscape input. I kept visiting the Hibiscus House library. After numerous visits and due to my sustained academic interest, Toseland and Fyodor finally invited me to walk their applied research project, the Oval Garden. I arrived mid-afternoon for a walk which was to begin at sunset. Portals? Insights for my design study? I was full of hope.

In the library, Toseland said, "First, we need to prepare. Let me show you to our garden antechamber. It is upstairs. There we will relax for a while, have something light to eat and drink."

"Prepare? Eat and drink? What kinds of preparations?"

"Not to worry. Very simple. Basics for sensual exchanges with plants. A mix of vegetal supplements to relax you. Also to strengthen and enhance your sensual receptors so that multi-dimensional plant input will flow smoothly into you."

I didn't really know what to expect; but I was a willing participant. Toseland commented about the light and the time of day, "As the sun sets, and as soon as it drops below the horizon, a very auspicious—a magnificently enchanting time—you can then enter the Oval Garden and walk at your leisure. Till your heart's content."

He led me out of the library, around a corner to an inconspicuous, altogether ordinary door. Once through the door into the small closet-like space, I had but one path. I followed Toseland to a steep, narrow, wrought iron spiral staircase, then slowly up the long flight of stairs.

As I reached the top of the staircase, I was in a glasshouse, surrounded by a large number of floor-to-ceiling plant trays and stands. Strange, exotic, quite tropical foliage I had never before seen. Intriguing shapes and forms.

"Carnivorous plants. Specialties that Fyodor collaborates with in his research. The antechamber is where he rests them," Toseland explained.

He continued, "I can tell by your eyes, these plants are all new to you, let me give you only the dominant genera of those now surrounding us: *Aldrovandra*, *Nepenthes*, *Cephalotus*, *Dionaea*, *Drosera* the pygmy species. These are portal plants on numerous levels—beautiful to the human eye, and certain death for smaller life forms. And most intriguing, Fyodor applies their natural excretions in his portal research."

That was interesting, but what captured my attention first was the air I inhaled. Enriched oxygen. I felt added energy as that inhaled air reached every corner of my lungs. I was excited. I felt good. I was ready.

***

Antechamber

The garden antechamber felt like an expansive glasshouse extension. It was twelve sided. Five sides were connected by solid walls to the villa second floor. The balance seven walls were glass, providing an expansive overview of the gardens and the dramatic regional landscape beyond. The landscape view included the Strait of Gibraltar in a wide northern horizon from the north east all the way around to the west north west. I could see both the Med and the Atlantic Ocean. But there was nothing of Tangier or its neighborhoods in the view—blocked out by tall mature trees.

The antechamber had three comfortable armchairs, separated by side tables, displaying fat, squat candles, obviously of long and regular service. They were lit. Next to them were a couple smallish oriental incense burners, smoke lightly curling up to ventilated openings in the glass roof above. I bent to sample the incense smoke. With my hand I wafted the curling smoke toward my nose—frankincense and myrrh—a fragrance soft and sweet with a timeless gravitas, somber just like in a Catholic church.

And all around us there were more potted plants. I paused to observe these new plants. The patterns and colors on these new large leaves took me somewhere in between Aldous Huxley's *Doors of Perception* and lively iterations of Frederick Law Olmsted's plans for Riverside in Chicago.

"*Caladium hybrids,*" Toseland said, "my hobby. Some of these are linked back to Louis Van Houtte's original hybrid work from more than a century ago." I saw, in between these caladiums, numerous pots of small ferns. I had no idea what they were.

Toseland took my arm and led me to the glass windows that provided a prospect over the garden below, the Oval Garden. He showed me the set of double French doors opening out onto a terrace. Those doors were locked but I could see that they were in the centre of the small terrace, more like a long narrow balcony, for no more than eight people to stand, shoulder to shoulder, at the same time.

The narrow terrace had a granite balustrade, connecting at each end to staircases which curved down to the garden. The top of each staircase had two matching granite posts. Each post supported a low profile, patina'd bronze fire bowl. A total then, at the terrace ends, of 4 fire bowls with burning flames gently licking upward—lighting the path from the antechamber down.

The two curving staircases, emptying down into the Oval Garden, opened onto the narrow head of the gentle oval pathway. At the bottom of each staircase were two more matching granite posts, four in total, each again topped with lit patina'd bronze firebowls. I could see therefore a total of eight lit firebowls lighting what would most likely become my way, via either of the two staircases, to the garden's oval pathway.

That oval pathway structured the entire garden arrangement. The long axis of the oval was easily fifty meters, probably longer. I noted the fountain at the end of the oval was softly lighted and the water was lightly dancing.

Toseland said, "There are soft lights throughout the garden, should clouds cover the moon."

Then he said, "When you finish your walk, return to this antechamber. I will be waiting for you, to answer any questions and then to lead you to the door, so you can return to your flat."

Toseland suggested we sit down and begin preparations. On a table, between our two chairs, was a collection of serving articles—looked like tea caddies. He opened one and took out a small box which he offered to me. I held the box— dark, aged walnut, carved flowers on the outside, like a Brienz box from Switzerland.

"Before you open the box, this is the beginning of the vegetal supplements—very simply these supplements—a combination of chocolates, herbs and absinthe, will heighten and refine your sense perception. Like I mentioned in the library, you might experience extra sensory perception. In all dimensions, keep your mood respectful of the plants."

Then I opened the box. The smell of dark chocolate flooded my nostrils. Inside the box were six bite-size, round chocolate wafers set in a soft, chestnut color, tissue wrap. On the underside of the lid, I found clasped a hand lens.

Toseland told me to take one wafer now, and if I have thirst in the garden, the white marble fountain at the far end offers potable water for my refreshment. He added, "Carry the remaining five wafers in the box for rejuvenation during your walk in the garden." The hand lens, he suggested, might prove useful during the walk, should I wish to examine anything in detail.

As I put the wafer in my mouth, he instructed, "Let it dissolve on your tongue.

"Engage your thoughts on the plant—its growth, flowering, fruiting—*Theobroma cacao*, which provided all the components that you are tasting. Hold your concentration on that taste, explore the taste until the taste is no longer." We did not talk while I tasted the dark chocolate wafer.

I found it sweet at first. Then, after 15 minutes, ever so bitter in the end. The bitterness overcame my meditative efforts.

Toseland then poured a glass of room temperature white chocolate milk and offered it to me. The aroma had the faintest, yet rich, sweet promise of well-prepared white chocolate—must have had the slightest amount of cocoa bean solid because it had an undeniable bitter base. Over that bitterness was an herbal note— couldn't quite identify those components but their scent—magnetic. I took a swallow, then, while listening to Toseland's explanations, I gradually drank it all.

The attractive herbal mixture, according to Toseland, included cardamom, camphor and all-spice. It was refreshing, almost cleansing.

Toseland instructed me to savor and meditate on the source plants that provided all the tastes and aromas I experienced in the 15cl of white chocolate liquid.

After I had finished the white chocolate milk, he cleared away my glass and opened a tantalus that contained a decanter of green liquid. Absinthe, a distilled spirit, he called it. He handled it religiously, as if a sacrament. Out of the tantalus he took a single glass, a perforated spoon, a carafe of iced water and a small bowl with rough white chunks of fine grain, cane sugar.

He talked again about the importance of focusing on the history of the plants and processes that he would now assemble for the absinthe drink.

He told me that the locked doors to the garden would open automatically at sunset. I should enjoy the absinthe drink and engage my eyes, all my senses, gross and subtle, my mind and intelligence in the beauty of the plants as the sun was setting. Then, as the door opens, surrender myself to the plants I would meet on my walk.

From a sideboard on my right, Toseland rotated out a wood table into its position just above my lap, at the height of my elbows. He placed the ice water carafe and the empty, clear glass on the table.

Then, overhead, he turned on a small LED spotlight and adjusted it so that it sparkled on the tall, thin, but wide-mouthed empty glass sitting on the table in front of me. He placed a measured amount of the pale green absinthe spirit into the glass—not quite one-third full. Then he placed the perforated spoon, strainer-like, over the mouth of the glass and selected, with tongs, a solid chunk of the white sugar which he placed in the centre of the spoon's small perforations.

He set the carafe directly adjacent to my glass so that when he opened the stop cock on the side of that ice water carafe—Toseland called it a fountain—the drips fell squarely on the sugar chunk. He adjusted the stop cock to allow what seemed like one drop every three or four seconds—very slow drips. I was to remain seated and shut off the dripping when the sugar was fully dissolved, which should be approximately a ratio of two measures of water to the original measure of absinthe.

As he made these preparations, he talked me through the mixing of water, sugar and absinthe with its herbs: star anise, *Illicium verum*; wormwood, *Artemisia absinthium*; fennel, *Foeniculum vulgare*; green anise, *Pimpinella anisum* and a selection of minor botanicals to establish its unique bouquet and transcendent enjoyment. Transcendent enjoyment!? His words exactly.

Toseland, very peacefully and almost in slow motion, explained the absinthe preparation sequence. He told me the louche was an esthetic experience of delicate nuance. In his words, it was a multi-dimensional, liminal mixing of the two liquids.

He instructed me to watch the glass carefully as each drop of cool water fell through the block of sugar into the absinthe spirits, releasing alchemical potencies.

What I saw, as each drop fell into the absinthe, was first, a timeless three-dimensional graphic, wherein liquid marble cat's eyes appeared, turning and twisting until their fine wispy threads became Mandelbrotean shapes which themselves began their own twisting and turning—almost dancing as they dissolved into clouds. Not just any clouds—these were a soft mixing of alchemical herbs and water and spirits, de-concocting and uniting. These clouds were dancing. And for the inner ear only, the cloud edges emanated an ethereal music.

I became absorbed in this dance. I heard no more talking. I heard only a soothing internal music that had to have been inspired from the dance I was watching. All my other senses shut down as the louche, the cloud, developed, materializing and dematerializing, until the aromatic anise fragrance increased and took over. Finally, the rematerialized cloud took over all. The sugar fully dissolved, I closed the ice water carafe.

It was time for me to fully sample the fragrance. Filled my lungs with its sweet, earthy, licorice-like alchemical aroma. Then I sipped—slowly, as the sinking sun turned the colors of the day into the colors of the twilight. Before long, the dancing light rays of sunset animated every part of every plant and filled my head with their glories. It was all so wonderful.

**

Chocolate Trance

I did not see Toseland leave; and next, I heard the self-opening of the doors to the garden.

I stepped out on the terrace, looked out over the oval lawn, the oval pavement, the tall oval hedge. This was the Oval Garden. This was the adventure I sought. I noted the unusual placement of the gloriettas along the oval path. Their placement was not symmetric. Neither were they equally spaced. It was hard to tell how many there were. More than three—but more than five?

I examined the Oval Garden's large flat lawn as I descended the curved stairs. At the bottom of the stairs, I paused briefly next to the last pair of softly glowing flame bowls. Then, I started to my left and, walking the oval pavement, followed the path toward the closest glorietta. A slight breeze brought *Jasminum polyanthum* from that glorietta. I let that fragrance carry me forward, and the next thing I remembered, I was back in the antechamber. I held the empty chocolate box. Apparently, I had eaten all five remaining bitter chocolate pieces. I couldn't remember anything of the walk except the jasmine at the first glorietta.

Toseland was sitting next to me. "You have been two hours in the garden, how did you find it?" Toseland asked.

"I don't know. I don't remember anything!!?"

We talked it round and round. To make a long story short, we reached two conclusions. First, he told me to go back to my regular daily activities and the memories would likely emerge on their own. Second, he told me that if I had been habitually eating processed food or, on a regular basis, been taking too much intoxication, the pineal gland may not have functioned properly. He suggested we talk with Fyodor and, perhaps, schedule a second walk in the Oval Garden.

In hindsight, I was looking for that special portal and I would have done anything to experience that garden and its plants... that plant-assisted movement to a portal, across a threshold I had only heard about.

I had so much anticipation—such a buildup for this walk and I came back empty. A mystery. Hope and pleasure had turned to uncertainty and deep disappointment. I was puzzled beyond description. Regarding speaking with Fyodor about lack of memory, Toseland told me to come by the next day, in the afternoon, and we would see.

Toseland, slowly walking me to the Hibiscus House entry terrace, saw me off. I felt hollow as I made my way to the Petit Taxi stand. I had somehow stepped away from reality in that garden; and I had not truly returned yet. I needed to ground myself in a reality I could understand, so I took a Petit Taxi to Brahim's for a sandwich.

Hung out by myself for a while at Brahim's at a quiet table in the back, lingering over my sandwich, trying to settle. This Oval Garden mystery could have become a vein of content for my revised design study or could remain as it was—a big zero—a huge disappointment.

All I had wanted was to get inspiration to turn my plant fragments into plant stories but what had I got? Nothing but deeper into a rabbit hole.

No memories.

Nothing.

I was definitely moping when Brahim came up said hi, sat down and asked how I was doing.

I told him straight out, "Nothing is working for me or my study..."

"Tell me."

I retold what was going on and while I was telling it, I thought I should ask him. He knew Tangier. He knew life in Morocco. So, still struggling with my green in Tangier floundering

396

design study, I asked.

"You have a successful business, no?"

"*Hamdulah*," he said.

"What about family?" I asked.

"I'm living in the medina but I come from Chechaouan—last of five sons. Have three younger sisters. Father injured in the fight for independence in the 1950s. I send money to him to support."

"How about you? Married?"

"Still saving, still looking..."

Then I shifted, "What do you do for fun—there are no parks in the medina..."

"Some days I hang at the beach... other days, some friends and I go fishing... sometimes out past Malabata... sometimes near Larache..."

I was getting confused again. Brahim described an almost normal life. Hard work for self and family—taking a break with friends. I didn't have the nerve to bring up the subject of teeps. I thought they were almost like extraterrestrials here just to cause trouble. Brahim excused himself as a crowd of people entered needing all hands on deck.

Me, confusion aside, well I could always find a shred of hope.

I took a Petit Taxi home for the night. And believe me all I had were the thinnest of shreds.

***

Decompressing

Ihad to share my baffling Oval Garden experience with Sachy. I needed more grounding and comforting. I needed a sympathetic ear so I could decompress.

<u>Parsec/muse404 Text Exchange 11 Oct 2000</u>

muse404: You in?

Parsec: Hi, what's up?

muse404: Walked the Oval Garden.

Parsec: And what happened?

muse404: Not really sure.

muse404: The whole thing's a mystery.

Parsec: Tell me, good or bad?

muse404: Both, the procedure for entering the garden just like an H. G. Wells story.

Parsec: Whoa!

muse404: And the garden, entrancing.

muse404: It had a glow.

muse404: Mediterranean sun quality--I entered at sunset--the crepuscule--splendid.

Parsec: Sounds like heaven.

muse404: Here's where it got strange--I walked the oval path and came to a pergola, they call them gloriettas.

muse404: The glorietta was covered with jasmine in bloom. The fragrance grabbed me from my nose and filled my lungs to their deepest regions.

muse404: As I was observing that, I became entranced to such an extent...

Parsec: Yes, yes, what happened then?

muse404: ...and then my memory fails.

Parsec: What!?

muse404: Next thing I remembered was being back indoors two hours later.

Parsec: What!?

muse404: No memory at all and that's really frustrating.

Parsec: That, let me say, that sounds like you were under the influence of drugs.

muse404: Not so fast, not that simple--the important thing is that I can't remember anything about my walk after the fragrance at the glorietta.

Parsec: What'll you do?

muse404: You'll like this, the guys at HH have said that the memory loss could be from too much regular intoxication.

Parsec: Maybe I was on the right track--so?

muse404: Apparently it hardens the receptors in the pineal gland, so, I need to put an end to Seagrams, smoke and amphetamines.

Parsec: Uh huh.

muse404: Yeah, just like you were saying, I'm going to stay off all intoxication until I have a second Oval Garden walk in a couple days.

Parsec: Good, good.

Parsec: Good, keep clean.

muse404: I'm so disappointed not to have any memories.

Parsec: I can only imagine....

muse404: I figured after all the explanations from the guys at HH that I'd find real plant content, at least a key to turn my plant fragments into stories; but I've got nothing.

Parsec: Patience CJ, you're still on the path, right?

muse404: Yeah...

Parsec: ...and you're going to clean up your intoxicated metabolic system, right?

muse404: ...yeah...

Parsec: I can't hear you! Your going to clean up, right?

muse404: Right, definitely.

Parsec: Clean up and talk to those guys. Be patient. You'll clear, I'm sure. Anything else?

Muse404: Okay, I'll hold on, I'll clean up and I'll be patient. I'm seeing them again tomorrow. I'll get back with you after I have more talks at the HH and hopefully take the second walk.

Closed the texting after some personal exchanges. Took the airs on my garden terrace. Decompressing had begun, but... still no memories. Patience? I'd give it a try, but... time was short... Went to sleep.

***

Tangier Home Theater

Next day, I returned to Hibiscus House. I went through the usual entry procedure and met Toseland on the front terrace.

He greeted me, saying, "Call me Tolly, if you like."

They had just finished lunch. He explained they always finish lunch with espresso, a plate of sliced fresh figs, and Armagnac, then invited me to join. He walked me through two of the hibiscus display lounges to I didn't know where.

Then he parted damask curtains to reveal a passage to another part of their house. He led me along a windowless, dimly lit narrow corridor and after a couple turns, through a thick heavy door into a small but modern media room—a home theatre.

The room was indirectly lit from the reflected cove lights around the edge of a graceful dome above. The dome was night time dark with pin light sparkles as stars. This media room proportions and detailing had the comfortable feel of an intimate, private Turkish *hamam*, like I had regularly seen in Ottoman architectural history books.

Fyodor was already seated—he welcomed me. I needed to use a toilet before I did anything else. Tolly pointed me to the toilet door in the back of the room as he and Fyodor began discussing what to watch.

A toilet's just a toilet, right? Not exactly. Turkish squat and drops over a hole in the floor—standard for public toilets in the medinas. In the European parts of Moroccan towns toilets looked more like the porcelain bowls I had grown up with; but there was always an extra piece of porcelain equipment—the bidet. Neither was the case at this Hibiscus House toilet.

The outer door had angularly set wood slats that acted as ventilation. They also emitted a soft glow from between the slats that I noted as I approached the door.

As soon as I opened the door, lights became brighter and I confronted a free-standing, tightly geometric patterned, wooden screen that blocked any view into the toilet. The screen reminded me of pictures I had seen of Persian mushrabiya. I walked round the screen and found myself in a wash room.

At the far end of the wash room was another door. As I opened it, lights and a ventilation fan turned on. The toilet room was small but had two stalls, each with door. Bingo. Finally, down to business.

As I exited the toilet room, I noticed a distinctly calming influence... like a whispering.... It was a fragrance I had encountered once before when I worked on a hospitality destination in the Persian Gulf Region during my summer internship with the planning and design firm from Fort Lauderdale. The light fragrance was oud, known by some as agarwood.

Agarwood, *Aquilaria species*, is a pleasing, yet complex scent—very soft, fruity and floral with something very deep and mystical running through it—definitely rich with the oriental "Ali Baba and the Forty Thieves" character. Relieved of my toilet needs, I paused to look around the washroom.

This media room toilet was another world of its own. I thought, will this place ever stop amazing me? Above the wash basin sink, I saw a patina'd bronze framed mirror with matching vertical sconces on either side. Overhead in the centre of the room hung a bronze arabesque chandelier shaped like an outlined assemblage of filigreed mocárabe vaulting, containing within multiple low wattage bulbs.

On the sink sat a stack of folded, fine weave, cotton towels. Across from the sink I saw a storage sideboard, with a spotlight above. The spotlight highlighted an assemblage of five large, empty vases. They were glazed and were of beautifully intense colors with well detailed flowers. I walked over to them to examine them more carefully. I found a note in front of them. The note read "These are original William Moorcroft Florian Ware vases, featuring flowers we wish we could grow here".

After I finished washing at the sink, I stepped away and the vertical bronze sconce lights at the sink turned off. I turned toward the exit and, in the now very low light of the wash room, I heard, from beyond the outer door, a rather heated discussion going on between Fyodor and Tolly. I paused to listen.

What were they saying... it sounded like they were arguing about what movie to watch. Then their conversation grew quiet. I moved closer to the door and tried to hear—they were quietly talking about me!

Fyodor was saying, "...we need the money... and... I'm not sure it is safe to have him spend the night. How do you know we can trust him?"

Tolly said, "We've been through this before—he's just a typical naive young American university student who rather surprisingly likes plants—drop it."

"But we shouldn't take a chance..."

"You yourself have said how many times that we need to test our garden on a suitable subject, right?"

"You're right."

"Well, this young man is perfect."

"But what about what what's his name... Joey?... said?"

"You mean Mr. Grimaldi? He's just a transporter. Like I said, drop it. Pick out a good movie and let's relax."

I wasn't really sure what I heard but it sounded... queer, maybe even nefarious? I put it aside. It was time for me to return to them in their media room. And what I needed was to talk with them more about my lack of memories from yesterday's Oval Garden walk.

25-Stomata

The Garden of Allah

I had to ignore that strange conversation I'd just overheard between Fyodor and Tolly, and keep in mind why I was here. I needed to get to grips with my study, my hoped-for plant inspiration and my missing garden memories.

Whenever I visited Tolly and Fyodor, the subjects of plants, people and portals dominated discussions. But I had yet to make this all fit into a design study...

It wasn't easy. Fyodor's descriptions of his work regularly led me down into a dark hole—didn't understand what a portal really meant—in real life. Just words? Hope? No hope. Maybe Fyodor's portal and Bo's transfiguration...? Couldn't get it all together in a direction that was useful.

It sounded interesting, but I just couldn't follow Fyodor's technical stuff. He talked portal details and I had no idea what was a portal. Maybe it was just a distraction. Maybe I was putting too much into it... but the concept of portals interested me. Especially here in the Hibiscus House where they had to do with plants; but... as I was thinking about it... their media room details captured my attention.

In the media room the seats—like first class airline seats—were broad and comfortable with wide arms suitable to safely hold drinks and ashtrays—the accoutrements of gentlemanly enjoyments.

There were no windows. Lights were low. Seats in two staggered rows. Four in front. Five in back.

The perimeter of the room was chockablock with sideboards and their glass doors. I could see their collection of media disks of all sorts. Fyodor was still working through an onscreen menu when Tolly brought in three espressos without sugar.

We sat together in the front row. Sipped espressos while they discussed, for the nth time, what to watch. Tolly took away our espresso cups and brought back a plate of sliced fresh figs to share, along with three small, clear, tulip-shaped glasses and a decanter of Armagnac. He poured three. We saluted and sipped.

Fyodor took down the house lights. Then, for our enjoyment, and quintessentially apropos, he started rolling *The Garden of Allah*, one of the first Technicolor movies, an early David Selznick film from 1936 starring Marlene Dietrich, Charles Boyer and Basil Rathbone. Tolly made an introduction, saying, "It is not really about Islam but you might divine some of the North African mood of the crowds and minor characters herein."

And we began. I was quiet through most of it. Tolly was right; even though it was filmed in the US, Arizona, the minor characters and scenes definitely recalled some of my current off-putting cross-cultural experiences.

I did ask my hosts, "Charles Boyer was looking for what in Allah's garden—a portal? Was he looking for why it is okay to throw away his faith in God? Both of you guys have Christian background, what do you make of it?"

"Maybe you are too young to know; but, in life, everyone goes through a crisis of faith, sometime or many times," Tolly said.

This movie was weird—it made me question. "Allah's garden—no plants—just like every medina I've seen—what's the point?"

"A devout Muslim would say there is no need for beautiful gardens during our short stay on earth because in Muslim paradise is a glorious garden," Tolly replied.

That was good enough for me. Fyodor piped up with a couple tedious broadsides at my profession again, chipping away at landscape architects not knowing anything about their key design element, plants. I guess he wasn't so much into the movie.

Me, I was always looking for the slightest clue that would lead me out of my conundrum. A clue to turn plant fragments into stories. Maybe it was staring me in the face? Maybe it was—but I didn't see it. That's for sure, I didn't see any clues or even a handful of plant fragments. I really needed to focus our discussions on my design study needs.

***

Fyodor's Portals

The movie finished, we wound our way back through the dark hallway tunnel to the main villa and sat in one of the hibiscus lounges. Their house intrigued me—rambling California bungalow combined with classical Mediterranean style villa. Could have been found up in the Hollywood Hills where all past owners made their own unique extensions. The most recent extensions here in the last twenty years were by the Brit and Rooskie to enhance their botanical and horticultural efforts.

Tolly told me his father bought it in the 1950s from the Italian family of Baron Luigi Parilli, who had bought it in the 1930s from the Portuguese Ambassador. I learned a bit more about these guys over a second Armagnac. As Tolly refilled our glasses, Fyodor went to one of the sideboards and brought out a humidor. They each selected a thin crooked cigar and then offered the humidor to me. Not my style.

"No thank you; but I don't recognize those cigars..." I was curious.

Tolly said, "These are from Switzerland and are called '*krumme*' made by Villiger."

They both lit up and inhaled deeply sending the smoke toward a ventilation fan in the ceiling. Then Tolly got into family history.

In summary, Tolly's most recent ancestry had been associated with Malta in both world wars.

Fyodor was, distantly, of the Russian royalty—but definitely connected. His great grandfather was a fisherman who married a black sheep Russian princess. Their first son, Fyodor's grandfather, became a fisherman and married another fisherman's daughter. Fyodor benefited immensely from his great grandmother's bequest. But I was distracted—not interested in their history—I still had problems with my study.

I changed the subject and brought up my issues about cultural strangeness impacting my study and Fyodor talked about cultural impedance.

"Cultural strangeness is real—like the cell wall in plants. Though inside each cell, all the components may be the same, they are surrounded by what is called a cell wall that varies in its construction but in all cases impedes movement in and out of a cell and between cells." Fyodor was into this and he had more to say.

"It is there," he said, "...seek the stomata... seek the places where movement between the two occurs. Learn how to use those stomata to your needs."

I wondered... stomata, portals?

"There is an innate impedance in any media," he said, and he continued, "this impedance is friction. That friction is an innate unwillingness to allow, to permit internal exchange between team members and external exchange into the environment between members—impedance in both cases."

Fyodor said, "That is the cultural impasse you are dealing with. And here you are trapped in the cultural no-man's zone. The interzone—a mental place that does not recognize the difference between cell wall and stomata. Anomalies are not anomalies—they are portals or they are signposts of errors in our assumptions. There are more things about humans and plants that you should know, my young American friend."

Fyodor carried on about Stargate-like portals in nature that are very limited and very difficult to find and enter because... in his words.

"The human nature is unstable, always uncertain. The mind is restless and the intelligence is a labyrinth, formed differently in each person.

"Everything around you is made of elements that scientists

have studied in quite some detail only over the last 200 years. Recent understanding breaks down when these elements are subjected to high pressure and temperature. Now, using an advanced theoretical understanding and extreme conditions, researchers have converted a basic, such as table salt, into exotic chemicals that are causing anomalies, rethinking of basic scientific assumptions. So, in truth we find the contemporary field of chemistry trapped in a 'the world is flat' stage."

Okay, okay, I thought, I still could not understand why I had no memory of my walk in their Oval Garden. Fyodor was in another world. I had to interrupt, my impatience getting the best of me. I said, "But my memories—what about my memories?"

Tolly said, "Come back tomorrow. We can examine that then."

Inside, I was frustrated; but I thought at least I was an invited guest in this villa, rich in botany and horticulture—certainly my plant fragments and stories would emerge.

As we wrapped up our Armagnacs, they excused themselves; they had to prepare for a business guest coming that evening.

We said goodbyes.

***

Oval Garden Redux

I had just received a truckload of input—I really didn't know how much I understood—and we hadn't even talked about my missing Oval Garden walk memories. Trying to separate the peripheral from the useful, my head was overflowing. Maybe I was looking too hard. Maybe I was in the land of "can't tell the forest from the trees". Impatience grew.

I came back the next day, determined to get more insights on my loss of memory. I had been depending on drug-induced experiences to search, to discover plant-related perspectives for my study. I had been eager to find a breakthrough in the Hibiscus House. At least, those were my thoughts and hopes.

We got off to a good start. Tolly was helpful. He recalled the antechamber preparations, reminding me, "Those preparations were for easy access to the pineal gland. And therein I believe is the root of your Oval Garden walk loss of memory." Okay, the conversation had finally turned my way.

"Today," he added, "some say that if the pineal gland has been abused by frequent intoxication or improper diet, it can withdraw during attempted access." They had told me this before. My impatience grew.

He and Fyodor, after considerable back and forth, concluded that was likely what happened. I was still uncertain what was going on. I only knew I had taken my much-anticipated walk in the Oval Garden and remained without memories. Where were those memories?

Tolly and Fyodor were convinced about their efforts and their conviction strengthened my fading hope. But Fyodor thought my memory problem went much deeper—in his words—to my weak understanding of my profession.

Fyodor said, "Listen, my young American friend, if you want to build gardens, you have to maintain gardens. You have to start with understanding how many ways humans interact with plants. Otherwise, how can you bring humans closer to plants to come in contact with the Stargate-like portals of the plant world, to open the doors to heaven?"

In retrospect this comment went over my head—Fyodor had tried to answer my memory concerns by saying that if I had a more complete understanding of human-plant relationships, then I would not have the memory problem. I should have asked him to be more specific; but Tolly got involved and the discussion moved in my favor again.

"Exactly—the doors to heaven," Tolly emphasized.

"Doors to heaven—how do I learn about this?" I was sure I was on the verge of something essential—transcendental, portals, transfiguration or similar—to my design study theme and stories.

Tolly asked me, "Are you serious?"

"Definitely."

He looked at Fyodor, their eyes connected in understanding, and he said, "As we briefly discussed yesterday, if you'd like to take another walk in the garden, come after dinner at the end of this week, pass the night here in our guest accommodation and stay away from intoxication. The walk at sunrise will suit you. The sunrise experience is always a softer walk than sunset, especially for people who are good hearted, like you."

I was in. I hoped this time would be better—rememberable.

***

Osmotic Stargate

I spent the next days in the Hibiscus House library I got to spend more time with Fyodor. I had never met a Russian before. Fyodor was the first. There was a power in his persona. Did it represent Russian cultural roots? He came from the St Petersburg region. Or did he derive it from the plants? With conviction and power, he took me through his work with plant portals. I have tried to summarize, quoting from Fyodor to the best of my memory.

He started me off once again with his summary of the gateway in the movie Stargate. A person passing through the gateway was able to escape the restriction of time and space by crossing a threshold and moving through some wormhole to another already located gateway.

He said, "You may find it helpful to think of plant portals like gateways. Humans passing through an 'osmotic' membrane— where a time and space displacement occurs.

"Osmotic portals are crudely known these days as stomata. That is how scientists describe in plants the movement of liquids, gasses, minerals, ions, electromagnetics—so many things moving—moving via infrastructure networks between the tip of the deepest root hair end and the tip of the highest growing cells of every leaf bud—flows in every direction through millions of individual cells, each equipped with perimeter coverings—protective cell walls.

"And scientists, even with all their so-called advanced equipment, still have not understood all the components, all the processes of each cell or the activities, exchanges and signals going on in each cell—what to speak of the intercellular spaces and transcellular flows throughout the entire cellular megalopolis.

"Instead of taking the best from Culpepper, Gerrard, Paracelsus, and earlier people who explored the subtler aspects of plants, when the scientific revolution entered the scene, they—how do you guys say—threw the baby out with the bath water." I'd heard that before—believable I thought. Fyodor was in a passion as he continued.

"Now after two hundred years of 'refined' scientific labors, 'accelerated' scientific revolutions—all we have with plants is crude pornography—let's look more closely at the sex life of plants—let's cut and play with their genitals."

I was dumbfounded. My eyes were glazed—they gave me away.

Fyodor shouted at me, "Are you listening to me? Do you know what I am saying? I am speaking English, no?"

I was stunned. Couldn't absorb it on the day. I finally got myself together and answered, "Look, I thank you and Tolly for your hospitality. I came here to read about the Hooker and Ball observations of plants and landscape in Morocco, to walk in your Oval Garden, looking for a usable rich vein of plants for my study; and you, if I must say, deliver in a plain brown wrapper to me, a thermonuclear explosive device of plant knowledge. I'm not sure how to respond.

"In the end, my business will be to plan, design and build gardens with plants, for people to enjoy. I have observed that most people never think about plants and gardens being anything much more than a contemporary design accessory or at best an extension of some kind of ecological network. I just assumed people wanted plants, gardens, landscapes that I would design and supply."

I was over the top. In retrospect, Fyodor and I weren't so far apart on plants. On the day however I could not see it. I was nearsightedly focussed on my missing memories, plant fragments and stories. And that was the end of discussion on that day.

***

416

Clarity?

In the quiet of my rooftop garden terrace flat, I pondered on Fyodor's descriptions. I appreciated his scientific vocabulary and wondered—plant stories wherein passing through some kind of transcendent osmotic portal gains access to the story world of... of what? Hadn't quite figured that out, yet... however...

On another afternoon that very same week, on my way home, after most of the day at Hibiscus House, I stopped at the Grand Socco fruit market and found a particularly good-looking batch of fresh oranges for sale—the kind that still have a couple healthy evergreen leaves attached to the stems—the kind that look so full of juice that their thin peels are bulging like full balloons—best oranges I'd ever seen. The vendor cut one open for me to try—superb. I bought two kilos.

As soon as I got back to my apartment, I squeezed a large glass full. It was past the heat of the afternoon. The sun was moving down into its last quarter. With my glass of orange juice, I sat down in my wicker chair on the terrace. I sat in the shade and observed the terrace garden plants still rejuvenating their resources in full sun.

The plants were absorbing the sun's energy; and I was absorbing the juice from solar energy production. Perhaps it was a 2+2=4 moment with solar energy in charge. The juice felt more intoxicatingly powerful than neroli attar; and it was so sweet and relaxing, yet energizing.

Shortly after having swallowed half the glass, I felt something in my head clear—don't know what it was but it felt like clarity had arrived. For the briefest moment, all of Fyodor's explanations fit into place. All the pieces of the puzzle fit. The picture was clear.

It was about a subset of liminality, a vegetal subset. When the proper conditions were met, a plant's supra-dimensional stomata would admit human consciousness while simultaneously removing the human's awareness of the human body—a stomatic transformation.

That was good; but now how could I fit that into my design study. Part of a story... a series of stories... could I even describe it as anything but a fantasy... a dream that could likely never be found in a garden or landscape—because of all the conditions that Fyodor said were required to be fulfilled for passage. Hmmm, went inside, finished my orange juice and puzzled—I was in the hunt, or was I?

Ever since I felt the power of Harlequin's stories, the idea of stories as a landscape design tool had been developing in my head. Harlequin's stories merged landscape and culture. I had serious cross-cultural issues overlaid upon my plants, gardens and landscape interests. The Zerhoun Sufis convinced me there was something in stories. And Neil bought into it. What was holding me back? Memories? Or...?

My original Design Study Topic Statement was: This study will examine the regional sociological roots behind the physical placement, ornamentation and use of water features in the Moroccan urban public realm, with a view toward a metric understanding of the cultural components in public realm design.

As I revised the study to landscape architecture design short stories, my provisionally titled *Annex of Tales* now had two basic components rooted into them: people and plants. I had lots of stuff on people and their cross-cultural weirdness; but plants—didn't have a handle on them yet. Ideas were evolving—except my Oval Garden memories—needed them.

My design stories could feature, from beauty discovered in plants, gardens and landscapes, links to the human senses. These links could lead to other worldly experiences beyond the five visceral senses, beyond emotion, beyond intelligence, passage through vegetal supra dimensional stomata. Or perhaps transfiguration, as my friend, Bo, had once described.

This was a two-fold problem—transfiguration or stomatic transformation—what was that? ...to and from where? How could I write about something I didn't understand? I needed something simpler about plants—magic realism was not my goal.

I ran this finally defined collection of discrete, but barely linked, short stories by Sachy. It worked within the "fragment" idea Sachy had originally suggested. I didn't have my hope for a clear "portal" design arc, but I had to move forward. Sachy pushed me to get it going—to stop "thinking with portals", stop "shooting for the stars" and start writing.

Sachy had agreed to help as development editor, line editor and proofreader. My Academic Advisor had bought into the "stories" format; but I still had to brief him on final content. My struggles for plant content continued.

***

Polovstian

On my second walk in the Oval Garden, I still sought usable inspiration for the plant aspects of my proposed short stories. That is, if my memory would function normally. Memory? What? The battle had been constant. Battle? What? My head was engaged somewhere else as Tolly led me through the rambling villa to my accommodation for the night.

I was battling something—cross-cultural—good vs evil—I didn't know what. But with or without intoxication, I could not put a coherent, replicable and doable plan together for my design study. It was a simple task—but once I had my original public realm water fountain plan undone—my ability to restructure—restructure?—how many times have I started to restructure? It had become a "Herculean" task. Why?

Here's why it shouldn't have been "Herculean". I was in one of the most well known urban conurbations—an Arab medina—in Morocco—on the Mediterranean sea— in one of the most salubrious climates of the planet—yet I was struggling for plants, plant fragments, plant stories—plant content. Why? In this medina public realm there were no plants. Maybe in that observation was the link, the arc, the clue of how to approach my plant content. Naw, I couldn't see it.

Okay, some of the medina homes were *riads*—but only those of the wealthy, like the old American Legation and David—where was the public realm green?! Before my Tangier Municipality fiasco, I had done some WebCrawler research and found that the density of human habitation in the Tangier medina was about 500/hectare—more than double the average density of Manhattan! Where was the Tangier medina Central Park?

At the same time I was getting an unexpected education, new insights into plants and people—specifically hearing and portals—both of those fascinated me to the point where I thought I had interest suitable for an invigorating design study. Here I was at portals again, I didn't know what to do or where I was going. But hearing, music, sound... that maybe had something for me. Refuge... relief... away from the medina din... safely in the garden beauty... the music of Manuel de Falla... the succor of "Blues" music.

There had been a persistent emphasis on the sense of hearing during my medina and Hibiscus House experiences. I could link that into my stories. Not sure how. Hearing? Could it replace portals as my design arc linkage?

Taking a ride on the music—taking a ride on the plants? Trance? In the zone? I was definitely not in the zone. I concluded to keep it simple about plants.

The stories might become only a couple about the rare plant experiences I had already had. Just that in a medina of no plants, inspiration was hard to come by.

Like a too-fast carnival carousel, thoughts spun in my head—whenever I tried to draw conclusions, I found only confusion. Tolly led me under a pergola patina'd with a huge wisteria in second flower. The vine had to be decades old—and the flowers' fragrance? Their sweetness at least temporarily, cleared my head... calmed me. And the flower colors... softly blending pastels of lilac, lavender blue, by their health and fulness, inspired me. Suddenly, I felt refreshed.

I was still searching to find a richer inventory of plant content for the stories. I recalled how others put hearing together with plants, gardens and landscapes—Washington Irving's silver lute, Paganini, Lorca and Mahler. Magic was there somewhere. It sure was not on the pedestrian byways of the medinas.

But I was on the best track here in the Hibiscus House. And my second visit to the Oval Garden would hopefully boost my restructured design study. Tolly led as we worked our way across the many hallways and verandas of the sprawling

Hibiscus House to their guest wing.

In the hallway of the guest wing, which I came to call the Russian Wing, I heard Borodin's *Polovstian Dances*, which most people know popularly as *Stranger in Paradise* from the movie *Kismet*. The music was both soothing and energetically encouraging.

Tolly noticed my interest and suggested I might find the associated lyrics enlightening. He unlocked and opened the door to my room for the night, then showed me around the ensuite guest accommodation. He told me that when he departs, my room door would be locked to allow me a most peaceful sleep.

"Your room door will open with the tingling of brass bells at 3:30AM; and I will arrive at 4:00AM to accompany you to the Antechamber. Sleep well my friend." As he left the room, he pointed out the *Flowing Dance of Young Maidens* lyrics on a card attached to the back of my hallway door. The music took over.

I floated on that music. The music actually wrapped the poetic landscape lyrics I was reading. Together, they enthralled me. Words and music dissolved the present place and, through my sense of hearing, moved me to another place, oh so distant. Amazing!

At the bottom of the lyrics sheet, I read the contextual notes about the piece and found it was about cross-cultural problems. Female allures and music were attempting to bridge cross-cultural difficulties.

In Borodin's piece, the external music flows carried me. In the Oval Garden walk the next morning, I imagined, or hoped, internal sound flows or thought flows, released by sensual garden experiences, would carry me. Carry me where? I hoped to find out.

It was still about freedom—the searching—the discovery—the answer... the relief. And it had to come from the inside, from the hearing that connected inside and outside. That was how I imagined it.

Could or would such richness come from a walk in the garden? And that freedom that leads to personal discovery? Is that moment just immediately before discovery... is it not a portal... a threshold? And have we not the freedom to cross or not? This search for plant fragments, stories, arcs, themes... had turned into fundamental existential questions. And I was trying to simplify my search...

And so, despite my ever-present confusion, once again with great hope, I would begin a walk, my second walk, in the Oval Garden, this time at sunrise.

Sachy had once explained to me from her Vedic readings that *brahma muhurta* was a special time of day. The *brahma muhurta* was the time of day before sunrise. It was the inverse of the crepuscule, the twilight after sunset.

According to Sachy, the morning, just before sunrise, was supposed to be the most auspicious time of day for spiritual activity—a quiet time—when hearing could be crystal clear. I interpreted that as the time of day when one could pass, with least difficulty, through a transfiguration portal. I hoped I could easily encounter and pass through a plant portal. Couldn't disarm my portal intrigue.

Here I was at *brahma muhurta* in the Oval Garden at the Hibiscus House. I was ready.

***

The Second Walk

Tolly arrived at 4:00AM. He walked me to the antechamber. From the antechamber, I saw there was just a peep of color in the eastern sky. The candles were lit. The censers were softly emitting thin smokey wisps—solemn spiritual fragrance. The carnivorous plants were looking healthy. A combined effect of subtle alertness. That effect was accentuated by a steadily brightening sky— an evolving slow-motion shimmering beauty—the earliest diffracted rays. Those clear sky first rays announced the yet-to-be-seen rising sun.

Tolly brought out the dark chocolate wafer box. I took one of the six as before and let it dissolve on my tongue as I immersed myself in thought about the cocoa bean and the tree that produced it.

Then he poured the spiced white chocolate milk, which I drank in the same mood of appreciation of the plants from which all ingredients had originated.

Tolly informed me the antechamber terrace doors would automatically open thirty minutes before sunrise. Then he rotated out the wood table from the sideboard, opened the absinthe tantalus, set me up as before and he departed down the spiral staircase.

In the antechamber silence, I respectfully prepared and drank the absinthe. As the terrace doors opened, I walked out. Before descending the curving staircase, I paused to absorb the prospect from the outdoor terrace.

The Oval Garden path looked just as I remembered the other

day. The low bronze flame bowls, however, were extinguished. The sky, instead of twilight sunset, was sunrise, gloriously bright. I chose to walk the oval paving counterclockwise this time.

I was flummoxed as I looked across the oval lawn. I could swear I saw, for the first time, secondary paths leading from the gloriettas. That was encouraging. From my first Oval Garden walk, I had no memories of secondary paths. Well, so much for analysis... because in a moment, my gross senses quickly shut down intellectual analysis. I had no choice. It was my sense of smell—captured by climbing pink and red roses in bloom on the glorietta directly in front of me. Magical. Fragrant roses.

The scent of roses—their essence, their attar—rose water—the scent that from time immemorial has captured the hearts of both men and women. I asked myself, how does a fragrance actually capture a heart? Is that a threshold hint, a signpost? Had I experienced a partial channel transcendence into the spiritual? Analysis disappeared as I inhaled deeply, I entered the glorietta... paused... I remember hearing only my heart beat... and then...

After that, I once again remembered nothing of the Oval Garden. My next memory had me sitting in the antechamber with the empty box of dark chocolate wafers grasped in my hand.

"It was the roses of the first glorietta," I said. Tolly stood next to me.

Proudly, he said, "Roses at the glorietta—our own sports, selected for fragrance and late, long blooming characteristics: *Rosa damascena* and *Rosa centifolia*, as well as '*Climbing Crimson Glory*', '*Paul's Scarlet*', '*Madame Gregoire Staechelin*', '*Guinee*'... and that's the last I remembered. I must have fallen asleep or something; and Tolly must have arranged for a Petit Taxi.

Somehow, I made it back to my flat—just barely—I was busted—the entire Oval Garden sunrise event completely drained me. I must have climbed the entire six flights of stairs in a daze. I must have immediately collapsed into sleep at my place, because my next conscious memory was in my own bed morning the day after.

Only one thing on my mind as I awoke—no result. No memory! Not again!!

26-Connectors

Ecological Time

The second Oval Garden walk gave me nothing. It was bad. I was floating. I had no connectors. Phone calls with Sachy helped; but they were not "feet on the ground", "eyeball to eyeball" real life connectors. And in Tangier, where I was in real life, "feet on the ground"—I had nothing.

And my study? Totally deflated. No plants. No portals. No inspiration. Nothing worked. Two walks in the Oval Garden and zero memories.

I had to find out more. In the afternoon, I went back to Hibiscus House, hoping to explore further with Tolly and Fyodor how all my Oval Garden walks' memories had been curtailed. They were helpful.

They wanted to test my memory faculties with some of Fyodor's lab equipment. I was desperate to recall my Oval Garden walks, so I said I'd try anything. Tolly and I, along with Fyodor, who was carrying a large wooden case, slowly climbed the wrought iron circular staircase to the antechamber.

Fyodor opened the case. He took out a strange mechanical instrument that looked something like glasses, like night vision goggles, but with, in his own words, some augmented reality features at the eyes and the ears.

He handed the headset goggles to me and helped me put them on. The goggles had some kind of mechanical/electrical ear buds attached by coated wires to the headset. The buds were softly cushioned and fit comfortably deep into my ears.

Then he started making attachments around my eyes. From the outside edge of the complex series of lenses in each goggle piece was attached, by coated wire, a small diskette upon which he placed some kind of ointment before affixing them to my temples.

Then he pulled out a third diskette, just like the two on my temples. He applied ointment and attached it above my nose right between my eyebrows, the third eye location. Then he connected a wire from that third diskette to the nose bridge of the goggles.

I couldn't see anything. The goggles fit so that I had no peripheral vision at all. For the moment, all was black.

"Comfortable?" he asked.

"Yes," I said. But, inside, I was nervous. Not sure what to expect.

Then he removed the opaque lenses in front of each of my eyes.

I saw it all, everything in front of me, the Strait of Gibraltar landscape, the Oval Garden. But it was in some kind of flux. The landscape was huge and changing over time—geologic time—nothing stayed the same—it all changed—it all changed simultaneously—ecological time. Sameness obviously was a short-term illusion. And the parade of human civilization and their cultures passed with barely a notice.

I saw the minutest details changing. I had enhanced vision and time was eliminated—my temporal frame of vision was dislocated—relocated—the hugeness of time and the hugeness of the landscape combined into a massive, nay unfathomable ocean of perceptions. My thoughts became mental quicksand. My emotions depressed—increased anxiety—existential fear—breathing fast—head hot—sweat all over. The scale of the changes I witnessed made human presence insignificant.

Suddenly my own efforts had nothing—nothing to offer—nothing of value—I was insignificant in this current reality. My life had useless goals and intentions—downward, downward—life was draining out of my heart. I did not exist in something approaching infinity—I lost all touch with reality—I had only my belief in God to hold onto.

I stared through the goggles across the Oval Garden below us. Landscape roiling continued. I was thrown out of existential balance. If I had been standing, I would have fallen flat. My knees were trembling, my hands were trembling.

I was shaking, suddenly I was part of the entire history of the life and times of every living entity, every plant in the garden—their glorious passion in creation—their good, their healthy maintenance, their stewardship, their battles for life—their sad pain of death. Such hugeness on every level of emotion and intellect.

I knew not what was going on! I didn't count in this world. I and my thoughts were nothingness in this huge world picture. Sweat had been rolling down my forehead and my shirt collar was soaking wet. I was feeling... meaningless, useless, worthless—what? I gasped...

***

Discoveries?

Fyodor reached over and adjusted some things. He rotated some filters into place. The roiling landscape froth steadied and I saw clearly the paths, the plants and all the places I had visited on my first walk into the Oval Garden. My breathing gradually became normal.

With Fyodor's help, I lifted the goggles up a bit so I could see, with my bare eyes, the Oval Garden. It was as before, an oval—nothing more, nothing less. I slipped the goggles back on. I could see the sequence of the walk I had followed via the first glorietta on the left. Good stuff. I became excited. Was a result coming?

Not so fast. How could I see these new paths but not have memories? I saw connecting paths at the gloriettas, some twisting and turning—others forking again and again—all seemed to disappear into a complex intermingling with Italian cypress hedges. Details emerged—but they were... illusion?

The Italian cypress hedges aligned and reinforced the Oval Garden structure—then they didn't. They grew taller and taller, greyer and bluer into the distance as they merged with the color of the sea at the Strait of Gibraltar. Again, dizziness overwhelmed me. My stomach tightened and churned. My breathing—shallow—faster. I grabbed Fyodor's arm...

In response, he adjusted the filters again. The dizziness momentarily settled. I saw my second walk. Yet... yet... I still had no memory of either of those walks. Perplexing replaced dizziness. Suddenly, frightful tingling on my spine, then fearful chills of frustration, quickly heating to mental indigestion, intellectual constipation. Thoughts did not move.

Originally, I told them I had no memory of those walks. They knew my intent had been to look for plants and portals in the Oval Garden and just as I appeared to encounter a portal—each time, the portals seemed to disappear. I had no memories of the experiences or of any plants. This time, I saw paths, but...

Fyodor said to Tolly, "His memory works." Then Fyodor began to disassemble the headset goggles apparatus, glasses, lenses, wires, diskettes, putting them away in his carrying case. As he left the antechamber, he began whistling his usual, Shostakovich's *7th*, and disappeared down the circular stairs.

***

A New Path

I was still sitting in the antechamber—in a daze—perplexed, dizzy, exhausted—without result. Thoughts flowed again. All we see has always been shown. But there are so many things that I've never known. None of it made sense. If human civilizations passed like clouds of dust, then what was that horrible current I was feeling from people densely packing the medina byways?

If I was feeling such electromagnetic intensity, how could it be so insignificant as dust? And was it coming from humans or the landscape—the urban landscape? I was confused. I was embroiled in something... but what? Tolly, adding his own form of common sense, brought me to my senses.

He said, "So looking at the paths you walked does not spur memory recollection? Let's try another approach. Do you have a garden at your apartment, not like this, but well established?" I told him I did, and he said, "Go, and at sunrise, sit in it, follow the same preparations as you did here."

Frustrating it had become. It was like paying for the best seat in the concert hall and, after sitting there for two hours, not remembering the music. I had lost all memory connections. But my interest remained strong.

Tolly told me what I must do.

"Before you leave," he said, "I will prepare in a picnic basket for you to carry the components for two weeks of home cleansing—dark chocolate wafers, white chocolate milk, an absinthe tantalus."

Tolly busied himself in the sideboards assembling the

ingredients. He gave me instructions at the same time.

"Follow the same sequence at the same time of day. In addition, this is very important, in this Lalique snuff box, we have given you some vegetal salve, an unguent which includes highly evolved enzymes from carnivorous plants.

"Take a thin finger tip of salve, and as the sun begins to rise, gently massage it into your forehead at the spot between your eyebrows. Massage it slowly and steadily for three minutes. During this time, please engage your mind, intelligence and emotions in a mood of thankfulness for the beauty and service that plants give to humans.

"Then follow with the dark chocolate wafer, the spiced white chocolate milk, and the absinthe as before. After the absinthe, wait for ten minutes, then apply a thin finger tip of salve again and gently massage the third eye area for three more minutes, closing your eyes and meditating on plants, especially those in your terrace garden as they serve humans—and humans, as they serve plants.

"So, in essence, a circuit of service is complete. Doing this according to this schedule, you should open your eyes and enjoy the changes in the plants of your garden as the sun rises and begins to fill your garden with its rays. If all goes well, your memories of your walks in the Oval Garden should become manifest. If it does not happen the first time, you should repeat.

"Stay away from intoxication—your system must eliminate all artefacts of that past intoxication. Be advised, it might take a number of days of these efforts. Your patience will be your reward.

"This is a cumulative process to open and cleanse the ports, the connectors to your pineal gland. Your experiences have been registered there, and you will be able to access them. Keep your mentality right. Just as Fyodor said—50% plants, 50% humans. Absorb the plants with humility."

In the Petit Taxi on the way home, I thought more about how I could have seen all aspects of that garden and landscape over a huge geologic span of time as if time was not involved. That had been beyond my ability to understand—definitely disturbing.

Well, at least according to Fyodor, my memory faculties were in order. His conclusion increased my enthusiasm to regain my memory of those Oval Garden walks. That enthusiasm was a brief respite before the harsh reality imposed itself—I was still without memories.

Everyone had suggested the solution would be to back away from intoxication—and I did that. Maybe I needed more time—but it was already nearing the end of October. And what I had just experienced in Fyodor's memory test had wrung out my emotions and intelligence. I had to get something together. I had been looking for plant details; instead, I was overwhelmed by the largeness and complexity of landscape over time.

The next day, first thing in the morning, I did home cleansing according to Tolly's instructions. I was enlivened, hopeful certainly—but no results. Then I updated my Academic Advisor with an overly optimistic SitRep.

20 Oct 2000

Dear Neil,

I've spent the last week, every day at Hibiscus House—long days with the botanists and walking their garden. Things are happening.

Building up a substantial collection of short story ideas based upon plants and human culture—cross-cultural design impacts and plants in everyday life. Working titles as I sent you previously. I trust you are good with all that. Unless I hear differently from you, I am proceeding.

Will be developing structure, form and detail in those stories between now and end of November. Sachy is helping on the editing and will assist right through the last proofread edits. Final report to complete before Christmas according to revised schedule.

CJ

Another email playing with reality. I just could not speak of my frustrations to Neil.

Everybody had been telling me to get off the marijuana, the amphetamines, the morphine, the Seagrams. I had finally backed myself into that corner. After the time machine memory tremors, and without the Oval Garden results, I definitely had to follow instructions. Personal cleanup had to continue; and I had to be diligent. But I had no guarantee of results.

Cold drafts of frustration brought chills—what part of this was useful for my study? A glorietta? Italian cypress hedges? Were these the kinds of useful fragments that Sachy had urged me to develop?

I was feeling like Ibn Battuta, sailing in unknown seas. He knew there were ports around, but he just couldn't find them. I wasn't even sure I was headed in the right direction. I needed something more... something reassuring... a confirmation of some sort.

***

Strange Morning

I'd had more than a few good cross-cultural story ideas, a bit of story development... but my thinking still felt like it had a restriction, a governor... something like a stiff plaster cast constricting the development of stories, especially plant stories. Could it be damaging cross-cultural roots still tightening—sucking on my energy?

Flows of good stuff not happening. Or could it be something else? The intoxication cocktails had finished; but what about the alchemical absinthe and vegetal unguent?

Then I had a strange couple of mornings.

Some unusual story ideas emerged; but they had nothing to do with my Oval Garden visit memories, or lack of them. So, what was the source of these ideas? To make it simple, I concluded the ideas resulted from the absinthe preps I was taking every morning. Was that conclusion an easy way out? Yeah... but any other explanation was weird... other worldly.

Bottom line, I wasn't remembering my Oval Garden walks. I needed those Oval Garden memories. But those Oval Garden days, experiences, journeys, had generated a huge mystery, or mysteries—Interzone, Morocco—every time something seems to make sense, the rules change or the characters change or perceptions change. Might my missing Oval Garden memories have clues to resolve those cross-cultural anomalies? Or is this it? Morocco never clear? Not a wisp of clarity.

I had nothing. Just a handful of things I didn't understand at all.... Nevertheless, I kept at it. Stayed in working all day, trying to get a handle on things. Another day with nothing.

The next day at sunrise, as Tolly had recommended, I patiently continued home cleansing. Following that, I was sitting on the terrace when I saw the struggle of these terrace plants, especially their hardened, their cramped roots. Almost a punishment!

The plants were alive and to the untrained eye looked healthy; but they were silently suffering. That was the lot of the plants. Suffer while serving humans. Circuit of service? What exactly did that mean?

As I sat on the terrace, I felt sorry for the plants, and their cramped roots—like having to wear shoes two sizes too small. Interesting. I asked myself if I or Striet had been negligent in our circuit of service responsibilities to those plants? Agh, that didn't help me with my missing Oval Garden memories.

But then as I thought about the constricted roots... wait a minute... like animals in a cage... these plants no longer had their roots in the earth, only in an artificial cup of soil... they no longer had the richness of that "hard wired" direct connection into the deep landscape earth. Maybe I found a plant story there; but it had nothing to do with Morocco. Thought I had something; but when I tried to grasp it—poof—disappeared. Gone.

I tried to get serious about my study—story writing, developing more content... but it was a struggle. Took a midday break to walk Striet's Tangier spine—same teep BS. On the way back to my flat, I stopped at Madame Porte's to pick up a couple pain chocolat from their French bakery next door. Anything to give me encouragement... to make me feel better. Alas, none left.

Demain matin, inshaallah. So they said.

Tomorrow morning, God willing. Those words epitomized my collapse into North African fatalism. In the Petit Taxi, I realized I was feeling sorry for myself. My attempts to sustain a little of Western order—pain chocolat—had been foiled. Back at the flat, I grabbed my MP3 player and earphones.

Midday had slipped by, so in the afternoon shade, I sat down on the terrace, in the wicker chair, put my feet up and tried to relax. Replayed the last played—Paganini *Caprice No. 6* solo violin—suited my mood. Western music, memories of Sachy. I listened to it over and over.

I let the tune weave a cocoon of Western culture around me. Was I slipping into a trance? What was I actually hearing? Can a caprice be sad? It should be lighthearted—but it was oddly sad—slow, almost dirge-like.

I nearly cried listening to it—was I hearing my North African misfortune rendered into music? I missed Sachy; but the beauty of the violin ignited within me the smallest kernel of hope—and it grew—the hope from which I needed to draw the strength to succeed with my study and return home, back to Sachy.

That growth of hope felt like a well of optimism pouring out abundant fresh water. And as flowing fresh water wonts, voices emerged from the flow. Before long I heard words. Then the words carried meaning.

I heard, "The garden of the Hesperides has the secrets you seek."

"How can I find that garden?" I asked.

"Do not try to find it, it will find you—it issues melodies sweet and strong that, once heard, become means of transport, strong and beautiful as trees, that will carry you and your heart to the very central core of the garden."

I couldn't believe my ears. The water of hope still flowed. I heard more. What was I "hearing"? Who was I "hearing"?

"But you need not worry about taking that voyage, or finding that door, because I, keeper of the Eden apple, too, have that message."

This was not the first time I felt spellbound during my stay in Tangier. Spellbound!? Hell, I felt spellbound since I crossed the stormy strait from Algeciras to Tangier... those thoughts were interrupted by my sense of hearing.

"Listen carefully to my words—in them you will find the key to unlock that for which you seek—the Hesperides were tasked with tending the grove—understand that and the blessings of the Hesperides will be yours eternally."

Neither that afternoon, that night, nor the next morning did I understand what had just happened. Such a strange

440

mystery cum dream? ...remaining to be solved. This felt quite like listening to a Faeryland story from Bree. The sun had set. The temperature on the terrace was Mediterranean Sea comfortable.

I was puzzled. What does the landscape contain that is part of the cultures inhabiting it? Hesperides. Faeryland. The Tangier teep street culture. Landscape good. Landscape bad. Landscape mysteries.

Then I had one of those nights where, as is the case with many people, sleep did not want to come. I felt something was about to emerge, landscape, gardens, plants... Fyodor. Could there be rootlets from the landscape emitting electromagnetic flows into humans?

Then I thought again. In my terrace garden I heard or rather sensed plant concerns over their root bound conditions—there was nothing natural about that. So, what was this riddle I just heard? Might it have been the growing effectiveness of the alchemical absinthe and vegetal salve intake?

Were these useful story fragments? These recent experiences... fragments... daydreams... trances... made me wonder about the breadth and depth of the landscape. Landscape was more than a freeze frame picturesque photo of natural beauty.

There were at least, and historically arguable, two intertwined forces of significant strength—natural landscape and cultural landscape. Were those two forces independent or were they linked—linked by other than ideas? The "linkages"? Real or imagined? Truly mysterious.

But my hope was, even though wavering, ceaseless. That was my strength. I expected stories to emerge at the furthest, ill-defined edges of those "linkages". Even with hope, my uncertainty remained weighty.

*** *

Botany Book

Absinthe, chocolate, carnivorous plant unguents... portals, music, landscape linkages... unfortunately, just wasn't coming together. And, I still couldn't get the plant memories, fragments, or stories happening so I went to Piliers Culturels, looking for a basic botany book, something like a school book. Perhaps by reviewing the scientific basics of botany, I could use those threads to weave into fragments for stories. That was my hope. When I arrived at the store, I was surprised to see out front, not Mme Zsófia but Mme Olga.

I said, "It is nice to see you. I am surprised to find you out front. Is everything okay with Mme Zsófia?"

"Christopher, it is a pleasure to see you again. Mme Zsófia? She had to step away for a moment. How are you and how is your design study?"

I thought back to our earlier conversations when I first met Mme Olga in the bookstore back room. We had talked about the old magic shop off the Socco Chico and the unusual young person who visited their shop back then. I remembered that Mme Olga had called him an "ancient". An "ancient" ... that had stuck with me.

Then I answered her question, "My design study? I'm still struggling..."

"Struggling? How so?"

"Roots. I'm entangled by cultural roots and despite having met the guys at Hibiscus House, I have no memories of walking their Oval Garden—so I am feeling strangled by roots I can't see and memories I can't find."

She took my hand and held it warmly saying, "Sit down, relax a moment. Let's talk. Maybe I can help. Tell me."

"Do you remember, a while back, when you and I first talked, you spoke about evileye and how the *Magreb* cleanses itself. Then you mentioned someone you met when you first arrived in Tangier when you were working in a small curios shop off the Petit Socco..."

Mme Olga interrupted me, "Stop right there. Here's how I can help. It is clear to me you have been and still are under its influence. It happens to a lot of young first-time visitors. We call that, rather harshly, due to their naivety."

"What?"

"Let me explain. In this part of the world there are too many legends about the past before the past..."

"What do you mean?"

"Who are the Berbers? What is Atlantis? Who were the Greek gods? Who were the Egyptian gods?"

She continued, "The stories, the legends are all the same. About good vs evil. That battle always rages in this place very near the surface. We breathe the dust of that battlefield and that dust can infect us." I had already figured something in my life was out of balance. Mme Olga had me listening intently.

"Protection comes in many forms; and the old lady from the curios shop told me that *Anquietas*, the ancients, had the powers to overcome, by various means, the evil."

"If I am infected, what should I do?"

"I do not have that knowledge. But I can tell you what I've heard. Return to your birth home and take the clean airs. In time they may purify the dust that rests in you." My back shivered as her words sank in.

"But what can I do now, I have to do my study."

"Just do it and put aside your worries. The worries feed the infection. That is what I hear."

At that moment, Mme Zsófia entered the shop.

"Oh, Christopher, nice to see you. It's been a long time. I hope Mme Olga has been helpful. Are you looking for a book or is this just for conversation?" Her words were soothing— brought me back to a visceral reality.

"I need a school book on the subject of botany, do you have anything?"

Mme Zsófia brought out a botany book in English. Used—a high school textbook. I paged through it. Lots of classic line drawings—all the basics. I bought it and headed back to my flat. I needed to be in a safe place. I needed to make my study work. I needed to finish then get back to Sachy and my homeland.

***

Cultural Hand-hold

But my trip to the bookstore for the botany textbook did not end there. Out of my simple visit to Mme Zsófia's normally comfortable bookstore, something else went awry. First Mme Olga confirmed that an evil dust might be infecting me—I tended to believe that. Then I found something in that Botany book, a folded-up piece of paper with a message—something that triggered me deep down.

It was not just a something—it had started recently at Hibiscus House when I was wearing Fyodor's memory glasses— the immensity of the landscape changes over time had brought to the forefront my persistent fears of existential nothingness—a soul-destroying uselessness—I thought I had snapped out of it; but my trip to the bookstore showed me how close to the surface was that nauseous depression. And that— after my good vs evil talks with Mme Olga?!! I had to call Sachy.

<u>Parsec/muse404 Text Exchange 27 Oct 2000</u>

muse404: Are you available to talk 10AM your time today? Need to talk. If yes, I will telephone you.

Parsec: 10AM today, my time, I'll be ready, can't wait.

At a critical moment in my study, this phone call exchange was pivotal.

"Hi LittleWing?"

She "read" my tone of voice and said, *"You sound lower than vexed. What's happened?"*

"I'm frightened… frightened of what I've become… My life here always leads me into meaninglessness. I hit some bottom—deep. Like an endless fog… Couldn't shake it. Can't shake it. In the used botany book I bought a couple days ago, I came across a folded piece of paper. I unfolded the paper and found an Edgar Allen Poe poem inside, 'A Dream within a Dream'. It got right down underneath everything that has had me down here. Remember when we texted the other day and you asked what is really at the bottom of all this?"

"Yes… yes…"

"Well, you know, I am not much into philosophy, but that poem led me to feel everything I am doing here, even my life, is just useless. And just this last week at HH, I was trying to recover my Oval Garden memories and fell into a horribly depressing funk where nothing mattered. I felt this once before when we were in that huge commercial lavender field one summer just outside the university. Remember?"

"Yes… but what about that back then has got you today?"

"Uselessness… then and now… as I remember it, back then we talked about my inner feeling of uselessness long and deep. We talked about my parents' separation and divorce which left me with an internal cavity, an emptiness. Maybe even a rot. I was missing something—related to being a young kid, weakened by the lack of a wholesome relationship without both parents at home."

"Yes, I remember…"

"Well, Poe's poem today fell into my hands by chance. I was trembling like in that lavender farm field… like at HH last week… and before I finished that poem—trembling—sweating profusely—nauseous—couldn't write—couldn't think. You might say it is just a poem; but his 'Dream within a Dream' poem is much more because I look at it on top of all the events during my time here in Morocco… the persistent way things here in Tangier undermine—choke my study. Well this poem brought them and

446

my life altogether in a painfully depressing way. That poem has crippled me.

"Crippled, I feel crippled will power. I feel like some incurable, relentlessly growing rot has attached itself to my deepest, already damaged tap root. I am shaking internally as I say these very words."

LittleWing said, *"As I begin, I do not expect you to feel anything like help; but as I continue, you might start to feel some relaxing of the depressive tension.*

"How many times have we sat on the porch in the summer on beautiful warm days enjoying the shade, the breeze, sharing a glass of lemonade, when up comes a change of weather, a storm. The wind rises, the sky darkens, first distant thunder, then soft lightning, then the roaring wind, rain, hail, violent lightning and cracking thunder. It goes and goes. Ear splitting. Vicious. Then it starts to relent.

"It continues its retreat, the sky lightens, blue sky streaks appear and before long the sun is out, the wind and rain storm is gone and the landscape is crisp, beautiful to see. The air is clean, wonderful to breathe. The wind is silent, only birdsong on gentle breezes.

"Remember those days?"

I said nothing. She had more to share.

"All of us feel that kind of mental, intellectual, that existential storm from time to time. It wrenches our insides with the most hopeless twisting. But it passes. Calm returns. Emotions are relieved. Intellect returns to make decisions. Normalcy in our daily life returns. Some experience this more frequently than others. It seems that some people who, like yourself, experience these very infrequently, are most heavily shattered by the experience.

"Different people turn to different religions. You and I find our soothe in plants, gardens and landscape.

"Do you follow?"

I felt sullen.

"Can you hear me," she asked, "I mean, really hear me, inside?"

I felt detached from her words, but I answered, "I hear most of it."

LittleWing continued, "The black, the dark is always there, we have the choice to sink into it or go toward the light. The light, remember? Find something that attracts you and do something positive with the time we have that we call life, you know?"

I sat, nothing but silence. Even my thoughts were silent.

She continued, "Just so happens that, recently, I have been reading about some Bengali poets. They were writing about the Ocimum sanctum. Remember, about a month ago, I told you about that Hindu religious plant Tulsi devi, as a way to think about plants. Remember?"

"Yeah."

"Well this one Bengali poet, Candrasekhara, had a very clear way of describing our human life with plants. Let me read the English translation:

> 'Tulsi devi, you engladden and shower your rain of mercy upon one who offers you service…
> And whoever takes shelter of you has his wishes fulfilled.
> My desire is that Tulsi devi will grant me residence in the pleasure groves.'

"This is your path. This has been our path. Pleasure groves have been what we've shared. It has been one of the bonds that makes us strong. Together we have been enlightened, enthused, recharged. We have been happy and jolly around plants, in gardens and landscapes. Is this not so?"

"Yes. Yes, of course."

"And do you not wish to share these experiences with me again? Because for me it is certainly my deepest hope."

"Yes, yes… of course I do."

"Listen please, you have a great approach to the restructuring

448

of your design study. The stories you have sent me are coming along nicely. And I think you are addressing the larger picture appropriately. The way I understand it you are taking plants, people and the stresses of urban cross-cultural realities and weaving a tapestry of short stories to enthuse landscape architect designers and the public to seek shelter in the beauties of plants, gardens and landscapes. Is that not so?"

"Yes."

"Well, take a deep breath or two. Enjoy the simplest pleasures of your terrace garden. Recharge from that. Set up your schedule so that all is complete and we can pass this Christmas and New Year together! I need you in my arms!

"You've got an agreed schedule with your Academic Advisor, right?"

"I do, right."

"Well, time to write what you can. Write what you have. Grind it out. You have concluded your author voice and narrator style, right?"

"Not yet, but I'm working on those."

"I can help with that. Let me know. Now start building out each story and craft the plot flow, sentence structure and grammar. Good craft takes time. Work on it as a discipline every day.

"And if you are troubled moving story ideas forward, move the plots from dark to light, or from confusion to clarity, or from complexity to simplicity. Keep it simple. Focus on plants, gardens, landscapes and the absence of access to them in the urban public realm. That's your domain, right?"

She added, "Grab onto those things that have brought joy and light to your life. Hold on tightly. They repay your steadiness."

That was how I remember the conversation. Her voice was like sunlight breaking through storm clouds. I brightened before we finished.

I had to turn that telephone call emotional uplift into "boots on the ground" result in real life in Tangier. Once again, I wasn't sure. I didn't have plant story stubs or fragments; but I did have hope—much stronger.

27-Production

Surfacing

I'd just about given up hope when it happened.

Memories of the Oval Garden surfaced for the first time. I must explain this word for word as I remember it.

I had been following the regularly scheduled discipline, the early morning pineal cleansing procedure.

This one morning on my terrace, as I watched the first rays of the sun break through palm tree fronds... before I heard the first autos down on the street, I was transported to my first walk in the Oval Garden.

Memories emerged. Everything I had realized during that first walk became clear and present in my memories. My memories were not details of plants or garden construction. Rather, I had clarity about the most essential component of garden exploration. And that component helped distinguish gardens as a distinctive subset in the landscape—a protected subset—a safe subset.

And in that safe subset, it was about sound. A garden was not proper until all I could hear were my own footsteps. No other human intrusions except the sound of my shoes on the path.

But even that was too much noise. Thus, I needed a bench, and one was nearby. The bench was required.

There was the noise of my steps, and there was the noise of my metabolic presence. Everything was pumping while I walked.

When I sat, when I sat quietly—no walking—no talking—additional wrappings came off my ears. I heard differently. I could hear the garden.

Slowly the channels of communication opened. As that quiet level was reached, new portals became accessible—at least, that is how I thought. My sense of sight seemed to focus on details of trunks, bark, stems, leaves, buds, flowers—each begging for deeper exploration. I was spoiled for choice. Like the fun of youth, the exploration spilled all over me. Time disappeared.

Later, when I tried to recall the details, they were missing. I was, however, able to maintain big picture memories. My first walk in the Oval Garden started with my sense of smell entrancing me into a state where only my sense of hearing guided my garden experiences. Before that day, I had seen objects of visual beauty as labels, only as labels.

Explanations had been thin. But objects previously only of visual beauty had become new worlds for exploration—where sound, never before heard, connected via pineal to deep memory. Where reality exploded with dreams, with visions, with insights.

What gardens were these?

Fyodor had once told me about a colleague of his who had concluded that certain plants had abilities—in his words, an electro-dynamic inverse doppler effect that enabled two-way communicatory connections or meta-communications with humans. Could that have been? Something happened—was it portals? Because, as a result, a richness of plant story ideas sat before me like the first view of a spectacularly flowering June English garden border. Richer than sight, fragrance and sound combined.

And as easily as I had entered into those memories, I exited. Take it for what it's worth. It did happen like that. My free will had evaporated. I had the memories briefly in my grasp... and then.... But I felt clarity strengthening—like a dawning sunrise.

Gardens were different from landscapes. Gardens were secure, safe. Free from aggressive animals, free from aggressive humans. They were places to relax, to listen without fear. I had an essence—an essence for my plant stories. I had the essence. Sound—the sense of hearing.

**

And More...

Shortly after the first resurfacing of my memories of the Oval Garden, a second batch of memories came to the surface.

Such enjoyment for me when memories of the Oval Garden walks resurfaced. Rich inspiration for stories, or so I hoped. The resurfacing memories strengthened my convictions to emphasize the place of plants in the urban realm for humans and in design for landscape architecture. I finally had actionable benefits from my walks in the Oval Garden. I had the inspiration for plant stories in my design study. And there was more to come.

My pineal gland must have softened into normalcy because the next morning, after following the pineal cleansing discipline, it happened again in my apartment, outdoors in the terrace garden. As I recall, it happened like the following.

I was inspecting the plants on the terrace, examining closely the flower petals of a particularly healthy and glowing *Osteospermum fruticosum*. The petals were neither white nor glowing magenta, but carried pencil-thin, deep purple parallel lines along the petal length with a white background.

As I started to inspect the glowing inner circle of bright yellow pollen-filled anthers and the outer circle of dark blood purple ovaries my perception of space and time started gently hiccupping. I could not clearly see the now.

The African daisy was stuttering—kind of like a flickering cathode ray tube television picture—getting worse, not better. I had to go sit.

Relaxing on my wicker chair, I closed my eyes, and consciously inhaled the Med air. I slowly filled my lungs. Suddenly, I was walking deep into the Oval Garden, well beyond the first glorietta. Through hazy sequences of narrow dark tunnels into open sunlit courtyards with uncertain passages of noisy water into expansive, though introverted, gardens with only a quiet tinkling of water discovered here and there. I saw it all. I heard it all. My memories were clear as real life.

It was quiet. Only the hum of insects. The songs of birds. The casual flutterings of butterflies. The singular zipping beauty of a hummingbird, and the sweet presence of happy, healthy plants.

I thought the first sign of freedom was the ability to choose how to protect myself, feed myself, and shelter myself. Yeah, gardens are protected places, free from fear. Landscapes, including urban landscapes, always have fear lurking. Natural fears—cultural fears—social fears—medina fears—countryside fears—always there. Thus gardens—as safe spaces—very important—nay—essential to human civilization. They are an existential essential! Then I had to ask myself the next question. Wouldn't that make riad gardens the smart essential solution for the Tangier medina?

And the first sign of intelligence was I didn't have to be engaged 24/7/365 in my protection, feeding or sheltering.

The first sign of wealth was that I could step aside from my protection, feeding and sheltering. I could move away temporarily without endangering those three elemental activities. I had such strange garden realizations. Those were my memories of my walk—more about the essence of human culture than landscape architectural details.

By those measures, as I sat in these gardens in Tangier, I was free, intelligent and wealthy.

Beyond those elemental conditions, it was just a matter of metrics. And it was a matter of sadness when any of those were taken to a greedy, selfish extreme. But taken to extreme was by and large the human nature. Never quite satisfied. Always looking for some new portal. Me, too? Not being satisfied by the minimum. That is not criminal, is it? The happy plants

457

around me erased my troublesome questions.

Then I heard a diesel engine, and a truck horn from somewhere. And then I heard a stubborn donkey braying nearby.

...oh yeah... now the day began...

I recognized I was sitting on my apartment terrace in Tangier, and the sun had risen just enough to pleasantly warm me.

I had crossed a threshold... and found missing memories.

***

Real Progress

The resurfacing memories continued to roll on—or was it real time results from successful pineal cleansing? I walked across the terrace. Looked at the plants. Time for water. At each pot I watched carefully at each and every plant as I slowly watered. The entire time of watering must have been an hour or more. After I finished watering, I sat again in my wicker chair on the terrace.

The morning had clouded, but somehow, as it is, in Tangier, often wont to do, the sun broke through, and beams of sunlight fell across the terrace plants. How could these plants have delivered a unified message to me? Maybe my ears adjusted their filters? Or, did I imagine this? Or, did I just want to hear it? Mysterious—communication reality.

Flowers, stems, leaves, ensemble told me that beheld beauty, by humans of plants, is a simple act. Spiritual refreshment from plants' beauties requires not one bit of complex thinking; not one bit of complex industry; not one bit of complex technology; not one bit of mechanical logistics.

It is simple.

—it is—

Flowers, stems, leaves, just are.

Humans have only to see, to hear, to smell, to touch, to think about plants in order to enter into the simplest of relationships with them. It does not cost anything. I was in a strange landscape. Simultaneously inside and outside?

No!

Wherever I was—I was beyond those simple dualities.

It was clear. It was refreshing. I returned. Returned? Returned from where? I had no answer—but my experiences were real. This must have been my passage through a supra dimensional stomata that allowed my consciousness to pass but removed my awareness of body, time and space.

Now I was ready to write.

The plants had provided a portal—never quite so clear as architectural doors and gates that humans built, but a portal just the same. Some may call enlightenment the crossing of the portal threshold. For me it was just seeing things clearly—adding the light of clarity—it was... thanks to the offering by the plants.

For me, those experiences caused realizations that were as plain as the nose on my face! The simplicity of plants as inspiration. The simplicity of plants' sensual, mental, intellectual accessibility. The multitudinous historical and contemporary layers of human-plant connectivity. All those realizations were high density, high intensity, real life. The real real.

I knew I was in the right direction. I was at the root of landscape architecture and it was my study. It was making sense. Had I been communicating with plants on my terrace? I sure had. Didn't understand how—but it happened.

I had encountered a portal and crossed. I wanted to know more about how plants facilitated this timelessly sought-after experience—clarity, trance, enlightenment—what to call it? I wanted to know more about plants and humans on this connection level. That thirst persisted.

In the final days of October, I utilized those moments of clarity and memory to develop my stories about plants. Before the first week of November, almost all stories had outline structures completed. I was working through rough drafts with some already into second drafts.

LittleWing's communications and edits had given me a sharper perspective, a deeper understanding and a peaceful foundation. She had suggested a narrower focus which had weeded out many of my disturbing and dangling stories. At the same time, she had shown me how to enrich my more useful stories. Now she was editing all.

I continued my morning cleansing routines, amazed by the story inspiration I had been receiving from plants. When these inspirational moments happened, I often could not tell the difference between dreams, imagination, real life... but ideas and perceptions flowed.

Dare I say, it looked like I finally had this restructured design study on its way to completion. Despite persisting internal questions and a range of external difficulties, I did come out of October and into November in production mode. And I was making progress. Neil was pleased with my SitReps.

My relationships with Tolly and Fyodor were at their best. I spent as much time as I could with them and in their library. But when I tried to get another walk through their Oval Garden, I learned they had no time in their schedule.

***

Trance Artisans

Some people call it enlightenment. Others call it trance. I liked trance. What had happened to me in my Oval Garden walks and their memories afterwards was, indeed, trance. Trance was a convenient word to describe the indescribable. We were in mystery country here. Suspension of disbelief.

I prefer to call it that place where "science" has not yet reached. Not dissimilar to the time in human history when everyone thought the earth was flat—and they were okay with it.

At the Hibiscus House, Fyodor and Tolly were exploring just beyond the boundary of contemporary science.

Answering my questions in the library, Tolly explained to me how, every November and December, he and Fyodor went to Europe where they acquired the basics for their antechamber preparations. He said they had individual specialists for both the absinthe and the chocolates. Specialists? I thought of them as trance artisans.

"So you guys go to Europe every winter for a two-month shopping trip?" I asked lightly.

Fyodor sniffed and chuckled.

Tolly answered, "Do I have to teach you everything? We do a little essential shopping but our destination is the Jungfrau Region of the Swiss Alps. It is a large landscape that for centuries has been lovingly cared for by its inhabitants. The result is a landscape of uniquely high inspirational quality. It is a regional landscape that gives transcendent portals very easily—so different from north west Africa. The Jungfrau

Region people sing with and to their landscape—quite unusual—quite enlightening."

"Maybe I will visit there sometime; but tell me more about how you get absinthe and chocolate, if you will?" I asked.

"The absinthe specialist comes from Spain, just north of Valencia. It is a processing and unusual blend of Mediterranean herbs yielding an absinthe with the appropriate amount of thujone that works in conjunction with the chocolate. Fyodor does the linking chemistry, the quality control, or I should say he does the linking alchemy between the absinthe and the various chocolates."

Regarding the chocolates, Tolly explained that they go to Paris to resupply their chocolate inventory. From a company in business for over a century, harvesting *Theobroma cacao* from all corners of Africa and the Americas. They inventory each batch, according to its very rarely found liminal qualities, through careful chemical and experimental analysis.

Then Tolly told me a brief story about one of Fyodor's colleagues whom they visit when in France.

"He is a specialist of French rose gardens, and by the way, provided the original roses we now have on the gloriettas. Anyhow and more importantly, he, after a student apprenticeship in the greenhouses and laboratories of Vilmorin, has been engaging in research tracing back the history of roses, you might call him a forensic botanist chasing the landraces of the Josephine roses. He now works behind the scenes in private greenhouses and laboratories in the gardens of Courances. His hobby is painting copies of Redouté's roses for sale in tourist shops.

"You must have heard about Redouté?"

He didn't give me time to respond. Rather he quickly continued on the subject of surrogate portals. He went on about Redouté's roses and Withers' orchids, wrapping it all up with another sling at me, asking, "Christopher, I am amazed that you've never heard of Redouté, Withers, Bateman, Cook or Banks. The golden age of plant exploration? And your American universities actually honor students with Landscape Architecture degrees without that historical understanding?"

That was one sling too many. I'd had enough of that. I had work to do. I excused myself and left for my apartment. Despite their tiresome nagging at Hibiscus House, I did benefit from my visits. My inventory of plant source fragments had grown ever so large. But, for me, a challenge yet remained—a trackable arc. My time was getting horribly short, but I couldn't deny my interest in an all-encompassing theme.

Trance, portals and surrogate portals? All gray and foggy. Still a struggle. A plant portal leading to trance—was it just a thought? Was it transfiguration? Was it a supra-stomatic cultural realization? Was it just the unexpected pleasure of exquisite, beyond reproach, beauty to be discovered in the components and character of plants?

And I had other questions—about the landscape. How does energy pass from the landscape into humans? And what is the difference in that energy transfer between farmers in the rural landscape when compared to medina people in the urban landscape?

For me, that hunt continued. But there was something growing in my expanding experiences and definition of landscape... might it become the glue... the arc that could link all my stories—people, plants, gardens, landscape?

***

Pearly Gates

As October drew to a close, I continued the sunrise absinthe and chocolate pineal cleansing. Likewise, I continued story writing—sent them to Sachy for edit—received her comments and cleaned up as appropriate. The process was working.

But I should have remembered... things in Tangier always unexpectedly twist away.

I was not so far from finishing. Neil liked my content and he gave approval to my newest restructured design study. And I had a bunch of stories and story ideas already under development, including the recently remembered plant content from my Oval Garden walks.

But the local culture? It had generated stories... but in real life, daily activity, it was still like an albatross—weighing me down. Fortunately, I had a pleasant place to work in my apartment and I could finish the final deliverable in Meknes, which was immeasurably easier on the street.

Getting into the nitty-gritty of my work, I still needed help. My mind just couldn't wrap around the details of story writing. I couldn't figure out why. I recalled my last phone call with Sachy and the existential trauma that had precipitated it. The trauma still lurked—a ghost over my shoulder. It was the diametric opposite of what I expected to find, what Bo expected, what all artists and musicians search for—the portal to joy—the portal to a place free from existential trauma—free from suffering—free from lying, cheating and hurting.

My mom and dad were both brought up Christian and

that was always in my background. Pearly Gates. That was it. That was the portal. And entering the Pearly Gates was the beginning of a joy not known at its fullest in the material world.

Fyodor and Tolly—they figured plants were there to give a taste of that Pearly Gate joy. Yeah, that was the Christian definition of a portal. A plant, garden or landscape portal would never be construed as a Christian religious alternative— but it may be considered like a sampler of that for which we humans existentially have sought throughout written history.

That did not quite come to grips with my adventure here in Tangier—my search for a portal—but maybe it was my surrogate. This local culture put me into such a traumatic displacement that I had to seek peace, I had to seek joy—thus my search for the portal experience.

That thinking was as close as I ever got to understanding anything in my six months in Tangier, Morocco.

***

Not Quite and Quite

Pearly Gates thoughts? I put them aside because I had to finish my stories. They weren't quite smooth yet. Trying to get them all into some kind of parallel structure, I had to concede that portals, Pearly Gates, would not be the unity glue. I sought more technical help from Sachy.

<u>Parsec/muse404 Text Exchange 28 Oct 2000</u>

muse404: You in?

Parsec: Right here, how're you?

muse404: Quick one. You got me thinking.

muse404: Short story author voice.

muse404: American student?

muse404: American expat?

muse404: Or indifferent Moroccan culture observer?

muse404: What do you think?

Parsec: All three fit you, so which has the richest emotional threads inside you?

muse404: Hmmm…

muse404: Indifferent cultural observer if I can maintain the indifferent bit.

Parsec: Make it a mysterious cultural observer that lets you add subjectivity and you can let the reader solve the mystery.

muse404: Not bad, definite potential. But I am an American student--I feel better with who I am. I'll go with that.

Parsec: I understand. Being yourself should permit easier flows of stories--go for it!

muse404: Second question, narrator.

muse404: First, second or third person?

Parsec: Go first because it lets you put the intensity of your experiences up front for the reader.

muse404: Yeah, that is what I was favoring.

Parsec: Anything else?

muse404: No, just wanted to text you. You happy?

Parsec: Yes.

muse404: I mean *really*?

Parsec: Definitely! Can't wait to feel you in my arms.

muse404: That's what I'm talking about. Now, I feel energized.

muse404: Thanks for your help.

Fiddled around with a couple stories, using LittleWing's suggestions. Some promise there—I could feel my direction and my stories getting stronger. Her structural support ideas were actually giving a unifying glue to my work. Things were coming together.
Finally at rest.
My contacts with Sachy had increased to an almost daily texting.

Parsec/muse404 Text Exchange 30 Oct 2000

muse404: You in?

Parsec: I was hoping to hear from you…

muse404: I'm good. Have had two great days in a row. Writing good. Energy good.

muse404: Your last edits were inspirational! But something has been niggling me in the background--and I wonder about it--it could be a part of a couple of my stories; but I want to get your thoughts before I use it…

Parsec: Something's got you--what is it?

muse404: I've had a couple, I don't know what to call it, dreams? Imaginary events? And they all seem to come in relation to a discussion I had with a Peace Corps volunteer maybe two months ago--I really didn't take it seriously…

Parsec: What is it?

muse404: It was a new Peace Corps Volunteer, recent graduate. If I had to put a label on her, I would say she might be a white witch…

Parsec: What?

muse404: She talked about what I would call mythology, fairies and their battles that coincide with cultural/geographical battles in real life.

Parsec: That sounds wild!

muse404: Wild it was. I just wiped it from my memory. But… but… I had a series of dreams, visions that could easily be linked to Greek mythology while seemingly relating to my study… c'mon, fairies? What do you think?

Parsec: Wow, you sure have gotten yourself into a real mixer there. As I think about it, I see two issues clearly. First, on the question of should you write about it--if it is a landscape item based in your regional geography of stories--why not, especially if you have the creative fire. Second, on the subject of fairies, white witches and, dare I say, the like. In the Vedic readings I have done, especially the Srimad Bhagavatam, there are loads of life forms that have existed on and around this planet during different ages and under the different modes of nature--goodness, passion and ignorance.

So there is that. I'd have to do some research to give any more details. Bottom line--write what motivates you. Send it to me for the usual edit stuff, ok? Is that helpful?

muse404: ...helpful? Yeah, but everything that happens to me here forces me to look at landscape, gardens and plants from new angles of vision. Somewhere, I'm just going to have to draw a line, otherwise my stories will have all breadth and no depth.

Parsec: You're not slipping, are you?

muse404: No, no, no... with the exception of that fairy stuff, I'm bright--I'm focused.

Parsec: So glad to hear that. Will you make your final deliverable schedule?

muse404: Yeah, I'll make it happen. It will be a push and there might be some difficulty because I will be finishing in the month of Ramadan...

Parsec: How will that be difficult?

muse404: Muslims' normal days are turned upside down for the month of Ramadan.

muse404: They fast all day, sunrise to sunset. Eating only at night.

muse404: So their daily rhythm is out of sync. But it should work out okay. I've already met the maalem, the craftsman who will make the leather covers and bind the final deliverable books.

Parsec: Listen, if you need any more editing help let me know, okay?

muse404: Yeah, thanks. It's good to know I've got back up from you, thank you.

muse404: What you've given me so far has been priceless. Thank you ever so much.

Relief all around. It's happening—the study, on the run.

***

470

Dystopian Nightmare

I could sense the finish approaching. It was a deep comforting feeling—on the verge of a major life goal—university graduation. I'd been through a lot, a real dystopian marathon of cultural and physical imbalance. Finishing this study and returning home was my dream of peaceful pleasure.

<u>Parsec/muse404 Text Exchange 4 Nov 2000</u>

muse404: You in?

Parsec: Yes, had to do shopping, just got back, you okay?

muse404: Yeah, no troubles.

muse404: How about you?

Parsec: I'm fine, you still on schedule?

muse404: On home stretch.

muse404: Plan to depart Tangier for Meknes final deliverable on 30 Nov.

muse404: Plan to fly out of Casablanca, via Brussels and NYC, home arriving 11 December in time for Christmas.

Parsec: Is it confirmed?

muse404: Still have to do that. As soon as I have it confirmed I'll email all the flight stuff.

muse404: You'll let my mum and dad know, won't you?

Parsec: Sure, be glad to. I'll give them this update and then send flight info after you confirm.

Parsec: Need anything else?

muse404: Well...

Parsec: Do you need any more editorial support?

muse404: Naw, it's all working out just fine. Thanks for all. Couldn't have done it without you.

The next day, I worked through my list of stories. Developed a couple second drafts. Good progress.

Paella time. Sidi Hamete knocked on the door. As usual, she had gone by the time I opened the door. Brought the hot paella *tajine* in and tucked into it. While eating the warm meal, I felt my confidence grow and I knew that I would complete my study.

That evening texted Parsec.

Parsec/muse404 Text Exchange 5 Nov 2000

muse404: You in?

Parsec: Yes, hold on, BRB.

Parsec: Sorry, am cooking lunch, how're you doing?

muse404: Yeah, good, all is well. After your edits, made good progress over the past week No problems here, you?

Parsec: I'm good, got anything new for me?

muse404: Naw, just wanted to check in.

Comforting. Took rest.

In the morning on the terrace I found light overcast and no direct sun. The plants actually looked relieved not to have full sun for a change.

Applied pineal unguent—only the unguent now—by Tolly's instruction before he and Fyodor went on their long European shopping trip. I found the unguent and subsequent meditative approach on the terrace led me to one or another of my stories. Showed me different perspectives on some. New paths on others. Made a smooth start for writing. Good day of writing. Stayed indoors all day.

The meditative unguent process has been interesting. Called it meditative because I disciplined my mind into thinking about the lives of the plants on the terrace. The mysteries of how sunlight, water, air and soil combined to produce the growth of leaves, stems, flowers, fruits; and how these were essential for all other life forms on the planet!

More than that. How the five senses, the mind, the intelligence, the spirit of humans all had some strangely curative relationships with plants! As I saw a new bud yielding a new leaf, or a new flower, I saw a communication effort from the plant to reach a human. When I realized this, each new leaf, each new flower brought an inward peace, an inward tranquility.

This emerged from the massaging application of Fyodor's herbal unguent on my forehead between my eyebrows, and my willingness to make myself, to make my senses available— open to communications from the plants on the terrace. The uniqueness of each plant brought to me intricate creativity. How? Still a mystery—but the reality was unmistakable. A sort of garden rapture.

New storylines emerged. The rest of my stories were well into second drafts. Stayed in again all day, except for a quick trip down to Souss brothers' bakal for the usual bread, butter, cheese, some fruit and a bottle of Moroccan-grown French red wine. Good progress on the study stories.

On Mosque Friday, I performed unguent meditations. Emailed my SitRep to my Academic Advisor, Neil.

10 Nov 2000

Dear Neil:

Progressing with study.

I had a very strong week.

On track for meeting November schedule. It is all about writing now. Glad I have that lit background. And I'm glad to have had almost daily support from Sachy this past month. It has made all the difference in my attitude and productive capacity.

I'm surprised how much I like writing about plants, gardens and landscapes--a natural extension of my explorations of same here in North Africa. :)

Thank you for all your support and assistance.

CJ

The next morning, I applied herbal unguent again. What is this stuff really about? The unguent, Fyodor's unguent? Plant substances that I rub on my skin. Plant substances that give something that passes, what, via stomata, into my skin?

Substances that somehow flow to my pineal gland. And that improve communication between me—a human—and plants? How does that work? Don't know—I'm sure that Fyodor tried to explain it to me many times—though I never got it. But apparently it has worked and most stories are just about into final proof reading.

I did Striet's Tangier spine walk in and walk back with virtually no teep hassling—finally. On the way home, I was thinking about how the *tajines* from Sidi Hamete had given me a dependable steadiness.

I was thankful; and as I passed through the Grand Socco, I saw on the edge, the row of Rif mountain Berber women, who had been selling goat cheese wrapped in palm fronds— and who had appeared in my dream. I turned away at first; but some of them had bundles of fresh flowers in front of them. I had to stop.

What did they have? My nose told me first—mimosa, *Acacia dealbata*, so yellow the small puffy flower balls, and so unmistakably Mediterranean in their heady, just on the edge of medicinal fragrance. Along with the mimosa, they had bunches of wild narcissus, *Narcissus tazetta*. I gave one lady ten dirhams and she gave me an armful of mimosa and narcissus. Both of these beautiful flowers were enlivening signs of Mediterranean spring—arriving three months early for a northerner like me.

As soon as I got back to my apartment building, I knocked on the doorframe of Sidi Hamete's apartment. I handed the armful of flowers to her, thanking her profusely for her steady support. First time I saw her smile. She accepted my gift.

Then before going upstairs, I went across the street to the *bakal*. Picked up some Coca Cola, and more Moroccan grown French red wine from the Souss brothers.

Through the next days, I tweaked some story lines, polished other stories. Stories were undergoing final crafting. Final drafts all good, I got into proofreading exchanges with Sachy. Stories—final title—North West Africa Stories.

Only two weeks remained in November when I went to Piliers Culturels. Needed a dozen end papers for the five copies of the final report. Mme Zsófia showed A4 size prints of Art Nouveau masters Gustav Klimt and Alphonse Mucha. Their work spoke to me about cultural conflicts between the Western world, the Arab world, and the deeply rooted African cultures. Beauty of plants. Essence of nature. Beauty of women, and there was always an edge. In the Klimt and Mucha works, I could always see something hidden—something to discover—that was me. Something to discover—like my time here in Tangier, in Morocco, in northwest Africa.

While I was there, I returned some books for resale and made final payments for the artwork.

This month, on a weekly basis, I worked closely with Brahim to set up a CD of my final design study stories. And for the final hard copy text, Brahim provided, through special order, a creme parchment paper. He would do the printing on his laser printer. I would then take that text on creme parchment to be leather bound as the final step in Meknes.

Brahim also provided the protective mailing wrappings for sending the final CDs to the US. Brahim was a big-time logistics supporter and facilitator for the production of my design study. I don't know what I would have done without him.

But for the appropriate time, I had saved a special gift with his name on it.

28-Ohrwurm

Olga and Zsófia

As I neared completion of my project and started my goodbyes, I was relieved, but also exhausted.

In Tangier, I could not stay away from the Piliers Culturels bookstore. It had been a steadying node of resources over my six-month Tangier timeline. For the insights gleaned, I was thankful, and when I was close to departure I stopped by the bookstore one last time.

Thanked Mme Zsófia. I suggested afternoon tea at Mme Porte's. She agreed, and surprised me. She suggested on the very same day, Sunday. She asked if I minded if she brought Mme Olga.

Of course, I agreed. We met at Mme Porte's at three. I had reserved a table in a quiet corner. Hoped we would have pleasant conversation. And we did, accompanied by Bergamot tea.

Sampled a variety of finger sandwiches, pastries, biscuits and scones.

Mme Zsófia and Mme Olga were of similar age. Both born of good families. They had come to Tangier in the fifties to live a full life, we might say, without pejoratives. Both dressed for afternoon tea in the bohemia of Eastern Europe with an overlay of haute couture from Paris. I was proud to be with them. Enjoyed their conversation immensely.

Mme Zsófia spoke about Delacroix, referencing Delacroix's *Moroccan Sketchbooks.* His investigations into the presence and absence of light as that special joy of women. She referenced Delacroix's expressive brush strokes in an intimate way, saying he explored the uncertainties of human life. He explored portals. He explored portals for their beauty on all sensual and spiritual levels. Were these the same portals I had been seeking? No, these were different. As I learned, these were sexual.

Mme Zsófia's demeanor was passionate—no Miss Marple here—her words carried the tremors of fond memories. She spoke of a crescendo within liminal spaces—crescendos that exceeded the most beautiful roses in the most beautiful gardens.

Her words and her own crescendos made a nonsense out of eating. For a moment, we all shared a kind of respect for the words. It was such an eloquent description of what I had come to call, only as crudely as an American could, pole-in-the-hole.

She helped herself to another scone and refilled her teacup. I took the cue and refreshed myself, too. I said no more.

After finishing her scone, Mme Olga brought up the bookstore... founded in 1949... a refuge for people of letters and other fine arts... a centre of respect for Morocco, for Tangier culture and for the people of the Rif. As I had grown accustomed to, Mme Olga also had a knack for the spoken word. This day she too was on top of her game. She used language like a literary craftsman. With words, she was an artisan that I could only hope to be.

Our discussions reminded me of the "Jacob's Ladder same but different" talks I had shared with Bo up in Belgium and France this past summer. The ladies talked about a certain strangeness, historical and contemporary, in art, in Delacroix, in North Africa. Something here was being perpetually reborn. Some kind of strange magic in its landscape, in its people. In their words, something here in this region tries to emerge in stories, in music, in painting... never clear, but always powerful. She used the author William Burroughs to illustrate, saying he addressed the complex, dark mysteries of the region in his book *Naked Lunch*.

On that she built the story of modern Tangier, as she saw it.

"Spies, bankers, black marketeers dominated the International Zone through the 20s, 30s, 40s, WWII and into the 50s until King Mohammed V returned to power.

"With the return of the Moroccan leadership in the 50s, the International Zone became, as has been coined by Burroughs in his *Naked Lunch*, the Interzone. The influence of both of the Bowles, and their coterie, caused the fine arts to flourish; but so also did a sub-culture of groupies. The Interzone became a big-time arts and social scene—and the other stuff—don't forget Tangier has always been a port town like Amsterdam, like Shanghai—sailors and traders—ladies, girls, boys and girlie-boys.

"And since the post-WWII European economic recovery, the cold, gray, dreary Europeans never tire of the warm sun and dipping their toes, their feet, in the soothing but threatening cultural currents of the Moroccan waters, the North African coast. They can't get enough of those odalisque paintings, floriferous plains, threatening sand deserts and the people who call these lifestyles, these places, home.

"They, and your North American compatriots, come here liking the dark side from a discreet distance—the dramas of misunderstanding. That all lives here in Tangier.

"And now, we have *une nouvelle* Montagne, fuelled by Gulf Arab oil money—that is our life today. It works for us. Many of these new people come to our shop looking for local information; and for the right people, we can be quite helpful—all very exciting. But all is changing—not always for the good."

I asked Mme Olga, "What kind of local information do they ask for?"

"You're in the business, I'm sure you know... who owns what and the like... most of the time, we refer them to an American who lives in the Kasbah... he keeps up with that sort of thing..."

Mme Zsófia interrupted, "Thank you for tea, Christopher; and now we must get back to the shop. We have inventory to do."

Aside from this last bit about contemporary real estate development inquiries from foreigners, these ladies, and their seductive locution, were the weavable cultural lamé, gently wrapping this Tangier tangled knot with their beauty, their knowledge and understanding. Such a strange place.

Such unusual people. A threat? A treat? Same but different—definitely not my home.

But I passed the entire afternoon with these wonderful women and their sensuous story telling. Left me emotionally breathless. We parted.

Back at my apartment, the stories of my study completed, I couldn't help thinking about what many might call the cultural richness of Tangier. But me, I saw this landscape, this urban landscape, this cultural landscape as filled with deep, eager, hungry roots. Roots that attached to humans, injecting a cultural energy that to many, perhaps myself included, felt like a systematic poisoning of the things some had valued in life.

What was I on about? Oh, how this place confused me.

Before taking rest, I reviewed, over and over, the logistic details essential to completing the digital and hard copy of my final design study report. I fell asleep dreaming of a white Christmas.

***

Brahim and David

I was very busy as November drew to a close with Brahim's Print Shop—proofed entire draft—checked pagination quartos, etc. Colors good. Layout good. Took it home. Double checked everything.

After all that checking, I gave Brahim the okay to print the final five copies on creme parchment paper. Burned and labelled five CDs.

Sat at Café de Paris and waited. Watched the crowd. Drank a fresh orange juice. Relaxed like I hadn't in a long while!

Picked up the five creme parchment finals from Brahim and paid for all. Slipped him a fifth of Seagrams. Had held one of the fifths that StoneSteve gave me, just for the purpose, as a form of business currency that might have a use.

Funny giving a Muslim a fifth of Seagrams. And Brahim, as I learned over the months, was a, how can I say it, a relaxed Muslim. He sampled those things in life that an orthodox Muslim would never touch.

Might say he counter-balanced the mad Muslim who threw a tantrum at the American Legation because an infidel, like me, took his picture while he was praying. Takes all kinds—that is life.

Walked back via Striet's Tangier spine—Place de la France—Grand Socco—home. A slow walk home, thinking about North Africa. Still had that silver Hand of Fatima in my pocket. Fingered it for the thousandth time.

Despite having finished the hard part of my study, just couldn't relax on the street. Never know who is the teep, who

483

is the fraudulent copper. Anyhow, with my alertness on full, I walked slowly home. Up the stairs.

StoneSteve's place was dark. I took rest.

The next day, I started to organize my things to get ready to depart. Started to clean up the apartment. Got some sun on the terrace. Spent time with the plants.

Finalized with the airline, confirmed reservation and arranged to pick up the ticket. About 10AM headed via Petit Taxi to the Bureau de Poste. Brahim had given me international bubble pack mailing pouches for the CDs. Mailed CDs to LittleWing, and Neil—a security precaution in case something got messed up in the binding process in Meknes, or in my baggage returning to the US.

Had to go to the Kasbah to see David. Despite all the unusual adventures I had had at his place and the Tangier Municipality, I did learn quite a bit from him about the interfaces of Islam and Africa here in Morocco... and his incredible riad garden. Again, with minimal teep disturbance, I walked Striet's Tangier spine from the European Quarter via Grand and Petit Socco to the Kasbah. I knocked.

David was home. Invited me in. Told him I had finished my study, was on my way home in the next two weeks, and wanted to thank him for his hospitality, his help and for his introduction to the culture of Tangier and North and West Africa.

He invited me to his place for his upcoming pre-Ramadan party. He called it... Ramadan Kareem Party. He explained his party had become a regular annual social feature in Tangier.

Asked him if Abdulwahab would be there and he told me the Chief Engineer had taken his family to Paris for Ramadan and the Eid—that was a relief.

I asked David to tell me more about Ramadan. He told me about how the first day of Ramadan is never really known for sure because it depends on sighting the first sliver of moon in the west after the new moon darkness.

"We don't know whether the party will be one night, or two days' worth. It is decided by eyesight, and is never known until the actual day. So come prepared for two days of partying."

he said.

I asked, "How do they tell exactly the beginning?"

"The same way as the end of Ramadan. They measure it by holding a white thread in their right hand, and a black thread in their left hand. The Muezzin at the main mosque holds the two threads out at arm's length, and then at the point when he can no longer distinguish white from black, he looks for the crescent moon.

"If he does not see it, he repeats the same process the next day at sunset. When he sees the crescent moon, they fire off a cannon, so everyone in town knows. Then the cannon is fired at sunset every night of Ramadan, marking the official beginning of eating and drinking, normal life so to speak.

"Good fun, hope you'll come."

I still had questions. "What about clouds, overcast?"

"There is a certain practicality to all possible situations; however, there is a lot of pressure these days to centralize the dates by referring to Saudi Arabia, and using the atomic clock as the basis for the official decision. No fun there! For now, here in Tangier, it is the two-thread technique."

Interesting, but I could only follow so much detail.

David's *riad* was as beautiful as it always was. Particularly quiet. The plants, the tree ferns, the kentia palms, the mud walls, the oriental glasses, the brass artwork—I loved it.

David had to excuse himself, and saw me to the door. He wished that I would come for the party. Before departing, I agreed.

***

Ramadan Kareem

David's Ramadan Kareem Party. I arrived just before sunset. Everybody was there. Erik, the Tangier Old American Legation Director who had got me through some tough cross-cultural issues, was there. Mme Zsófia and Mme Olga were there. A bunch of old established names from Tangier were there.

It was crowded. Moroccans and expats. Shoulder to shoulder. The large kentia palms were there; but all the pots of ferns, Arabesque lights and movable furnishings had been pushed to the edges. It was a real party atmosphere—twinkling lights strung everywhere—classic rock and roll on a high quality, high volume sound system—I think I was hearing greatest hits from the Hollies. Dark came and from somewhere in the Kasbah a cannon boomed. The month of Ramadan had officially begun. Was going to be a one-night only party.

Mme Zsófia stopped next to me and asked, "Have you heard? At midnight, the colorful Jajouka will arrive—with all their drums, reed horns, the *ghaitas*, and flutes. You remember those musicians—who can use music to bring health?—who can dissolve the spell of madness? Some say they can break the force about which we should not speak, that may have someone under its sway.

"They will make their music on foot from the Grand Socco, via the Petit Socco, and arrive here in the Kasbah, entering David's *riad* about midnight. Now you will have something to write about in your study, will you not?"

As she was finishing our conversation, Mme Zsófia was

already drifting over to another group. I saw the odalisque in the distance.

Yes, Zainab was there. Our eyes briefly met. But Erik was next to me and he started talking. He said he knew Zainab and changed the subject.

Erik got into the culture right away. He said, "Ramadan is too long to be a thing. It is a pillar of spiritual life. It has a presence. It is about being, not doing. The secularized Christmas and Easter these days are just boxes to be ticked, things. Muslims do not 'do Ramadan', they live it."

I was still curious about Ramadan. Erik gave me more local culture insight. He explained the good stuff about families, austerities, and how everybody tries to behave in their activities and business as normal. But, he said, "Humans being humans, toward the end of Ramadan, daily business hours begin later and later in the mornings. And everybody ends the business day before sunset without returning back to work after breaking the fast."

"And, at the end of Ramadan, Eid," he said, "...is a huge family holiday at least three days long when all the kids get new clothes and all extended families exchange visits with their extended family members."

I lost interest and started looking around. Looking was hard enough with the huge crowd. Moving anywhere around the *riad* garden was difficult. The place was jammed. More people were arriving.

I bumped into a delicately patterned burnoose with hood up fully covering wearer's head. The cloth texture, lavender color and contrasting stitching patterns were of fine noteworthy quality—caught and kept my attention—looked like something Marlene Dietrich might have worn in the movie *Garden of Allah*.

***

White Slaves

I excused myself for awkwardly bumping into that strange but beautiful burnoose; and to my surprise as the burnoose cautiously turned around, I recognized the face.

"Is that you, Bree?"

She slowly lifted her burnoose hood; yeah, it was Bree—she always had a bit of that Cyndi Lauper *Time after Time* look.

She said, "Am I glad to see you!"

"Likewise, what brings you to Tangier and to David's Ramadan Kareem Party?"

"Long story, but more important I really need help." She sounded desperate.

"Help? Tell me. Maybe I can help."

Distracted and a bit short of breath, she said, "I'm looking for Erik. Do you know him?"

"Yes, I know him—he's here. Don't worry. Calm down. Tell me what's happened."

We walked to a small cove at the side of the *riad*. I told her, "We are safe here, now relax and tell me, how can I help?"

"CJ, this whole Peace Corps thing has gotten so weird. The girl I replaced was named Brandi..."

"I met her back in July. Replaced? What?"

"She disappeared. Nobody knows what happened. Well, her assigned community area was intense. Nobody in that community wanted an American; and the men, they never gave me a moment's peace in public. Rick, the Director, invited me to stay at his place for a couple days—to calm down—to recover... but I really needed some people like you and Eileen.

488

But no way—Eileen was stationed 400 km away. I texted her—she told me to hang tough—if things really got bad look for Erik in Tangier. Well, things got bad. Rick told me that I could extend my recovery by taking a break at a volunteer horticultural project in Tangier."

"What?!"

"Yeah, see that huge harlequin type black guy over there?"

"Yeah, I know him."

"Well, Rick arranged for me to travel to Tangier with a guardian. The guardian, Joey, was identical in size to that harlequin, but he was an albino—clothes just as weird as that harlequin."

Unbelievable what I was hearing from Bree. She continued, "Look, CJ, I don't like this place. That harlequin gives me the creeps."

"Finish the story and then we'll find Erik."

"Joey took me to some garden dormitory here in Tangier—in the area known as La Montagne. All kinds of large villas and large gardens everywhere."

"I know the area. La Montagne. Then what happened?"

"I was shown to my bed. There were about ten beds in the room and I was told all the girls were all working as gardeners on some special project. Then Joey left and I went to sleep. No sooner had I fallen asleep, than someone shook my shoulder. I opened my eyes and a girl covered my mouth and said, 'Shhhhh...' Then, in a foreign accent, she said, 'You know what this place is? It is called Tangier Gardens—a halfway house for girls going to be servants to rich men in the Middle East or somewhere in Europe—white slave trade. It is impossible to escape—but that should not stop you from trying. This is Morocco and anything goes. Stay alert.' Well, I couldn't sleep after that. I remembered what Eileen told me about Erik and I became determined. It became the stuff of spies then. I went to the toilet and hid the toilet paper—went to the lady *guardienne*, who was watching our room, and told her I needed more toilet paper—then quietly followed her—she had to leave the dormitory building for an adjacent building—as soon as she was out of sight, I grabbed my burnoose and took off—had

489

no idea where I was going—just ran and ran—finally ended up not far from here at a Petit Taxi stand where one driver said something to me like—you looking for the Ramadan Kareem Party, that's where all the foreigners are—so long story short—here I am. Now where is Erik? And keep me away from that harlequin."

I took her hand. It was weirdly clammy and we walked the edge of David's *riad* until I saw Erik. I motioned to him to come over to us. When he arrived, I introduced him to Bree, saying, "She wants your help." He questioned her quietly for about five minutes, totally ignoring me.

Then he said to me, "CJ, keep all this to yourself. Bree and I must leave right now. Nothing, right? Say nothing about Bree to anyone!"

They disappeared.

***

Worst Trance

I was on my own again at David's bustling, noisy party. Then I saw Harlequin across the *riad*. Our eyes met briefly. But he was starting to dance wildly in a circle with another harlequin—same size and build. On the sound system, the Hollies belted out *I'm Alive*. The harlequin pair held each other's hands and spun wildly in circles as they sang *I'm Alive*. My attention was split between their dancing, Bree's story and just how David's tranquil *riad* garden had been transformed into a party room.

I found myself next to the tables that were filled with catered Ramadan foods, *Iftar* specialties, Eid sweets and a bar of exotic spirits. I was thinking about sampling some sweets when I ended up face to face with Harlequin. He led me to a somewhat quieter corner. I asked him who was he dancing with. He said it was his twin brother—identical except his brother was albino. Before I could satisfy my curiosity, he changed the subject, asking how was my study. I told him, in a sociable way, about my experience of not remembering my walks in the Oval Garden at Hibiscus House. That was a mistake.

He asked me to hold out my hands. As I did, he took each of my hands in his hands. Before I knew it, he was speaking with his falsetto voice into each of my ears simultaneously, "Hear with your mind, hear with your mind, hear with your mind..." His falsetto voice was becoming deeper and slower with each repetition, accompanied by a reverberation that disconnected my consciousness and awareness of the *riad*. A continuing deep reverberation penetrated my ears—each repetition slowed down more and more until... I was walking through the Oval Garden—I was by myself, walking eagerly, exploring, wondering what next—then Zainab shook my shoulders.

I was on my back, on a *banquette*, in some kind of candle-lit small room. In the distance, I could hear the party going on somewhere... below. I figured I was upstairs in David's Kasbah *riad*.

"Are you okay?" I could hear Zainab's voice.

She asked, "Can you hear me?" I nodded my head.

For once, Zainab looked like her Western name, Irene. Her Western female nature was comforting.

I asked her, "Can you get me out of here? I'm on my way back to my own real home and I do not want to get trapped here."

She took my hand and led me down a back stair, out a small, half-height door, through twisting, dark alleys and found a Petit Taxi. She helped me into the back seat and, somehow, she knew my apartment because she gave the name to the driver. She, closing the taxi door and leaning in through the window—said softly in my ear, "Remember me. Good will always prevail." When I turned to meet her eyes, she was the odalisque again. My ear accepted her breathy kiss. Then her tongue lightly touched the edge of my ear and, it set me on fire. As she backed away I heard her whisper, "I always come for you... and never forget... we are the Magi."

The Petit Taxi whooshed away. All I could feel—rushing cool night air—bumping byways. The taxi driver turned around, looked at me and smiled, asking, "You want more, my friend? I can get for you same, all night, all day, same like that if you like—boys, girls, men, women. What is your pleasure? You like beauty? I give you beauty. Yes, my friend, yes, I give you all!"

I heard more than I wanted. Nothing made sense. I pleaded, "Just take me home, fast!"

The taxi driver tried to drive me through the too narrow medina alleyways. Somehow, he squeezed through the Petit Socco. Then off the main route. The bumpy rolling alleyway went very dark and, as he turned one corner, our path was blocked by chanting men dressed in black and deeply aggravated about something. These were not Jajouka.

The driver said not to worry, no problem—but they saw my blond hair. Then they stopped the car and started rocking it. They were all over the car doors, opening them and grabbing at me, I heard—*hmuck kaffir*—crazy-non-believer. Dark was. Somebody grabbed my hand. And as it became terribly, terribly quiet, I was off to... never... never... land.

29-Dreamland

Hacking the Ohrwurm

I had wished only to get home, back to the US and I had been so close I was tasting it. But that night—my experience at the Ramadan Kareem Party and on the way back... inside/outside disorientation and confusion. I was lost in a psychological fog—just effing lost. Dreams? Realities? Realities made no sense. Nowhere safe—nowhere to hide. This had been like teeps with superpowers—powers that shape-shifted realities. That evening had been a carnival ride in a fun house—trapped into the beginning and no end. Overwhelmed in a fog filled fun house; and I was falling off the rails.

I'd had enough. I thought I was attending a friendly social event. First Bree, then Harlequin and his albino brother, then Zainab, then the mad chanters. No, no, no! Cross-cultural bullshit, over the top. I was drowning in my worst nightmares.

Somehow, I got back to my flat. I had ended up in some place where nightmares came true and reality was worse than the nightmare. Where reality became worse than the nightmare. Sidi Hamete knew what to do.

This story got so dark that I still hesitate to daylight all the details. I turn to my diary entries to aid my rather chilling recollection.

Beside me, on my *banquette*, Sidi Hamete was sitting crosslegged, cradling my head on her lap. She was telling me about *ohrwurm*, and how, once it is encountered by anyone, a weakness is implanted. That was the most I had ever heard her talk.

"What?" Stunned, I was stunned.

She said, "*Magreb geomagnetique* help *ohrwurm*; and this region is rich in *geomagnetique.*

"*Ohrwurm* eat discipline of host. Make them susceptible to immoral, unethical, danger, and horrible death."

Stunned and now worried, I asked, "Can I be fixed?"

"*Ohrwurm* weaken discipline. *Ohrwurm* then weaken will power. Then invite dark, invite zombie."

I pleaded, "Please turn my nightmare into sweet dreams."

Again I pleaded, "Can you fix me? And what about my Hand of Fatima charm, isn't that helpful?"

"Your Hand of Fatima is for tourists, and can I fix? Maybe. The first time I gave positive *marabout* powers and spells to bring protection, to bring normal to your life.

"Young man you have good heart. You must learn to protect it. Your time here in *Magreb* has taught you lessons of the street, lessons of the Africa. Do not forget them. Protect yourself. But do not harden your heart."

She had found me on the doorstep when she opened the front door at 5am. She knew immediately it was more of the same and worse—she walked me up the stairs. She had to clean me up. Deeply this time. I looked around.

I was clean. My clothes were off. I was covered, wrapped in large, freshly laundered, white terrycloth towels.

Around me I saw: candles, censers, mortar and pestle, a small gas burner stove, potions, and an open can of detritus, as well as a large porcelain bowl containing a moist mixture of cloths and herbs.

Sidi Hamete, looking concerned and helpful, gently put my head on my pillow as she moved to the floor and sat next to the *banquette.*

She continued, "We must finish this before you leave the *Magreb.* Once this *djinn* has you, it will never be vanquished. You are finished.

"Its connections are deep and everywhere. After the first time you are open, then inviting easy entry, any time, any place."

I asked, "But is it actually a worm?"

"Yes and no. At first it is the essence of worm, subtle,

alchemical. In time that essence grows and changes into dark that takes energy from your brain. Takes little by little your life. Your force. You cannot walk. You cannot move. You cannot see. You cannot hear. Maybe you can think, maybe not. The worm gets big."

I asked, "Could this be evileye?"

Very quietly, Sidi Hamete said, "I don't say no and I don't say yes. I don't say and we don't talk."

She continued, "Words like iron threads—fly direct to *geomagnetique*. Finish, okay—no more talking—now drink this tea."

Sidi Hamete reached out with a small cup of gelatinous tea. She told me sternly, "Do not smell it. Do not think about it. Grab this cup. Drink it fully. Fast! It is for your life! Now take it and drink!"

I did!

"Fast and hard!"

Gulped it all down!

In the split seconds following, I felt it moving down my esophagus and begin to settle into my stomach. Nothingness at first, then my thoughts started up again. Instead of talking, I started breathing—voluntary, controlled deep breathing. I had to gain strong control of my breathing to stop an aggressive repelling muscular action in my stomach that became a rasping noise in my ears.

The deep and strongly controlled breathing gradually settled the wrenching convulsions as what I swallowed had passed my choking esophagus, my convulsing stomach and finally moved quietly into my intestines. Then the rumbling began.

"Okay?" Sidi Hamete asked.

"Yes, but..." I put my hand over my lower abdomen.

"That is normal. It will clean and empty, day or two, okay?" she said.

I said, "Okay."

"Good, now just relax, and pray to your god."

"But what did I drink..."

"You do not want to know. You do not want to ask. Be

satisfied with my words. It is your own healing essence with the help from the plants."

"...and will I be safe to go home?"

"No more questions, now sleep, my friend, before long it will be like nothing happened."

I didn't want any repercussions from that night. So I stayed quiet about it. But after Sidi Hamete went downstairs, back to her apartment, and in my weakness, as I lay down to sleep, when I closed my eyes, clarity briefly flashed. One realization crystallized. This entire six months had been about a battle between good and evil. Feeling ever so vulnerable, like a young child, I folded my hands to pray and whispered:

Now I lay me down to sleep,
I pray the Lord my soul to keep,
If I should die before I wake,
I pray the Lord my soul to take.

***

The Morning After

Pounding, pounding, pounding!

What was it? I couldn't figure... I was dizzy... weak... couldn't sit up... the pounding.

Oh, I finally sat up. It was the front door. Then I heard Steve's voice shouting my name. I put my feet on the floor, struggled to the front door and opened it.

Steve's face was filled with concern, his voice, too.

"You alright?" he asked. "You must have changed the lock. My key didn't work. I was worried."

I invited him in and went back to my bed.

"You look like hell," he said.

I was weak, sitting on the edge of the bed.

He stood over me and asked again, "Sure you're alright?"

He continued, "Sidi Hamete knocked on my door early this morning and said you had partied hard in the Kasbah, and if she takes the time to talk it is important. She asked me to check on you. And if that wasn't enough, I got an email from Erik at the American Legation. I hardly know the guy. His message was cryptic. It was for you. He said that a girl you know, the PC volunteer—she is okay, she is safe. What the hell happened? Was that all about that party in the Kasbah?"

I didn't know where to begin. I hardly had enough energy to speak. I said, "Thanks for your concern and messages, Steve; but I feel weak. Let me go back to sleep; and when I wake up, I'll come over to see you."

"I'll be in town over the next week, no problem. You finished with your study?"

"Yeah, but we can talk later. I just need to sleep."

I reached over to the bed stand and handed my door key to him, asking, "Please lock it on the way out. Keep the key, I have two."

Then I collapsed on the bed and pulled my blankets over me. I heard Steve mumbling something nice as he left the room. Then I heard him locking the door before I fell asleep. Deep sleep.

It seemed like I slept for days. I started dreaming. In the dreams I saw Steve standing over me. Then one day I awoke and felt "normal". Sidi Hamete was right. I finally felt better; but it was evening. It had taken a couple days of complete rest and I had lost all track of time—like my internal clock had rebooted or something.

I felt hunger. Saw a bowl of oranges on the sink and grabbed a couple, cut them into quarters then walked out onto my terrace. I took the airs and looked thankfully at the plants. With them, I was with friends for sure! Sat down on the wicker chair and ate the oranges. Refreshing. Yeah, I did feel better.

I could see StoneSteve's lights were on next door. I went over and knocked. He let me in. He was packing. "How long was I out?" I asked.

"Two days—48 hours straight! I stopped in every once in a while. Sidi Hamete brought some oranges up in case you were hungry or thirsty; but you're looking good now."

"I feel much better, had a couple oranges before I came over. You packing? What's up?"

Steve told me he was departing till sometime in the New Year. Some kind of project combined with holiday.

Steve once again said he was surprised to get the email from Erik...

"Steve, I did see Erik and also that girl from the Peace Corps—she was part of my *Darija* Stage in Casablanca. She was stressed then and also at David's that night."

Steve looked at me long and hard before he started. "You're on your way home, right? You've finished your study and all that. Done with Tangier, done with Morocco?"

"Mostly, all that's left is binding the hard copy with a

craftsman in Meknes, then I'm outta here."

"You were close to Bree?"

"How did you know her name?"

"Erik and I do some things together from time to time."

"That's interesting because Bree told me her story at the party in the Kasbah that night—unbelievable. Then Erik told me to never talk about it."

"Well, CJ, Erik thought you might want to know that Bree is safe and she is back in the US now."

"What?"

"Here's the back story. You hungry? I'm gonna pour myself a bowl of Frosties."

"Yeah, I'm up for that." He poured two large bowls of Frosties then mixed up some Nido for milk and we both dug in.

After a bite or two, he started, "This is all about trafficking, and the US government attempts to kill it at its root. Erik filled me in. Anyhow, Erik made some arrangements and Bree was taken to safety that same night. All is well."

Maybe some more pieces were fitting into place for me now; but I had to ask, "First you told me you didn't know Erik, then you said the two of you work together... what's that all about?"

Steve took a deep breath, then paused before starting. "After I finished my undergrad civil engineering, I enlisted in the Air Force to use my degree—it worked out well and I became a squadron engineer in their Red Horse squadrons. I got to say only that stuff happened. They paid for me to go back to school for Resource Management studies and afterwards, I joined the Peace Corps here in Morocco. That was when I met Erik."

My head was spinning. This was all much more than 2+2.

Steve said, "I've told you too much already. Bree is safe. You are going home and none of this will impact your life. There is a saying, 'Loose lips sink ships'. Nuff said?"

I drained the sweet Nido milk from the remainder of my Frosties. I still had the work in Meknes to achieve. I thanked Steve for the Frosties, the update on Bree and for all his support over the past six months.

StoneSteve had been my go-to-guy—saved my butt from

the Tangier Municipality—maybe a friend for life. He kept the key copy to Striet's apartment and reminded me to leave my other key with Sidi Hamete before I left Tangier. No problem, I told him. We shook hands one last time, exchanging the usual niceties alumnae from the same university share. Then I went back to my apartment.

Two days later—finally! I was glad to be leaving Tangier once and for all. I thanked Sidi Hamete. I gave her the key to Striet's flat and reminded her about the plants. In my apartment, I had written and left an additional thank you note to her, detailing all the ways she had helped me in the past six months. I addressed the envelope to her. Along with the note, I included seven one-hundred US dollar bank notes.

I thought her help was more than money could buy. Her help, her skills... they were a mystery and always will be a mystery to me; but in part of the "dreams" I had in my recent two days of sleep, I saw a strange memory conflation where Sidi Hamete, sixty years ago, was the little kid in Olga's stories from the Petit Socco. Another dream. Too many dreams, too many nightmares these past six months.

I was on my way to Meknes for binding the hard copy report. If I had to keep riding on the cross-cultural carousel, Meknes was the place to be—relatively quiet compared to Tangier—actually very quiet.

At the end of her work on me the other day, Sidi Hamete had told me, "Before long it will be like nothing happened." How many ambiguities were hidden behind the words in that clause? I certainly didn't know; but I shuddered for years whenever it crossed my mind.

My memory was strong about that night and none of it was good. But LittleWing had, a long time ago, shared with me an approach to the dark things. She said to understand them as having three increasing layers of impact. Thinking. Saying. Doing. Her advice was not to let the bad, the dark, proceed any further than thinking. The saying and doing would invoke serious karmic repercussions. Nuff said.

504

30-Iftar

Hameed

I took the later train to Meknes. Because *Iftar*, no food service—no problem—until sunset, when they served dates and ¼ litre bottles of water. Austere, simple.

Such a relief to be on the train leaving Tangier and not having to return. Tangier seemed more and more to have been non-stop a bad dream. I felt, arriving Meknes Ville Nouvelle, I had returned to the "real" Morocco. In Meknes, I had measurable tasks to do.

Time to finish my term abroad design study. I had 15% of my study, the final hard copy, to complete in Meknes. Fifteen percent? Seemed like a lot but presentation-quality material was a main component of my landscape architecture education. I didn't want to be downgraded for presentation after all I'd been through in Tangier. Plus, I had found a great craftsman in Meknes to do the work, so I was psyched and confident.

The sun had long set before the train arrived in Meknes. Exiting the Meknes train station, I saw Hameed crossing the street, coming in my direction.

"*Comment ça va? Ça va bien?*"

"How have you been? How come you aren't working in Corsica?"

"*Ne marchait pas.* They did not get the work."

"What are you going to do?"

"I am talking to a person for work in the *banlieues* of Marseilles."

"Why are you working in a foreign country?"

"*Sauver la vie.*"

"*Qu'est-ce que ça veut dire, 'sauver la vie'?*"

Hameed launched into a long monologue in French—some of which I understood. Bottom line—it was up to him to make a success out of his life—not his father, not his family, not his government. Him alone. He seemed so different than those aggressive, envious teeps from Tangier. I was thinking that through when Hameed suggested.

"Let's have some tea."

"Good idea but not at that *keef* café."

We found a small counter serving tea next to the train station. A nice hot glass of mint tea. I held it lightly with my hands until it cooled to warm and drinkable. That was relaxing.

I asked, "And what about your cousin?"

"They let him go if he promised not to sell anymore."

"And?"

"He went to Tangier. And last week he sent me an email saying that he was waiting for someone to drive him to Amsterdam where he would have work."

"Sounds like he is still in the drugs."

"*C'est ça la vie.*"

We both took swallows of mint tea.

Then I asked Hameed, "You're 25, what will you do with your life? How will you *sauves ta vie?*"

His eyes were sad as he paused, then his eyes brightened with hope.

He said, "My grandfather has land in Taza. I will take money from my foreign work and build a house. Then I will marry and start a family. Taza is quiet, good people, no tourists, no drugs. *Pas de foules.*"

"When will you hear about the work in Marseilles?"

"Soon," he said.

"I wish you luck."

I finished my tea, said goodbye, and Hameed offered to take me to his home in the medina and said that I could stay there. I said I still had my university study to complete and I already had a room waiting for me nearby. I wished him *baraka*, luck, many times over as I parted company with him. Then I walked the five minutes to Tom and Marcela's.

***

508

Tom and Marcela

My friends, Tom and Marcela, were happy to initiate me into their Ramadan daily routine. They both kept Ramadan because they worked all day with Moroccans.

Thus I was introduced to the glorious end-of-the-day breaking of the fast that everyone partook of, a celebration called Iftar.

They gave me the key to move into my top floor studio. In the morning, Tom offered to accompany me to Maalem Hamid's shop in the medina if I needed to get started immediately. I did—perfect!

Tom and I took a Petit Taxi to the Place El Hedim in the medina and we made the short walk from there to Maalem Hamid's.

We sat with Maalem Hamid. Even though it was Ramadan, he offered mint tea. We politely said, no, because of Ramadan. We sat quietly.

Then he asked, in French, if I had my book text ready for work. I pulled out the creme parchment text and the decorative end papers. I gave him the five copies of text, organized in signatures of eight sheets each.

Maalem Hamid checked the signatures of all five copies, prepared them for folding, and gave them to the young trainee who commenced folding. As soon as one book's folding was complete, Maalem Hamid checked it and showed it to me for approval, which I gave, then he gave it to his trainee helper to begin sawing and sewing.

While the trainee worked, Maalem Hamid showed me the

goat leather samples, finishes and color options. I saw a very Meknassi yellowish color that I liked. Showed him the drawing for the front cover gilted image. He traced it. Showed me how he would do it—I was happy.

Then we checked the trainee's sawing and sewing—when Maalem Hamid was happy, he showed the work to me—the trainee was good.

We went back to the cover—I agreed two ribs on a rounded binding with a stamped pattern between the ribs and an anti-evileye engraving, suggested by the Maalem, on the bottom of the end binding. It was a Hand of Fatima—much more ornate than my mom's keychain—it was his own artwork—his personal trademark.

Then came the money discussion. Maalem Hamid asked for money, 75dh per book. He did artisan quality work. The price he asked was more than he had said last time; but now he knew exactly how much of everything would be needed.

Because of the fine quality of his work, I would have paid the price. But when I asked him if it would be finished in a week, he said, "No, two weeks."

He only had one trainee assistant.

"One week, and I will help with some of the simple work like folding signatures or gluing," I said.

Maalem Hamid said, "*Mumkin.*"

We had agreement. "*Humdoulah*," I said.

Then I offered his price, minus 25%. He gave, in return, his original price minus 10%. I agreed. Then agreed 50% to pay now, and the rest on completion. No problem. Said goodbye.

Tom and I returned via Place El Hedim and Petit Taxi to the Beau Séjour. Tom invited me to *Iftar* dinner at his place. Went upstairs to rest and clean up. Returned for 9PM dinner.

A Meknassi named Driss also came for *Iftar*. He had studied English with Tom's brother, Justin, at the USAID (United States Agency for International Development) English Language Centre in Meknes back in the 80s. He was an old friend. Tom and Marcela warned me he now was the proprietor of a place of questionable repute called Bar Californie, the other side of the tracks, behind the train station in the Ville Nouvelle.

We talked late about the history of Meknes, an Imperial City, and then a centre for French agricultural development. About its future, Driss was hopeful. Finished dinner and about midnight finished with all the social niceties.

Went back upstairs and took rest.

***

Maalem Hamid

I slept well. I had to go to Maalem Hamid's shop in the morning to help his trainee. The next couple of days were the same. I enjoyed working in the shop with these craftsmen. After about five days, Maalem Hamid invited me to *Iftar* at his house in the medina and to pass the night with his family. An honor. The night was Ramadan 11.

I have to call my overnight at Maalem Hamid's home auspicious. One auspicious occasion after six months of non-stop Tangier inhospitality? I am left still without comprehension of the whole.

And this was why I have concluded the inside-out, upside-down experience of this culture had driven me back home. Home to Western culture. Home to my roots, even though Maalem Hamid and his family treated me respectfully as an honored guest.

No one on the streets of Tangier ever showed me 1% of the respect each of his entire family showed me that day. And it was the public conflict, the contradiction between media "peaceful culture" hype and the on-the-street reality, that drove me away from Morocco. After all, I was into plants, gardens and landscapes. I was not into finding some kind of universal unity for humans.

Universal unity for humans? Nobody has found that in all of written history. And why? I don't know why, but unresolvable cultural differences have been thrown in my face every day since I took the ferry from Algeciras across the Strait of Gibraltar, to Tangier—from Europe to Africa.

And my stories? My North West Africa Stories? They reflected the reality of my public realm Moroccan experiences. The stories? They were inside-out, upside-down, about the humans, plants, gardens and landscape of this geography. They may inform design and they may challenge the landscape architecture students and practitioners. That was my straightforward intent—nothing more, nothing less.

Being a guest of Maalem Hamid and his family was the real thing. My diary entries clearly described the setting and my feelings.

As soon as I entered the Maalem's home, I was introduced to a bunch of men, brothers, uncles, like that, and also to women, his wife, some sisters, some daughters, some nieces. I felt as though I just arrived to a party already in high gear and they made me feel like now that I had arrived, the party had just begun—very hospitable. Overall, I must have met at least twenty people.

Everyone was quietly buzzing—waiting to hear a siren, which in the Meknes medina signalled the breaking of the fast on the day. As soon as we heard the siren, we all went upstairs where a plate of dates and small drinkable bowls of *harira*, a tomato and chickpea soup, were already placed on the tables for people to break the fast. People helped themselves. It was men only. The women were downstairs breaking the fast the same way. After the fast was broken, everyone shared jolly conversation. It was noisy everywhere in the house.

The Maalem's house was a *riad*, like David's *riad* in Tangier but without the lavish plants and other decorations—considerably simpler. The courtyard was smaller, no plants. The rooms around the perimeter were larger.

I observed the room in which we had broken the fast—actually, everyone was moving around again and talking loudly. The room? It was a larger rectangular room that had banquettes continuously around the perimeter and two large, low, round tables, one at each end. The room was bright, lighted by two large decorative chandeliers on the ceiling at each end of the room. No other decoration. Room walls and ceiling painted a sky blue.

Finally, everyone started quieting. The maalem took my hand and led me to his table. Maalem Hamid and I sat, then the rest of the *banquette* seats were taken by the men and boys I had met downstairs. Older men sat on the banquettes and younger boys sat, with cushions, on the floor. Told me the women would eat downstairs. Maalem Hamid's assistant was with us, too.

Two of the younger boys began the hand washing ceremony. One carried a bowl, the other carried a pitcher of water and a towel. Each guest in turn had water poured over his hands into the bowl, then was given a towel to dry his hands.

While this was going on, the cooking of preparations was being finished by the ladies downstairs, accompanied by lots of bustling, noise and excitement. Fantastic aromas filled the air, meat, vegetables, cinnamon, cumin and others I couldn't identify. Then came eight glasses and four 2-liter bottles of Coca Cola for each table. Then came the bread—*khobz*—four big, round, flattish loaves per table. Then in came the masterpieces, round trays—huge *tajines* with a mountain of meat and veg—one *tajine* tray for each table—placed in the very centre. Maalem Hamid, at my table, and the oldest man at the other table, broke each loaf of bread into halves and quarters, then distributed them.

Preparations complete, everyone waited and watched Maalem Hamid. He paused, the room was silent, then the Maalem said loudly, "*Bis-mee-lah!*"

Boom—everyone dug in, using torn-off smaller pieces of bread like a spoon. The burst of energetic eating kept the room silent.

Maalem Hamid pulled apart pieces from the whole young sheep in our *tajine*, making sure I had meat in front of me. Onions, lemons, almonds, carrots and I don't know what—all sweet and spicy. Cinnamon, cumin and raisins burst in my mouth with every bite.

Gradually people began talking again. Everyone pressured me to eat more and more with the intensity of the teeps on the street; but here... here it was all good natured. It was fun. It was all jolly.

During dinner, Maalem Hamid and one of his nephews, Moha, who spoke good English, explained how the night would work. We would eat well; and because it was an important night when I was a special guest, we would stay here, enjoy sweets and then get a good night's sleep until *Suhor*.

At about 4AM, there would be a drummer, passing through the street to wake everyone for prayer and *Suhor*, a reduced version of *Iftar*. And that was how it worked.

***

I Thought It Was Over...

Af/fter feasting and upstairs on the roof top, Moha showed me to my small, private room—a *banquette*, a couple wool blankets, sheet, pillow and one low wattage lamp on a small table. I tucked in to sleep. But something so inexplicably strange happened that night. Strange? Not really. If I looked back at everything I had encountered in Morocco over the last six months. I thought it was over... but not... and this was definitely strange.

First of all, I had eaten big. Think of your largest Thanksgiving dinner—I had that, plus 50% more. I was stuffed and I had fun all the way; but these guys just kept telling me to eat, as if my manhood was at stake.

I was so full, I could barely walk as I was shown upstairs to my small room on the roof. Then my bloated stomach kept me from easily falling asleep. My mind wouldn't stop. Behind my eyelids, thoughts raced like spinning rolodex cards. Where did these thoughts come from? Before long, I was bouncing without control between the strange memories, thoughts and dreams...

...way back in high school, the school day began for most students at 9AM. But the school also had an advanced placement program for select students of promise. For them— an extra hour of school each day, beginning their day at 8AM. I was part of that group. We were proud of our status, maybe too much so. We gave ourselves a nickname—The Breakfast Club, like the movie.

We thought ourselves to be pretty hot—in reality we were

a ragtag bunch of geeks. Budding libertarians, we thought we were above the politically correct socialization blanket that smothered normal high school classes. Those normal classes we called "Dreamland"—a place we thought was out of touch with real life—a place where Orwell's *1984* was in process. Before long, I was slipping into... I didn't know where...

***

Dreamed To Death

Like rising flood waters, sleep gradually came to me. I had eaten so much I couldn't move. At first I welcomed sleep. Then those rising flood waters became infinite in breadth and depth. I was, against eternal infinity, useless, pointless... I could not escape... I twisted and turned and then deep sleep did finally come... sleep and dreams.

In the dream I was still at the feast—still eating, digging into the *tajine*—tearing off more pieces of *khobz* to sop up the juices.

Then... it all started slowing down—I was eating in slow motion—all the guys were cheering me in slow motion—I started thinking they were conspiring to stuff this infidel, stuff this *kaffir* to death—I had to get away.

On the excuse to use the toilet, I snuck out the front door—didn't know which way to go—heard my hosts yelling my name—started running—looked over my shoulder—they were all running after me, making all kinds of ugly sounding shouts.

Neighbors opened their front doors wondering what was the shouting—they started shouting too—they started running after me too—each *riad* seemed like a bodily organ releasing deleterious fluids into the byways—all flowing after me faster and faster, noisier and noisier. I didn't know where to go, where to turn—I was looking for plants, for gardens, for the agricultural landscape—nothing—they were catching up—I had to hide—I ran uphill, downhill, turning this way and that—a cacophony of thousands shouting and chasing—the medina byways became darker, more secluded—the searing shouting and liquid were lapping at my heels.

Then I saw a door I recognized. David's *riad*—didn't knock, just burst in. Breathless. Soaked in sweat. Heart pounding. Lungs empty. Slammed the door behind and bolted it shut.

Turned around and what did I see?

Inside, all the potted plants and furnishings had been pushed to the side. The place was loudly filled with the most painful Andalusian Gypsy flamenco singing. And who was dancing? Harlequin and Joey. Wildly round and round with each other in fast circles—then Zainab arrived in her silks. She stood next to me for a moment and she spoke to me in a voice so sweet, I thought I heard the shuffle of angels' feet, "Just stand here, don't move and you'll be safe."

As she stepped forward I saw a tattoo on the back of her neck, "Tell 'em that God's gonna cut them down." Then before I could blink she reached down between her breasts and pulled out a huge sword, swung it above her head, and shouted, "I know your works!"

Then she proceeded to lop off the heads of the each of the dancers and Gypsy musicians in one unimaginable sweeping blow. With heads bouncing and rolling around on the floor, she turned toward me. I did not know what to expect. Until a waft of unusually intoxicating neroli fragrance overcame my nose, lungs, heart and mind for when she was, at least so I hoped, leaning over to kiss me, I saw not Zainab, but Sachy. Were my eyes open or closed? Was I dreaming?

***

Neroli: Oranges or Sachy

I was 100% into my dream. As I so eagerly leaned to share that kiss with Sachy, I closed my eyes wishing I really was with Sachy. When I opened my eyes again, Sachy had gone—instead I saw the most beautiful orange tree. I blinked and I was in a huge orchard of orange trees—this dream would not stop. Must have been June—trees full of plump oranges and fragrant white orange blossoms.

Sun bright, sky without clouds—needed shade—needed to be in the shade of all those evergreen orange trees—but I couldn't—I had to give a lecture—as part of the "Break It Down" Series—entitled Landscape Architecture.

I began—first you have hardscape and softscape.

In softscape when I came to talk about plants I announced the subsection as "Plant Materials".

Immediately there arose hissing, booing, whistling from every one of the quincunx-arranged orchard of orange trees stretching as far as I could see—from among the orange trees, I could hear words forming—we are alive—we are alive—noisy decibels that started hurting my ears.

That noise turned into the medina cacophony; the trees crowded closer, and before I knew it the trees were the people who had chased me from the medina.

Tolly, smoking a short, thick cigar, appeared and said we'd better get out of here and together we started running.

The ground started rolling as we ran harder—the rolling turned into ocean-like swells raising us above the orange trees.

The grove disappeared.

Then each swell was in colors—fuchsia then hot red then blinding orange—the colored swells pushing like huge waves.

Then the waves over each swell got larger and larger—surfable and each wave was its own color—these were waves of bougainvillea—one after another after another—one color then another and another—I became dizzy from the colors.

First the surfing was fun—then the waves got huge and unruly.

As they crashed they became noisier and noisier until they sounded like an amplified medina cacophony.

Finally a huge fuchsia wave sent us tumbling head over heels—I could no longer see Tolly, and I was going under... Tolly had gone one way and I went another—I felt nauseous—suffocating, drowning.

Then I lost all self-awareness. Suddenly I was with a bunch of other people who were nauseous and blowing lunch. I was in the hold of the ferry in rough seas crossing the Strait of Gibraltar. And there was Bo—he said come upstairs to first class it is not so bad. We talked, like before, about Stairway to Heaven and the room in which the stairway sits.

"Your stairway lies on the whispering wind," Bo said.

"My spirit is crying for leaving..." I added.

"Enough dreaming, let's get down to it. Shake it off, let's talk about rooms," Bo said.

Bo and I talked about rooms and I refined his Art Nouveau plant room ideas.

"As landscape architect, Bo, I have to put your rooms speculation into the proper domain—do you catch my drift? No design concept involving plants can work if the plants are not healthy, not flourishing. So here's how I define the domain in which the rooms concept must fully and comfortably sit. Right plant, right place, soil, water, sunshine—health above all—monitor and adjust all as plants grow and develop."

I looked Bo in the eyes. He was following me. I took advantage of his interest by continuing.

"Then the room concept starts simply with two components—mass and specimen. The mass becomes the structural plants—the floors, walls and ceiling of the room. The specimen is the focal point of display within that structurally defined room—for example—if the structural mass is made of evergreen plants then the color and texture of the foliage should by contrast allow the specimen to stand out like a cut diamond on a black velvet background."

I was getting into it when an especially strong wave hit our ferry, almost knocking me off my feet. I became queasy—felt faint—things going black—grabbed onto a rail to support myself, at which time Tolly, with his cigar putting out huge clouds of sweet-smelling smoke, grabbed my shoulder, asking, "Had enough, yet? Need some calm? Follow me, I've just the place."

Just as I started following him another huge wave rocked the ferry again almost knocking me over. As I regained my balance, Tolly said, "C'mon over here and take a seat."

I barely blinked and the storm was gone.

I was in the dragon's blood tree forest on La Montagne in Tangier at the villa *Loins du Monde Réel.* Tolly was sitting on a wicker chair enjoying his cigar and told me, "Sit down, let's share some iced lemonade."

I was unsure about everything until I saw the stone plaque with the Tolkien engraving.

"I felt a curious thrill, as if something had stirred in me, half wakened from sleep."

Tolly sat quietly as I read and reread the Tolkien quote. The words from the quote "...beauty is an enchantment and an ever present peril..." tumbled and rolled through my head. Then Tolly asked, "And what has my young American friend learned about plants?"

I shook myself, trying to clear my head, before I answered.

"Maintenance development—always evolving—without excellent plant health there is nothing. It is personal between us and the plants."

Tolly smiled and said, "Fyodor is waiting for you. We'd better make haste."

We walked into the villa and straight to the media room. All became quiet. Tolly and I sat in the front row.

Fyodor was standing in front of the screen facing us—the

house lights were up—he started pacing back and forth—he was perturbed. "So what did you want to tell me, my young American friend?"

I started explaining, "...plant portals are doors that plants offer to certain humans to relieve their existential anxieties and the certain humans were people who gave of themselves to the very plants. And this is the basis for excellent planting design."

At the end, Fyodor walked up to me, shook my hand. And as I stood up, he said, "Well done." Those were the first kind words I had ever heard from Fyodor and it tickled me. I felt tickles, goose bumps, tingles all over my body.

At that point, I woke up, finding myself on the *banquette* upstairs in the Maalem's house. I turned on the desk lamp. The tingling I felt was from bedbugs that by dozens were covering my body. Brushed them off as fast as possible and they, along with scores more on the *banquette*, disappeared into the shadows underneath and behind the *banquette*. And that was no dream!

Just then from out on the medina byway below I heard the *Suhor* drum beat. And, before long, there was a knock at my door.

12 Ramadan had begun.

31-Home Sweet Home

Dreaming of a White Christmas

On the twelfth day of Ramadan, Maalem Hamid and I arrived at the shop about 8AM. Maalem Hamid finished the outstanding work. I watched him do the final touches. I helped where I could; but I was tired and mostly watched. He did a lot of detailed tooling; his assistant did leather stamping.

When they finished the first book, the *Maalem* proudly offered it to me for examination. I took it. I hefted it. I felt it. I inspected it. I paged through it. Yes, it was beautiful—content aside, it was every bit as delectable a product as I could have ever hoped for.

About two in the afternoon, when he had finished the details, he wrapped the five books in thick brown paper himself. Then he ceremoniously presented to me the final five books. I placed the balance of what was due for his services in his hand. Then we shook hands. He was proud. I was proud.

And honestly, it had been such a pleasure to watch the exceptional craftsman handle his tools, and produce such a refined result in appearance, in touch, and in technical strength. I thanked him.

He walked with me to the Place El Hedim where I took a Petit Taxi. He and I both waved until out of sight.

Almost sunset when I arrived in the Ville Nouvelle. Lights on in Tom's place. Knocked and showed them one of the final copies. My time in Morocco was up. Over the past six months, Tom and Marcela had given me shelter every time I needed it. I owed them.

Arranged to have dinner together at a 5-star Ville Nouvelle hotel restaurant the next night.

I spent the day packing. I took Marcela and Tom for dinner at the Hotel Transatlantique with a full-blown late-night Ramadan *Iftar* buffet special, filled with more options than I could list. It didn't make much difference to me because all through the *Iftar* dinner I was dreaming not just to be home for Christmas, but of a White Christmas.

***

White Christmas

The morning of the fourteenth day of Ramadan—couldn't believe it—my personal last day of Ramadan—my last day in Morocco!

Tom drove me to Casablanca airport. We left early in the morning when it was still dark. Three hours on the road—a Moroccan autoroute. Raining and gray, low clouds all the way. The earth was sucking in all the moisture. Plants looked happy. The ride, though, was a slog.

I was emotionally depleted. My last Moroccan memories like the first—sensually extravagant. We had parked and I was walking. Just at the pedestrian entry to the airport terminal— my sense of smell was assaulted by—clusters of *Eriobotrya japonica* trees in flower—excessively sweet to the place where fragrance meets odor. Goodbye Morocco.

Finally, I was off the ground. Casa-Brussels-NYC-home. I was outta there! Phew! Never thought it would happen. Relief.

But then there was also sadness. *Ma'salama*. I'll never be the same. But then I mentally blinked—twice—reset.

Wonder what Santa will bring?

Back home. I paused in transit in New York, had to go through passport control and customs. Outside, it was snowing. Thanked my lucky stars to be standing there where at least I hoped I could live happy in the land of the free. The country where we can sleep in peace at night when we lay down our heads.

Last flight... after gathering my luggage, I looked around and thought, I am starting again. LittleWing was the first I saw, then Kate and Sam—they all met me.

Sachy—eyes all aglow—a huge smile on her face—ran up to greet me and wrapped her arms around me Hugged me hard and in my ear she whispered, "Home for Christmas!"

I stepped back, looked deeply into her eyes. It was her, Sachy, in real life, in front of me. Could this be? I held Sachy by her shoulders and said, "Lovely weather for a sleigh ride!"

Kate joked, "Look who got a Med suntan."

Sam observed and, with a smile on his face, gruffly asked, "Did you order this winter wonderland snowstorm?"

I put my arms around Sachy again, pulled her ever so close and, in the tightest of hugs, I whispered in her ear, "This is not a dream—my heart is warm—I couldn't have done it without you!"

32-Curious Tales

Epilogue

For more than six months, I had forgotten what was a warm heart—where had I been? And I wasn't sure that I had truly left wherever I had been; no this was not the end.

Yeah, I got home... but the story was not over.

Exhausting—that was my six-month term abroad design study in Morocco. Be forewarned, if anyone tries to summarize Morocco, it's a lie.

In an ideal world, I suppose my stories, my study, would have accomplished two tasks. First and foremost, the stories should have satisfied my term abroad design study requirements. They did because I passed the course and graduated.

But the second task was more personal because the landscape, plants and people of northwest Africa made major impacts on my personal life. And the impacts were far from pleasant—lying, cheating, hurting, suffering. I have tried to indicate those impacts, challenges, changes in my stories; but I was not clearly successful. Why? Difficult to answer. Partially because some of the impacts are ongoing. And some other impacts were and still are... well, unknowns that defy knowing.

Better, let me try to explain how my perceptions changed. Plants, once only Latin names and visual characteristics, became my doors to freedom. Gardens, once only places of work, became my refuge. And the landscape... instead of an 18th century romantic ideal... became deeper and broader than I ever imagined.

The northwest Africa landscape became the source of

all my fears—my undoing—and almost the end of my career aspirations. And the culture, the people, my cross-cultural disturbances? They became extensions of the landscape.

My final conclusion in the design study was rather mundane—a retread of conclusions historically well documented by people better than I. Cities need plants and gardens to reduce the sociological tensions of humans living very close together. Cities need publicly accessible green. That's it.

But I added an asterisk.

Based upon the new realities I experienced in my Tangier gardens, I felt obliged to note for public consumption that plants communicate with humans and doing thus provide humans an essential existential peace. Again this was something, over the centuries, that had been noted by many greater than I.

And under the circumstances I found myself in north west Africa, plants saved me. Do not underestimate the power of this asterisk.

In mid-January 2001, back in the US, I publicly presented my study as required. Essentially, I just read my stories. Well, some member of the public took issue saying that I made unfair statements about Morocco. He said it was a wonderful country and the people were very friendly. I couldn't contain myself. I said all that happened, happened. Believe it or not.

He continued to rail on my depictions. He said he had a tourism business and I was undermining his customer base. I told him if he wanted to call me a liar, come up and say it to my face. When he stood up and walked forward, some students and professors stopped him and asked him to leave. Despite the brouhaha, I passed and graduated.

Then Sachy and I married. We worked in our university town. I was aiming to get my professional license as quickly as possible. I wanted to start my own business. But, since my return from north west Africa, brouhahas became my ways of life at work and home. Brouhahas deeply nagged me. They pestered me. They had become like shape shifting teeps had been in Tangier.

These troubles regularly brought back memories of what

Mme Olga once told me about a cure, "take the airs of my birth home landscape". The university town was not my birth home. I had to do something about that.

Upon reading the stories, you may think I write fantasy? Fantasy? My six months in Morocco were not fantasy. At least, that is my conclusion. They were real life.

Cultures are not demonstrably uniform or unifiable. They are unique. They are different. They also have a unique time scale presence in the landscape. I concluded that cultures are rooted in the landscape. How are cultural thoughts and energies flowing through landscape roots? Can't answer that. Foreign culture, foreign roots, rife with misunderstandings. Not for me.

I have concluded, therefore, to work in my own culture. A place in my birth landscape where my roots are the strongest.

So I left Morocco. I left north west Africa. If I had been watching TV, one might say I just changed the channel, from watching something I could not understand and therefore did not like, to a channel I understood and liked.

I will work as a landscape architect in my own culture in my own landscape. And there, I will design and build gardens where people can sample the extrasensory communications that plants offer.

Illustrations

1-Kingdom of Morocco (also in front matter)

2-The Strait

3-Tangier Medina Spine (also in front matter)

4-Café de Paris

5-Medina Public Fountain (also in front matter)

6-The Medina

7-Fancy Protection

8-Co-ca Co-la

9-Cyber Club

10-La Ville Nouvelle

11-Art Deco Remnants

12-Marabout

13-CJ'sRooftop Garden Shelter (also in front matter)

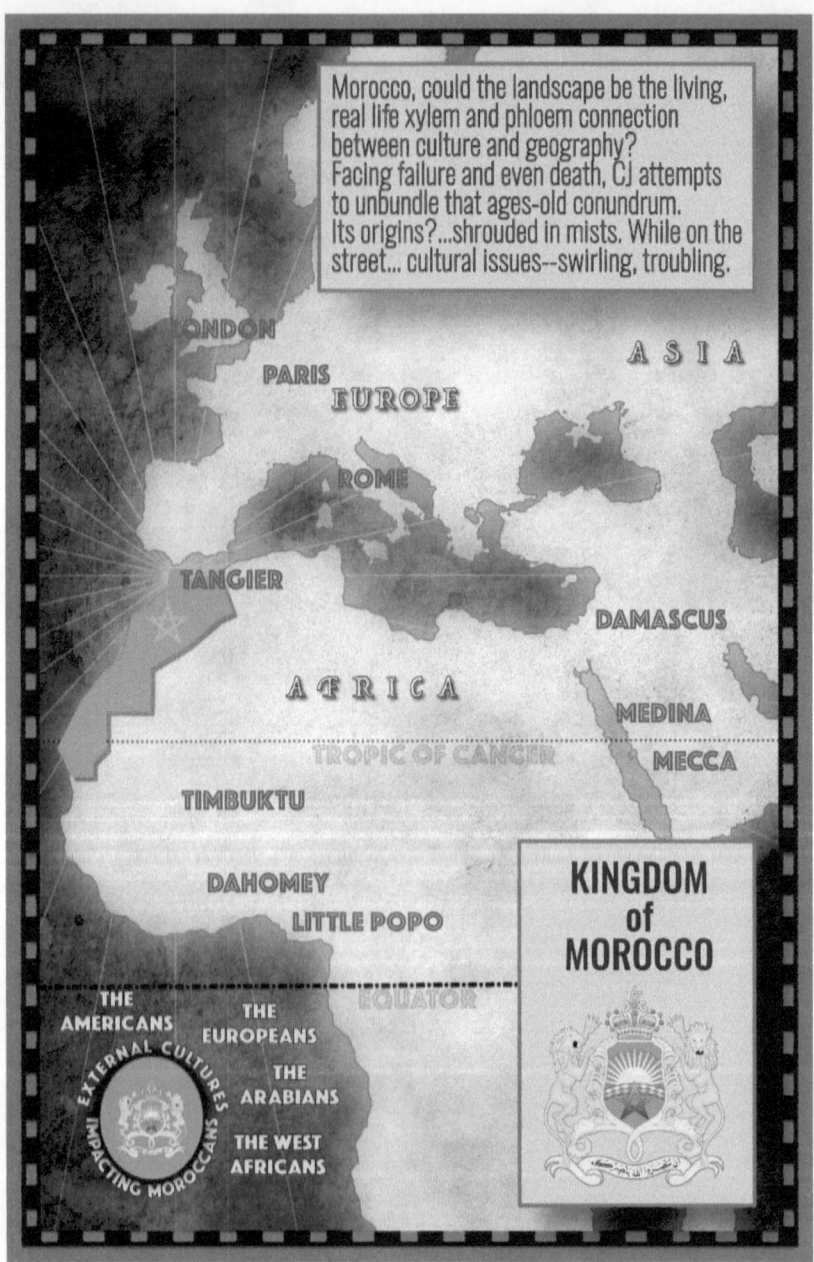

Morocco, could the landscape be the living, real life xylem and phloem connection between culture and geography?
Facing failure and even death, CJ attempts to unbundle that ages-old conundrum.
Its origins?...shrouded in mists. While on the street... cultural issues--swirling, troubling.

LONDON

ASIA

PARIS
EUROPE

ROME

TANGIER

DAMASCUS

AFRICA

MEDINA

TROPIC OF CANCER

MECCA

TIMBUKTU

DAHOMEY

LITTLE POPO

KINGDOM
of
MOROCCO

EXTERNAL CULTURES IMPACTING MOROCCANS

THE AMERICANS

THE EUROPEANS

THE ARABIANS

THE WEST AFRICANS

EQUATOR

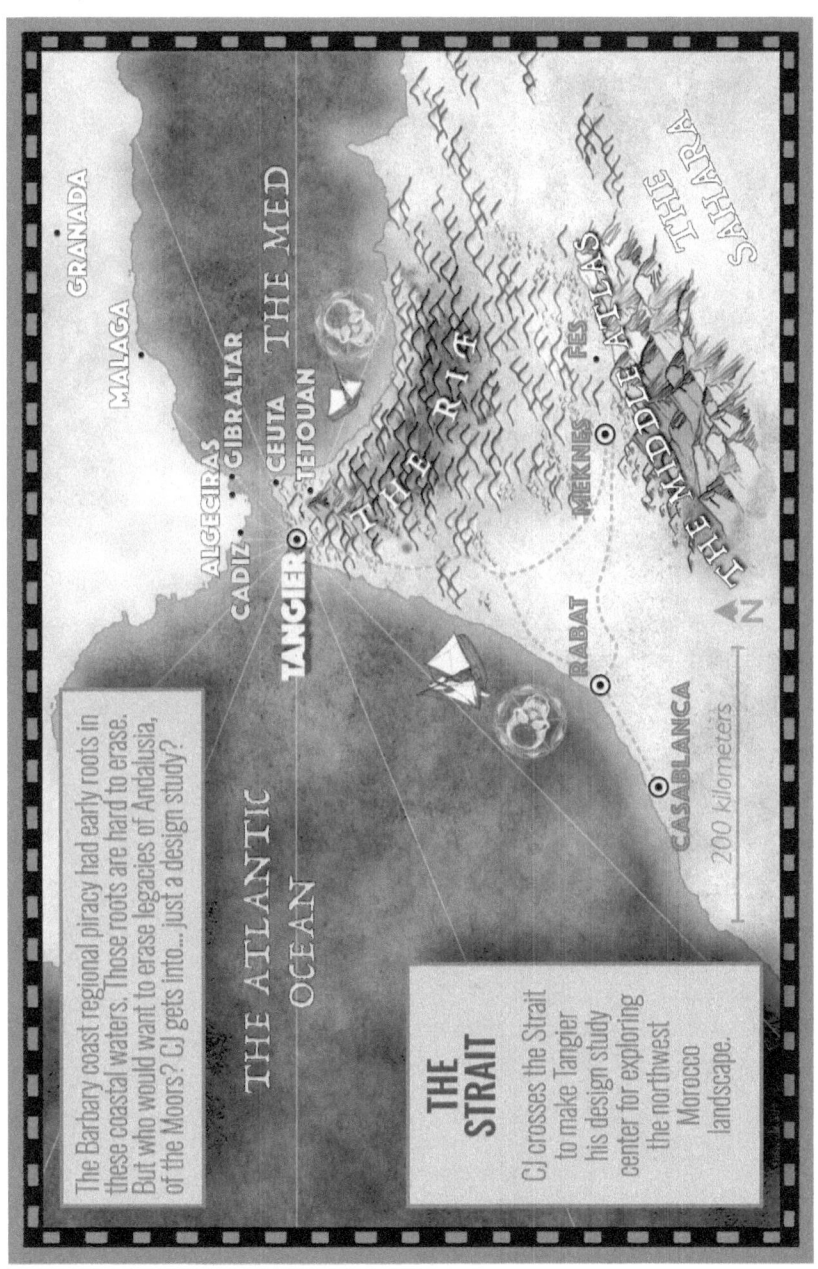

The Barbary coast regional piracy had early roots in these coastal waters. Those roots are hard to erase. But who would want to erase legacies of Andalusia, of the Moors? CJ gets into... just a design study?

THE ATLANTIC OCEAN

GRANADA

MALAGA

ALGECIRAS
GIBRALTAR
CADIZ
CEUTA
TETOUAN
THE MED

TANGIER

THE RIF

MEKNES
FES
THE MIDDLE ATLAS

THE SAHARA

RABAT

CASABLANCA

200 kilometers

N

THE STRAIT

CJ crosses the Strait to make Tangier his design study center for exploring the northwest Morocco landscape.

THE STRAIT OF GIBRALTAR

N

2 kilometers

CAP MALABATA

LA BAIE DE TANGER

TANGIER MEDINA SPINE

Herb Striet showed four landmark nodes to help CJ understand the ever so mysterious, ancient medina & European Tangier.

REVEALED

MEDINA PATHS

PLACE MECHOIR

SOCCO CHICO

GRAND SOCCO

CAFE DE PARIS

500 METERS

LA MONTAGNE

CJ'S ROOFTOP FLAT

GREATER (EUROPEAN) TANGIER

CAFE
DE
PARIS

An invisible gateway
in Tangier...
an inherent, strong,
social and geographic
presence since
the 1920s.
In 2000, CIs haunt.

MEDINA PUBLIC FOUNTAIN

This is what CJ
remembered.
This is what he
based his study on.
This is what
he was looking for.

THE MEDINA

Built approximately
500 years ago...
...la ville ancienne...
public ways narrow...
closed in by
three storey buildings,
hardly any daylight.

**FANCY
PROTECTION**

The rare
residential windows
at ground level
in the medina
have protection...
...from everything.

CYBER CLUB

The future slowly works its way into the medina.

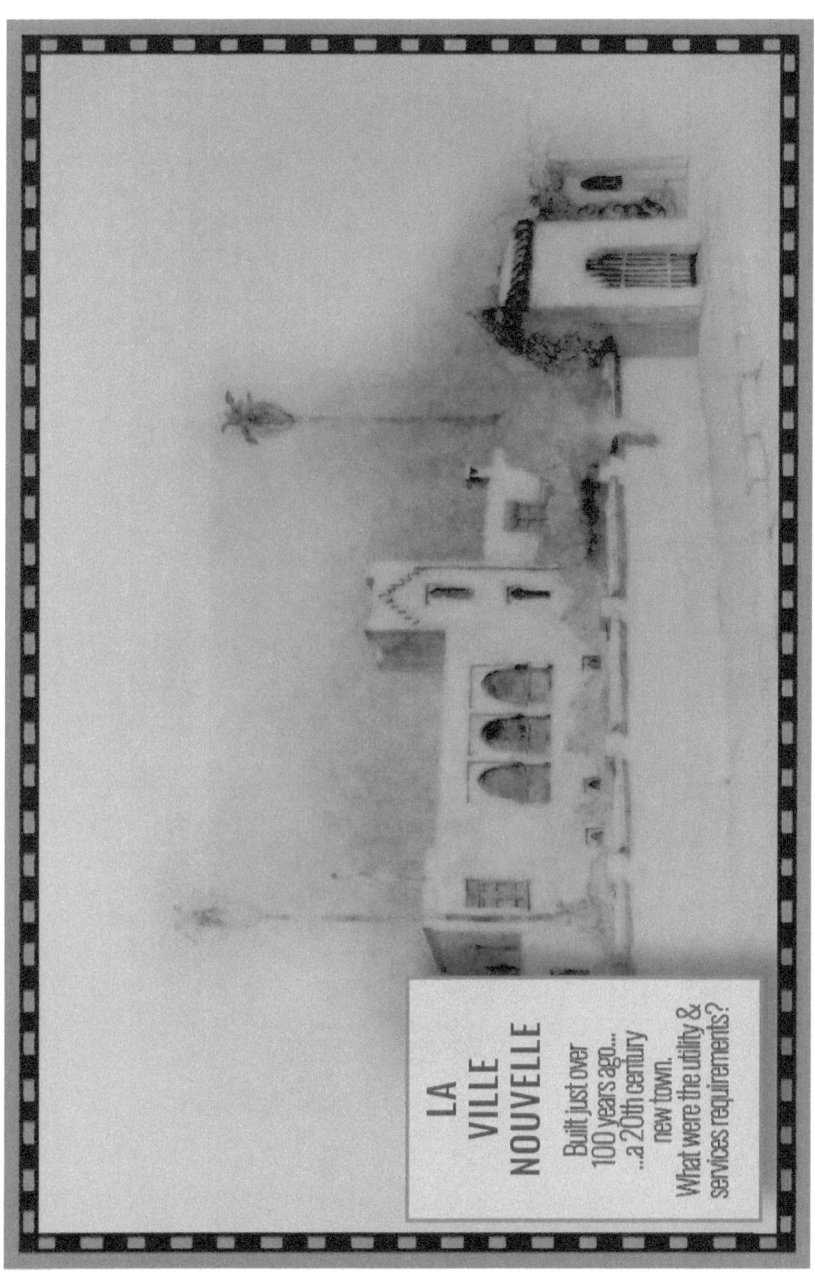

**LA
VILLE
NOUVELLE**

Built just over
100 years ago...
...a 20th century
new town.
What were the utility &
services requirements?

ART DECO REMNANTS

In the nouvelle ville are many decorative and functional art deco remnants.

MARABOUT

Landscape roots.
Never know what you'll
find inside.
Northwest Africa
landscape remnants.
Real?
...or imagined...

VIEW TO THE EAST OVER THE TANGIER MEDINA, LA BAIE DE TANGER, CAP MALABATA, THE STRAIT, SPAIN AND THE ROCK OF GIBRALTAR. CJ COULD SEE IT ALL.

STONESTEVE'S PLACE
next door, no garden

CJ'S ROOFTOP GARDEN SHELTER

Herb Striet, a landscape architect with a green thumb, rented his flat to CJ, if CJ would care for these outdoor plants.

ROOFTOP TERRACE GARDEN

CJ'S RENTED FLAT
his shelter

4 meters

FRENCH DOORS

CJ'S WICKER CHAIR

WINDOWS

"The Landscape Architect" Series

The Landscape Architect series is about CJ, Christopher Janus. He wrote it all. The six stories are his collected memoirs. He was into asking questions, discovering and writing. And above all he was a landscape architect deeply intrigued by foreign cultures, landscape and design. The six stories track the arc of his beginning interest in landscape architecture followed by his growth in the profession.

Who is CJ? CJ is an American, born in the Midwest, raised in New Mexico—a hard worker who found his muse in the landscape. At university in the late 1990s, he grew to embrace landscape, literature and all the fine arts with humanitarian, environmental and spiritual sensibilities.

He became a landscape architect and despite his heart-felt attraction to the New Mexico landscape—inspired by the works of Ansel Adams, Georgia O'Keeffe, and the writings of JB Jackson—he travelled the world because, like it or not, life had its own plan for him. CJ's personal life and professional landscape architecture career are woven through with drama in landscape, foreign culture and design—all presenting him with unrelenting dilemmas.

The series reveals the twists and turns in his professional landscape architecture development. But the series explores further. CJ, drawing upon his fine arts history, becomes obsessed with experiences in nature and the landscape beyond the five senses. Beyond the five senses? The paranormal? He recognizes his limits yet always strives to achieve more.

CJ chases nature, its landscape and plants to their existential roots. He describes his interactions with cultures, landscapes, gardens and plants of the world—where the unexpected and downright strange become daily facts of life.

CJ, like his landscape architecture profession and its practitioners, obsesses over design. In one of the major themes in the series, he tries to get to the root of the gossamer, ever-evolving landscape design theory.

Unique in this series, CJ, not a tourist, uses his expatriate life across the Middle East, North Africa and Europe, attempting to weave the threads of his foreign landscape and cultural experiences into a pragmatic design theory.

Throughout his adventures and to his surprise, he discovers, on the good days, not the normal landscape architecture world, rather an enlightening and exciting ethnobotanical world influenced by the likes of Lord Byron, HG Wells, Algernon Blackwood and Rod Serling. And then there are the "not-so-good" days... strange cultures and even stranger landscapes.

In the next book, *Curious Tales*, CJ shares 44 short stories that he wrote as part of his final term-abroad design study submission.

Acknowledgements

All photos, artwork and illustrations prepared by the author, except the marabout photo in Illustration 12 which was provided from Jean-Claude Latombe at: https://ai.stanford.edu/~latombe/mountain/index.htm. Base maps from 2022 Google Earth: https://earth.google.

Colophon

Books are crafted. Colophons are the end credits of literature.

Books have a typographical tradition that to this author go nearly as deep into human culture as does the landscape.

So when it came to selecting the manuscript text, Baskerville, originally by John Baskerville in the 1750s, was my clear favorite because it reaches back into history where alchemical roots still had gravitas.

Baskerville has an enduring elegance not unlike an attractive landscape—crisp, high contrast, generous proportions and refined beauty.

When it came to chapter headings and scene headings, Matthew Carter's relatively modern Skia provided a Mediterranean anchor. Skia is Greek for shadow and the letter forms take inspiration from stone-carved 1st century BC Greek writing. Roots in the Mediterranean, a definite multi-cultural strength suitable for this story.

At the ends of chapters you'll find a protective charm—the Hand of Fatima:

Cover Art

On this book's cover, upon examination, you will find a sonata of cultural clues as found by CJ in Tangier gardens:

1. There are leaves and fruit from *Ficus carica*, the historically prominent common edible fig of the Mediterranean Sea basin;

2. There are mesmerizing geometric textile patterns hand-woven by northwestern Morocco country folk;

3. There are the *zellij* patterns from the public Meknes medina water fountains—once the only source for medina water and an animated social gathering node; and, last but not least,

4. There is the Hand of Fatima, offering protection from the evileye.

All were daily influences in Christopher Janus' life while he was restructuring his design study in Tangier Morocco.

Dedication

Dedicated first of all to my wife, her photographs, support and understanding. Then to everyone who has interest in landscape, culture or the profession of landscape architecture.

About the Author

An international award winner and frequently invited conference speaker, Edward Flaherty practiced landscape architecture over the past five decades on very large projects where he has lived as an expatriate in Africa, Europe and Asia.

In Morocco, he has made his home in both Meknes and Tangier.

Professional details at LinkedIn: https://rh.linkedin.com/in/edflahertyl

Discussion Guide for Tangier Gardens

As I wrote this story, a couple big picture items kept me busy. I never fully resolved them, so I ask you, the readers, to discuss them and share your thoughts with me by commenting on my blog via this link: flahertylandscape.com.

1. Does human culture relate to the landscape? If so, then how?

2. What is the power in plants, gardens and landscape that induces peace in humans?

3. How do human cultures change? How do ecotypes in nature change? What happens at the edges of adjacent ecotypes and the edges of adjacent human cultures?

I look forward to hearing from you. Thank you.

Call to Action

Tangier Gardens is the first book in the fictional autobiographical series, "The Landscape Architect". In the series, CJ tracks the intriguing events he experienced in his expatriate professional career in landscape architecture across Europe, the Middle East and North Africa.

If you liked reading about CJ's coming-of-age adventures in Morocco, please write a short review and share it on my blog flahertylandscape.com.

Join my email list if you want to read more about CJ's Moroccan adventures.

This includes his bike trip from Brussels to Pamplona, his landscape impressions from his daily diary entries and periodic journal summaries:

A. In Northern France in the fields of the WWI Battles of the Somme
B. In Monet's water lily gardens in Giverny just outside Paris
C. In Frank Gehry's Guggenheim in Bilbao Spain
D. In Granada with Spanish Landscape History professor.

You might also enjoy reading my other books in "The Landscape Architect" found on my blog flahertylandscape.com.

READ THEM ALL